Broken Arrow

Written by Azaria M. J. Durant

Printed in Canada

First Printing, 2018

ISBN 978-1-7753311-0-0

Imperatrix Publishing
311 Ling Street
New Waterford, NS B1H-2W5

www.imperatrixpublishing.com

To all the bright and imaginative minds out there. Never change!

Part One

"The Slave"

Chapter One

D eep beneath the surface, beyond the winding staircase, and through to the end of the narrow passageway swathed in shadows, lay the meeting place. The figure descending the staircase knew its every turn and crevice. Its gaze swept unflinchingly over the grotesque, leering visages of stone ghouls that leapt from sudden curves and clefts in the walls— images rumoured to have been endowed with dark magic in ages past. Phantoms crafted to reflect the heart's deepest fears rose from the statues and swirled around the figure as black shadows. The figure glided through them like a blade through mist and the shadows fled before it.

The hour was late. No doubt the meeting was already in progress. Though the Master was terrifying, the figure did not dread his wrath. A face of iron and a nerve of steel left no room for fear, even of their creator.

Two oaken doors barred the entrance to the inner room where the meeting was taking place. Though time had left its mark upon the splintering wood, the ancient inscriptions remained as legible as the day they were embossed. The figure did not pause to admire the unique craftsmanship as it once might have, but threw open the doors, its cloak billowing out behind it as it strode into the circular room.

The light of the torches guarding either side of the doorway was first to greet the figure. Flickering, the glow gathered in the dome of the ceiling, playing with the shadows nestled in the wall's archaic mouldings. A stone pentagram was raised on the floor directly beneath the dome, an ancient monument that once served as an altar for rituals of the original council of Gaiztoak. Dark stains marred the cracked surface of the pentagram, remnants of even darker days.

Thankfully, the present purpose for it was much less brutal.

At each tip of the star sat a figure in a high-backed chair and draped in a heavy mantle. Every head was bowed, each face hidden in the folds of a large hood. Four of the five were mortals, useful pawns to the fifth figure, who presided over the meeting.

He was their Master, and they feared him.

"Bellator." His voice was light, but the newcomer could sense the rage beneath his calm.

The figure fell to one knee. "Master."

"You are late."

"I apologize, Master. It won't happen again."

The Master did not acknowledge the apology, nor did he accept it. "Begin your patrol."

Bellator rose and commenced pacing the perimeter of the room. The task was pointless. There had never been a whisper of trouble during any of these meetings, and Bellator doubted there would be any today. The fools around the altar wouldn't dare raise a hand against the Master. Bellator was merely a tool he used to further intimidate his players.

"Continue, Avia," the Master said.

Of course, this was not the man's name. The Master addressed each mortal as the country they represented. Two rulers, an ambassador, and a governor were present this evening, each of which – however insignificant their rank – held major sway over assets the Master had use of.

The man called Avia cleared his throat as a guise for composing himself. "P-production from the mines has been c-cancelled, my lord— for the time being. It was the queen's order. The holidays are upon us, c-celebrating the festival of *Dragoi Magni*, and—"

The Master raised a hand and Avia was silenced.

"See to it personally that the supply is tripled next month in recompense," he ordered. "Valamette?"

Bellator frowned. It was unusual for the Master to pass over a chance to make an example of Avia for such a failure. Clearly, there was something else pressing on his mind.

"My Master, *our* holidays are not until wintertime," Valamette boasted. "We'll be certain to supply you with twice the gold and lumber that you require."

Bellator's fists clenched. Across the table, Avia's shoulders sank, and to the Master's right, Zandelba let out a low growl. Valamette's smug attitude gained him nothing but disdain from his peers.

"Lavylli?" The Master's voice was impatient.

The figure to his left, who had no doubt remained silent and attentive since the meeting began, spoke abruptly in a strong, plummy accent. "The tunnels are underway, my lord, but we are making swift progress. Regarding the payment of precious gems, it has been sent. You will have what you need to stamp out all resistance when the time arises."

"That time is already upon us," the Master stated, rising to his feet. "Many nights now, my gaze has been turned to the stars. The constellations Heroi and Retsu are aligning for the first time in two and a half millennia. Prophecies connote these coming years as the last of mankind. This is the opportunity I have been waiting for. I must not fail!"

His eyes glowed with the passion his words expressed, and murmurs of agreement echoed through the room.

"Our toils have been rewarding and our preparation has been long," the Master went on. "Yet we must not deceive ourselves into thinking that our position is secure."

The murmurs fell to silence. The Master had never spoken so freely of such things before. The most this council had ever discussed were the brief updates concerning the progress of each respective country and its assets. There was the occasional new order from The Master, but such a thing was rare, and was always followed by a long, tedious discussion concerning the politics of the task, and thus was never interesting.

"It has been predicted that there is one who has the potential to stand in my way; one who may have the power to end my supreme rule before it has begun."

"My lord, who could possess the power to rival you?" Valamette asked, bewildered.

The Master lifted his gaze to glare at Valamette from beneath the shadow of his hood. "You of all people should know."

Understanding dawned on Valamette. He nodded slowly. Bellator glimpsed the other figures, looking to find a shred of understanding among them. But they too turned to look at Valamette, hoping to glean what they could from his bearing.

"The boy, my lord?" he asked.

"Yes," the Master replied. "The boy."

Bellator was intrigued. When had a boy ever entered their conversation?

"But my lord, how could *he* be a problem? Didn't we do away with him as an infant? How is it possible that he still draws breath?"

"Does it matter how?" the Master snapped. "What matters is that he lives and that he will pose a threat if we aren't careful to hone his abilities to our favour."

"I can do it." Valamette took a breath. "I can kill him, if you wish it. I will not fail you."

"No!" The Master's fist slammed on the altar. "If I wanted him dead, I would have let him die! I wouldn't have kept him safe all this time."

Valamette recoiled. When he dared to speak again, his voice came as a whisper. "You kept him safe?"

The Master raised his chin. "I will have his allegiance."

"Forgive me, Master," Zandelba interjected eagerly, "but won't you allow *me* to capture this boy? I'm the best man for such a task."

"Fool," Bellator scoffed so suddenly that all around the altar started. "If His Majesty refused Valamette, do you really think he would accept you?"

"I suppose you assume he'll elect you for the task?" Zandelba retorted.

Bellator's voice turned to steel. "Your head would be at the end of my sword if my master elected to give the order."

The Master's eyes blazed crimson from beneath his hood. "Be still, Bellator!"

"My lord," Bellator said, stepping forward, "just give the word, and this boy will be at your feet by morning."

"As much as I appreciate your enthusiasm, your request is denied. This boy is unknowingly under the protection of the Council of Buentoak. Their skill in the art of magic is unparalleled by all present but myself." The Master slowly lowered back into his chair. "No, *I* must be the one to retrieve him."

Exclamations of alarm were stifled around the room, and Bellator stepped back, confused.

"You, my Master?"

"Yes, me."

Zandelba cleared his throat, choosing his words carefully. "Do you think it' wise, my lord, to venture so far from your sanctuary? If you were to encounter any difficulties—"

"Ha!" the Master scoffed. "Do you think me so weak that I cannot hold my own in the world of mortals? Or perhaps you believe I have only survived this long because of your cautionary tales?"

"My only concern is for your well-being, my master," Zandelba muttered, ducking his head.

Valamette fidgeted uncomfortably. "My lord, once you have the boy... what will be done to him?"

The Master considered the man before him. When he spoke, his voice was determinedly cold. "Whatever it takes to persuade him of where his loyalties should lie."

"And if he isn't persuaded?"

Bellator sensed the smile that almost imperceptibly altered the Master's features. "One way or another, he will be."

Chapter Two

Long ago, I promised myself I would never give anyone the satisfaction of seeing they've hurt me. That's why, when the hot iron is pressed to the back of my hand, I don't make a sound. Teeth clenched, breath held, I gulp back bolts of pain that echo the beating of my heart. I can stand the pain. Just a few moments longer...

The poker is removed, leaving behind a sooty line of blisters. I clench my fist and lower it deliberately, my face a mask of indifference.

The master chef's mouth is a line of cruel mockery. "Think on that, and mayhap your worthless mind'll keep to the task at hand!"

"Yes, Master Lye," I mumble, my 'worthless mind' suppressing a good number of things I'd like to say.

He tosses the poker into the bin beside the hearth. "The spices for the poultry, now! Dinner's in an hour. We don't got time for any more of your mishaps!"

I nod and obediently turn toward the spice counter, flexing my fist in and out to ease the throbbing of the burn. Afternoon is the most hellish time of day for the scullery, even without Lye in such a bad mood. The endless clattering of pans, the heat of the crackling fires, and the chatter of the maids as they exchange the daily gossip- it's enough to make my head pound. Even so, it's better than field work, where I'd be in the hot sun from morning to dusk tilling the land; or worse, cleaning and gutting fish at one of the foul-smelling fisheries by the docks.

The air is thick with steam from boiling vegetables. There is one thing I could never tire of, and that's the tantalizing aromas that sing like music to my senses and cause my mouth to water in longing. Normally, I would weigh the dangers of swiping a roll or meat pastry from the counter before Lye makes his final count. Right now, however, I won't dare risk it. I'm usually a little clumsy, but today is worse than ever. I keep getting dizzy with no warning. Most likely I'm coming down with something.

I reach the spice counter and begin to portion the correct ingredients into a wooden bowl, anger boiling in my chest.

Yes, I'm angry. Angry that I've been punished, true, but angrier still about what the punishment represents. I've never understood. They don't have a problem with themselves, or with full under-dwelling Lavyllians, so why am I so abhorrent being half of both? I'm not that different from them. Am I?

"Half-breed!" Lye's voice smashes through my thoughts as forcefully as when he swings a rolling pin at my head.

Instinctively, I duck, and the sack of ground peppercorn falls into the bowl, mixing with the thyme and sage already measured out. I sweep up the bag with an inward groan. If he sees what I've done, it'll be the whip.

Again.

Fortune favours me for the first time in a good while. His back is to me as he hangs his apron on a peg by the door. "Stop dawdling and get to the fire with the seasoning! That bird *will* be cooked by the time I get back."

"Yes, Master Lye."

He leaves the room, letting the door slam shut behind him.

I breathe a sigh of relief and quickly scoop the excess peppercorn back into the bag. An added fistful of salt, and I'm done. I make my way back toward the fireplace, where a large pheasant is skewered over a simmering fire.

A frazzled, pasty-faced maid spins in front of me, a steaming pan in one hand and a spoon in the other. I try to dodge out of the way, but she charges forward, slamming into me. The bowl flies from my hands and clatters to the floor, the fine powder scattering in all directions. The maid jumps back, her lip curled in disgust.

"Watch where you're going!" she cries shrilly, cuffing me upside the head.

Mumbling a quick apology, I drop to my knees to salvage the seasoning from the wooden floorboards. The scullery is small as it is, but it seems to shrink to half its size. My hand gets trodden on twice. The bowl is kicked halfway across the room. A maid with carrot orange hair drops a ladle on my head, and when I get it for her, she snatches it from me as if I'd stolen it. I even get a frustrated kick in the side when I find myself in the path of the young assistant cook. All the while, they're chattering on and on about the master of the house's son, who's apparently something to look at.

When most of the spices are retrieved, I give up the rest as lost. Sheltering the bowl in my arms to keep it from spilling again, I cover the distance to the fireplace and crouch down before it.

Finding a jug of oil on the hearth, I drench the golden skin of the roasting pheasant, and then sprinkle the spices over it. The warm firelight licks my face, but serves only to increase the burning of my hand.

Regardless, I determine to stay focused. The punishment for burning the borscht was bad enough. Of course, it wasn't my fault. I was too busy to check on it, what with Lye shouting at me to stoke the fires, carry water, scrub the floors, and tidy every little mess made during that time.

It's my lot in life, it seems, to take the fall for everyone else's mistakes. If only—

A log in the fire coughs, sending sparks into my eyes and I blink. When I blink, the world changes suddenly before my eyes.

I no longer see the sizzling skin of the pheasant and the blackened stones of the oven behind it. Instead, I stand between the brick walls of a narrow, dead-end alley. The ground beneath my bare feet is dirt instead of rough wood and putrid city air replaces the savoury smells of the scullery. A cool, midsummer breeze finds its way to me over the high walls around the alley, caressing my clammy skin, bringing with it the buzz of late afternoon hustle and bustle on the street outside. Yet somehow, I can still feel the heat of the fire on my skin and hear the familiar sounds of the scullery behind me.

My attention is quickly drawn to movement at the dead-end of the alley as a beggar emerges from the shadows. He has the looks of a man in his thirties, yet his dirty face is cut with more scars than a warrior twice his age could've acquired. A tattered cloak is wrapped around his shoulders, mostly concealing his ratty green tunic and patchwork trousers. An eye-patch covers his right eye. He steps softly, his shoes simple cloth bound around his feet, and surveys the walls cautiously with his good eye. His gaze passes through me as though I wasn't there.

Knotted, dirty-blond hair whips his face as he jerks his head to look up the alley and his lip curls in a fierce snarl.

I recognize the beggar at once. Though I haven't met him in person, I've seen him often enough to imagine him a figment of my own imagination. In every city, in every town I've ever worked, the beggar has always been there – lurking behind corners, in dark alleyways, in every crowd – and always, always watching me. But he's never there long enough for me to see him on second glance.

This is a dream. It has to be. I survey my surroundings once more and the cool breeze greets me once again. *A very vivid dream. Maybe I've fainted.*

Whatever is happening, I seem to have little control, so I decide there isn't much else to do but accept it.

I begin to start forward, my goal to get directly in the beggar's way, but something binds me in place.

A rough, throaty voice rings out from the mouth of the alley, and a shiver shoots down my spine.

"Banner!"

The beggar whips aside his cloak, putting a hand to the spiked club attached to his belt.

An old man limps into view, leaning on a stout, gnarled walking stick. He picks his way along the downward slope, lifting the hem of his drab grey robes clear of his feet. A pointed beard and sleek white hair peek out from the baggy hood draped over his head. His face sags with deeply set wrinkles, and his eyes are narrow, squinty, but there is an authority gathered in the indent of his brow. A beaded braid of leather is tied around his forehead, the tails of which dangle down the side of his face, and I contemplate how annoying that could get over time. There's nothing threatening about his appearance at all, and I wonder why I shivered at his voice.

A sudden chill, obviously. He's just a friendly old man. Not everyone is out to get me.

Recognition dawns on the beggar's face, and he relaxes his grip on the club. "Ulmer? This is... unexpected, to say the least! Why have you come here?"

The old man – Ulmer, I infer – begins to speak slowly. "Listen to me. The boy is in danger. I think it prudent that we get him to safety. Tonight."

The beggar sighs, nodding. "I knew I felt something amiss."

"Your intuition serves you well." Ulmer glances around, lowering his voice. "Zeldek is coming for him."

As he says these words, a raven screeches from the rooftop and soars into the air, disappearing beyond the thatched peak of the building next to us. Dread washes over me, and I look up enviously at the raven that can fly away so freely. *Zeldek.* The name sounds vaguely familiar, but it is meaningless to me.

"Why now?" Banner's voice is tremulous, yet resigned. "He could have come for him at any time. What is he planning?"

"My source was unclear. Simply that he plans to capture the boy himself." The old man shakes his head. "I must inform the council of this development. We may not have the numbers to wage war against him, but we can distract him while you get the boy to safety. We will reconvene at this location at midnight. Be sure he is with you then. If Zeldek gets to him first, I fear he will be beyond our help."

Banner nods. "I will protect him with my life."

"I know you will, little brother," Ulmer says, resting a reassuring hand on his shoulder. "I must be off."

"All speed to you," Banner returns, lines of worry sinking into his brow.

Ulmer pulls the hood down over his eyes and slips into the crowded street outside.

No sooner has he gone than I feel a tugging on my shoulders, and I am jerked back into the wall. Next thing I know, I am once again breathing in the heavy air of the scullery, the flames of the fire dangerously close to my face. I stumble backward, my eyes stinging from smoke. My foot catches on a loose brick in the hearth, and I hit the floor before I even realize I'm falling. All air flees my lungs.

When everything comes back into focus, the alley is gone.

The scullery, on the other hand, is too real. All five of the maids have stopped their work and are staring at me, agape, as if expecting me to sprout wings or turn into a worm.

"What's it doing?"

"Stop that! Stop that, you hear?"

"Loretta, do something!"

Beads of sweat form on my forehead – whether from mortification or exhaustion is hard to say. A wave of nausea overtakes me and I feel suddenly very weak. I run my sleeve over my face, widening my eyes in a futile attempt to clear my vision.

"Sorry," I mumble, trying to scramble to my feet.

My knees wobble and buckle underneath me. An awkward pause hangs in the air while the maids hang back, motionless.

Come on! Get up! It's a dizzy spell. It'll pass.

If anything, more of my strength is draining away.

"Are you alright?"

Stunned, I crane my neck in search of the owner of the kind voice. Faces swim before my eyes, only adding to my confusion.

And now I'm hearing things. Maybe there is something wrong with me.

The voice comes again, louder this time. "Are you alright?"

The face of a girl appears above me, genuine concern in her clear grey eyes. Even through the fog in my mind, I know her. She's the maid that was hired yesterday. The strange, quiet girl with the pure white hair, like that of the aged – though she's still quite young.

"May I help you?" she asks.

I stare at her, bewildered. "M-me?"

She laughs, a soft sound, like the strings of a harp. "Who else, silly? The pheasant?" She nods her head in the direction of the roasting bird, a wide smile on her face. "I don't think I'd be much used to him now."

I begin to answer, but stop myself. I know the rules better than anyone. People who fraternize with half-breeds tend to get hurt, as do the half-breeds they associate with. I won't see her get in trouble on my account.

"Sorry, miss," I mumble, bowing my head, "but I can help myself."

"Are you sure? You look a little pale." Her voice isn't so light now.

Pretending not to hear her, I grab the edge of a nearby table and pull myself to my feet. I fall into it, knocking a bowl of leeks onto the floor. No one moves to retrieve it.

"Did you pass out?" the girl persists. "Maybe you should lie down."

"Please, miss," I hiss, my gaze darting to the other maids in the room. The lot are eyeing the girl with collective suspicion and disgust. "Let me alone. I can take care of myself."

She steps back, her brows furrowing. "I'm sorry," she says. "I was only trying to help."

"Annalyn!" barks an unusually deep, raspy female voice from across the room.

The girl jumps at the sound of her name and backs away as a thin, sour-faced hag with a long, skinny neck and a terrible under bite charges toward us.

Watchdog.

That's what I call her, anyways. Her real name is Loretta, but she takes it upon herself to be Lye's eyes and ears while he's out of the room. If the two of them aren't already married, there is certainly something going on between them, and since she knows Lye has a vendetta against me, she's taken it upon herself to treat me with just as much contempt.

"Back to your work, half-breed lover," Watchdog growls to Annayln, "before I give you more trouble than you're worth!"

Annalyn flushes a deep red, and biting her lip, she turns back to peeling potatoes.

Watchdog turns on me. "What do you think you're doing, filth?"

I open my mouth to make an excuse, but she backhands me across the face. The force of her blow sends me spinning to the floor again.

I've only been down a moment before she jabs a foot into my ribs. "Up, now!"

I try, but I'm too slow for her.

"I said *up!*"

She snatches a wooden spoon from the table and raises it to strike me. As she brings it down, a strange wave of energy shoots through me. My vision snaps clear. Before I know what I'm doing, I've caught the spoon in my hand and twisted it from her fist.

Gasps and shrieks ring out. Watchdog's mouth drops in alarm and she stumbles back. The orange-haired maid turns and flees the room.

I stare down at the spoon in my hand, frozen.

How did I do that? Why *did I do it?*

Watchdog grabs a knife from the counter. "Drop the spoon," she orders shakily.

I throw it aside, putting up my hands. "I'm so sorry!" I blurt. "I didn't mean—"

The scullery door bursts open, and Lye enters, the orange-haired maid close behind. I gulp and shrink back.

Things just got a whole lot worse.

Chapter Three

I've never seen Lye so furious. Puffing and spitting, he takes in the scene, his face turning so red it could easily be mistaken for a beet. Even his moustache, two tongues on either side of his upper lip, frays at the ends as he prepares to blow.

"Half-breed!" he bellows so loudly that my ears begin to ring. "What are you doing? The bird is burning, you idiot!"

I back away, glancing at the remains of the pheasant. He's right. Curls of smoke rise from its blackened surface. As I watch, it bursts into flames.

Lye throws back his head with a cry of distress. "Ruined! What will the master have now?"

Watchdog is at his elbow in an instant. "The half-breed's gone savage! I've heard of it happening before, but I never thought I'd see the day. In my own scullery! The look in its eyes, like a wild animal it was. And glinting—"

"What are you babbling about, woman?" Lye sputters. "Can't you see? Dinner is ruined!"

She points a finger at me. "The half-breed attacked me! I warned you, didn't I? When they put it to work down 'ere, I told you it was no good!"

Lye's face, once red with fury, has turned white. "Attacked you? How?"

"There!" She points at the offending spoon lying near my feet. "Snatched it right outta my hands. Scared the devils outta me. I grabbed this 'ere knife to defend myself. It had blue death in its eyes, I saw it! And the maids, they can attest!"

"That's a lie!"

Annalyn's face is red with indignation and she wipes her hands on her apron. Lye turns to her, shocked speechless. It's not every day that he's confronted, least of all by one of his own staff.

She takes a deep breath, straightening herself up. "Sir, it isn't his fault. He only took it to stop her from hurting him. If anything, it was self-defence."

"It's a half-breed! It don't got the brains to be deliberate." He jabs his finger at her. "And you don't got no right to speak to me that way, missy!"

Her eyes blaze and she opens her mouth to protest.

"I did it on purpose." The voice is shaky, but clear, and I realize it's my own.

If anyone's going to get in trouble for this, it's me. No need for her to join my punishment.

I jut out my chin. "There, I said it. Pleased?"

Lye lunges at me, grabbing the collar of my shirt. "You dare mock me, whelp? I'll put you in your place once and for all!"

He yanks me around the table, shoving me toward the exit. I stumble along without protest, pretending I don't care what happens to me, that I'm not afraid of getting whipped for the second time today. I'd rather Lye take out his rage on me than have *him* find out.

Lye kicks open the door and pushes me out into the courtyard. Rainwater drenches my face from a deluge that must've only just started. The door slams behind us, and he shoves me forward. My feet slip on the wet cobblestones and I fall on all fours. I scurry to my feet, but he throws me down again with a blow between my shoulder blades. My ankle twists beneath me and I gasp as pain vibrates up my leg.

Lightning flashes in the sky.

"Really?" a familiar voice calls over the pattering of the rain. "Him again?"

Fear rises in my throat like bile as I search for the owner of the voice. I soon find him leaning against the trunk of the large oak tree in the centre of the courtyard.

Ralcher.

A relatively young man, perhaps in his mid-twenties, Ralcher is the son of the master of the household, Lord Thane. Whatever the maids say about him, he's a devil who takes cruel pleasure devising unusual and painful ways to hurt things so he can break their spirit. He was the one that bought me. Said he saw a lot of spirit in me.

Lye picks me up by the collar of my shirt and holds me at arm's length. "Master, this half-breed of yours is nothing but trouble! He ruined dinner, set the pheasant afire, and attacked Loretta!"

Thunder cracks. I glare defiantly at Ralcher through the long straggles of hair that have freed themselves from the tie at the nape of my neck. I feigned some remorse for Lye. Ralcher gets no such privilege.

Ralcher lets out a deep chuckle, a wide grin showing his crooked teeth. "Does my little half-breed have anything to say for himself?"

I bare my teeth.

Lye cuffs me upside the head. "Answer him!"

Ralcher holds up a hand. "That will do, Lye," he says with an easygoing smile. "You may return to your post. Dinner still needs to be served, after all."

Lye releases me with a shove. "I suppose I've got to make new arrangements for the main course," he grumbles.

Turning, he retreats indoors, his anger appeased.

When the door to the scullery has closed once more, Ralcher straightens up and starts toward me with his usual off-balanced swagger. I don't dare move as he grips my face in his hand and peers into my eyes with his wild, chestnut ones.

"The rebellious spirit lingers still." He shakes his head, letting out a low chuckle. "I've never had one as young as you last for so long."

I struggle to breathe without shaking.

He pushes back my head, moving my hair out of my face. His eyes glint with a sadistic ire, and his dark hair hangs in wet strings, framing his face and accentuating his appearance of insanity.

"I'll win, eventually. I always do."

I want to run, to get as far away from him as I can. But he'll only catch me. And he'll make me pay. Instead, I grit my teeth, and brace myself.

He seizes a handful of my hair and drags me across the wet grass to the tree. Throwing me backward into the rough bark of the trunk, he brings his fist into my gut. I double over, but his hand closes on my throat, and he slams me back against the tree again. His fingers dig into my skin, cutting off my windpipe.

I sputter, trying to take a breath. He waits, that casual smile still playing on his features, until my chest feels like it's tearing itself apart. Then he lets go. I double over, gulping air, but he grabs my hair again and slams my head back into the tree. White light shoots across my vision. When it clears, I'm on the ground at his feet. Pain splits my head. The dizziness is returning.

"You're pathetic!" he spits, sending a sharp kick to my stomach.

Gasping, I paw at the wet leaves scattered on the grass, searching for something solid to cling to.

He kicks me again. "Quiet, wretch!"

That only sets me to coughing, and when I remove my hand from over my mouth, it is specked with blood.

"What is it that you cling to? Freedom? Hope for a better future?" He stands over me, rolling me onto my back with his foot. "You want the pain to end, don't you?"

I nod faintly.

"It will. But first, you must understand; you are nothing. You never will be anything. Embrace it. Then the pain will end."

It's a lie. I... I can still be something.

I struggle to my knees, and he lets me, a cruel smirk twisting his features. I look up, blinking through rain that pelts my eyes.

"Do what you want," I breathe. "You will *never*—"

Down on the grass, fingers in the soft dirt, I am unable to finish my pledge. A shock of cold rushes through my arms, gathering in my palms, and blue lightning flashes from the sky. The ground around me explodes, throwing Ralcher back onto the cobbled path. Rocks and dirt shower down on me, and I fling my arms over my head to shield myself.

Crack!

The sound is followed by muffled screams from indoors. Forgetting about myself, I look up toward the building. Although my vision is blurred, I can see that it is undamaged, which is more than I can say for the rest of the courtyard. The cobblestones have been ploughed up, the grass left in ravaged clumps, and the oak tree has been uprooted and thrown against the now crumbling wall that surrounds the estate.

My gaze falls to the ground close around me. Though scattered with dirt and stones, it is otherwise untouched.

The rain pours down harder than before.

Ralcher picks himself up off the ground, stumbling in a full circle before his mad eyes come to rest on me. "You did this!"

I shake my head, shocked. That feeling of exhaustion is taking me again, and I blink, trying to keep focus.

My voice is weak. "I didn't."

An insane glee takes hold of him, "You're a sorcerer!"

"No, I'm not. I swear!"

"But you are! I saw your eyes glow. You're a sorcerer!" He pauses, realization dawning. "You just tried to kill me."

"No, please!" I cry desperately with aching lungs. "I didn't!"

"This has gone too far, I'm afraid," he says, and leaps over a mound in front of him, charging toward me.

Terror rips through me, giving me strength to run. I bolt for the wall, scrambling over turned-over boulders, dirt, and roots. Ralcher is close behind, but I manage to scale the wall before he reaches me. I leap down the other side, ignoring the pain prickling in my ankle as I stumble toward the opening of a nearby alleyway.

The world is spinning around me, but I manage to stay on my feet. I bump into the corner of the wall beside the alley before stumbling onto the dark, grimy pathway, clinging to the wall for support.

I've got to be invisible before the city guards start looking for me. As soon as they receive word of a sorcerer loose in the city, they'll be after me. They'll close the city gates until they catch me. There's no way I can get out in time.

They will catch me, eventually. No matter what I say, they won't believe that I'm not a sorcerer. Ralcher's the son of a powerful lord. I'm a nobody.

Panic begins to creep in. Unless I figure out a way to escape the city, I'm doomed.

Chapter Four

Night descends swiftly over the city. The rain lets up a little, but the streets are already crawling with men in the red and black livery that marks them as the city's superior security. I perch on a rooftop, watching from the shadow of a chimney while a squad of nine guards rushes past. Their leader barks directions. They split into groups of two to search the surrounding alleys and streets, leaving him to wait for their return. He stands with his back to me, his hands clasped behind him. I recognize the silhouette of the Great Black Bear glinting on the back of his armour.

Ancient mythology speaks of the Great Black Bear and the battle that raged between it and the Phoenix of the neighbouring country, Valamette. Both animals were Bereziak, charged by Irla, goddess of life, with the task of creating their own people groups to inhabit Theara. The Bear and the Phoenix both claimed the western side of the Tireth River as their own. Instead of settling the dispute through negotiations, the Bear challenged the Phoenix to a battle. In the end, the

Phoenix struck a mortal blow to the Great Bear, and carried his body to the other side of the river. With his dying breath, the Great Black Bear swore vengeance upon the Phoenix, and using his own blood, he created a people that were as strong and fierce of heart as he was. To this day, Zandelba values brute strength, arrogance, and power above all, although they prefer to call it courage, patriotism, and loyalty. They honour the Great Black Bear and have sworn to one day reclaim the land that is now the country of Valamette.

My take on it is that they're using the legend to claim right to land they so fiercely covet, and I'm guessing it has something to do with the rumoured veins of gold running through Valamette's mountains.

The guards return and the squad moves down a few blocks to continue their search. Once they are out of sight, I swing down from the rooftop and drop lightly to the ground. My feet hit the wet cobblestones with a splash, and I dart into the shadows. Keeping close to the walls, I make my way further into the area already searched. They aren't likely to retrace their steps until morning, so I should be safe until then. But just in case, I need to find an adequate disguise and an out-of-the-way place to sleep for the night.

Lord Thane's estate is in the wealthy sector of the city of Weisport, Zandelba's largest port city. There, the streets are clean and orderly, so those of the upper class can imagine the rest of the city is as well-to-do as they are. But the further I go into the city, the more I see the poverty of its underworld. The rows of cobblestones grow uneven and dirty, and the gutters run with sewage. Beggars, street urchins, and drunks are standard spectacles, and the evening air is filled

with the loud music and brawling from taverns on every other street corner.

I enter one such establishment for long enough to filch a cloak from a man

who is too drunk to notice. I say a silent apology as I leave, hoping he doesn't have

as much a need of it as I do. Throwing the cloak over my shoulders, I pull the

massive hood down over my face, gagging as the sharp pungency of spirits fills my

nostrils.

Even with the cloak as a disguise, I stay close to the shadows. It's easy to spot

me because of my stature, which Ralcher will surely have told my pursuers. I'm

short for my age, just a few inches shy of five feet tall. There aren't many young

children out in this part of town after dark to blend in with.

"Halt!" a voice rings through the air behind me. "You there, turn about!"

I don't look to see who said it; I bolt. A singular pair of footsteps pounds on

the pavement as the owner of the voice chases after me. My heart hammers in my

chest and the only thought in my head is to live another day.

I reach the mouth of a dark alley and dash into it with a burst of speed. Even

as I do, a wall looms out of the darkness in front of me. I slam into it before I can

stop myself. Dazed, I spin around, throwing my back against the wall, and look back

up the alleyway. My pursuer is nowhere to be seen. Breath held, I listen, but the

sound of his footsteps has all but vanished.

Relieved, I lean back into the wall and let myself breathe, silently begging the shadows to cover me. But fate is against me tonight. The moon bursts from behind the clouds and casts its pale glow upon my face.

Something about the alley looks hauntingly familiar. The shadowy dead-end, the upward slant to the street outside, the dirt beneath my feet; this is the same alley I somehow saw from the scullery.

This can't be a coincidence.

I step away from the wall, scanning the shadows. The beggar had come from the left corner, which is more shadowed than the other. He could be there now, watching me as he has always done. If he is, perhaps he can explain why I have been drawn to this place.

Afraid yet determined, I take a faltering step toward the corner and peer into the darkness.

"Banner?" I whisper, then flinch, envisioning the beggar rushing out with his spiked club lifted to strike.

But all is still.

"Who is it that you seek?"

Deep and ageless, the voice echoes as if from within my own mind, penetrating a dimension beyond sound. My heart bounds into my throat, and I spin around.

A man in a dark velvet cloak smiles down at me. His face is shadowed by a deep hood, but what I can make of it is long and ghoulish. His chin is pointed, his nose oblong, and his complexion has a lingering white pallor that differs from the bluish pale of the half-breed. A deep scar cuts across one side of his face, crossing over his left eye.

Despite his fearsome looks, his composure is dignified and his clothing is very fine. He is fully attired in black armour that glints in the moonlight. An expensive, dragon-hilted broadsword hangs at his side, upon which he rests his hand. Though his attire is dazzling, my eyes are at once drawn to the glittering black signet ring on the middle figure of his right hand. On it, a fierce dragon with eyes of ruby is trapped within a circle of silver chains, its wings lifted in flight, and a goldon ring dangling from its fangs.

I step back from him distrustfully, pulling my cloak further around my shoulders. "I seek no one."

The man chuckles good-humouredly, which does nothing to ease my discomfort. He seems delighted to have found me here, though I don't judge him to be the type to go after a runaway slave for the reward money. My eyes scan the walls for the easiest path of escape should it come to that. I'm not a fighter, but I'm swift on my feet. This man may have a sword, but I doubt he's as agile as I am.

"Who is this Banner?" he asks.

"Just a beggar that lives here." I speak as though I'm sure of myself. I've heard that looking people in the eyes means you aren't lying, so I do that too. "I owe him some money."

He raises his scarred eyebrow in concern. "You? But you're just a boy!"

I straighten up, as if somehow that might make me look older. "I'm fifteen!"

He doesn't look convinced. "Where are your parents?"

"Don't have any."

Feigned sympathy replaces his suspicion, and his earlier good humour fades. "I am sorry. Perhaps I can help you find your friend?"

I shake my head, annoyed by his false kindness.

His mouth turns down in mild disappointment. "You certainly are a mistrusting child... Ealdred."

My façade fails me. "H-how do you know my name?"

I've never told anyone my name. Not that anyone has bothered to ask. I have held it as a deeply cherished secret.

He steps forward and appraises me. If I'm going to make a run for it, I should go now. But then I see something that makes me freeze. His eyes, which had been shadowed only moments before, now glow crimson.

"Don't be afraid, Ealdred." His voice is a biting mockery as he emphasizes my name a second time. "I only want to talk."

"Who are you?" I demand. "What are you?"

He throws off his hood, revealing a crown made from some sort of black metal on a head of long, wispy white hair. The crest of the crown renders two dragons facing one another, each with a foot on an oval ruby between them. Tiny rubies glisten in their eyes and all the way around the scaly circlet of the crown.

"I am Zeldek," he cries, his voice booming in the still night air, "Lord of Gaiztoak, Keeper of the Aemurel, Ruler of the Vaelhyreans, and King of Theara; and I will have your allegiance!"

My mind works out the details on its own. Zeldek came here to wait for Banner and Ulmer to return with their charge and found me instead. However great my fear, I quickly decide that the best way to handle this situation is not to stammer like an idiot.

"King of Theara, you say?" I ask, my voice quavering in spite of myself. "I'm not sure I've heard of you."

He stiffens and his eyes spark with anger. "It matters not who you have or haven't heard of, half-race! You will bow to me!"

"Why?" I scoff. "What good would the service of a lowly half-breed be to you? I'm a nobody!"

A hint of a smirk turns his lips. "You truly do not understand your own worth, do you?"

I shrug, and my words are as biting as the truth itself. "I am worth nothing."

"If you were worthless, I would not be here to retrieve you myself."

"I apologize for being so bold," I say with deep irony, "but you're wasting your time. I really am not worth anything. Please, I'll be on my way before I cause you any more trouble."

Where the sudden courage came from, I cannot say. All I know is that deciding to scorn a powerful magician who claims to be king of Theara and then attempting to walk away unscathed is probably the stupidest thing I've ever done.

He draws his sword and bars my path. Fire leaps from the blade as he drives me back against the wall.

"You dare treat me with such disrespect? You have lost the privilege of my kindness!" His voice deepens to a harsh growl. "Tell me what you know of this Banner!"

I glance down at his sword, finding a growing need to muster up more courage. My voice comes out as a squeak. "I told you—"

"You're lying! You know this beggar is a Vaelhyrean. Don't you?"

"No! I don't even know what a Vaelhyrean is!"

He pulls back his sword until its tip is pointed at my chest. I gulp, staring at the sharp edges of the blade, and put up my hands compliantly.

"Tell me the truth, or I will cause you such pain that you will wish you were never born!"

He says this as though I don't already deeply regret my birth.

"Please," I gasp, "I told you the truth."

The tip of his sword touches my shirt and the fabric melts away. The red-hot metal begins to scorch my skin.

I grind my teeth, forcing back my distress. *Focus. Remain calm!*

"I swear, I've never met him before in my life!"

"But you've *seen* him, haven't you? I know you have. You heard him speaking in the vision you saw this afternoon."

I inhale sharply as the blade cuts into my burn. Sweat rolls down my neck. "How do you know about that?"

He smiles through his teeth. "You can hide nothing from me, half-race. I know more about you than you know yourself."

"Let the boy be, Zeldek!"

The voice is loud, clear, unafraid. When I look past Zeldek, Banner's form fills up the entrance to the alley.

Zeldek whirls to face the beggar, drawing the sword away from my chest. Somehow, the release is almost more painful than when it was burning. "Ah, Banner. So very pleased you could join us. It's been a while, brother." He spits out the last word as if it left a sour taste in his mouth.

Of course, they would *be brothers.*

Banner approaches with a cautious step, holding up his hands to show his goodwill.

"I am surprised to see you so alive," Zeldek taunts. "You should've faded long ago. I suppose I owe that to Ulmer and his incessant watchfulness."

Banner dismisses his words with a wave of his hand. When he speaks, his voice is surprisingly placid. "Leave the boy be, Zeldek. He is under my protection, and I will do everything in my power to keep him safe."

Wait, protection? Me?

Zeldek scoffs. "False words from a weak will. If it was protection you bestowed, why does he wear the scars of his masters' abuse? Why has his life been under the daily threat of extermination under your watch?"

"It was for his own protection that he had to endure such pain." Banner's passivity is beginning to grate at me now. One would hope a protector would show a little more passion, especially if their charge is currently in the clutches of the enemy. "I don't want to fight you. I merely ask that you give him more time. He's still a child."

More time for what? For this Zeldek to kill me?

Zeldek draws himself up, towering above me. "Try and stop me, I dare you!"

Banner bows his head, and when he looks up again, his eye not covered by the eye patch is glowing purple. "I wish it hadn't come to this."

"*Saurekin erre!*" Zeldek cries, throwing out his hand toward him.

All I can do is stare in bewilderment as flames shoot from the bare skin of his palm and roll down the alley toward Banner, threatening to engulf him. But Banner, who I am sure is a sorcerer as well, puts up his hand just in time.

"*Desxeo!*"

A violet flash counteracts the flames, engulfing them until they are extinguished. Banner then raises his right hand, and with a shout that I can't quite make out, he sends a wave of purple light toward us both.

With a casual flick of Zeldek's hand, the light fades to an ebony mist. It touches his long black fingernails, and in an instant, the mist is sucked into them.

I stare, eyes wide. *That's... not normal.*

"*Zikinkeria!*" Banner cries, causing the cobblestones between us to explode in a shower of rocks and dirt.

A large root shoots out of the ground and twists around Zeldek's sword to wrench it from his hand. But the blade bursts into flames, incinerating the root, which falls in ashes to the ground.

Banner sways on his feet, and he grasps the wall for support.

Zeldek laughs with scorn. "You are as weak as you have always been!"

"Zeldek, I beg you!" Banner's plea has become desperate. "Leave him be, for another year. You owe me at least that!"

"I owe you nothing." Zeldek's voice is callous. "I will wait no longer!"

Taking the hilt of his sword in both hands, Zeldek points the blade at the beggar. Banner throws up his hands as a wave of flames rolls toward him, a shield of purple mist surrounding him.

"Run, boy, run!" Banner shouts as the fire engulfs him, but I am rooted to the spot.

How can I flee from a man who's in danger because he's trying to protect me?

Banner's shield fails him. His garments catch fire and he throws himself to the ground with a cry of anguish. I leap forward to help him, but Zeldek shoves me against the wall and pins me there with his left hand.

Regaining control of himself, Banner puts his hand to his chest, and the flames disappear. He raises his head feebly, attempting to pull himself up. But his strength leaves him, and his head lolls to the side.

"Your power is pathetic," Zeldek mocks. "You cannot protect yourself, let alone your last hope of redemption! Crawl back to Ulmer before I change my mind and cause you to suffer a fate worse than death!"

Anger wells in my chest. If there is one thing I despise, it's a person who torments someone weaker than themselves. This Zeldek, king or no king, is no exception.

I struggled against the hand still holding me to the wall enough to reach the dagger on his belt. I snatch it, bringing the blade across the back of his hand, hard, leaving behind a sparkling trail of black liquid. Zeldek jerks it back with a yelp of pain, knocking the knife out of my grasp. Yet as he does, he loosens his hold on me, giving me the chance to twist myself free from his grip. I race around the crater created by the root's growth and run to Banner's side. His good eye has gone back to its normal shade of hazel and his face, where it isn't scorched, is very pale.

"Get away, fool!" he rasps.

"No." I crouch down and take his hand as gently as I can in my own. "I'm staying with you."

"He's here for you, not me! Go while you still can!"

I shake my head. "I can't leave you here alone. Not after you risked your life for me."

His gaze darts to Zeldek, who is rubbing his hand in suppressed rage as he stalks towards us. "You don't understand. I have to protect you!"

I lean closer. "Why? Why are you protecting me? I need to know."

He struggles to get the words out. "You are Elroy."

I furrow my brow, not sure that I heard him right. *Who is Elroy?*

"Enough! You've said your goodbyes!" Zeldek is upon us now. He grabs my arm, digging his long fingernails into my skin, and jerks me away from Banner's side. "I leave you alive now, Banner, so that when next we meet, the one you 'defended' for so long will be the one to thrust the knife into your heart."

Then he raises his fist in the air. Dark mist comes in long wisps from the ring on his finger and encircles us. I try to struggle, to shout, to scream, to wake up from this nightmare I'm trapped in. But this is no nightmare. This is real, and I am powerless to stop it.

The darkness envelopes us and all else fades into oblivion.

Chapter Five

The darkness clears and I find myself emerging from a heavy slumber. My head pounds and my eyelids feel like lead. It takes me a moment to remember where I am. The alleyway? No, I'm somewhere else now. Somewhere warm, but closed off. I am completely alone – I can sense it.

My arm aches, and I recall Zeldek digging his claws into it. I am lying on my back in the middle of a square space of floor. A grey smoke-like mist, like the kind you get when you blow out a candle, floats in the air above me and sheds an eerie light on my surroundings. The room in which I'm trapped is small – about twice as tall as I am in width, length, and height – and empty. The walls, ceiling, and floor are made of black marble as smooth as glass. There are no windows, no doors. No way in or out.

No way to escape.

It's as if someone built this cage around me while I slept.

I sit up with a groan. My chest stings where Zeldek burnt me with his sword, and I put a shaky hand to it. The cut has clotted now, and the skin around is enflamed, but it will heal.

Taking a deep breath, I run my hands over my face, wiping away the tears that crusted it while I slept. My entire body is fragile, trembling, as the weight of my situation falls upon me.

I've been kidnapped by a psychopath.

What could he possibly want with me? For that matter, why did Banner risk his life to keep him from taking me? None of this makes any sense.

I have to get out of here.

My legs don't want to move, but I make them as I climb painfully to my feet. They prickle as I turn in a circle, scanning the walls for a way out.

Nothing.

I stagger toward the nearest wall. The mist swirls to avoid me. I wonder if its purpose is solely to light the room, or if there's something more.

Mustering up my strength, I slam my hands into the wall. The moment my skin touches the glassy stone, a powerful force grabs me by the waist and throws me backward. I slam into the floor on my side, and quickly scramble back to my feet, searching for the attacker. But a quick glance around the room tells me it's still empty.

Empty, that is, but for the mist. As if it can hear my thoughts, it grows suddenly restless and rears up before me, taking form as a hideous monster with rows and rows of sharp fangs, and huge, flapping wings. Worse still, the mist tinges yellow as the air becomes unbearably hot, radiating from the jaws of the mist phantom. I leap back, throwing up my hands to shield my face. I break into a cold sweat, unable to move, to think, to breathe.

The heat diminishes as suddenly as it came. I peer through my fingers. The beast has also gone, but the mist has become something else – *someone* else. A tall, robed man turns toward me, his face long and sour, his hair wild and grey. I don't know who he is, or why he fills me with more terror than Ralcher ever could, but he's a character in every one of my nightmares, his beady eyes staring through me, his lip curled in derision, his only desire to hurt me. He takes a step forward and I trip over my own feet in my hurry to get away from him. I roll over to face him and scramble backward into a corner. His eyes blaze out in streaks of grey and white as he raises his fist to strike me.

"Don't!" I squeak, putting up a hand to shield myself.

But his blow never falls. When I dare to look again, the mist is back to floating peacefully about the room. I let out my breath in a rush, shaking uncontrollably. A lump clogs my throat and I grasp my knees to my chest, fighting the tears.

A whisper echoes in the silence, soft as the mist and just as malicious. "What's wrong, little one?"

I look up, searching for the owner of voice. Once again, nothing.

"Z-Zeldek? Is-" I gulp. "Is that you?"

A deep chuckle.

I take a shuddering breath. "Where- where am I?"

"You are my guest, for the time being."

I swallow. I want to hide my fear, to act strong like I did in the alley. But I'm still too shaken from the phantom in the mist, and my words come out with a tremor. "W-why did you bring me here?"

No reply.

"And how did I get in here? There isn't a door."

"The place where you are imprisoned is enchanted, without time. There, the mist has been instructed to keep your magic from you. The only way in or out is by my word. If I am to release you, I must have a reason."

Once again, I am at the mercy of the whims of another. Will I never be free of it?

A yearning for freedom helps rebuild the final pieces of my composure. "What must I do to prove myself?" I ask.

"Wise answer."

The mist charges toward me, swirling, and expands, forming a funnel that hides the walls from my view. Then, just like that, it is gone.

I get to my feet slowly, awed. The walls around me have vanished. Now, I stand on the end of a long, red carpet in the centre of a great hall. And the sight of the hall takes my breath away.

On either side of the carpet is a line of pillars. Each pillar is a statue of a robed and hooded figure holding a lit torch in both hands, their heads bowed low on their chests. Every stone person is different, too. Some are short, some are tall, some are men, and some are women. There are twelve of them in all, six on either side of the carpet. The flames in their hands light up the faces beneath the hoods, revealing the dark scowls that twist every face, and the ultimate self-importance to each tilted chin.

The torches only give off enough light to dimly illuminate the path between the pillars, leaving the rest of the hall cloaked in darkness.

Two incense burners burst into flames at the opposite end of the room from where I stand. Between them ascends a flight of stairs. At the end of the stairs, set on a large dais, is a black throne. The back is spread out in two large wings, creating the impression that the man sitting on the throne is some sort of winged beast. The light of the burners casts shadows around the throne, obscuring the man. But his identity is easy to guess.

With my hands stiff at my sides, fingers clutching the hem of my shirt, I bow my head to acknowledge his distinguished position.

"Step forward!" Zeldek orders.

I start up the carpet toward the dais, taking a quick glance over my shoulder. Two large doors bar any chance of escaping from the hall. I am trapped.

For now.

As I pass the unsettling pillars, I can't shake a sudden feeling that someone is watching me. I peer into the darkness, but nothing presents itself. The stone eyes of the statues seem to glow suddenly red in the torchlight, and I can't help but shudder.

They aren't alive. They aren't watching you. Just keep walking.

When I reach the foot of the stairs, I bow again, more out of habit than respect.

"Welcome," Zeldek declares, "to Gaiztoak, my home."

I glance around again, and I'm sure I see a figure move behind the nearest pillar to my left.

"It's nice, sir." I look back up at Zeldek. "It suits you."

"I take that as a compliment." He leans back into his throne. "You will be at home here, then?"

I attempt a small laugh that gets stuck in my throat. "Must I stay? What I mean is, sir, how could *I* be of service to you?"

"Don't you want to stay?" He sounds genuinely confused. "To live here in my palace will certainly be better than facing execution for sorcery by your master, will it not?"

"That's a matter of perspective, sir."

I don't know why I say it. It's true, I would much rather work in a palace than ever have to face Ralcher again. Yet there is something about Zeldek that chills me deep in my bones.

Zeldek rises from his throne with a deep chuckle that causes the ceiling to rumble, and starts down the stairs toward me. The glow of the firelight is finally cast upon him and I behold his face once more. He looks the same as I remember; only now, his eyes no longer glow, and instead of wearing a black cloak, he wears a blood red robe that trails behind him as he walks.

He begins to descend the stairs. "You have a bold tongue, boy. I admire that."

I take two steps back for each one he takes. Cowardly though it may be, I can't bear him coming near me again.

Reaching the bottom step, he pauses between the braziers, his hands clasped behind his back. "You wish to be free. I understand that. But that freedom is up for you to decide."

My mouth goes dry. "How?"

"I've told you already."

"You want me to give you my allegiance. But I don't understand why."

He releases my gaze, turning to the fire. "I have been observing you for many years. Do you know what I see when I look at you?" He pauses for but a moment. "I see—"

"I don't want your lies," I snap, my temper flaring. "You see a dirty half-breed, same as everyone else!"

"No." His voice is firm, yet soft. "When I look at you, I see myself. I see a boy filled with raw potential, who has everything to prove, yet no one to prove it to. I see a boy who has been alone for his entire life, who has learned to harden himself to the world because all it has ever done is hurt him. But you need not be afraid any longer. I wish to look after you, to call you my son. I will place the world into your hands to do with as you please! All you have to do is put your trust in me."

His words disarm me. Whatever false compliment or veiled threat I expected from him is gone, and the sharp reply I have ready falls from my mouth.

He's right. I do want a father, and a mother. The two people who were supposed to love me the most were the first to leave me. Was I an inconvenience to them? Did they not want a half-breed for a child? Or am I only the product of slave breeding?

"You have more courage than many of my elite followers," he continues, and his tone is almost kind. "You stood up to me when the odds were stacked against you, and stayed with the beggar instead of taking the chance to save yourself. If I could gain that loyalty from you – that trust... I would be more than proud to call you my son."

My mouth hangs open and I don't bother to close it. What am I supposed to say? Only moments ago, this man was a villain in my mind. Now, I'm sorely tempted to accept his offer. Who else has ever wanted to give me so much for simply the price of my loyalty?

Which is as clear a sign as any that there's something not right about this. He must have more to gain than just my loyalty. But what?

There is only one way to find out.

"I don't believe you," I say quietly.

He turns his head to look over his shoulder. "Pardon?"

"I don't believe you," I repeat, louder this time. "You want me for some purpose, a reason you don't want to share with me, and you think that tickling my ears with false promises will convince me to serve you. Well, it's not going to be that easy."

Anger flashes in his eyes and I know I'm drawing closer to the truth.

"Why would I *want* to be your son?" I continue. "How do you expect me to trust you after you almost killed my guardian for protecting me, then threatened me, and then kidnapped me for not bowing down and kissing your feet?"

His face reddens and he holds up his left hand, palm toward himself, as he takes an angry step toward me. I leap backward, but even in my movement, the gash that I made across the back of his hand is very visible. "And should you expect me to be so gracious to a boy who injured me when I was trying to save his life?" he demands. "No! I am bestowing upon you an honour beyond your worth because I see potential in you. Do not take my generosity lightly!"

I look him steadily in the eyes, although his back is to the flames of the incense burners now, and his eyes are cast in shadows. "I don't believe you."

He seems to be assessing me, and an odd smile turns his lips. "Your courage continues to astound me, half-race. Most would be on their knees before me, begging for my forgiveness for even the remotest affront. Yet here you stand and defy me openly?"

"My respect must be earned before it is given."

"Indeed," he says, his mouth curling into a sneer. "And you assume I would strive to *earn* your respect?" He says the last word with contempt.

Turning on his heel, he strides back up the steps to his throne.

"It's unlikely," I venture to reply.

He reaches the top of the stairs and spins to face me, casting the train of his robe to the side. "I do not crave your respect, half-race!" His booming voice ricochets from every corner of the hall to create a very impressive resonance. "I crave your obedience and I care not how I get it!"

He sits upon his throne, clutching the armrests viciously. "I will give you time to consider my offer. I bid you think your answer over carefully. In the meantime, I leave you in the expert care of the commander of my elite bodyguard, head of the dark outlaws, and leader of the Alliance of Shadows; Bellator."

Chapter Six

My expectation of what will emerge from the shadows and what actually emerges are complete opposites. The name Bellator brings to the mind's eye a broad-shouldered man with rolling muscles and a disposition prepared for war. I would never have imagined the short, slender form that steps into the light, but I'm relieved at the difference. That is, until he starts forward with such a dangerous and confident deportment that it causes my heart to leap to my throat, and I instantly know I once again misjudged him – which is to say, I misjudged *her*.

Clad from head to toe in glinting black armour, Bellator wears the stare of death itself on her countenance. A face streaked with jagged scars is delineated in the flickering glow of the firelight. Her eyes are dark in the shadows, her nose is small and refined, and her jaw is rigid. A sable cape decorates her shoulders, billowing out behind her as she strides up the carpet. She holds a helmet under her arm, leaving bare a head of dark brown hair wound around her scalp in a practical braid. The only loose hair is a patch of ragged bangs, which falls down her face to partially cover her right eye.

But the most surprising thing about her is her youth. She can't be more than a few years older than I am, yet she has a bearing that speaks volumes of her adept experience.

Her lip curls in distaste as she casts her gaze briefly upon me, and I nearly trip over my feet in my hurry to get out of her way. I have barely stepped off the carpet when she sweeps past me, leaving the scent of blood roses in her wake. She halts abruptly at the foot of the stairs, and falls to one knee before Zeldek, bowing her head reverently.

"Sire," she begins in a strong, brazen tone. Her head remains bowed as she speaks. "You must forgive me, but I've just received word that there is an important matter in the forest that calls for my immediate attention. I'm afraid I will be unavailable to do as you've requested of me."

Even hidden in the veil of shadows, I can see Zeldek grow tense. His pupils flare like hot embers and he lets out a low growl. Yet when he speaks, his voice is determinedly calm. "More important than my orders?"

Her chin snaps up. "It may be."

"By all means," Zeldek says derisively, "tell me what is so important as to distract the mighty Bellator from carrying out her master's commands?"

Bellator lowers her gaze to the topmost step. "I meant no disrespect, sire," she says quickly. "But as you are aware, it is forbidden to leave the boundaries of our sacred grounds without your permission. One of the families in my care—"

"If it's so important to you that this be dealt with now, I shall take care of it in your stead."

"Sire, that's not—"

"Necessary? Oh, I think it is. In the meantime, you will do as I have commanded you or you will learn to regret your impertinence. Do I make myself clear?"

Her eyes travel back up to her master and she nods. "Crystal, sire."

"Go," he orders coldly. "We'll discuss your wilfulness later in more detail."

She rises to her feet and bows her head to him once more. But as she turns to me, she tightens her jaw in irritation.

"Bellator," he adds, a warning to his tone.

She doesn't turn back to face him. "Yes, my lord?"

"If you so much as think of harming him, I will know."

"Of course, sire."

Her gaze passes over me. There is a savage glint in her ocean blue eyes, and I know that she doesn't intend to heed his warning. She seems to guess that I know this, because a sudden smirk forms on her lips.

"What's your name, then?" A note of spite is concealed in her falsely pleasant tone.

I blink, my mind suddenly blank. I was not prepared for such a question. In my memory, no one has ever asked me that. "Uh," I stammer, and I find myself flinching as I look up into her face.

She lifts a mocking eyebrow. "You don't know?"

"Yes. Yes, of course I do." I pause, taking a gulp of air to clear my mind. "Ealdred. My name is Ealdred."

"I'm surprised that you have a name at all," she remarks. "Half-breeds normally don't, you see."

She says this as if I wouldn't already know.

The flames in the incense burners flare slightly, and Bellator stiffens. Inclining her head once more towards the dais, she starts back down the carpet toward the doors at the opposite end of the hall, telling me to follow her.

I steal one last glance at Zeldek, who is once again fully masked in shadows, before reluctantly turning to follow Bellator. I quickly fall in step with her gait. Each of her steps is quick and sharp, yet there is an uncanny sense of grace to her movements.

As we near the doors, they begin to open for us on their own. Bellator halts suddenly, and putting a rough hand on my shoulder, she jerks me from the carpet. She draws aside as well, leaving space for the figures outlined in the doorway to step into the room.

Slowly, trembling, a man enters the room, followed closely by a woman carrying a little girl in her arms. The girl appears to be very young – maybe two years old – and extremely ill. Her fair hair is drenched with sweat and her eyes are

listless as she rests her head upon her mother's shoulder. All three are dressed in

drab, ragged clothing, carrying with them the scent of heavy toil.

They approach the foot of the steps and fall to their knees before Zeldek. The

flames rise again, the glow casting itself eerily on his face. He examines them for a

moment and then says in his omnipotent, earth shattering voice, "You are the

family that sought to abandon the humble shelter of the forest in which I have so

graciously allowed you to take shelter?"

"N-not perman-nently, your g-grace," the man sputters, drawing his wife

closer to his side. "W-we were merely—"

"Silence!" Zeldek roars. "Are you so daft that you think I *care* what you were

doing?"

Bellator's fist clenches and unclenches.

"You disobeyed the laws of Gaiztoak," he continues coldly. "No one passes in

or out without my permission! Therefore—"

"Wait!" Bellator barks, and even Zeldek starts at the abruptness of her voice.

She continues without waiting for a reply from him, but her voice has softened

considerably. "My master, this family is under my jurisdiction. Please, allow me

the pleasure of flogging them in your name for their rebellion."

Zeldek leaps from his throne. "You were given an order, Bellator! I suggest

you follow through with it immediately!"

Bellator opens her mouth, but prudently snaps it shut again. She turns to leave, dragging me along by the wrist. As we pass under the archway of the door, the man takes advantage of Zeldek's silence to speak.

"Sire, please, have mercy! Our daughter is ill, and we were searching for an herb to make her well."

Bellator stops so suddenly that I slam into her. She doesn't turn around, but stays fixed in place.

"Is that so?" Zeldek says, his voice dangerously quiet.

There is a sudden whooshing sound, and I glance back in time to see the little girl vanish from her mother's arms and appear in Zeldek's clawed hands. He looks down at the girl, clicking his tongue in mock sympathy, and then runs a knife through her tiny chest.

A cry of alarm escapes my throat, only to be quickly suppressed by Bellator, who slams her fist into my stomach. But there was no need. My voice is drowned out by the girl's mother, who shrieks, and her father, who cries out in despair before collapsing in a heap on the floor. Zeldek, however, revels in their sorrow. He chuckles, and casts the girl's lifeless body down the steps. It comes to a halt at her parent's feet.

"There." His tone is indifferent. "I have found you a cure."

Unmitigated hatred for Zeldek burns in my chest, and I open my mouth to curse his soul to the devils when Bellator claps her hand over my mouth and throws me from the room. The doors slam behind us, cutting off the sobs of the heartbroken parents.

I free my mouth from Bellator's hand, and she releases her grip on me. I turn in a circle, clutching my head, overwhelmed by the horror I just witnessed. "What kind of a—" I begin, and cut myself off, swallowing back the overpowering nausea that engulfs me. It isn't the first death I've witnessed, but never have I seen a young child so carelessly and brutally murdered. "That man – that beast! He's the devil!"

"Walk!" Bellator says coldly, shoving me away from the door.

"But—"

"Now!"

I have no choice but to do as she says, and the only reason that I don't thoroughly despise her for it is that despite her pretence of carelessness, I have a feeling that she may have tried to intervene to protect them.

The only sound that follows us as she directs me through a maze of dark halls is the echoing of our footsteps, which seem to reflect the despair growing inside me, both for myself and for those poor parents. The scene replays itself over and over in my head as the silence continues, and I know that it is forever branded in my mind. But no, I cannot allow myself to dwell on it. I have to push it from my mind. I must if I want to remain sane.

There's one thing I know for certain. There is no way that I will ever give my allegiance to that monster, no matter what he promises me.

After we've passed through two levels of empty, torch-lit halls, Bellator stops

in front of a door. She pulls it open a crack, and a surge of steam pours from the

room, dampening my face with warmth. I jerk my head backwards. Bellator,

however, remains quite still until the steam has passed over her, and then peers

inside.

"Curse him!" she cries in exasperation, throwing the door fully open.

"Where's that good-for-nothing knave?"

Inside, the light of the torches on the walls shimmers on the surface of the

pool in the centre of the room. Towels, soap, a scrub brush, and other such bathing

materials lay on the tiled rim of the pool. I recognize it as a very civilized bathing

room, having had some experience attending to a few of my more prestigious

masters while they were washing.

Bellator shoves me into the room. "Get cleaned up. Well. You smell like a

slave." And she slams the door in my face.

I glance back at the closed door, feeling separate from my body. One part of

me is too numb to feel anything, while the other part grows indignant at her words.

I take a few more steps into the room. The tiles are warm against my bare

feet and the movement of the water is alluring. It has been a good while since I last

had a proper bath, I realize. I begin to undress, taking off the oversized cloak, which

still has a strong scent of liquor hanging about it. My ratty tunic and bulky

trousers hold no sentiment in my mind, what with them being large enough to fit a

grown man. I've had to tie the trousers up with a rope since I was given them by an auctioneer, who thought my previous ones were too worn to be considered decent. And he was right.

I untie my knotted, shoulder-length hair and comb it out as much as I can with my fingers. Then, after a moment's hesitation, I step into the pool. The warm water engulfs me, caressing my tired, aching muscles, and forcing me to relax. The nausea finally fades, and I inhale deeply. In the next few minutes, I use the brush and soap from the side of the tub to scrub away the layers of dirt and grime that darken my skin. I'd forgotten the fresh touch of the air on my skin, and just how pale my complexion could be. I feel new, and I like it.

Just as I am contemplating getting out of the pool, the door swings open. Embarrassed, I sink down to my neck in water as a red-haired boy is thrust into the room by Bellator.

He curses at her, but she merely curses back at him and slams the door in his face. He swears louder, kicks the door, and then utters a yelp of frustration and pain.

"Um... hello?" I say when he has quieted down some, shivering from the cool air let in by the open door.

The redhead turns and spits at me. Fortunately, he is too far away to hit anything but the floor.

"I ain't no stupid half-breed's servin' boy!" he shouts, either to me, or to Bellator, or perhaps to the both of us. His accent is strictly Avian – he's obviously a native, though he doesn't have the characteristic dark skin – as he has a habit of drawing out his vowels and skipping half of his consonants. "I won't be!"

"Y-you don't have to be," I stammer. "I don't mind."

"You shut it!" he shouts, throwing the bundle of clothing in his arms onto the floor.

His face is almost as red as the freckles that speckle his skin, and he stomps his foot angrily on the dark tiles. But it seems as if his shouting is to no avail, because after letting out another grumble of frustration, he snatches up my old clothes and carries them toward the door.

I bolt upright. "What are you doing?" I cry, starting out of the pool.

He turns back to me, his anger switching to confusion in an instant. "What's it look like? I'm burnin' this sad 'scuse for clothes!"

"Just... one moment," I say, pulling a towel around myself in case Bellator decides to open the door again.

I pick my way across the wet tiles toward him.

He hesitates. "What for?"

I snatch the trousers from him and feel along the inside seam of one of the legs until my fingers find the hidden lump. I rip open the seam, and an amulet rolls out into the palm of my hand. A perfectly round pearl the size of an eyeball is embedded into a maze of silver lines that curve and swirl into the shape of an eye. It hangs on a simple metal chain which is wound carefully around the amulet. This amulet is the only precious thing that I possess. I've had it for as long as I can remember and I know it's the only link I have to the identity of my parents.

I close my fingers over it and throw the balled-up trousers back at him. "There, now you can throw them out."

But his gaze is fixed on my hand. "What's that you got?"

"Nothing," I reply, turning back toward the pool.

"Oh, it's somethin'," he says, starting after me. But a sudden pounding on the door redirects him and he hurries out of the room.

I snatch up the clothing he brought me, and quickly pull them on: a black tunic and trousers; a black doublet with golden stitching; black stockings; a pair of leather boots; a belt; and a blood red cape that fastens at my shoulders. Each article of clothing fits as if it were made for me – a foreign feeling, as I've never worn clothing that fit me before.

When I am fully clothed, I put the amulet around my neck. It feels as if it's suddenly gained ten pounds of weight, but when I pick it up in my hand, it is as light as ever. I haven't worn it since I was very little. I don't know where it came from or why I was allowed to keep it; I am sure it could be worth a fortune to the right buyer.

The door opens, and I slip the amulet down the neck of my shirt. It feels cold against my bare chest. The redheaded boy enters again, looking just as annoyed as he had when he left.

"How do I look?" I ask, turning to face him.

His critical green eyes flit over me, and he shakes his head with a nasty grin. "That hair's gotta go."

"What do you mean?" I put my hand to my hair, which is dangling in wet strings over my neck.

"You look like a girl, that's why!" He pulls a stool from against the wall, and sets it in the middle of the floor with a bang. Then he taps the seat. "Sit yerself down and I'll give you a more manly haircut."

I hesitate. I don't want that boy anywhere near my head with a knife. "Can't I just tie it back?"

"Sure. Might 'swell braid it too. Look like fancy pants captain girly out there for all I care." He shoots a glare at the door. "Just sit down and get it over with!"

I give in and sit down on the stool, clutching the seat beneath me with both hands. He takes a rusty knife from his pocket, and begins cutting away at my hair, making a point of jerking at it as much as he can. After a few long, painful minutes, he's finished. I look down at the tangled black locks scattered on the tiles and can't help feeling a tinge of sadness. But as I run my fingers through the tousle of hair left on my head, I decide I don't mind it short as much as I thought I would.

"Now," the boy says, casting an admiring glance at his work, "get outta here. The 'general's' awaitin'."

I stand up. "Thanks," I pause, and turn to him. "What's your name?"

He glares at me, his sour mood returning. "What's it to you, half-breed?"

I stare at the floor, weariness washing over me at the sound of the hated insult. "Nothing, I guess."

His suspicion fades slowly and he attempts a crooked smile that ends up looking more like a sneer. "The name's Uri."

"Well, thanks Uri." The next words come out of my mouth without deliberation. "I'm Ealdred."

A grin flickers over his speckled face. "Well, Ealdred, welcome to hell."

Chapter Seven

When I exit the bathing room, Bellator is waiting outside. Leaning back against the wall across from the door with one foot crossed casually over the other, she folds her arms over her chest and casts a careless glance over my new appearance.

"Trying to make you into a prince, is he?"

I shrug. I know she isn't asking because she wants an answer.

"He's wasting his time."

She pushes off from the wall, coming to stand directly in front of me. I look up at her, but for some reason, I don't withdraw or lower my gaze. I feel steady as I look her in the eyes, and a new confidence is born within me.

"I will admit," she adds, "you'd come closer than most from your background if it came to acting regal. You have an unusual confidence about you for a slave."

"As do you, for one who serves a man like Zeldek," I say. "Back in the throne room... with the little girl... he did that to spite you, didn't he?"

Her eyes flash and she folds her hands behind her back. "Lord Zeldek does not tolerate disrespect, and neither do I. You will learn your place here, or you will have me to answer to. And I promise, I won't have as gentle a touch with you as the Master has had thus far."

Spinning on the heel of her boot, she strides back up the hall, barking over her shoulder, "Now follow!"

I trot after her obediently, and we are soon ascending a wide flight of spiral stairs. They end abruptly at a short walkway that halts before a small door. Bellator draws a key from her belt and thrusts it into the lock of the door. It grinds in the keyhole as she turns it, and there's a resounding snap as it unlocks.

She throws the door open. "Welcome to your new prison."

I stumble over the threshold, expecting to see a dingy, dark space with straw on the floor and a small barred window that would barely let in any sunlight. Instead, I am greeted by the dancing light of crystal chandeliers, the soft touch of red carpets on stone floors, and the brilliant hues of black, red, and gold in the elaborate tapestries decorating the walls. In the centre of the floor is a small, circular table with a single chair beside it.

"Sit!" Bellator orders, closing the door behind us.

Caught in a daze, I walk over to the chair and sink down onto the cushion. A black, velvet tablecloth trimmed with golden lace graces the surface of the table, and silverware is set out upon it. I reach out, my fingers barely touching the prongs of the fork. They have been polished well so the candlelight reflects on them like tiny stars. I've never had such a privilege before, to use eating utensils. I hope I don't embarrass myself too much if I don't know what to do with them.

"This apartment is a triangle of three chambers," Bellator explains jadedly, leaning back against the wall beside the door. "This is your dining chamber. To the left is your living chamber, and to your right is your bed chamber. You will be staying here indefinitely, unless otherwise summoned. Zeldek wants to appear non-threatening, but the reality is that you are a prisoner. Get used to it."

At least she's honest.

The door to the apartment is pushed open, and a maid enters. Her arms are laden with a tray of food, which she carries carefully toward me. The pleasant aroma of roasted fowl fills the air, and my empty stomach grumbles eagerly. It's been weeks since I've had a full meal, and days since I've eaten anything more than the scraps Lye left for me.

The girl sets the platter in front of me and places a crystal goblet of wine to the left of it.

Wait! How does she know that I am left-handed?

"Thank y—" I begin, glancing up at her nonchalantly. But my voice dies in my throat.

She averts her gaze, the blood rushing into her rosy cheeks. A ringlet of white hair falls from the snowy braid wound around her head and rests on her cheek. She cringes, as if expecting me to blow up.

But I'm not angry. I feel as if I've been punched in the gut, and everything I feared falls into place with a sickening thud in the pit of my stomach.

"Annalyn?"

"I'm so sorry, Ealdred!" she blurts. "I had to do what the Master told me."

That only makes me feel worse.

She didn't know my name. I never told her my name!

"You were sent to spy on me." But it isn't a question.

She bites her lip. "Not spy, exactly. My assignment was to relay information regarding the effects of—"

"That's enough, girl!" Bellator snaps. "Return to your duties at once."

Annalyn backs away. "I'm sorry," she whispers. "I had no choice."

Then she's gone.

Once the door has closed behind her, I turn to Bellator, my fingers twisting the stiff lace of the tablecloth. "Why did Zeldek send her to spy on me?"

Bellator shrugs, crossing her arms over her chest again. "Why are you so worked up about it? The Master has sources everywhere, and Annalyn happens to be one of them. How else did you think the Master knew so much about you?"

I feel betrayed and I don't know why. I should've guessed that Annalyn was up to something, that her kindness was merely a facade. I should've remembered that no one is just nice to a half-breed.

"Oh, spare me the tears, half-breed. Go on and eat while you still can." Then she adds under her breath, "And preferably choke to death while you are at it!"

My gaze drifts down to my plate. The food on it is far richer than anything ever set before me. But I've lost my appetite.

"Just eat!" she bellows, clearly working out her own frustration by shouting at me.

I grab a roll from the platter and cram it into my mouth, following it with a gulp of wine to help it go down. But even that threatens to come back up. I push away my tray and put my elbows on the table, resting my face in my hands. I run my fingers through my unfamiliarly short hair, trying to regain some sense of calm.

Why is this upsetting me? I know better than to put my faith in anyone but myself.

"Well, it's not my problem if you want to starve," Bellator says, and pounds her fist on the door.

Annalyn returns to take away my food, but she doesn't look at me as she gathers up my tray, silverware, and goblet. She carries them away, and the room is lost in silence.

Bellator fumbles with the hilt of the dagger in her belt, staring at a section of floor with a dark scowl. I wait for her to give me an order, or at least say something. But she doesn't.

At last, I push back my chair and stand up.

Bellator's glance is hostile as it flashes to me. "Where do you think you're going?"

Halting, I slide my chair back into its place at the table. My life thus far has never been in my hands to decide. I've always had masters telling me what to do, forcing me to follow their rules. Yet now I am expected to make a decision that will undoubtedly mean the difference between my life and my death? I need help from someone. Someone who, quite possibly, has made such a decision.

I clear my throat.

"Bellator," I begin, and then wince.

Why is she so hard to talk to?

She stares at me blankly, waiting. I take it as leave to continue. "I- I was wondering; if you were me— no... not that you are me, but if you were ever in my... position," I pause, taking a breath to untie my tongue. "What would you do? About Zeldek's offer, I mean. Would you agree to it?"

Her expression doesn't change.

I realize that I am nervously twisting the amulet under my shirt, and I jerk my hand away. A quiet moment passes with no response. "Y-you did hear me, right?"

"I did." She tosses her head to the side, knocking her bangs out of her eyes. "Why are you asking me? You either want it or you don't. What I would do has no sway over what you've already decided."

I wet my lower lip. "I know, but it's just that he killed that girl without a thought, didn't he? Refusing him would be asking for the same – or worse – treatment."

She raises an eyebrow. "Scared to die, are you?"

I cross my arms to shield against the very notion. "Aren't you?"

"Oh no. There are things far worse than death." She outlines the deepest scar on her face with her finger. "I should know."

I don't know what to say to that.

"Don't believe me?" She pulls out her knife and turns it over in her hands. "You'll find out soon enough without my help."

Without so much as a warning, she leaps forward and hurls the knife at my head.

My hand shoots up without deliberation, catching the knife by the hilt, the point inches from my nose. I feel an icy chill retreating up my arm, and the hilt of the knife is warm in my palm. Heart pounding, I look from the knife to Bellator. Her expression is one of restrained shock, her eyes withholding a glimmer of admiration. At least, that's what I hope it is.

"For a simple half-breed, you have excellent reflexes." Her tone is accusing and I don't know what to make of it.

"It's a nice knife," I say lamely.

But my statement is true, at least. The knife is of remarkable craftsmanship. The pommel is a scaly silver circle with a black crystal set in the centre of it, the grip is redwood embossed with a spiral of black silver, and the cross-guard is a depiction of two blackened silver dragons. Each dragon faces outward, their tails entwined around the first few inches of the foot-long blade.

"It should be," she says with pride. "I forged it myself."

"Ah," I nod, my breath catching up with me. "You're a blacksmith?"

Her thick brows draw into a steely glare. "In my spare time, yes."

She looks at the knife in my hand.

"Oh, sorry." I hold out the handle to her, but keep a close eye on her movements in case she decides to impale me again.

A brief look of wonder crosses her face. "You would give the weapon back to your attacker? That's remarkably stupid."

But she doesn't move to take it back.

"Oh no, it's yours," she explains when she sees my confusion. "You caught it, you keep it. Who knows? It might come in handy some time soon." She grins unnervingly, then turns to the open doorway to the living chamber. "Come. The Master wishes to speak with you."

The pit of my stomach drops and is rapidly replaced by a burning indignation.

What more could he possibly have to say? I've already seen enough to know how despicable he is. Nothing he does or says will convince me of otherwise.

I follow her cautiously, my grip tight on the handle of my new knife.

The adjoining room is sparsely accommodated with two crescent sofas with a low table between them. They face out toward a set of crystal doors that open to a dark balcony. On either side of the doorframe is a torch, which combusts into flames as soon as I set foot into the room.

Bellator steps aside, her hands clasped behind her back, and nods to the balcony. "He's over there."

I skirt around her, watching her out of the corner of my eye. I might've caught the knife when she threw it at me, but I doubt I can do much if she decides to stab me in the back.

It turns out there's no need to worry. Once I've passed her by, she turns on her heel and exits the room. The doors click shut behind her, leaving me alone in Zeldek's dark presence.

Chapter Eight

I squint past the bright illumination of torchlight to the darkness of the balcony, only able to detect a slight haze of movement. But I know Zeldek is there.

"You wanted to speak with me," I say a bit too stiffly.

The flames rise in their posts, brightening the entire vicinity. The light reaches the balcony, and I can make out his dark form. He stands at the edge of the parapet, his back to me. His hands rest on the balustrade as he surveys whatever is below.

"Half-race," Zeldek greets tonelessly. "Has Bellator been kind to you?"

I am too angry to laugh at the ridiculous question. *Is Bellator even capable of kindness?*

"That depends on one's definition of kindness, sir."

"You're alive, aren't you?" I can hear the smile in his voice and I despise him for it.

"Yes."

"Then she has been kind to you."

Despite the humour of his words, I feel my fists clench at my sides. "I thought you gave me time to think about your offer."

He turns his head to the side. "I did."

"Then why are you here?"

There is a slight pause. "It is of another matter which I have come to speak."

I wait for him to explain himself, but he doesn't.

"What is it?"

He turns to me at last, coming to stand beneath the arch of the doorframe. "You."

"Me?" I echo, unease filling me. "What do you mean?"

"Sit and I will explain myself," he says, gesturing to the sofas.

I don't move.

He frowns. "I see. Well, if you won't sit, I will."

He takes a seat, crossing one knee over the other, and leans back with a deep sigh. A wave of exhaustion washes over his sunken face, and for a moment, his age catches up with him. But the moment is brief.

"I have not been as forthcoming with you as I should've been," he begins, entwining his fingers together. "My intention was to break all of this to you slowly to avoid overwhelming you, but I see my caution has only caused you confusion. The truth is, Ealdred – and you might have guessed this already – you are not as ordinary as you may have thought."

I eye him suspiciously. "What do you mean, ordinary?"

He rubs his chin between his index finger and thumb. "I suppose I should say it plainly." He clears his throat. "You are a half-race."

"Yeah, really hard to miss that," I say, furrowing my brows. "What with being a slave because of it."

"Not half-*breed*. Half-*race*. Half-breeds are individuals that are descended both from those who live in the darkness beneath the ground and those who dwell under the sun, but are humans nonetheless. A half-race is one who is half human, half Vaelhyrean."

That piques my interest. "Half Vaelhyrean?"

He nods.

"What, exactly, is a Vaelhyrean?"

"*I* am a Vaelhyrean."

He turns to stare out through the balcony doors, his face growing downcast.

"Long ago, before the five races of humankind were formed, my people, the Vaelhyreans, came from over the northern sea to inhabit Theara. We were splendorous, beautiful beings of great power, which we carried with us from our homeland. We were Irla's – that is, Earth's – guardians, sworn to protect and serve her, and as a reward for our service, she granted us control of the elements. We were bound to protect the new land we had found and to command its elements with wisdom. Over us ruled King Emyr, the wisest and most powerful of all the Vaelhyreans. He directed us with foresight and justness."

A deep sorrow wells in his dark eyes.

My anger begins to slip away quite against my will. "What happened to you?"

Heaving a great sigh, he glares into the flames of the torches and his voice is bitter as he continues. "Upon the creation of humanity, King Emyr made a pledge to Irla that we would welcome this new species to live amongst us, and that we would use our magic to safeguard them. But there was a rebel among us called Caderyn who cared nothing for the humans, desiring only to dominate them. He swayed a council of twelve Vaelhyreans over to his way of thinking and together, they went in search of the ultimate source of power – the Aemurel, a substance made purely of dark magic. King Emyr had trapped it in a sceptre and locked it away in an abyss, the entrance to which was hidden in a chasm deep beneath the crust of the earth. Combining their power, they took possession of the sceptre and the insatiable malice within. A great battle ensued between those loyal to Emyr and the forces of Caderyn and it lasted for over a century. Many on both sides were lost and many of the elements were destroyed. One, ice, was lost to insanity and had to be locked away." The terrible recollection haunts his eyes and he shudders. "In the end, my four siblings and I were among the few left to defend Emyr."

"Banner and Ulmer are your siblings, aren't they?" My voice is accusing, but he doesn't seem to notice.

"Yes. We also had two sisters, Batuel and... Sylvia."

"Had?"

His expression turns to stone. "They are dead," he says, and his voice grows only more frightening as he continues. "They did not understand. No one did! Caderyn had to fall, and fate saw fit that I be the one to end him. I slew him in the great hall of this very palace and the Aemurel presented itself to me. It showed me a way to save my people! So I took it and I used its power to wipe out the remaining traitors. But when I returned home, I found that I was too late. King Emyr had been killed." His fist clenches and he bows his forehead to it. "You see, that is why my brothers hate me. Those who had once been my allies blamed me for his death. They saw my possession of the Aemurel as a threat and tried to make me destroy it. But I could not part with it. It had saved us, and I was not like Caderyn; I could control it! But my own family, all of them – they betrayed me, attacked me, and I could do nothing but retaliate. They saw my strength then, too late. I drove them into hiding, where they have stayed for the last two thousand years, licking their wounds and biding their time."

Knowing him for even this short time, I doubt he was as innocent in the matter as he claims. But I don't dare say this aloud.

I clear my throat. "Why are you telling me all of this?"

"Because it is your legacy! If you swear your allegiance to me, you will be my heir, and this the cause that will carry you forward. You will live it, breathe it! It will determine the rest of your life and your rule long after I am gone."

Apparently, he has my entire life planned out for me. "And what cause is that?"

"To rule the world as was once intended, spreading prosperity to those worthy, and weeding out those who are a detriment to that prosperity."

"And who would that be?" I dare to ask.

He narrows his eyes. "Anyone who stands in our way."

I recoil, trying not to show that I have no inclination toward going along with this plan.

A long, unbroken silence hangs in the air and he stands, turning to stare into the darkness beyond.

I swallow, working up my courage to speak again. "So... you think I'm half Vaelhyrean?"

"I don't *think* it," he snaps. "I *know* it!"

"But how do you know?"

"I know everything about you. I told you, I've been observing you since your birth. You see, I knew your father."

My breath catches in my throat. "My father?"

"Yes, your father. The very same man that sold you into slavery all those years ago."

I am stunned. *My* father *was the one that sold me into slavery?*

"The only reason that you are alive now is because I was watching over you, although my foolish brother seems to think it was his work."

"But... well, wasn't it?" I venture to say. "Even in the alleyway, the only danger seemed to be you. Banner just wanted to protect me."

"In the alleyway, perhaps, but what else has he done for you? This whole time, I've been the one protecting you from yourself!"

"From myself?" I echo. "What are you talking about?"

"The earthquake, the sharpened reflexes, the vision; what do you think caused these things? Your master was right to call you what you are: a sorcerer, and a powerful one at that!"

"I—" My voice falters, horror filling me. "I *did* do that?"

"Indeed. Each time, you drew on the well of energy stored within yourself, and you were able to do extraordinary things. These early stages are crucial for learning to control these powers for the rest of your life. If you do not, you will do yourself more harm than good."

I don't want to admit that he is right. A half-breed sorcerer? I would never be able to show my face anywhere ever again without someone wanting to enslave or kill me.

"So... so I can use magic?"

"Not just any magic," he said. "Petty witchcraft done by mortals is weak and fleeting. No, what you and I possess is elemental magic, which is the most powerful magic of all. You were born with this ability, though I took it from you as a child to keep it from getting you into trouble. But such a thing cannot stay absent forever if it is rooted deeply within you. Your magic began to come back to you the same day that I took you from Zandelba, when you unknowingly almost brought down your master's estate. You could not control it, and your fear and anger made it very strong indeed. It will only grow stronger as time goes by. You will need a master to teach you to control it." He turns to face me, an intent look in his eye. "I would be pleased to oversee your training, if you accept my offer to join my cause."

And that is something that I will never do.

Trying to buy some time, I quickly change the subject, and ask the question nagging in my mind.

"Sir... you said that you knew my father. Can you tell me who he was?"

His expression turns to disappointment. "It doesn't matter who he was. He didn't want you as a son! Isn't that saying enough?"

"But I need to know."

He goes on as if I'd never raised the question. "To aid you in cultivating your magic is the reason I brought you here. I must be the one to train you, or you will be of no use to me at all."

"Use?" The word is bitter to my tongue. "To what purpose?"

He pauses, finally turning back to face me. "Your destiny, so to speak, is a great one in the eyes of many. If you give me your loyalty, I will equip you as best I can to accomplish it."

I take a deep breath. "And if I refuse?"

His cold smile sends a chill down my spine. "There are other methods to get what I want. Methods that would break the spirit of even the strongest warrior."

"T-torture?" I can barely mouth the word.

"Like nothing that you can imagine. I warn you, things will not go well for you if you get it into your head to be stubborn. I have had many years to plan for this and I do not intend to fail now."

No one ever intends to fail.

"Think it through carefully. I expect an answer by the end of the week. Do not disappoint me, *Elroy.*"

With that, he disappears in a cloud of thick, black smoke. It lingers in the air for only a moment, and then the flames in the torches are extinguished, cloaking the room in gloomy darkness.

I feel my way over to the sofa, and sit down, letting out my breath in a rush. He called me Elroy, the same name Banner used before I was taken. It isn't that I don't like the name. On the contrary, it has a very nice feel to it. But why? Why had they both called me by that name? Is it a key that will unlock the secret to my past? A title, maybe?

No matter how many questions I ask, the answers do not come.

I can use magic; that much is clear. Magic that I don't have even the beginnings of an idea how to use. It almost got me executed back in Weisport. I must learn to control it. But I cannot stay here. Zeldek is cruel and I refuse to serve him. Yet he will demand an answer from me, and I doubt the one I'll give will please him very much. Then he will torture me, and I'll end up serving him anyways.

What choice do I really have?

Conflict raging within me, I wander out onto the balcony. The sky is overcast with dark clouds that snuff out all light. A thin mist hangs in the stifling air, shedding a ghostly light on my surroundings. A parapet cut from grey stone extends from the smooth obsidian of the building's outer walls, guarding the edge of a drop.

I approach, wrapping my fingers tightly around the balustrade before leaning carefully to peer over the edge.

What I see takes my breath away.

I am standing at the top of a tower that looks out over the edge of a cliff. Stretching out as far as the eye can see are the grey, stormy waves of the sea. They chase each other to the foot of the cliff and collide into the side of it. The spray shoots up, bathing the base of the tower in foam, and then cascades back into the depths of the ocean in time for the next breaker to follow it.

Over the roar of the ocean, there comes a faint beating sound, almost like a sheet flapping in a strong wind. Suddenly, a huge, black creature flashes across my vision, piercing the air with a wild screech. A dagger shoots past me and clatters to the floor of the room behind me. I stagger back in shock.

The creature circles above the water and starts back toward me. As it comes, I notice Bellator sitting on the creature's back, smirking down at me. She pulls another dagger from her belt and raises it to throw.

I turn, my heart pounding in terror, and dart through the doors, slamming them behind me. Seconds later, the knife shatters through one of the crystal panes and falls to the floor at my feet. Gasping, I put my back to the doorframe and grasp my knife in both hands.

"What's the matter with you?" a voice drawls.

I spin around, pointing my knife in the direction of the voice.

Uri stops in the doorway opposite the balcony and throws up his hands. "Hold on, would you? It's me!"

I lower the blade. "S-sorry."

Seemingly forgetting the incident in an instant, he yawns and stretches himself out on one of the sofas. "That's a real live dragon, in case you don't know."

I try to relax, but my tense muscles refuse to obey. "What was?"

"Hmm? Oh, the beast you was runnin' from. The Master keeps a few 'round as pests. Part of his plan to take over the world." His voice is dripping with sarcasm. "When he gets his power back, he's gonna get revenge on the lot of us for not kissin' 'is feet, and terrorize us 'til we repent of our sins."

So how do I fit into this? These powers that I have… clearly, they are the reason I am here in the first place. Not because he wants a son. He needs them for something.

I won't be used like that. Not as a weapon.

"I don't think he'll never get it back," Uri continues, closing his eyes and settling into the cushions, "so we don't got nothin' to worry about. He's been a tryin' for the past few thousand years now, but ain't got nowhere."

"What happened to it?"

He opens one eye. "To what?"

"His power. I thought he had it."

He shrugs again. "Oh, he's got some. I don't really understand it, to be honest. But he's got a hankerin' to get the rest back."

"I take it you don't support his cause?"

His tone grows bitter. "It don't matter what I think! I'm only here 'cause my cursed pap traded me for a fleet of ships and the rank of pirate captain for Zeldek."

I feel sorry for him. As I have recently discovered, the only thing worse than not having parents is having them abandon you.

Chapter Nine

I lean against the back of the sofa, my mind only half awake. My eyelids are heavy as I attempt to keep my gaze fixed on the broken window pane in the balcony door. The night has come and gone under my sleepless watch, and it is only as morning approaches that I begin to feel drowsy.

The pitch darkness of night has brightened into a grey haze, but it is still laden with the same dense hopelessness as before. Usually morning gives me a small glimmer of hope for my dreary future, and reawakens dreams of freedom in my heart. But here in Gaiztoak, the very air clouds my mind with doubt and fear.

A dark shape passes across the broken pane, and I bolt upright. It disappears around the tower before I can make it out, and I become aware of the same sound of beating wings that I heard last night when Bellator and her dragon attacked me. Only this time, it isn't followed by that bloodcurdling screech.

I rise to my feet and draw my dagger, watching the entrance to the balcony for any sign of movement. My heart races as the beating sound continues, but I see no sign of the dragon.

Suddenly, a smaller, dark figure drops lightly onto the balcony, stooping quickly to its hands and knees. It stays that way for a moment, and then rises slowly and silently to its feet. Even though the figure is blurred by the glass in the door, I know who it is.

Bellator pushes the doors softly open, and tiptoes into the room. Her helmet is on her head now, and she is fully armed with her bow and a quiver of arrows at one side, a belt of daggers around her waist, and a sword at her other side.

She stops short when she sees me and puts up her hands in mock surprise. "Whoa! Easy there, half-breed. I thought you were asleep!"

"Would you prefer that I was?" I demand coldly. "Perhaps so you can more easily kill me?"

She clicks her tongue, wagging a finger at me. "Someone's a little cranky. Didn't get much sleep last night, did we?"

My irritation grows. "What are you doing here?"

"Oh dear. You don't look too good at all. Were you up *all* night?"

I point my dagger at her. "Answer my question!"

The corner of her mouth turns up in a smirk. "Were you frightened?"

"You would be too if you had to worry about someone coming in and trying to kill you while you slept."

"That's why no one knows where I sleep." She wipes her bangs under the rim of her helmet. They are damp with perspiration and a thick strand sticks to her forehead. "Put the knife away and come with me."

I eye her with suspicion. "Where do you plan to take me?"

"I think you'll like it. If you're brave, that is."

I hesitate. "You're not going to try to kill me again, are you?"

She snorts, but doesn't make any promises. "Come on! Fyra is waiting outside."

"Fyra?" I repeat, casting a nervous glance into the sky.

"Fyra, my dragon."

I slide my knife into my belt, not feeling very encouraged. But I keep my hand close to the hilt in case she tries anything.

Bellator goes back to the balcony and steps up onto the parapet, spreading out her arms to both sides like a bird in flight. Glancing over her shoulder, she beckons for me to follow. I approach warily and look up at the sky. The dark shape of her dragon is nowhere in sight.

"Follow me!" she cries, and dives over the edge.

My stomach drops with her, and a shocked cry escapes my throat. I throw myself to the railing and look down. Her body is plummeting toward the sharp rocks at the foot of the tower, stretched out like a leaf in the wind. I expect at any second to see her crash into the cliff side, and fall forever into the depths below. But then a black form almost too swift for the eye to behold shoots past me and is beneath her in an instant. It opens its wings, stopping itself mid-dive, and she lands on its back, unharmed. She leans forward, resting a hand on the beast's head, and they sweep around as smoothly as if Bellator were just another extension of the dragon's body.

"Your turn!" she calls as they begin their ascent back toward me.

I must be a fool for even considering this.

And yet I find myself climbing up onto the railing. My knees wobble and I fling out my arms to catch my balance. The rocks below seem to sharpen their teeth and the water opens its foaming mouth to receive me. I am well aware this is probably a trick on Bellator's part, trying to get me to commit suicide, or something equally as cruel. But a small voice within urges me to jump anyways.

As though she hears my inner voice, Bellator shouts, "Jump!" as the dragon soars past me.

I look down again, and the small voice grows still quieter. I'm not an imbecile. And yet I long to be able to jump like that. To feel like I am flying for even a brief moment. To grasp that kind of freedom. The thought exhilarates me.

Besides, Bellator was right. There are things worse than death, and serving Zeldek is one of them.

I take a deep breath and let myself fall forward.

The next few moments are both magical and terrifying. The ground rushes toward me and the air sweeps past me. I feel like a bird, floating through the air at my own leisure, free at last! A shout of exhilaration and pure joy escapes me, and I let it. I don't remember a time that I have felt so happy. But as the ground

continues to approach, panic begins to replace my joy. I force myself to remain

calm, waiting for the dragon to swoop underneath me. But it doesn't. The ground is

so near that I can almost feel myself crashing into it, and all that I can do is brace

myself.

I hit the ground, but it doesn't hurt nearly as much as I expected it would.

Once the air forced out by the impact refills my lungs, I realize that I didn't hit the

ground after all. I am still in the air. I am, in fact, floating upward. I feel pressure

on my chest and when I look down I see four of the dragon's formidable, scaly talons

wrapped around my body.

"I didn't think you'd jump!" Bellator calls, looking down at me over the

dragon's neck.

She sounds impressed.

But I don't have time to answer. Bellator disappears again, and Fyra dives

over the edge of the cliff. We speed right for the water until we are almost

swallowed up by it, then stabilize abruptly to hover over the rocky waves. The

spray of the ocean drenches me to the skin and my dangling feet cut a line through

the surface of the water. Then, without warning, we shoot back up into the sky.

Something entirely foreign to me comes out of nowhere and fills my throat.

Laughter. It comes out as an odd croaking sound, but it is laughter nonetheless.

And it feels good. So good that I find myself wishing that I had cause to do it more

often.

Fyra does a summersault in the air and glides back toward the tower, which is by now barely visible in the mist. As we sweep over the spire of the tower the mist clears away, and I gasp in wonder at the landscape below us.

Beneath us is Gaiztoak in all its splendour. Nestled in the rocky surface of a mountain is a large, five-pointed star which makes up Zeldek's palace. Between each spike of the star is a steaming pool of lava entrapped by a circular wall that surrounds the star. A jagged tower protrudes from the centre of the star, seeming to scrape the sky itself. At the tip of each spike is a smaller version of that tower, but each is magnificent nonetheless. One of these towers is the one that I am now forced to call home.

Surrounding the pentagram is a rough mountain range that acts as a natural protective barrier. Zeldek has made good use of it. Defence towers and beacons have been built into it at fitting intervals and a walkway snakes across the mountaintop between each of them. I can see a dark hollow in the centre of the mountain where a tunnel has been built to allow access to the outside world, but it is barred by a huge iron gateway.

The flatland between the mountain range and the pentagram is dry and barren, and dotted with what appear to deep pits. Wisps of smoke twist from them, joining the rest of the haze above Gaiztoak. Even more curious are the dark shapes that move among them, disappearing into the pits and emerging from them at their own leisure. The only thing clear of the pits and shapes is a large, oval-shaped stretch of ground near the ocean's side. Toward this Fyra swoops.

As we near the ground, the dragon opens her talons and drops me. I barely have time to gasp before I land. I roll through the dust, skidding to an abrupt halt a few meters away. Pain vibrates up the side of my body that I landed on, but not enough to indicate that anything is broken. I push myself to my hands and knees, coughing the dust from my lungs.

Fyra settles across the arena from me. Awe sweeps over me as I get a clear view of her for the first time. She is all around the biggest, most majestic creature that I have ever laid eyes upon. Armoured with a coat of shining black scales and equipped with razor sharp spikes on her head and at the end of her lizard-like tail, she is very much as dangerous as her rider. A long, forked tongue flits in and out between her sharp fangs as she pants from her exertion, and she folds her massive, bat-like wings to her sides. Her red eyes sparkle like rubies and there is a deep, ageless look in them that I've never before observed in a living being.

Bellator leaps from the dragon's back before it has fully landed and strides toward me. She pulls her helmet from her head and tosses it to the side, her hair falling about her face in tangles. She pushes it back with one hand to reveal an annoyingly mysterious smirk.

"Well, what do you think?"

For a moment, I think that she is talking about herself and I am grasping for something to say when I realize that she'd gestured to everything in general.

"Oh!" I stammer, glancing around. "Right! Yeah. It's nice. Has a lot of interesting detail. And fire. Who would have thought to use a mountain range as a wall?"

She grimaces in irritation. "I was talking about Fyra."

I try to speak clearly, but my tongue won't let me. "Oh- oh, right. Her. She's great too. Flying is amazing!"

My stammering only makes her more irritated, driving away the sliver of friendliness behind her tone.

"Oh, shut up!" she snaps.

A menacing glint sparks in her eyes, similar to the look she had when she threw the knife at me last night.

My mouth goes dry and I back away, beginning to see my immediate surroundings more clearly. The ground is packed solid, as if trampled down by many feet over a long period of time. Battered targets are set up along the precipice walls and the splintered remains of arrow shafts litter the ground around them. I realize for the first time that I am standing in the middle of a fighting arena.

I gulp. "Why did you bring me here?"

I expect her to smirk, to mock, to gloat. But she doesn't. Instead, she gives me a long, blank stare. "So, you have magic," she says at last.

"I'm told so."

"No!" She shouts it so suddenly that I jump out of my skin, scurrying backward. "You must *know* so with all of your being, or you will achieve nothing! Erase the doubt from your mind, and accept it. *You have magic!*"

"I- I have magic."

She advances toward me, her hand on the crook of her bow. I retreat a step with every step that she takes. "Do not hesitate! These powers will be with you for the rest of your life, whether you want them or not. So far, they have sharpened your reflexes to create a defensive shield around you, but they won't end there. You'll be able to see things no one else can see, hear things that no one else can hear. You'll be able to move things without touching them, make things happen without meaning to. Your power is a gift as well as a curse; you must use it with wisdom. If you do not, you will only destroy yourself and everything around you and everyone you touch!"

Fear lumps in my throat.

Somehow, she senses it. "Do not fear it. Welcome it! Fear causes you to lose control, and that is something you must never do when you possess such power."

I nod, swallowing back my fear. But my heart replaces it in my throat as she jerks an arrow from her quiver, nocks her bow, and directs her aim at my chest. She releases it, and I throw myself to the ground in a panic. The arrow barely misses and strikes the ground a few feet behind me.

"Get up!" she orders, pulling another arrow from her quiver.

I scurry to my feet just in time for her to loose the second arrow at me. A cold wave of that new energy flashes through me. My hand goes for my dagger and I slash her arrow out of the air.

Bellator straightens up, a sudden look of interest glinting in her eyes. "Ah, I see it now."

"W-what do you see?"

"Your eyes flash blue when you use magic. I wonder what your element is..." She dwells on this thought for only a moment. "Now, fight back!"

She has already slung her bow back over her shoulder and is holding a drawn sword in her hands. My vision sharpens. I note how she is standing, her exact footing, and what she is going to do the moment before she does it. When she leaps toward me, bringing down her blade toward my head, I am able to block it with my knife. She quickly follows it with a thrust, which I knock to the side. But then she whirls around, slashing at me. I underestimate the length of her sword and the tip of her blade cuts through the left sleeve of my shirt. I gasp as the warm metal pierces my skin. My focus cracks. I put my hand to the cut and try to stop the steady flow of blood.

"Pay attention!" Bellator snaps, thrusting her sword at me again.

"Wait!" I gasp, barely stopping her sword with my knife.

But she doesn't. She slashes at me again and I duck just in time. Her blade passes over my head, but when she brings it back, she puts it under my guard, cutting across my right thigh.

My knife slips from my hand and I have to bite my tongue to keep from screaming. I lose my footing and stumble to the ground. Blood darkens the fabric of my trousers. I clutch my leg, my breath hissing through clenched teeth.

She points her sword at my chest. "Get up!"

I try to push myself up, but my leg has grown weak with shock. I fall to my hands and knees, shaking my head.

"I can't!"

"I don't care!" she shouts, thrusting her sword at me again.

I attempt to block her blow, but I am too slow. Her blade pierces my side. This time I do scream, pressing my fists over the wound.

"You have to trust your abilities!" Bellator shouts, her eyes afire. "You have to feel the power flowing through you at all times! And you certainly must never give up during a fight! Do you understand me? Never! You're a natural fighter with an incredible gift, but none of that matters if you are going to give up as soon as you feel a little pain!"

Angry tears sting my eyes. "I don't want to be a fighter!"

"That doesn't matter!" she shouts just as angrily. "If you expect to survive for much longer, you have to be one! Fight through the pain! You won't get anywhere if you sit around whining when you get a little cut up!"

"You think you're the first person to hurt me for their own amusement? It's like I was born to be hurt! When's it gonna stop?!"

Her cheeks flush a dark red. "Never! People will never stop hurting you until you make them. I'm trying to show you that, but you're too busy wallowing in self-pity to listen!"

I feel a pang of guilt. She is right, and I know that. But the anger is still there.

"I never asked for your help."

The venom in her voice doubles, but the volume of her tone lowers decidedly. "I don't care what you asked for! You will either learn to control your magic, or you won't. But I would rather see you learn and free yourself from the bonds of your kind than have you waste away in misery! Why? Because I'm not the heartless beast that you apparently think I am, although I am tempted to be flattered that you think so highly of me!"

"You can't blame me for having a hard time trusting you, Bellator!" I say her name with spite. "Not only have you tried to kill me three times in the past day, but you're also the right hand of the man who's threatening me with torture if I don't give him my full and undivided loyalty for the rest of my life!"

Her anger fades like water over embers. When she speaks again, her voice is subdued. "It was never my intention to kill you. I was merely testing your skills. On my word of honour, I would never kill a half-breed."

I'm not sure whether to take her seriously. "What is your word worth to me?"

She glances around as if someone might be listening, and then looks back at me. "A half-breed once died so that I would not lose my hand. I can never repay the debt that I owe him."

My anger, my pain, my bitterness; it all drains away with her words, replaced by a dull numbness. "Your hand?" I ask quietly as a memory from years long passed stirs in its slumber.

Her eyes find mine for just a moment. "What would you know about it?" she snaps.

Now that the memory has stirred, it moves to full consciousness quickly. It becomes vivid, though it is of an event that happened over eight years before, when I was in the employ of a butcher in the city of Sustinere, Zandelba. It was in that city that I realized just how badly normal people treated their own. Sustinere had a lot of orphans and beggars roaming its streets, and thievery was common. I was beaten many times and missed more meals than I cared to count for meat that had been stolen from the storeroom.

One day, the butcher caught one of the thieves. It was a little girl in ragged clothing. Her dark hair was knotted and messy, her cheeks were hollow, and there was a vicious, hungry look in her eyes. I remembered seeing how thin and frail she was and I realized that she was only stealing so that she wouldn't starve to death.

The butcher wasn't so inclined to compassion. He called for the city guards and they were dragging her away to cut off her hand for thievery. What struck me most was that she did not scream, or plead, or even beg for mercy. Her eyes echoed the hopelessness that had seized her soul, and mirrored the terror that ripped her apart from the inside.

Reckless as I was even then, I leapt forward, calling for them to stop. They did, surprised and angry that a half-breed dared to speak to them.

"I told her she could take it. The other day," I'd lied.

The butcher was furious. "And why did you feel the need to do that?" he demanded.

"She's hungry, is all. She shouldn't be punished for just trying to live."

Both the butcher and guards flew into a rage. They turned to beat me instead and the girl managed to escape. I would have lost my own hand that day had the butcher not known I would be worth more at market with two hands than with only one.

Brought back to the present by a sharp jab of pain from the gash in my hip, I find myself staring into the wild eyes of the same little girl. Only now, there is much more than mere terror trapped behind them. In the years that have passed since then, she looks as if she has suffered the cares of a thousand lifetimes, felt the pain of a thousand deaths. The only thing that has kept her going is that same vicious desperation, now masked by a bitter, driving anger.

And I can't help but wonder what she must have gone through that caused such a change in her.

The realization of our connection is dawning on her face as well, and her colour drains. "No," she says, shaking her head. "It- it can't be!"

I open my mouth to say something, but quickly have to close it again. The intensity of the pain is making me sick. I clench my jaw, pressing my hand more firmly on my bleeding side.

"It was you?" She is angry now.

I can only nod.

A battle rages on her face as so many differing emotions clash over her tight features. She senses her vulnerably, and panic flashes through her eyes. Spinning around, she snatches up her helmet from the ground and bounds toward Fyra. She swings up onto the dragon's back and they shoot into the sky, leaving me behind in the pit.

Chapter Ten

"Wait!" I call after them, but my voice is too weak to carry over much distance. "You can't leave me here! Come back!"

It does no good. Within seconds, they disappear into the smoky haze far above me.

I collapse onto the ground and the pain of my injuries takes full hold of me. My fine clothes are soaked with seawater, sweat, and blood, and my throat aches for even one drop of fresh water. It takes tremendous effort to retrieve my knife from the dust, and with shaking hands I cut three strips from the hem of my cape. My hands are cumbersome as I wind a strip tightly around each injury to stop the bleeding, tying them off as best as I can. I barely manage to slide my knife into my belt before I fall sideways. It feels so good to be able to rest my pounding head, just for a moment. *When my strength returns, I'll be able to get up.*

But my strength does not return. Instead, I grow weaker as the strips of crimson fabric are darkened by my blood. Black spots fill my vision whenever I open my eyes, so I leave them closed. The world is spinning around me without ceasing, and I am alone. All that I can do is hope that Bellator returns to help me before it is too late.

I don't know how long I lie here half-conscious and immobile, sinking in and out of a fitful sleep. The sky begins to darken as the clouds thicken, and for the hundredth time I think that I see a shape flying overhead. The sound of flapping wings reaches my ears, and I feel a breeze as the dragon lands nearby. My eyes close heavily and I drift away.

Then someone is stroking my forehead, whispering something to me in a faintly familiar voice. I am lying on something very soft. Restless and sweaty, I turn my head from side to side on a fluffy pillow, batting my arms wildly, trying to push the hand away. But the hand remains firm and the voice grows louder. I cannot comprehend what it is saying. A calm comes over me as the voice continues a chant and I slip into a dreamless haze.

I awaken some time later, but all is dark. The air is too hot, and a warm, heavy bundle is pressed against my side. I turn over, everything about myself feeling heavy and languid. My eyes close.

The next thing I know, I am opening my eyes. The dim light hurts them, but my vision has finally cleared. Annalyn looks down at me with a relieved, yet anxious smile as she dabs my forehead with a damp cloth.

"You're awake," she says. "How do you feel?"

I bolt upright, gasping as a stab of pain shoots from my side, and take in my surroundings with a frantic glance. The room is mostly bare, except for the bed I am lying on, the nightstand beside my headboard – where Annalyn's bowl of water is set – and a large wardrobe across the room from me. I must be in the third and final section of my triangle of apartments; the only one that I haven't already explored. Other than Annalyn and I, the room is empty of any other people, which is a relief. It would be unnerving if Zeldek, or Uri, or – worse still – Bellator, were standing around me.

Annalyn gently pushes me back down. "You need to rest," she says, and offers me a cup of water from beside the basin.

I let myself sink back into the soft pillows and allow her to put the cup to my lips, taking a gulp of water. It's lukewarm, but it wets my parched throat and washes away the dust that coats the inside of my mouth.

"How did I get here?" I ask, my voice hoarse.

"We don't really know. We found you in your bed two days ago, wrapped in bloody bandages and very dehydrated."

"Two days?" I repeat, incredulous.

"It was mostly due to the fever, but the blood loss played a part as well. Your injuries are flesh wounds and will heal quickly without much scarring, but it seems you were bleeding for a while before we found you."

Scarring is the least of my worries.

"Uri noticed you were gone in the morning when he brought you your breakfast, but he didn't think anything of it until evening, when I came in to bring you supper and you still hadn't returned. The Master was organizing a massive ar— er, *search party* to find you when Uri and I decided to check your bedroom again, and found you."

"It was Bellator," I say. "She did this to me."

"We know." Her tone is grim. "It seems as if Bellator also hadn't been present for her duties, so the Master grew suspicious. She only turned up again yesterday afternoon, long after we found you, and admitted to what she had done. The Master was furious at her taking such rash and unauthorized actions, and they had a terrible argument. She is receiving punishment now."

"You mean to say he *didn't* put her up to it?"

Annalyn shrugs. "Apparently not."

She offers me the water again and I down the rest of it. She seems to take her time setting the empty cup on the nightstand, and I can tell there is something on her mind.

When she speaks at last, she struggles over the words. "The Master has been worried sick about you."

I remember the rift that is still unresolved between her and I, and the walls of tension are reinforced.

"He told you to say that, didn't he?"

"Yes," she admits in a very quiet voice. "He wants you to trust him."

"Why? What does he really want with me?"

She pulls the cloth away from my forehead and rinses it slowly in the bowl of water on the nightstand. When she returns it to my burning skin, it is soothingly cool. But she avoids my gaze.

"I don't know," she says carefully, thinking over each word before she utters it. "When he sent me to observe you, he told me to watch for any sign that there was anything abnormal about you."

"And was there?"

"Oh, there were many things right off. I've never met a— someone like you— before. I mean, I've seen slavery. None of it was new to me. Just, seeing it all up close..." She shudders. "I was impressed by you. No matter how the others treated you, you took it, but you didn't let it affect you. You were kind. That's why, when you collapsed, I tried to help you." Her eyes implore me to understand. "I was genuinely trying to help you then."

I find her words patronizing. *Does she really expect me to believe that?*

She doesn't notice my doubt. "The way they were treating you was wrong. Pushing you around, starving you for no reason, piling blame needlessly on you just to see you hurt. It was nothing short of barbaric. Although," she adds self-consciously, pushing a curl of hair behind her ear, "in the end, I was the cruellest of the lot. It's because of me that you're here now, after all."

She looks down at her hands, her guilt genuine enough. "Apparently the Master was waiting for something supernatural to happen, and I only discovered afterward that he was expecting some spell he'd put over you to wear off."

"A spell to hold back my powers," I remark. "He mentioned that much when we last spoke. From what I've gathered, he wants to use me for something, but I don't know what."

"Well, if he's come up with it, I guarantee it won't be anything good."

I knit my brow. "So, you too are against him?"

"Oh yes! He's absolutely dreadful!"

I give myself leave to feel sorry for her. "The other day you mentioned you had no choice but to do as he told you."

Her gaze is fixed on the folds of her apron, which she is smoothing out with her fingers. "Not everyone can afford to be as brave as you. No offence, but you haven't got anyone. What I mean is, the only life you have to worry about is your own."

I have to fight the urge to respond defensively. "Who are you protecting?" I ask.

"My parents. The Master took me from them when I was thirteen. He never told me why. For the past two and a half years, all he's had me do is work in his scullery, cooking for him and his elite. But he has promised that if I remain obedient and do what he says, he'll let me go back to them someday." She pauses, finally looking back at me. "That's why when he told me to spy on you, I did it. I thought that maybe, once I'd finished this task, he would let me go home."

"But you were wrong."

She sighs heavily. "When I returned, he merely congratulated me and sent me back to work. Only now, I also get to tend to you."

"Have you ever tried to escape?" I ask, and the hideous recollection of the murdered little girl that Zeldek killed comes to mind. I quickly force it away again.

"Yes," she replies, growing even more sullen. "On the first day I was allowed to walk freely about the castle after my capture, I made a run for it. I didn't make it any further than the entrance to the palace before Bellator caught me and dragged me back to the scullery. I had to work in irons for a month after that, and Uri still won't shut up about it. He was brought here a few months before I was, you see. He at least got as far as the lava pits when he tried." She huffs, crossing her arms in annoyance.

"Well," I say, thinking furiously, "is it possible that one could successfully leave Gaiztoak without Zeldek knowing about it?"

"I don't really know how much Zeldek actually pays attention to the security of his palace," she replies with a shrug. "The one you have to get around is Bellator. She's everywhere, and if she isn't, her men are. They inform her of everything that goes on, and she informs Zeldek. You make a wrong move, she'll know about it. Besides, even if you were lucky enough to be able to escape Gaiztoak, there's a band of outlaws waiting on the other side of the mountain to kill anyone who—"

There is a slam as the door to the room outside is opened, and she quickly falls silent. Loud voices reverberate off the walls, filling all three chambers with vehemence.

"Your incessant excuses bore me, Bellator!" There is no question the first voice belongs to Zeldek. "I only care that you appear contrite and stay your jealous hand from rising against him in the future."

"Jealous?" Bellator sputters. Her voice is strangely ragged, but twice as rancorous. "I did what I did because I thought it's what you wanted! If you would only explain to me—"

There is a dull thud, and then a choking sound. "I do not need to explain myself to a spoiled child!" Zeldek growls. "You will do as you have been commanded, or I will not think twice about breaking what little spine you have!"

A moment of silence, then Bellator gasps for air.

One set of footsteps starts toward the door to my room, and the other follows more reluctantly. Annalyn pulls the cloth from my head and quickly turns to rinse it in the water. A moment later, the door to my room is thrown open, and Zeldek enters. Bellator shadows him, seething, her helmet under her arm and her head bowed dejectedly. Her ragged hair falls in her face as she stares fixedly at the floor, and she doesn't bother to swipe it aside. Zeldek gestures for Annalyn to leave. She curtsies, takes the bowl of water from the nightstand, and hurries from the room.

"You live!" Zeldek says to me, a fake note of cheerfulness in his tone. "For a time, I was afraid we would lose you."

"I'm sure that you would have been devastated," I mutter. The more I see of this man, the more I despise him.

He chuckles. "In a sour mood, are we?"

I shoot him a disdainful glare in lieu of a spoken response.

He waves his hand dismissively. "Ah, well. It's to be expected from one back from death's door."

I sit up and throw aside the blankets. I notice with a start that I have been changed into a long black tunic and a pair of loose trousers, and I decide not to think about it too hard.

"What do you want now?" I grunt, placing my feet on the floor. My knees are wobbly and the wound on my thigh stings, but I manage keep my balance as I limp toward the door of the sitting room.

His cheerful disposition cracks, much to my relief. It was starting to unnerve me. "You will show me due respect, half-race! Face me when I speak to you!"

I stop with my hand on the door handle, and turn back to him. "What? It isn't like you're actually concerned about my well-being."

Bellator glances at me, but only for long enough to shoot me a warning glare. My mouth almost opens in alarm when I see her face. Both it and her neck are streaked with dark bruises, and there's a new cut on her right cheek to add to her collection of scars.

"I came," Zeldek is saying, "to assist my general in apologizing for her rash and cruel behaviour toward you. I assure you, she will not be allowed near you in the future."

Bellator fidgets with annoyance as he casts her a steely glare.

"She has," he adds, "and will continue to be sufficiently punished for her heinous actions."

"I can see that," I mutter, and Bellator's hand unconsciously goes up to cover the darkest bruise on her face.

"Now, just relax," Zeldek says in a pleasant tone, ignoring once again that I spoke. It seems to be becoming a habit for him. "Your dinner will be brought up for you momentarily."

At the mention of food, my stomach rumbles with eagerness, and I realize that I haven't eaten anything but that roll and a gulp of wine for at least four days. But I remain stubborn.

"Listen," I offer, "in Bellator's defense, I was partially to blame in the matter. I chose to go along with her."

Bellator's gaze shoots up, full of its usual venom. "Do not defend me, half-breed!"

"Be silent, you stupid girl!" Zeldek bellows, and whirling around, he backhands her across the face.

A red welt forms across the whole left side of her face, but she barely even flinches. She gives him a cold glare, and turning on her heel, she strides out of the room. A moment later, the dining room door slams thunderously.

"But she is right," he adds, turning back to me. "You must not defend her. You couldn't possibly have known what she had planned for you, or that I had not authorized her visit."

"She told me to jump off the tower and I did it," I say blandly. "I'm pretty sure I knew what I was getting myself into."

"Then you are more foolish than I assumed," he says, a smile briefly flickering over his hollow features. "And she is a foolish child who can be very headstrong at times."

Apparently, he and I see her very differently.

"I'll break her will, eventually," he continues, more to himself than to me. "I only hope it is done in time to stop her from doing anything too rash. I fear my trust in her has failed considerably since your arrival. She has always been vaguely rebellious, but never has she gone directly against my orders until now."

"Your orders, sir?" I ask, hoping that he might be so generous as to share with me what they were.

I am disappointed. He merely nods, his thoughts clearly elsewhere.

"Now," he says after a moment, "I trust you have had sufficient time to come to a decision about my offer. Three days at least."

I blink. "But sir, I was unconscious for most of that time!"

His gaze hardens. "But you know what you want, don't you?"

I grip the door handle a little tighter. It would not be wise to tell him my answer now, especially with me in such a weak state. I need more time; time to figure out some alternative, some way of escape.

Ducking my head, I mutter, "Give me a few more days, please."

There is a long pause, and I steal a glance in his direction. He is staring at me with a hard frown.

"Fine," he consents at last. "You have two days. But I will have an answer by then."

With that, he turns on his heel, and exits the room by the other door. It closes behind him with a slam, and I let out my breath. I allow myself to slump against the door, and then slide to the floor. If I don't figure out a way to get out of here before then, I'd rather pitch myself from the highest peak of the tower than discover what he has planned for me.

The door behind me is jerked open, and I fall backward onto the floor. Uri grins down at me through crooked teeth.

"Dinner's ready," he says.

Chapter Eleven

Zeldek was pouring over a thick, leather-bound book when the polished wooden door to his tower creaked open. The table around him was in disarray, scattered with a cache of papers that were both stacked neatly and spread out over every inch of the table. A page or two had fallen and lay abandoned on the floor, and a single candle burned low on the table, dripping wax over the papers beneath it.

He didn't seem to notice the figure that stepped into the room until it cleared its throat. He glanced up distractedly from his book, and a slow smile curved his lips.

"Ah, Bellator. Come in."

Bellator obeyed, and with a flick of his hand, the door slammed shut behind her. Her shoulders tensed, and she cast a quick glance at the door.

"You summoned me, my master?"

"I did." He leaned against the back of his chair and examined her face for a moment. "I would like to ask you something, and I want you to be completely truthful in your reply."

"Then ask," she said, and then added quickly, "my master."

He picked up a quill from his desk, and scribbled something on one of the scraps of paper beside the book. "How do you feel about the boy?"

"Excuse me, sire?"

"You have had more time than I would have liked to observe him. What is it that you see when you look at him?"

"I see a half-breed, if I can make it past his level of stupidity."

Zeldek's eyes narrowed. "He may be foolish, but his courage makes up for it."

"If courage is a sufficient substitute for foolishness. I've always seen them as synonymous."

His eyes flashed. Lately, it didn't take much for him to grow angry with her. "*You* are a different case entirely. Now answer my question!"

"If you want me to consider his character—"

"I do."

She sighed. "His will is strong, as is his mind. He has a sharp tongue that he is quick to use, and yet at the same time, he feels very deeply. He has a strong grasp on what is right and wrong. If he feels another has been wronged, I believe he will fight for them to his very last breath if need be."

"Which can be used against him very easily," Zeldek remarked, a malicious glint shining in his eyes.

Bellator drew closer to the desk, scanning the papers that littered it. The majority of them were scrawled with notes, most likely from books that the Master had pored over in recent past. Amongst them, a faded drawing of an arrow on an old parchment caught her eye.

Her gaze darted back to Zeldek before he could see her interest in his notes. "Why have you brought him here?" she demanded abruptly. "What purpose are you serving by it?"

Zeldek bent over his book once more. "I told you before. He stands in the way to my rise to power."

"Then why bring him here?" She rested her hand on the papers on his desk. "Why not leave him to be worked to death by the ruthless masters you took him from? You know as well as I do that he will only pose more of a threat now that he knows of your existence."

"It is true." Zeldek's gaze was now lost in the light of the candle. "It *would* have been easier, and I don't expect one such as you to understand my reasons for making him aware of his destiny."

"'One such as me' might understand if you actually told me anything," she remarked cuttingly.

"Such feeble remarks," he said, still gazing into the fire. "Small acts of rebellion that only tighten the chains that bind you even more."

Her nostrils flared. "I can speak however I want."

"You belong to me, Bellator." He was smiling now, and Bellator's insides recoiled. "You will always belong to me. You are my greatest creation, and one day, you will have no choice but to see that."

Bellator forced all emotion from her face. "I know, my master. Forgive me for my impertinence."

"It will be the same with the boy. Once I have harnessed his power, he will be forced to do whatever I say, and I will at last be able to secure my future. With the two of you under my control, and my full strength returned, I will be invincible."

"And you are so confident that you will be able to break him that easily?"

"He has one day left to decide his fate. If he refuses me, I will spend his power until there is nothing left of him, and then I will cast him into the abyss to stay until the end of time."

Bellator shuddered. She had seen the abyss once, from a distance. It wouldn't be a place she would want to spend the rest of eternity.

"You are certain that he is the one, then?"

He nodded. "I have been searching for one such as him for many years. One whose heart is so pure it is almost incorruptible, so that I may have the pleasure of corrupting it."

Bellator's mind worked quickly. *One who's heart was incorruptible... where had she heard those words before?* And that's when she finally knew why the Master wanted this Ealdred.

"And if the boy does accept your offer, will you make him your son like you promised?"

"My dear general," Zeldek said with a chuckle. "If he accepts my offer, I will know that he is not the one I have been looking for."

So his fate is inevitable, she thought to herself, once again disgusted with the Master's methods.

"Is that all you wanted me for?" Bellator asked.

"Yes, that will be all. You may retire to the forest for the evening."

"Actually, I will be in my room in the palace tonight." She had to force out the next words. "Have a nice evening, sire."

He didn't bother to return her blessing.

With a bow, she turned and left the room. When the door slammed behind her, she didn't look back.

Her mind was made up.

Chapter Twelve

M y knife is in my hand as I jerk awake from a light, restless sleep. Through the thick darkness, I cannot make out what just awakened me. But I can hear its slow, muffled breathing in the warm night air. The mattress creaks above my head and a foot shuffles against the floor beside me.

Someone is sitting on my bed.

I put my knife flat against my chest, quietly kicking my blanket off of me. Then I roll out from under the bed. Leaping to my feet, I pounce in the direction of the breathing, slashing wildly through the darkness in front of me.

My blade clashes with something metal, and a peal of mocking laughter fills the air. I step back, pointing my knife in the direction of the untimely mirth.

"You sleep under your bed?" Bellator scoffs.

My heart leaps into my throat at the sound of her voice, and I retreat another step.

"You!" I work to keep the fear from revealing itself in my voice. "What are you doing in my room?"

"Put that knife down, half-breed. You use it too much."

"Why should I?"

"Simple. I am trained to fight in the dark. It wouldn't be a fair fight for you."

Based on previous experience, I don't think that she cares about what is fair and what isn't.

"I didn't come to fight with you, Ealdred." The mockery in her tone as she says my name is hardly convincing. "Sit down before I lose my temper!"

But I don't sit down. "I don't trust you," I say.

"Good. I wouldn't trust me either." She waits. "Listen, you can keep the knife, but sit down! We need to talk."

I don't agree and I don't budge. "Whatever it is, it can wait until morning."

"No, it can't!" she snaps. "I don't want Zeldek knowing that I'm here. Even the Lord of the Aemurel needs to sleep sometimes, and he's asleep right now."

"Yes, well you aren't supposed to be talking to me," I remind her. "He told me so, and for once, I agree with him."

She makes an irritated noise in her throat. "He also told me not to let you leave your tower. And did I listen to him then?" She doesn't give me a chance to answer. "For pity's sake, sit down already!"

I give in. She has remained surprisingly patient thus far. I'd hate to see what would happen if I push her any further. Feeling around in the darkness, I find the edge of the bed and perch on it, my dagger at the ready.

She strikes a match. A flame shoots up, lighting a small portion of the room and casting long shadows on the wall. She ignites the candle on my nightstand and flicks out the match. Then she sits down across from me, leaning back into the pillows.

The bruising on her face has faded slightly since last I saw her, but she has a tired look about her that is unnatural to her usual reserved appearance. Glinting armour and sable cape aside, she wears a stiff black and gold dress with a black leather cincher around her waist. Aside from being militaristic in style, the dress has a somewhat Avian design, leaving one of her arms bare while the other is draped with a black and gold embroidered robe. Only her arms are still covered by tight black fabric that she wears in long sleeves and all the way up her neck. Her hair falls down her back in a tight braid. Around her neck, she wears a necklace with a pendant of a little dragon holding a ruby teardrop protectively in its tiny claws. She wears long black gloves that go up past her elbows and a thick gold bracelet over her right wrist. This is apparently what she used to block my knife with, as she's also unarmed to all appearances.

"Nice room, by the way," she says with a nod, glancing around.

"What do you want?" I demand.

"To the point. I like it." She adjusts her bracelet with a thoughtful frown. "Zeldek only recently informed me that you have one day left to decide your fate. Is that correct?"

I nod.

"Believe it or not, half-breed, I understand what you're going through. Only a few days ago, you were a nobody barely managing to survive in a world that deemed you unimportant and useless. Now, you are faced with an impossible decision. Whether you accept this offer or not, you will end up a slave to Zeldek. Your refusal will only guarantee you unspeakable pain, but in the end, the result will be the same."

Her words only add to my stress.

"When I first came here," she continues, "I was never given an ultimatum so tempting as the one you've received. I was only a child when he discovered me – or rather, one of his followers did – and took me to him. As a child, I was foolish enough to think that being brave, like you have been, was the right thing to do. I soon realized my mistake."

She stares past me at the memory, and her eyes are haunted echoes of the pain she was forced to endure. "Do not think me weak. No one could withstand such torture for very long and remain steadfast."

I know she wouldn't thank me for pitying her; instead, I clutch my free hand to my opposite arm. "Are you here to tell me that I should agree to his proposition?"

"And give him everything he needs to accomplish his life's work? I'd kill you with my bare hands before I let that happen."

I recoil.

"I don't mean I will," she adds quickly, the fire in her voice dying down a little. "Your coming here is most opportune, actually. I see in you the same longing for freedom that lives in me. Every chance you get, you look for a way to escape. I saw you climb onto the roof of the tower earlier. I admit, you do have pretty decent climbing abilities."

I chew the inside of my lip, ignoring the compliment.

"Zeldek does not own me." Her words are fierce, a lifeline almost, as if they are the only thing holding her to sanity. "And I certainly hold no allegiance to him. I want to get away from him, to make him pay for every time he mocked me, hurt me, controlled me, made me do his dirty work. But I can't do it alone. I've tried." She takes a breath, trying again. "What I'm saying is that perhaps it will benefit us mutually if we worked together on this."

I watch her distrustfully, not ready to reply.

Her gaze turns imploring, and she tries her hardest to appear sincere. "Listen, Ealdred, I'm truly thankful for your help all those years ago. Now that I know you're still alive, I understand that I owe you a debt. Let this be the payment of that debt."

I shake my head. "You don't owe me a thing. I didn't do it to get anything back."

She hesitates. "Consider making a deal with me, then. A bargain that, if you prefer, starts with *you* owing *me* something."

"Even if I did, I don't trust you to keep your word."

"At least hear me out!"

I think it over. "Alright. What are you proposing?"

"Your freedom. I suppose I don't need to remind you how important that is."

I raise a sceptical brow. "You'll get me out of here?"

She nods.

"In return for what?"

She reaches under the robe that is draped over her shoulder and pulls out a folded piece of paper. "This," she says, handing it to me.

I take the paper from her and unfold it, spreading it out on the bed beside me. On the weather-stained, smudged parchment is a faded drawing of an arrow. Above it, *The Arrow of Arnon* is written in delicate, cursive writing. Below that it reads:

> *Deep in vaults of hidden gold*
>
> *Caverns steep and halls of old*
>
> *Hidden from the fires and coal*
>
> *Rests the arrow and my soul*
>
> *Three bright stars of purest form*
>
> *Do await the coming storm*
>
> *Guarding day and night the shrine*

Until it my heir does find

He of dark and he of light

For his own soul he shall fight

And if the curse he can unbind

Much darker things shall unwind

"What's this?" I ask, marvelling at the elegant simplicity of the poetry.

"What does it look like, idiot?" She snatches back the paper, refolds it, and slips it back underneath her robe.

"I know it's an arrow. But what does the rhyme mean?"

"Ah, but it's not just *any* arrow." She looks at me with a glint of mystery in her eyes. "They say that the Arrow of Arnon is magical, and that it used to belong to Zeldek's sister, Batuel. When he took the Aemurel, he grew hungry for the power that the arrow possessed, and so murdered her and her entire household, including her children, to get it. But as she was dying, she cast a spell on it designed so that only one of her own descendants would be able to free the arrow. Thus, it would never fall into Zeldek's hands. In return, Zeldek cursed her spirit to eternal torment until the arrow was his. But because of his curse, the goddess Irla grew angry with him. She took much of his power from him and will keep it until the spell on the arrow is broken and Batuel is freed from Zeldek's curse."

"But," I point out, "if Zeldek killed all of her children, the spell can't be broken. He'll have lost his power forever."

"Ah, but he didn't kill all of them. One survived. Her youngest son was just a baby when his nurse dove with him into the Tireth River, hoping to save his life. She did not survive, but the boy was found by a fisherman in Zandelba, who raised him as his own. Of course, the child was unaware of who he was. He married, had children, and died, and soon the bloodline of Lady Batuel was spread throughout Theara. Zeldek was only able to trace them all quite recently, and slaughtered all but one." She pauses, looking right at me. "A little boy, who had been abandoned by his father into slavery. You."

My breath catches in my throat. Now it all makes sense; this is why Zeldek wants my allegiance! He wants to use my power to break the curse on the arrow so he can claim it for himself.

I vow to myself that I will never let this happen.

"But," I object, the thought occurring to me, "he said that I'm *half* Vaelhyrean."

She shrugs. "There must be Vaelhyrean blood on your father's side too. It was your mother who had Batuel's bloodline, after all."

I grow suspicious. "How do you know all of this?"

"Because, Zeldek told me while I still had his confidence. He never suspected I would tell you." She shakes her head, her voice hissing through her teeth, "He's too self-absorbed to see how much I hate him!"

I jump at the change in her tone, making yet another mental note to keep clear of her anger in the future. As it is, I decide it'd be in the best interest of my health to steer our conversation into safer waters.

"So, what is the plan?" I ask.

Her scowl lessens only slightly. "I will help you get out of here," she says, "in exchange for you finding and breaking the spell on the arrow."

"Wait!" My voice is louder than I meant it to be, and I quickly lower it. "You *want* me to break the spell?"

She nods, as if I should have already known that.

I blink, not sure whether to feel confused or stupid. I decide on both.

"But that will give Zeldek his power back."

"An astute observation, genius," she retorts. "Fortunately, you'll have the arrow, won't you? It was powerful enough to keep Zeldek at bay for a long time before he was finally able to capture and kill Batuel, and he was only able to do that because Batuel decided to lock the arrow away. With someone of your – er, *talents* – wielding it, you could be unstoppable."

"Sounds to me like you want to take the arrow for yourself."

She rolls her eyes. "Think for a moment, will you? If the arrow is powerful enough to fight back Zeldek, what do you think it will do to a poor nobody like me? Besides, if I help you get this arrow, it'll be like spitting in his face. I'll get satisfaction enough from simply that."

But I notice she doesn't deny it.

"So, our deal is what?" I ask. "My freedom in exchange for helping you find and break the spell on this arrow?"

"Yes, as well as my protection of you afterwards."

"Alright, I'm in. But I have one condition," I say.

"What is that?"

"We take Uri and Annalyn with us."

Her growing excitement fades into an angry scowl. "No! This quest must be done quickly and with stealth, and that's something that they – Uriah especially – do not possess!"

"I never said they needed to be involved in the plan. We can get them out of here, take them to their separate homes, and then leave them to go search for the arrow ourselves."

"That will take too long! If Zeldek discovers what we are doing, he'll try to take the arrow as soon as we break the spell."

"Then we'll take them as far as we can, but we can't leave them behind."

"No!"

"Then there's no deal."

Pursing her lips, she stares at me, a spark in her eyes. At last, she throws up her hands. "Fine! But if we are caught because of them, I'll go ahead with killing you."

I decide not to risk anymore of her anger. "We won't get caught."

She gets to her feet. "We leave tomorrow at midnight. Meet me out on the balcony. Be sure your friends aren't late, or we're leaving them behind."

"Got it," I reply, and in the darkness around me, a ray of hope fills my soul.

Bellator bends down to blow out the candle, but then stops and turns to me with an eyebrow raised in something close to amusement. "Why *do* you sleep under your bed?"

I shrug. "So that no one knows where I sleep."

She grins. "Helps you actually get to sleep, doesn't it?"

I find myself smiling too. "Well, it did before you found out."

She chuckles and blows out the flame. I don't hear her leave, but in a few moments, I hear the beating of the dragon's wings as they fly away.

I lay down on the bed with a relieved sigh. The mattress is soft and warm against my back, and my tense muscles begin to relax. I put my face against the feathery pillow, which still has the scent of that rose oil Bellator smells of lingering on it, and take a deep breath.

Everything is going to be alright. Bellator is going to get me out of here. Not only will I finally be free, but now I also have another link to who my family was.

But I am still trembling inside. I know that it can't be true.

Nothing is ever going to be alright.

Chapter Thirteen

"**C**ome on," I whisper to the empty sitting room, tapping my foot anxiously on the floor.

My stomach twists and turns into intricate knots as I glance over my shoulder toward the door for the hundredth time. Uri and Annalyn still have not arrived. Both had their reservations when I told them of Bellator's plan to free us, neither trusting her the slightest bit. In Uri's words, she's trying to trap us into cutting our own throats. However much I agreed, I assured them of her good intentions. We're taking a big risk, it's true, but if Bellator is truly sincere, I don't want them left behind to face Zeldek's wrath after we are gone. It was this fact alone that convinced them to agree, and I told them to be here before midnight.

But they aren't, and neither is Bellator.

I glance out through the balcony doors into the haze above. The night sky is still empty, and besides the distant roar of the water below, the air is silent.

Something's wrong. They should be here. Why aren't they here?

The door creaks open behind me. Heaving a sigh of relief, I turn to greet my new travelling companions.

"The hour is late," Zeldek says, and the door clicks shut behind him as he glides into the room. "You should be resting."

I stagger back, shocked. "L-lord Zeldek," I stammer. "What brings you here?"

"You have walked the floors in a restless state these two nights now," he replies. "Your unease troubles me."

"Right." I cast a nervous glance into the sky. "It's nothing. Nothing at all. Only I've rested too much lately, what with the lack of work to keep me busy, and my injuries, and... things."

Crimson light flares up in his pupils as he searches my face, his lip curling into an amused sneer.

He doesn't believe me. He knows. Bellator has told him. This was all a test, and I failed. I should never have believed her false promises of freedom.

"Your stupidity continues to astound me," he says at last.

I back away, shaking my head. Fear creeps up my spine as he clenches his fists. Flames leap from them, expanding in the air around him.

"What is it that I have done?" he demands. "I had it all worked out so carefully. I offered you everything you've ever wanted! Why does your resolve remain so strong?"

I swallow back my fear. "I- I don't trust you."

"What is trust?" he spits. "A fleeting premonition? What have my brothers offered that I can not also give you?"

"It isn't about what you can or can't give me! Can't you see? What you are, what you stand for; it's all wrong! You act like you mean well, then turn around and show me just how despicable you truly are. I cannot and will not blindly pledge my life to a man who has given me no good reason to do so!"

"I see you think yourself as brave," he growls, looming over me. "We'll see how much of your courage is left when I'm finished with you, and you've been driven mad by pain. It will be interesting to see how long it takes for you to break."

"You are an evil, twisted tyrant!" I shout vehemently the words I've wanted to say since the day I met him. "I would rather suffer the most painful death than give you my allegiance!"

His temper erupts and the flames around him explode. Fire rolls through the room, igniting everything in its path. Zeldek seems to grow taller with the flames and his eyes light as red embers. He throws me back against the wall, black smoke binding my wrists to the hot stones.

"I will destroy you!" Gathering fire in his hand, he holds it out toward me. "I will destroy every bit of you until there is nothing left! Slowly, painfully, until you are grovelling at my feet, begging for mercy. But you shall not receive it. You have refused me your soul, so I will pry it from your very being until you are nothing but a mindless servant of my will!"

Heat scorches my face. Turning my head, I press my cheek to the wall behind me. The air is stifling. Smoke burns in my lungs and I cough. My vision blurs. Then, a flash of cold goes through me, spreading relief from the heat and renewing my energy. Blue light fills my hands, driving away the smoke from my wrists. I straighten up, feeling bolder again, and turn back to face Zeldek.

He pulls his hand away in surprise, and his fire dims.

"Try all you like." My voice is level, yet powerful. "You will never destroy me."

"Enough!" he roars, throwing out his hands. Flames spiral around him and the heat begins to fight through the cold.

"Stop!" a voice cries from behind Zeldek. "Release him, tyrant!"

Surprise registers on Zeldek's face, but he cloaks it with a sneer. "You insult me, young one," he says, turning about.

Annalyn stands in the archway to the balcony, a bulky cloak wrapped around her shoulders. I never imagined she could be so fearless in the presence of Zeldek. Yet here she is, unflinchingly facing the flames that rise around her, looking as if she's ready to take on Zeldek all by herself.

"Threatening me in my own palace? You have more guts than I gave you credit for," he scoffs.

She lifts her chin. "I said, 'release him'!"

"You do not command me!" he roars, preparing to launch a ball of fire.

"Stay your hand!" Bellator charges into the room from the balcony. Her bow is nocked, and the arrow is trained on him. "Or I shoot!"

Alarmed, he lowers his hand for but a moment. "Bellator? What is the meaning of this?"

"Treason, my master, of the highest degree," she says through her teeth, her finger quivering threateningly on the string.

"How dare you raise a hand against me?" he cries. "I see now that I have given you too much freedom too quickly. A mistake I will not make again."

"Save your breath. From this day forth, I no longer answer to you."

"What defence do you have? You know mortal weapons cannot harm me."

Bellator crooks an eyebrow. "You know me, sire. I don't really follow the rules."

As though it were a signal, Annalyn throws aside her cloak. Blinding light emanates from an object around her neck, filling the room with white light. Zeldek cries out, throwing up his hands to shield his eyes. Black mist encircles him as he tries to block out the light. The flames all but fade away and the smoke binding me to the wall disappears.

"Ealdred, this way!" Annalyn cries.

I stumble in the direction of her voice, putting my hand in front of my eyes to shade them from the light. A rough hand grabs my arm and jerks me toward the balcony. As Annalyn follows with the light still glowing, flames rise up in the room again. Zeldek lets out a roar that cracks the ceiling and shakes the very foundation of the tower.

"Jump!" Bellator says, shoving me toward the parapet.

I don't have to be told twice; I dive over the edge. Fyra swoops beneath me and I land on her back, smashing my face into her hard scales. Blood fills my mouth, but I swallow it back.

"Where'd you get to?" Uri drawls from where he clings to the reins around Fyra's neck.

Annalyn lands beside me with as much grace as I did, the ball of light now extinguished. A moment later, Bellator lands lightly on her feet on Fyra's neck.

"Fyra, fly!" she shouts, snatching the reins out of Uri's hands.

The dragon screeches and leaps into the sky. Zeldek appears on the balcony with fire raised above the palm of his hand and hurls it after us. It grows to a massive ball of flames, which Fyra only narrowly escapes. She changes direction abruptly, sweeping around the peak of the tower. I lose my hold on her, rolling sideways, and slide down her side. My foot catches on a loose scale, halting my fall. Annalyn leaps forward and grasps my hand. She pulls, and I scramble back up.

"Thanks," I say shakily. "I owe you one."

Bellator looks over her shoulder. "Sit up and lock your knees on the dragon's sides. And hold onto each other!"

We follow her instructions as the dragon makes for the large tower in the centre of the star.

"Shoot them down!" Zeldek's voice booms around us, strangely amplified. "Shoot the beast down!"

"Curse him!" Uri mutters, now behind me.

Arrows begin to whiz past us from below. Those that don't miss us break on Fyra's iron scales.

"Hold on!" Bellator orders, pulling her bow from her shoulder.

She nocks an arrow on it and directs her aim below.

"Who's shooting at us?" I ask Annalyn, who is sitting in front of me.

"The outlaws, I think," she says, leaning forward to grasp the scales better. She casts an anxious glance back at the tower as we fly away from it. I tighten my grip on her, while Uri's grasp cuts off the circulation in my shoulders.

"I think I'm gonna be sick!" he shouts in my ear as the dragon makes a sudden dive downward.

As Fyra dives, she does something unexpected. She opens her jaws and blows fire out of it, covering the ground in flames. Then she does a sharp turn and leaps back into the air.

"Whoa!" I gasp, sitting up. "Did you see that? She just breathed fire!"

Annalyn nods grimly, as if it was a perfectly normal thing for a dragon to do. "Yeah, but it won't hold them. Everything in Gaiztoak is immune to heat."

A whistling sound follows us and an incandescent glow shines on our backs. I glance over my shoulder in time to see a huge wave of fire coming straight toward us.

"Bellator!" I cry.

"I see it," she says, her brow knit in irritation.

Slinging her bow back over her shoulder, she slides the reins from the crook of her arm to her hand. Then she rolls sideways from the dragon's neck. Fyra folds her wings over us and swings to the side, turning over in the air. Uri gasps, Annalyn whoops, and I hold on for dear life. The fire passes harmlessly by and Fyra stabilizes. She opens her wings in flight, revealing Bellator standing once more at the base of her neck, and flies furiously for the mountainous wall.

Fireballs take the place of the flaming arrows, hurled more accurately and speedily than the former had been. Bellator concentrates her full attention to directing the dragon. I doubt she planned for Zeldek to find out about our escape *before* it happened.

As we near the wall, the dragon shoots upwards toward the peak of the mountain. Fireballs crash into the mountainside, and showers of rocks explode into the air. One boulder hits Fyra's right wing, but she only swirls around once before persisting.

We reach the top of the wall and cross over it, passing directly between two watchtowers. As we reach the other side, I look down and see a dark forest stretching out for miles beneath us. Fyra folds her wings over us and dives toward it.

There is a flash of light, a loud bang, and a sudden jolt throws me from my tight hold astride the dragon's scaly back. My hands slip from Annalyn's shoulders, and I am tossed in the air for a split second before I am caught by the leathery folds of Fyra's wing. I grasp for something to hold onto, but nothing presents itself. The dragon's movements are spasmodic and uncontrolled.

Fyra utters a rasping screech and we begin to lose altitude.

We crash into something and I am flung forward again. My face smashes into the hard scales. Something sharp pierces my forehead and hot liquid spurts into my eyes.

Fyra thrashes her wings, struggling to climb back into the sky. But I know it is no use. With one last wild beat of her wings, she gives up with a roar of agony, and we plummet toward the trees

Chapter Fourteen

"Fyra!" The cry rips from Bellator's throat with wild desperation. "What have I done?"

We crash through the treetops and tumble toward the ground. Annalyn curses loudly, and Uri screams. Wood splinters, branches snap. We are tossed about like straw in the wind, protected from harm by Fyra's limp, armoured body.

The dragon hits the ground with a jarring crash and the forest echoes with the sound. When it fades away, the silence that follows is deafening.

My heart drums in my ears as I untangle myself from the contorted position I was thrown into when we landed. The gash in my forehead stings, but beyond that, I have miraculously evaded any serious injuries.

Steam rises from the heaving body of the dragon and the scent of something unpleasant burning mingles with that of the ferns we undoubtedly trampled during our collision. I search the darkness for an outline, a shape, or a blur of movement to betray the location of any of my companions. But the air is as still as it is dark.

I clamber to my feet, wiping blood from my eyes onto the sleeve of my tunic.

"Bellator?" I whisper. "Annalyn? Uri?"

Someone whimpers off to the right of where I stand.

I stumble toward the sound. "Annalyn? Is that you?"

"I'm not Annalyn!" Uri groans indignantly. "Get me outta here, would you?"

"Where are you?"

"Over here!"

"Keep talking. I'm almost to you."

"Hurry it up! I got a whole tree on top me!"

Something jabs my leg and I bend down to discover what it is. My fingers find the sharp edge of a stick and I yank on it. The large branch it's attached to shifts a little.

"Ow!" Uri hollers.

"Shh! Not so loud. Listen, I've got a hold of the branch that's on you – it's a branch, not a tree – and I'm going to try to get it off you."

"Make it fast! And do it careful-like, would you?"

I feel around until I find the main stem of the branch. Grasping it, I pull on it with all my might. It remains stubborn for a moment, but with another tug, it loosens and breaks free. I lug it off of Uri and drag it out of the way.

"Ow," Uri moans. "I said do it careful-like!"

"Sorry," I say.

"A lot of good this dragon did. We're gonna be caught for sure! I shoulda never agreed to this."

There is a sound from behind us like a leather blanket being yanked aside, and blinding light shines in my face. My eyes sting and I put up both arms to shield them.

"Hey!" Uri shouts. "Put that out, would you?"

"Quiet, Uriah!" Bellator snaps breathlessly, but the light lowers to face the ground.

My eyes adjust to the blazing glow.

Supporting an unusually pale Annalyn with one arm, Bellator is holding the ball of light in her other hand. Annalyn's knee is wrapped in a sloppy bandage already soaked through with blood. Apparently they had gotten trapped between the folds of one of Fyra's wings when we landed, while Uri and I remained on her back.

"We need to get moving," Bellator says, helping Annalyn down off the dragon's back. "They likely saw us fall, so we won't have much time – if any – before they come after us. The gateway is only a couple of miles from here, so we still have a head start."

Uri shoves past me and leaps down after them onto the mossy forest floor. I follow more carefully.

"I don't know about you," Uri grumbles, "but if we get caught, I'm gonna kill the half-breed myself."

"Enough!" Bellator snaps. "We're not going to get caught."

Once on the ground, I can see the source of the light. It comes from a necklace which Bellator pulls over her head to hang next to her dragon pendant.

"Um, Bellator," Annalyn objects politely, "if you please, that's *my* necklace."

"Not anymore."

"But my mother gave it to me!"

Bellator turns on her, her eyes flashing. "Listen to me! You have no idea what damage this firestone could do in the wrong hands. It's best kept safe with someone who can protect it."

Annalyn opens her mouth to protest, but Bellator cuts her off.

"That's my final word," she snaps, and then turns to the panting dragon.

Crestfallen, Annalyn pulls a strand of loose hair behind her ear, staring hesitantly at Bellator's back. Her chin drops dejectedly, and turning away, she limps over to where Uri is examining the remains of a large tree that Fyra splintered during our fall.

"*Sentitzen dut, nire laguna,*" Bellator says, reaching out her hand and pressing it to the dragon's muzzle.

For a moment, I think that she is performing some kind of spell, but when nothing happens, I realize that she is merely speaking in another language.

The dragon's eyes open at her touch, its pupils retracting.

"*Hau nire errua da,*" Bellator continues almost lovingly, drawing near and stroking the dragon's face with her other hand. "*Pena eman al didazu, eta duzu minik dut.*"

Fyra moans in dismay, raising her head feebly. With a gentle hand, Bellator lowers it back down.

"*Atseden orain,*" she whispers.

She straightens up, and taking a step back, she pulls her bow from her shoulder. "*Zure arimaren bakarrik eramango dut, beraz, egun batean itzuli ahal izango duzu.*"

"What did you say to her?" I ask, marvelling at how smoothly the ancient syllables roll from her tongue.

Bellator bows her head. "I said goodbye."

She nocks the string, directing her aim at the dragon's head.

Alarmed, I grab her arm. "What are you doing?"

She spins around, slapping me across the face. The impact throws me to the soft ground and my face stings. I watch helplessly as she aims again and looses her arrow. It enters the dragon's ear and buries itself up to the feather in her skull. The creature lets out one last groan and goes still.

Bellator slings her bow back over her shoulder and turns on me, nostrils flaring. "Don't you *ever* lay your hands on me again!" she hisses. "Do you hear me? Not ever!"

I nod, mute with terror.

"Good! Now get up!"

I pick myself up off the ground and watch after her as she turns back to the others.

"We travel in darkness," she announces. "The light is a weapon that we must save for the most dire of circumstances. Hold onto each other. Annalyn, you take my cloak. Redhead, hold hers. *Half-wit*," she emphasizes this new insult with disdain, "you bring up the rear. If any one of you lets go, you fend for yourself. I won't bother to find you."

As if to punctuate her threat, a horrible guttural bellow rings through the trees from a distance.

"What in hell was that?" Uri exclaims.

"Ezixs," she hisses, beckoning for us to get in line.

We follow her orders, forgetting in our fear any objections we may have had to the arrangements. As soon as we have hold of one another, she covers up the light.

"Not a sound!" she hisses from the pitch darkness, and we take off at a run.

However quiet her footsteps are, we make up for it as we trample after her. Together, the three of us somehow manage to step on every twig or branch as often and as loudly as possible. But our speed is not hindered by the noise, and soon the sounds of our mysterious pursuers have faded away.

With the danger also goes my panic and I begin to feel the stitch in my side. Annalyn and Uri don't sound like they are doing all that well either, and our combined gasping is deafening in the still air. Our pace slows almost to walking speed, until at last we are merely stumbling after Bellator as she drags us along after herself. But at last, after what feels like hours of straight running, even she has to stop.

"Finally," Uri wheezes.

"Shh!" Bellator warns breathlessly, and I can hear the creaking of a bow as the string is pulled back.

I muffle my breathing in the sleeve of my shirt, and listen intently. Besides the puffing and gasping from Uri and Annalyn, the warm air is quiet.

As Bellator uncovers the necklace – I think she called it a firestone – the light blinds us again. I force my eyes to stay open so they will quickly grow accustomed to the light. Even before they have, I can make out the circle of human archers that have us surrounded. Their weapons fall from their hands as they put them up to shield their eyes from the light.

As a whole, their forester attire is ragged and somewhat grubby, but it is uniform in colours of grey and olive. Even so, each one has a unique look to their appearance. Some wear patchwork fur hats and wraps, while others have strips of more ratty fur sewn onto the hems of their cloaks, tunics, and boots. Their faces are dirty, their weapons handmade, and they all have, in some way or another, an almost feral mien.

One man stands out among the rest. For the most part he is dressed in the uniform colours, but his doublet is iron as opposed to leather, and he wears a navy-blue cloak clasped loosely around his shoulders. He looks to be in his late thirties, and his face has sharp, murine-like features. Patches of roughly cut scruff sprout over his chin and muddy-blond hair shoots out in spikes from beneath the hood of his cloak.

He barely flinches at the sudden illumination, and his bow remains trained on Bellator.

"Reevan," Bellator says to him with a tense nod.

"General," the man replies, nodding back to her.

The air is tense as they eye each other and Bellator's hand clasps the handle of one of her knives. Then the corner of Reevan's mouth twitches and his lips part in a yellow grin.

"I hear Zeldek's put out a warrant for your arrest," he says, lowering his bow. "Finally drove him mad, did you?"

Bellator relaxes her grip on the knife. "In a manner of speaking. I am kidnapping three of his prisoners."

"I see it's all going according to plan."

Bellator's brow darkens. "He killed Fyra."

A hint of concern passes through his hazel eyes. "I'm sorry. I know how much that creature meant to you."

"This is no time for sympathy," Bellator snaps. "We are being hunted by at least one squadron of ezixs – although I suspect that more are on their way."

He tugs his whiskers uncomfortably. "What do you want me to do about it?"

"I expect you to honour your word."

He chuckles, handing his bow to the woman beside him. "Honour my word," he echoes, coming to stand in front of her. "You would rely on the word of an outlaw for your security?"

"Perhaps," Bellator replies, stiffening.

"Perhaps?" he mimics, and throws back his head, laughing harshly. "Then you have learned nothing!"

"I know only what you taught me," Bellator says. "You know what game I'm playing."

"Aye," he agrees, looking down at her with superiority. "But you should know that flattery won't work on me."

"It was worth a try," she says with a shrug.

Her attempt to lighten the mood passes unnoticed. Reevan's disposition turns to brooding. He begins to pace around her, his body language confrontational.

"Tell me, Bellator," he says, stopping before her once he's made a full circle. "Why shouldn't I turn you in? I can guarantee that the Master will pay a pretty price for your capture and safe return to him. He'd restore me to my position, being no longer able to trust you, and it would cost me nothing. If I help you and Zeldek finds out, it will be the end for me. You know that we only stay in these woods by his generosity." He sounds faintly sardonic as he forms the last word.

Bellator raises her chin, glowering at him.

He commences pacing. "I can sense your fear. You'll never admit to it, I know. But behind your eyes, I can still see that weak, whimpering child given into my care so many years ago. You have every right to be afraid. Your plan has failed. The Master will not take your betrayal lightly. You know the pain he'll inflict upon you in punishment for your disloyalty."

"It isn't that," she growls. "I *am* afraid – yes, I will admit it. But it isn't pain that I fear. Oh no. I can withstand a world of physical pain, and he knows it. But he doesn't intend to torture me. Not this time. This time, he intends to *break* me."

Reevan stops in front of her once more, crossing his arms over his chest. "He'll try, but I'm not convinced he'll succeed."

"Don't patronize me," she spits. "You asked me to convince you to keep your word, and although I had hoped to find more honour in you, I'll humour your request."

He gestures for her to continue.

"When I was brought here, everyone thought that I was useless, that I wouldn't amount to anything. You were the only one who believed in me. You have taught me everything I know now – that has kept me alive all this time – and I respect you for that. But ever since I've known you, you've been trapped serving a cruel tyrant whom you despise. I don't want to waste my life like that. I am willing to pay the price for my freedom."

"I can understand that. But what's in it for me?"

"Whether I'm captured or whether I escape, you'll get your old position as general back. And if I succeed with my quest, I will be able to get you out from under Zeldek's control."

Reevan ponders this for a moment. "Alright. Say you did get what you're after; what of these others? I know the Master would pay an even bigger price for that one." He jerks his head toward me.

She moves defensively between us. "I need him."

"Hear that, Ealdred? She *needs* you," Uri whispers, jabbing me with his elbow.

I don't find it as amusing as he does.

"Silence, Uriah!" Bellator snaps.

"And the other two?" Reevan asks.

"It's all of us or none of us," I say, coming to stand by Bellator.

She glances at me and her scorn noticeably returns. "Yes, yes, useless though they may be, they have to come too."

Reevan strokes his chin thoughtfully.

"I need you to make your decision quickly!" she snaps. "You may take your time, but the ezixs won't."

He throws up his hands. "Fine. Let's get moving, then. I'll take you as far as the Plains of Beldir, but after that, you're on your own."

She nods, which I am sure is the closest she will ever get to saying thank you.

"However," Reevan continues, "I'll need to make this believable to avoid any blame."

"Do what you must," Bellator says.

Reevan steps back, and pointing at us, he calls out to his men, "Secure them."

Bellator turns to us hurriedly. "Come quietly," she whispers, "but be on your guard. This may yet be a trap."

Uri frowns. "How come we didn't take the ocean way out? Then we wouldn't have to deal with no outlaws."

"So says the pirate," she says with an exasperated sigh. "Did you not notice that the balcony Zeldek was on overlooked the ocean for miles? He would have shot us down in an instant, and *then* where would we be? *Think* next time before you decide to contradict me, Uriah!"

"I told you, it's Uri, not Uriah!" he grumbles, but she turns away without another word.

Rough hands seize me, and my arms are jerked behind my back. The familiar coarse twine of a rope is forced around my wrists, and wound tightly at that. Another outlaw tries to force Bellator's hands behind her back, but she gives Reevan a sharp look, and he orders them to stop.

"No ropes," he says. "Rogue or not, Bellator was our general."

Bellator pulls her hands free. The outlaw backs away from her and rejoins the others. Reevan orders for torches to be lit while Bellator puts out the firestone and tucks it away under her cloak.

Once the new arrangements have been made, the party sets off. Annalyn, Uri, and I are kept close together in the middle of the throng, and no one bothers to speak to us. Bellator, however, is allowed to walk up by Reevan. All is silent save for the occasional grumblings of the outlaws around us, and the low tones in which Reevan and Bellator converse.

It is only as daylight begins to brighten the smoky sky that the woods thin out, and we reach our destination. An even larger group of outlaws is waiting for us in a makeshift camp in a small clearing.

A scout runs to meet us as we approach. "Sir, have you captured them?" he asks.

"Aye," Reevan replies, glancing warily at Bellator. "Fetch some horses. I'll be taking them back to Gaiztoak straightaway."

"I'll give the order right away... General," the scout says, bowing his head respectfully to Reevan.

Reevan then turns to the party who captured us. "You may disperse. I'll take them from here."

A chorus of 'yes, General', and his orders are quickly followed.

"I could get used to this," he says as they all hurry away.

Bellator glares at him. "Don't."

In a few moments, two stallions are brought forward. The first is pure white, while the other is a glossy black.

"Here you are, sir," says the groom. "Majax," here he nods to the white horse, "and Nimro are the fastest horses that we have."

"Fool! There are five of us, not two!" Reevan says, irritated. "Fetch three more horses at once!"

The groom ducks his head. "Sorry, General. Only, I assumed—"

"What did you assume?" Reevan interrupts challengingly.

"I just thought that the Master would only want the general back alive—"

"Fetch three more horses, now!"

The groom nods. "Yes Gen "

But his words are lost in a long, guttural bellow that rises from the woods nearby.

Bellator stiffens, glancing over her shoulder into the woods from which we just came. Leaping forward, she snatches the reins of the horses from the groom. The poor man staggers backward, terror etched into his face, and throws up his hands in a plea for mercy. But Reevan knocks him out from behind with a swift jab to the back of his neck.

Spinning around, Bellator jerks out a knife and cuts our bonds. "Half-wit, you'll ride with the girl. Redhead, you're with me. Quick!"

She thrusts the reins of the white horse into my hands and swings herself up onto Nimro with ease.

"Up, Uriah!" she orders.

I hold the white horse still while Annalyn scrambles up onto its back.

"Be careful with this one," Reevan says, coming up behind me. "Majax is young and has a mind of his own. He's swift, but he hates being ridden."

I glance up at him, and have the feeling that he is trying to intimidate me.

"Thanks," I say. "I'll remember that."

He takes the reins from me and holds them while I climb up behind Annalyn. I have handled many horses during my time as a slave, having been a stable boy in more than one of my many masters' estates. But I have never actually ridden a horse before.

Reevan hands Annalyn the reins, offering her a reassuring smile. Then he grabs my arm, pulling me down so that his mouth is next to my ear. "I am not risking everything for this to fail, half-breed," he hisses. "Break that spell, and make sure that no harm comes to Bellator. Do you understand me?"

I nod.

He releases me with a savage glare as Bellator and Uri approach on Nimro. He turns to them. "Any last orders, general?"

She shakes her head, looking worried for the first time since leaving Gaiztoak. Taking a knife from her belt, she hands it to him. "Thank you, Reevan. You've done enough."

He smiles faintly, accepting the knife, and opens his mouth to make a reply. But his voice is drowned out by an ear-splitting bellow, and our pursuers charge into view.

Chapter Fifteen

For a moment I am paralyzed with terror as I watch an army of hideous, human-like creatures gallop toward us. Each beast is at least seven feet tall, with dark grey slug-like skin, and wearing spiked armour painted black and red. One small, red, sunken eye peers out from beneath each iron helmet, and two large sabre-like fangs protrude from the bottom jaw of every snarling mouth. As if their looks aren't dangerous enough, the creatures are armed with massive longbows and crossbows, and long scimitars with jagged spikes along the blades.

"Ezixs!" Bellator's shout jerks me back to my senses. "Ride!"

Annalyn clutches the reins and kicks her heels into the horse's sides. "Hold on!" she cries as Majax rears and dashes after the others.

We zigzag through the remainder of the woodland, arrows firing around us, and burst out into a vast plain that opens suddenly before us. I glance back in time to see Reevan thrust Bellator's knife into his own leg. Grasping it, he staggers out of the way of the charging ezixs and collapses against a tree. The ezixs close ranks around him, blocking him from view.

An arrow whips past my shoulder, cutting through both my cloak and tunic, nicking my skin. I gasp and lean forward, locking my knees more tightly around Majax's sides.

The landscape before us is dry and barren, sweeping down into a narrow valley before it slopes back up into another rocky hilltop. We thunder down the first slope, arrows striking the ground around us. The ezixs are smart enough to see their advantage, and stop at the top of the hill, directing all of their attention and effort to shooting at us. It's clear that their aim isn't as accurate as Bellator's, but the arrows still fall too close for comfort.

An arrow hits the tip Majax's ear, barely missing his head. He whinnies, putting on a burst of speed, and we are quickly gaining on Uri and Bellator. As we approach, I see an arrow graze Bellator's elbow. She reacts at once, grasping the injury with her opposite hand, and thrusts the reins into Uri's fists. With an angry roar, she flips over his head, landing on her feet on the horse's flanks. Drawing her bow, she lets loose a volley of arrows at our attackers. Each arrow finds its target in the centre of a little red eye.

An uproar rises among the remaining ezixs, and they direct their aim only at her. It is a matter of seconds before an arrow finds its mark in her shoulder. She topples off of Nimro's back, tumbling down the rest of the hill in the dust kicked up by the horse's hooves. Unaware, Uri keeps on riding into the valley.

There is a guttural whoop among our hideous assailants, and a group of them start down the hill toward her.

"Keep riding!" I order Annalyn as we approach Bellator's prone body. "I'm going to see if I can help."

"Ealdred, no!" she shouts, reaching back to stop me.

But she's too late. I launch myself backward from the horse. I hit the ground on my back, and the wind is knocked out of my lungs. Struggling to breathe, I pick myself up and stumble toward where Bellator lies. She is sprawled on her back, unmoving. The shaft of the arrow in her shoulder was broken in half during her fall and a jagged end sticks out at a different angle than it entered.

Suddenly, a ball of fire strikes the ground between us, exploding into a raging fury. I jump back as the heat scorches my face.

Laughter issues from the flames. "You fool!" Zeldek's voice scoffs. "Did you really think it would be that easy to get away from me?"

"Ealdred, you idiot!" Bellator yells from the opposite side of the spreading inferno. "Get out of there!"

Zeldek chuckles. "Oh, Bellator. Always the warrior," he mocks. "Still fighting your destiny? You know that the more you fight, the more I win."

"Run, half-wit, run!" Bellator shouts. "He isn't there!"

Confused, I follow her voice around the flames.

"Wait!" Zeldek cries. "No one leaves without my permission!"

A flame in the shape of a fist shoots from the inferno and hits the palm of my left hand. The fire scorches my skin, burying itself deeply into my flesh, and I scream. I am being sucked toward the fire and I can't pull away. Terrified, I pull out my knife and slash at the flaming hand. My blade passes through it, and Zeldek laughs again.

"Mortal weapons cannot hurt me, half-race!"

The pain intensifies one last time before the flame finally releases me and disappears back into the fire.

My whole body is trembling as I draw away. I look down at my injured hand. A ring of flames burns in a circle on it, igniting a new brand from the base of my thumb along the breadth of my palm. It is the shape of a dragon inside a circle of chains with its wings spread out above it, and a ring hanging from its fangs. The same shape that is on Zeldek's signet ring.

I blow on it, hard, panic welling in my throat. The fire goes out, leaving the brand a glistening red. The muscles in my arm and hand tremble and jerk. I clap my palm to my mouth, wetting it with my tongue to cool it down. The relief is short-lived and a metallic taste lingers on my tongue.

A heavy foot hits my back, throwing me to the ground and holding me there. Dust fills my mouth. A loud growl comes from above me and I almost forget to spit out the dirt. Two large feet step in front of my face, and I follow them up to their owner.

A very large ezix stands above me, its teeth bared. The long claws on its hands are extended, razor sharp and polished. I search for my knife with my uninjured hand, but it is trapped beneath me. The ezix draws its scimitar from its side and slams it into the ground inches from my head.

"*Jaikitzen!*" it shouts.

I don't have a clue what that means.

The ezix that has its foot on my back grunts out something, and the one in front of me grows angry. It jerks its sword from the earth, and raises it threateningly above my head.

"*Jaikitzen!*" it roars even louder.

"*Lortu kanpoan zion!*" For the first time since I met her, I'm glad to hear Bellator's voice. "Or I will kill you!"

Apparently, they elect to disregard her words, because a moment later, both ezixs fall dead beside me.

"Get up!" Bellator orders, her voice strained.

I grunt and try to push myself up with my left hand. I remember too late that it is injured and yelp as the pain returns with full force.

Grabbing my elbow, she jerks me to my feet. "Blame yourself, half-wit."

I look around. The fire is spreading quickly along the dried grass of the valley floor, and the ground around the inferno we stand by is littered with dead ezixs. It seems Bellator kept busy while I was getting burned.

"Where's Zeldek?" I stammer.

"Still in Gaiztoak," she says bitingly, "as I kept trying to tell you. This was all an obvious distraction so the ezixs could catch you, and it would've worked if it weren't for me!"

"So, he's not here?"

"No! Creating so many fireballs will have weakened him enough to keep him from leaving his power source in Gaiztoak for some time. Do I have to explain everything to you?"

"I d-don't think so." I hesitate. "His power source is that Aemurel thing, right?"

She gasps, her face twisting in pain. "We don't have time for this!"

I notice the broken shaft sticking out of her shoulder and remember that she's injured too. Blood leaks from the bent hole in her shoulder guard from which the arrow still protrudes, shining as it streams down her breastplate. Part of the braid around her head has fallen loose and the end is drenched in the stuff. She presses one hand to the wound below the arrow and grasps my arm in her other, dragging me behind her as she sprints down the hill.

It seems Zeldek isn't finished with us yet. A ball of fire collides into the ground directly in front of us. The flames leap out to make a wall before us as far as I can see in both directions. Beyond the wall, I can make out Uri and Annalyn on the ridge above us. They've reined their horses and are turning back toward us, indecisive.

Behind us, the hillside is black with ezixs, but they aren't advancing. They stand in rows, jeering at us, pounding their weapons into the ground. They are mocking us. They know as well as we do that in the end, we'll have to turn back to escape the flames. Then they will capture us and drag us back to Zeldek.

"A curse on you and your fire!" Bellator bellows furiously.

I look to her for guidance. "What do we do now?"

"Oh, shut up!" she sputters, turning on me. "This is your fault! Neither of us would be trapped right now if you hadn't wanted to play the hero and save the damsel in distress!"

"I thought you were hurt!" I protest.

Her eyes spit fire, and I'm suddenly struck by how beautiful she is, even with the scars that tear her face apart. Beautiful, but terrifying.

"My welfare is no concern of yours!" she snarls. "You've never even held a sword, let alone ended a life! You would be dead if I hadn't come and saved you!"

"I'm not going to apologize."

Her fingers dig into my arm. "Never again, half-wit. I don't need help from you or anyone else. You hear me? Not *ever*."

I believe her.

She turns back to the flames and glares into them. "I won't give up! Not when we're this close!" A pause, then she nods sharply. "We're going to run through it," she announces. "Do you think you can do that without getting yourself killed?"

"You seem to think that I can."

"We'll see about that," she scoffs, pulling her hood over her head. "Just follow my lead."

Drawing her cloak over her arm, she brings it up in front of her face. I follow her example. Together we take a deep breath and plunge into the flames.

It is the strangest sensation, to be in the midst of a wall of flames. I expected heat, yet all I feel is a strong wind that rushes around me and then suddenly fades as we come out on the opposite side. There is a roar of confusion from the ezixs on the hill as we disappear from their view, but we don't stop to gloat. Letting our surprisingly unscathed cloaks fall from our faces, we make a run for the horses, which Uri and Annalyn are spurring toward us.

As they approach, Bellator releases me and sprints toward Nimro. She waits until he's passing her before grabbing his bridle and swinging herself up onto his back in front of Uri. She snatches the reins from him and turns the horse back up the hill.

Majax passes me and I grab for the bridle with my right hand, but catch the saddle strap instead. Annalyn turns Majax just as gracefully as Nimro was turned, but I am not nearly as graceful as Bellator. I manage to get my arms over the saddle as we ride up the hill, but it isn't until we slow near the top that I am able to pull myself up.

I barely have time to catch my breath before Annalyn confronts me.

"How could you be so reckless?" she blurts, turning in the saddle to slap my arm. "That was stupid and careless! You scared me to death when you jumped off like that!"

"I'm sorry," I say, alarmed. "I didn't think. They shot her, and I thought she needed help, so—"

"*Bellator* need help?" Annalyn asks incredulously. "Trust me, she could've taken care of herself. You, on the other hand, are untrained and weak and— and not a fighter! You could've died! Have you no thought for your own life?"

"Why are you so upset?" I exclaim. "You aren't obligated to be nice to me anymore. You don't have to keep pretending you care!"

If we weren't escaping from a horde of terrifying monsters, I am sure that she would have stopped the horse. As it is, her face dons a mask of pity.

"You think that I am pretending to care about your safety?"

The words come before I can stop them. "Well, it wouldn't be the first time."

Her cheeks redden with shame.

Guilt stings me.

"I'm sorry," I blurt. "I shouldn't have—"

"Just don't do anything like that again, alright?" she says, looking forward again.

We start down the other side of the ridge, entering a vast plain that stretches out for miles before us. We don't waste any more time. As soon as the ezixs figure out that we have escaped, they will be after us. And we need to be as far away as possible by then.

The further that we get from Gaiztoak, the more the darkness begins to lift. The overcast sky grows lighter and a fresh, cool breeze finds its way to my face through the hot, stale air.

The distant clamour of the ezixs in pursuit drives us on, and after over two hours of hard riding through dry, rocky ravines and mountainous terrain, we reach the border of another dark, haunting forest.

"Dismount!" Bellator orders, halting her horse at the edge of the woods.

Uri groans. "What for?"

"Now!" she barks, startling Uri so much that he falls off Nimro's back.

I slide to the ground, stretch my sore limbs, and then tend to the throbbing burn on my hand by wrapping it in a strip of cloth that I rip from my tunic. Annalyn draws the back of her hand over her damp forehead and glances with distaste into the dark recesses of the forest. But she doesn't dare complain. Bellator has already made it quite clear that she isn't in the mood for it.

Annalyn dismounts while Bellator walks along the outskirts of the woods, surveying them.

"Well then!" Uri mutters, dusting himself off. "She's pretty cranky all the sudden."

"All of a sudden?" Annalyn snorts. "When was the last time you saw *her* all sunshine and roses?"

"I guess she ain't much meaner than always," he relents, shooting a dirty look in Bellator's direction.

I find myself coming to her defence. "Well, she does have an arrow through her shoulder."

Bellator turns back and beckons sharply for us to come.

"Can't rest for even a moment," Uri sighs, leading Nimro toward Bellator.

I take Majax's bridle and follow. Annalyn trots along beside me.

"I found the path into the woods," Bellator calls as we approach. "Hurry it up! We aren't safe yet. Our pursuers are only a few miles behind us."

Not even Uri argues this time. I doubt that any of us want to ever meet up with an ezix again.

Chapter Sixteen

The forest turns out to be just as bad as the ezixs and fire combined. Never in my life have I seen so many kinds of thorns. The trees, the shrubs, the bushes, the vines, the moss; they all reach for us, grabbing at our clothing and tearing at our skin. All four of us have weapons drawn as we hack at the thorns to create a passage. Bellator has her sword, I have my dagger, Uri has his rusty knife, and Annalyn has one of Bellator's blades that was lent to her with great reluctance.

Our pace is slow going and I worry that the ezixs will catch up to us. When I voice this concern to Bellator, she points out that the thorns are weaving themselves together behind us, and my mind is set at ease.

"How much of this we got left?" Uri asks for the hundredth time since entering the forest. Bellator had him bring up the rear of the group, so he feels the need to shout over the rest of us.

"About a mile or so." Bellator slashes violently through a vine of thorns in her path.

He is silent for only a moment. "Where abouts are we, anyhow?"

A vine catches the jagged end of the shaft in Bellator's shoulder, and she gasps. She rips the vine aside with her sword, then pounds her fist into her shoulder right below the wound.

"The wilderness," she snaps breathlessly.

Uri doesn't seem to notice her tone. "Well, thanks a lot," he grumbles. "'cause everyone knows where 'the wilderness' is, don't they?"

"Be more specific with your question, and I'll be more specific with my answer!"

A thorny branch catches his sleeve, and he bats it away with his knife. "What I mean was, whereabouts in Theara are we? What countries are close?"

"The far north!" Her breath is wheezing, and I begin to worry.

She's pushing herself too hard. She needs to rest, or at least to bandage her wound.

"We just left the Plains of Beldir, and we're nearing the forest of Sylvaria."

Uri catches Annalyn's eye and raises an eyebrow in confusion. She shrugs and shakes her head.

Bellator gives an exasperated sigh. "On the map, we're in the vast forestland above the country of Valamette, and nearing the border of Lavylli – although in actual fact, Lavylli is beneath our feet."

"My parents own a tavern in Valamette," Annalyn offers helpfully.

"Well, my pap's a pirate captain from Avia," Uri boasts, but there is more bitterness than pride in his tone.

"Who cares where your parents are from, or who they are, for that matter?" Bellator says gruffly. "I don't know mine and I've gotten on fine without them."

I am pretty sure that everyone present would disagree with that last assertion.

We walk in silence for a bit longer, miserably fighting the thorns. I want to ask Bellator if she is alright, but I doubt that she would take it very well. But after she has dropped her sword twice and collapsed against a tree another time, I decide to risk it.

"How's your shoulder doing?" I ask in a whisper so the others won't hear.

"I'm fine!" she snaps. She doesn't look at me, but I can tell her face is very white.

"I can take over in the front for a while," I offer. "Maybe you should ride one of the horses for a bit."

She slashes through a branch in her way. "I said I'm fine!"

But she isn't. Her hands are shaking and her breath comes quicker and shorter. The other two are too busy arguing about how similar outlaws and pirates are to notice her predicament.

In another hour, we finally reach the end of the thorns. We all file out into a wide clearing, and the thorns weave themselves back together as if we had never been there.

It's as if we walked from a land of darkness into one of light. The trees are tall and slender with mint green leaves, and the rays of sunlight that bathe the ground have a silvery iridescence. The air is sweet and cool, but with a touch of mystery.

"Come," Bellator says after we have all drank water from canteens that we find in the horses' saddlebags. "We'll mount up again. It'll take the ezixs longer than we did to get all of them through here, but they will manage it. We need to get as much distance between them as we can." She takes Nimro's bridle from Uri and nods to me. "You'll be riding with me this time, half-wit."

I groan inwardly, and Annalyn doesn't seem to like the new arrangements any better. Bellator may be frightening, but Uri is overbearing, and he and Annalyn already seem to dislike each other enough.

Bellator swings up onto Nimro's back, then holds out a hand to me. I take it reluctantly, and she pulls me up behind her.

"You'll have to hold onto the horse with your knees to stay on," she says, "because I won't have you touching me."

Uri and Annalyn ride over on Majax, and Bellator turns to Uri with a nasty grin. "Oh, and by the way *pirate*, these woods are haunted. Just thought you might want to know."

Apparently, the stories of superstitious sailors are true, because the effect on Uri is instantaneous. His face blanches and he glances warily around at the pale, peaceful woods. Despite her pain, Bellator is still chuckling to herself as we start out.

"Why is the forest haunted?" I ask.

She snorts. "Don't tell me that you're scared too, half-wit."

"No. I'm just curious."

She doesn't seem to want to answer at first, and I think the only reason she does is because talking distracts her from the pain of her shoulder.

"This forest used to be home to a race of humans called Sylvarians. Mythology has it that these humans were the closest things to Vaelhyreans – that is, they had mild magical capabilities. But the entire race was wiped out in this very forest during the second great war."

"The *entire* race?" I echo. "Dead?"

Her silence is confirmation enough.

It is nearing evening when we leave the pale forest behind us and enter a slightly darker and denser stretch of trees. Large carved stones blanketed with dark green moss and fallen leaves protrude from the ground. The cracked skeleton of what looks to have been a magnificent archway rises before us, wedged between a grove of birch trees that appear to have grown many years after its destruction. Beyond that, I can make out the distant structure of a ruined fortress. Broken pillars rise from what remains of a stone courtyard, blending in with the trees and proving a lasting monument to a lost and conquered civilization.

Bellator reins the horse abruptly, and my face knocks into her back.

"We've gone too far east!" Her voice is unusually high.

"Wha'd'you mean?" Uri asks as Annalyn reins their horse beside us.

A sudden breeze rustles through the trees, carrying with it an odd whispering sound. The hair on my neck raises and I shudder. Both horses spook at once. Majax bolts toward the archway and Nimro rears. My knees lose their grip and I tumble off, hitting the ground on my back. The air is knocked out of my lungs, and before I can take a breath, I am jerked to my feet. Nimro and Bellator have already disappeared through the trees.

A woman in a long, shapeless grey robe stands in front of me.

"H-hello," I stammer, backing away from her.

She stretches her palm out toward me and whispers, "*Vincular!*"

Something snakes around my body, pinning my arms to my sides, and shoves itself into my mouth like a gag. It is covered in dirt and tastes bitterly like tender bark, and I realize that it is a root of some sort. The woman lifts her hand toward the sky. I rise into the air until I am dangling a few feet above the ground.

An agonized scream rips through the trees from the direction of my companions. I fight my bonds furiously, but despite my efforts, they only tighten further.

"Hold still, boy, or I'll snap you in half!" the woman growls.

"Alois, wait!" cries a familiar voice from behind me.

Shocked, I try to turn about. But the ropes – that is, roots – hold me still.

"What is it now?" demands the woman, who is apparently Alois.

"Release him."

Her hand drops to her side and the roots disappear. I flop to the ground as gracefully as a dead fish.

"Are you alright?" Banner asks, holding his hand out to me.

I bring my face out of the leaves, and look up at him. His appearance is subtly different. No longer is he wearing his filthy street rags, but is wrapped in a shapeless grey robe akin to the one worn by Alois. All that's left to signify his other life is the ratty eye patch over his eye, and the burns and bruises on the left side of his face from his skirmish with Zeldek in the alleyway. Yet he seems to have lost weight, and there is a sickness hanging about him.

"I'm fine," I say, taking his hand, which is wrapped in a grey bandage.

He helps me to my feet. "Sorry about that. Alois oversees the security of the place. She's a bit rough around the edges, but she has a good heart."

Alois growls.

"I see that you managed to escape Gaiztoak," he adds with a relieved, yet very tired, smile. "I'm impressed. That is a feat not many can boast of."

"I had help," I say. "The ezixs are still after us, but we're a few miles ahead of them."

He glances in the direction that we came from, his brow wrinkled with worry. "We'd better get you inside, then. Come with me. Quickly now!"

He starts toward the ruined castle, but I don't move.

"Banner, where are my friends?"

"They will be taken to safety as well," he assures me. "They will be given sanctuary with us if the council deems them worthy."

"Worthy?" I echo.

He nods. "Aye. The council will judge them according to what we know about them, and according to whom their loyalties lie. No need to worry. The council is reasonable."

Despite the assurance of his words, his tone relays uncertainty. But it's better than nothing.

I relent and start after him.

"Aren't you forgetting something?" Alois says, holding up a strip of cloth.

Banner glances back. "Oh, yes. That." He turns back to me. "I hope you don't mind, but we're going to have to blindfold you. It is regulation."

My shoulders tense, but I nod my consent. He gestures to Alois, who pulls the cloth over my eyes and ties it behind my head. A hand grabs my wrist, and I am pulled after the rustling sound of Banner limping through the leaves. We have only taken a few steps when the air grows suddenly cool and damp, and there is an earthy smell to it. The ground beneath my feet becomes hard like rock, and I would think we've reached the fortress had it not been so far away before.

The creaking of doors resounds through the air around me and the hand lets go of my wrist. Banner and Alois's footsteps fade abruptly.

I stop in my tracks.

The doors click shut. I feel as if I am standing on the edge of a cliff and remain as still as a statue. I wait for instructions, but none come. A moment longer, then I reach up to take off my blindfold.

"Come forward," booms a familiar voice.

I take a few faltering steps forward and stop. The blindfold is jerked from my face and I gasp, looking around. I stand alone in the middle of a bare hall crafted entirely of grey marble. Age clings to the walls, to the cracked ceiling, to the worn floor. There doesn't seem to be an immediate source of light, yet it is just as light as it was outside, almost as if the stones themselves were illuminating the room. Two steps lead up to a dais at the head of the hall, on which there is set a half crescent of five stone thrones.

The five thrones are filled by five figures dressed in the same dreary grey, shapeless robes. Three of them are men and two are women, and all of them look – in one way or another – as ancient and solemn as the hall around them. In the very centre throne is Ulmer, looking just as aged as before, and he is still wearing the bothersome headband. Banner sits in the throne to his right. To his left, the pointed face of Alois peers down at me from beneath the hood of her robes. As one, they appraise me with vaguely interested expressions, and a feeling of foreboding casts its shadow over me.

"Welcome to Buentoak," Banner says with a welcoming smile.

"Brethren," Ulmer says slowly, gesturing to me, "this is the child. The boy, Elroy, whom Banner has insisted on protecting for these past fifteen long years." He speaks directly to me. "We have been expecting you for some time now."

The other four council members incline their heads in unison.

I clear my throat. "Um, right then," I say. "Where are my companions?"

"They will arrive shortly," Ulmer replies, resting his hands stiffly on the arms of his throne. "But first, we wish to speak with you. Alone."

I cross my arms uncomfortably. "What about?"

"Your loyalties, of course," Alois snaps.

"Peace, Alois," Ulmer says.

"No need to spare the boy's feelings, Ulmer," Alois replies. "We would all thank you to say it plainly and be done with it!"

Ulmer casts her a reproving look and addresses me once again. "As Alois has just suggested, we wish to fully understand your position on my brother's proceedings in Gaiztoak, as well as to consider—"

"You want to know whether or not I gave Zeldek my allegiance," I cut in.

There is an awkward pause.

"Well," Ulmer says hesitantly, "so that there is a complete understanding between us, yes. We would wish for you to clarify that for us."

I look from face to face. There is a look of unexplained reverence and understandable suspicion on every countenance.

"I did not join him," I say, and there is a general sigh of relief. "But that doesn't mean that I am on your side either. I would rather be left out of whatever is going on – and that goes for all of it."

Disappointment replaces their relief in an instant.

"Just our luck, isn't it?" Alois says.

"Alois," Ulmer says warningly.

"It doesn't matter what he wants, does it? He has no choice in the matter!"

"What matter?" I ask.

"It's nothing," Banner says.

Alois rises from her throne. "You must understand boy! We're your only hope. Zeldek will continue to hunt you until you are either on his side or dead! You can't fight him on your own!"

"Mutila aukera du!" Ulmer shouts, and the room echoes with the sound. "Now sit down! You're making a fool of yourself."

Stunned, Alois lowers herself back into her throne.

There is another moment of silence, and then Ulmer speaks directly to me again. "There is one more thing I must know before I allow you to leave."

I wait.

"Did he mark you?"

I look up, startled, and instinctively clench my wounded fist. "What do you mean, 'mark me'?"

"I mean to say," Ulmer clarifies, "that there is a mark of a dragon in chains on his signet ring. Did you receive this mark on your person in any way?"

I swallow. Even Banner looks worried now, and all four of them observe me with distance.

"No," I lie. "But if he had, what would you do?"

"There would be nothing we could do," Ulmer says gravely. "You would already be too far gone for us to save."

Too far gone? What does he mean by that?

He flicks his hand, and the door behind me begins to open.

"Now," he continues, "we will judge your friends."

I turn to the door.

Uri and Annalyn enter, led into the room by two more grey-robed guards. Their eyes are still blindfolded, but while Uri comes along quietly, Annalyn keeps trying to peek under hers. I wonder where Bellator is.

She better not have gotten herself killed trying to fight them when they tried to capture her.

"You can remove their blindfolds," Ulmer says, and his order is quickly obeyed.

They look about, blinking, and Uri's mouth opens stupidly in wonder.

"Ealdred, you're safe!" Annalyn exclaims, relieved.

Uri glares at me. "Why's he here first?" he demands.

"There's no need for that, child," Banner says good-humouredly.

"And who d'you think you are?" Uri demands.

"Uri," I warn.

"Oh, it's alright," Ulmer says, waving his hand dismissively. "They were both unwilling slaves in Zeldek's household and so are worthy to receive our protection." He nods to the guards. "Escort them to their rooms for the evening and give them whatever they ask for."

Banner's eye twinkles as he adds, "Within reason."

They are both led right back out, while Uri protests that I should be coming with them. The doors close again behind them.

"Sir," I say, turning to Ulmer, "those weren't all of my—"

"Come now," Ulmer interrupts, beckoning for me to come and stand between his and Banner's thrones. "You will want to stand out of the way for this one."

I follow his directions, but I feel my heart sinking. I know what is about to happen.

Sure enough, the doors swing open at his command, and Bellator is brought into the room.

Chapter seventeen

No, 'brought' isn't the right word to describe how she makes her entrance.

She is dragged.

Two grey-robed guards haul her into the room by her arms, and she hangs limply between them. The jagged half of the broken arrow has been pulled from her shoulder, and her armour glistens with a renewed flow of blood. It drips in a trail behind her as they drag her toward the stairs. They throw her down at the foot of the steps and rip the bloodstained blindfold from her eyes. For a long moment, she doesn't respond, and I think she might be unconscious. Then, slowly, she pushes herself to her knees and looks up at us.

I gasp at the sight of her and quickly put my hand to my mouth to stifle it. Her face reminds me of a corpse. Her skin is beyond being pale; it's grey. Her eyes have a dull, glassy look to them. Blood dribbles from her mouth and runs down her chin.

Ulmer's expression, however, is without pity as he rises from his throne.
"Finally!" he says in a cold voice that booms throughout the hall. "After all of your
efforts, you have finally evaded us for the last time, Bellator!"

She blinks weakly, and her mouth twists into an unmistakable smirk. "And
yet," she says slowly, her words garbled, "I had to be in this state before you could
finally catch me. Such a great achievement, isn't it?"

Ulmer's face reveals nothing but disgust, and he looks at her as if she were
some loathsome creature less than human. "There is no honour in a beast like you,
and so none shall be used regarding you."

She counters his disgust with resentment. "If you think that you have bested
me, go ahead and kill me. I warn you, I will put up one last fight!"

"We will kill you," he returns, clasping his hands behind his back, "for your
crimes against Vaelhyrean-kind and for the wars you have waged against us at the
command of your master!"

She doesn't try to deny the allegations. "If you want me to beg, you are
wasting your time!" she spits.

"Even if you did, it would make no difference. Just like those who were slain
at your hands, you shall receive no mercy!"

He sits back in his throne, a satisfied smile turning his lips. I can tell that he
is taking great satisfaction in this, and the feeling of dislike already sparked within
me grows still more.

Bellator's gaze shifts from him to me, and her smirk fades. "Hello, half-wit," she says tiredly. "Come to watch the show?"

My throat is dry and I make no attempt at answering. I know that she is a killer. I witnessed her kill at least a dozen ezixs on the Plains of Beldir, after all. But something about this all seems wrong.

"Kill her," Ulmer commands.

One of the guards draws his sword and approaches her. Bellator presses both of her trembling hands against the floor, squeezing her eyes shut. The guard stops beside her and raises the sword above her head. She opens her eyes slowly, bravely, and looks at me again. There is no fear in her gaze.

The sword begins to come down.

"Stop!" I cry, and the guard does, the blade inches from Bellator's neck. "For the love of Irla, just stop!"

"What is it?" Ulmer asks, turning to me with a concerned frown.

I step out from between the thrones, and back to the edge of the dais. "I can't let you do this!" I say. "Whatever her past sins, she is the one who helped us escape from Gaiztoak in the first place. I wouldn't be here if it wasn't for her. I should think that a warm bed and care for her wounds is what is in order here, not execution!"

Ulmer's face remains stony. "Did you not hear that she has murdered our people?"

"I can't deny it," I say slowly, formulating my words carefully. "But you said yourself that it was at the command of Zeldek. Perhaps she didn't have a choice in the matter. Perhaps he forced her to do these things against her will."

"One always has a choice," Ulmer replies, his voice cold and emotionless.

"Not when Zeldek is involved!" I respond heatedly. "What kind of a choice does one have when forced to decide between being tortured until one submits to him, or merely submitting to him? You may think that one choice is more noble than the other, but what difference does it make if the end result is the same?" I take a deep breath as I look at each in turn, imploring for them to see reason. "I only just escaped having to make that choice, and it was because of the girl you are now trying to kill! The one whose blood will forever stain this ground if you murder her. Please, I beg you to spare her. If not for me, do it for your own consciences! And ask yourselves, if you were in her place, would you have been able to do any better? She did what she did to survive. You can't judge her for that!"

Three of the other council members lower their gazes, and Banner nods approvingly. Only Ulmer remains unmoved.

"Please," I continue, "I beg you, give her the same chance you would give yourself."

Silence reigns as my words fade in the echo of the room. Then Ulmer sets his jaw. "Step aside, boy. It is for your own good."

"No," I say evenly.

"Fine!" Ulmer nods to the man. "Proceed."

The man raises his sword again, and I act without thinking. I leap between him and Bellator, putting up my hands in front of me, palms facing outward. A transparent blue dome surrounds Bellator and me moments before the man's sword hits it. There is a metallic clash followed by a swell of light that throws him back against the wall.

Ulmer is on his feet again, his jaw dropping in shock.

Banner stands up with a chuckle. "It seems he's determined to protect her, brother," he says, patting Ulmer on the shoulder. "Perhaps it would be wise if we took his advice for the time being. You must agree, if she is no longer under Zeldek's control, the girl won't be much of a threat to us any longer."

The two nameless council members agree with him, and at last, Ulmer relents. "Alright," he says gruffly. "We will pardon her, for your sake, boy. But do not question our judgement again!"

I make no promises.

When I lower my hands, the blue shield disappears, and I kneel down beside her. Whatever notions I might have had of her thanking me, I am sorely wrong. She glares at me, however weakly it is, and as I put my arm around her to help her up, she hisses, "I had that under control."

"Can't you ever say thank you?" I mutter as she rises unsteadily to her feet.

"Take them to their rooms and tend to their needs," Ulmer orders, but his voice is monotonous now.

"I'll be checking on her frequently," I say. "Don't even think about harming her!"

Ulmer sinks back into his throne with a grimace, and everyone but Banner looks very worried. As we leave the room, I hear him say cheerfully, "I mentioned that he had spirit, didn't I?"

The guards lead us down a stone corridor to a cold room that feels more like a cell than a bedroom. There is a low bed to the wall across from the door. I help Bellator to it. She lowers herself painfully onto the clean white sheets and rests her head on the pillow with a sigh. Relief washes over her face.

I straighten up, but she grabs my arm.

"Why didn't you let me die?" she wheezes. "I would've if I were you! Then you wouldn't have had to fulfill your end of the bargain. You would've been free!"

My throat tightens. "Well, I'm not anything like you."

Her eyes flash, and she grabs my hand as I turn toward the door. The burn throbs and I gasp. Noticing, she pulls back the binding. Her eyes widen when she sees the brand and she almost bolts upright. With a hurried glance at the guards behind me, she pulls me closer with a frantic look.

"When did you get that?" she hisses.

"On our way out, when I stopped to help you."

Her jaw clenches. "I'd hoped I could get you away before he gave you his mark." She reaches down and peels her blood-soaked glove from her left hand, thrusting it into my hands. "Put that on and keep it on!" She pulls off the other

and gives it to me too. "Don't let them see the brand."

I glance back at the guards, but they don't seem to be paying us any mind. I

lean closer. "Why not? What is it?"

"It's Zeldek's mark of ownership," she whispers, her voice barely audible. "He

gives it to those special and powerful people whom he claims belong to him. People

like you who he will stop at nothing to either bring to his side or destroy. The

council recognizes this and will see you as a threat. Whether it's true or not, they

lump all with the mark together with the followers of Zeldek."

I put the pieces together on my own. "And they kill the followers of Zeldek."

She nods, then gasps from the pain it causes her. "They want to destroy

Zeldek once and for all, and I don't blame them. Before he lost most of his power, he

almost burned the world down. They do what they need to do to keep him from

rising again."

One of the guards clears his throat impatiently. "Is everything alright?"

"Yes, everything's fine," I reply.

"You'd better go," she mutters.

I quickly pull on the leather gloves. They are too big for my hands, of course,

but at least they conceal the brand. "I'll be back to check on you in a while."

Turning to the guards, I order, "Get a physician in here at once to tend to her

wounds."

One hurries away to follow my order, while the other escorts me from the room. As he leads me to my room, my thoughts process the information that Bellator just gave me. But my mind also lingers on something else. As I turned to leave, my eyes caught on the palm of her left hand. Zeldek's mark had been burned into it as well. It isn't red and blistered like mine – it must have been given to her many years ago – but it is distinctly the same one. And I have the feeling that there's more to Bellator than just her will to survive.

·

Chapter Eighteen

Two days pass before Bellator begins to insist she's fully recovered from her wound, but it is three before the physician pronounces her well enough to get up and walk around. She is still very pale from the loss of blood and her composure isn't nearly as put together as usual, but she is tough. I make sure to check on her every few hours for the first day and a half, which annoys her greatly, but as she grows stronger, it becomes clear that the council will respect their word not to harm her.

Uri and Annalyn, on the other hand, are very much enjoying their stay. Annalyn's knee has been tended to and is on the mend. Uri complains constantly about the grey robes they've provided for us to wear, and Annalyn says that the place is too cold and bare for her liking. But the council allows them to explore every little bit of the underground stronghold, which they take the liberty to do, and that makes their dispositions more cheerful. Since even dinner is served to us in our respective rooms, I rarely see them.

As for me, I spend most of my time in my room, at Bellator's side, or pacing about alone in the corridors. Both the council members and the very few Vaelhyreans they preside over try to avoid me as much as possible, and if they do end up running into me, they apologize profusely, anxiously avert their gazes, or just completely ignore that I exist. And I haven't seen anything of either Banner or Ulmer since the day we arrived. I've never been treated quite so strangely in my entire life.

It is on the fourth morning since our arrival in this solemn place that I am finally able to speak with Banner again. I am pacing in a long, ghostly hallway of unlit torches when he limps into view, carrying an armload of scrolls and parchments. He stops when he sees me and smiles the first genuine smile I've received from any grey-robed figure in days. He seems to have grown less pale since I saw him last, but he is just as thin and haggard as ever.

"Ah, Elroy," he says, tucking the parchments under his arm. An amused smile flickers through the weariness that clouds his face.

"What is it?" I ask.

He chuckles, shaking his head. "You're a wonder, you are."

Not sure what to say to that...

"Um... thanks?"

"You certainly have a way with people, at any rate. The council's scared half to death of you, you know."

"Yeah, I think I've noticed," I say, scratching my ear. "What I don't understand is *why*? What is it about me that makes them so nervous?"

"It's nothing about *you*, per say," Banner says dubiously. "It's more the magic you possess that has them in a tousle."

"My magic?" I echo. "But aren't you all Vaelhyreans? Certainly the lot of you could outmatch a novice like me, no matter what the circumstance. I really don't have a clue what I'm doing."

"Perhaps," Banner admits. "But, Elroy, you did defy Ulmer before the council the moment you arrived. He is our leader, after all. And you challenged him. This does not bode well to the others."

"You understand, though, don't you? I couldn't let him kill her."

He opens his mouth, closes it, then tries again, speaking his words with conviction. "I think the girl is dangerous. She has caused us much sorrow in the short time she's been in Zeldek's service. But you did what you felt was right. I cannot judge you for that. Who knows? You could be right about her."

"I believe that I am."

"Only time will tell. Fair warning, though, the council has labelled you reckless. They will be keeping a close eye on you from now on."

"That's just my luck," I mutter.

"Don't be so quick to judge them for their caution, child," he chides. "In the days of old, there were many half-races. The mixture of Vaelhyrean and human blood created unusually strong and powerful heroes. But many were corrupted by the promise of power that Caderyn offered them, and they turned against us in battle. It was because of their betrayal that we almost lost the war against him. It isn't in our nature to be trusting anymore."

"But I'm not like that," I protest. "I don't want to hurt anyone."

"I know. You are the only half-race that I know of in existence, and that is why I chose to protect you; to keep you from being discovered and used by Zeldek. That is also why we fear and respect you so." He heaves a great sigh. "But we have lived in fear for too long. The curse weakens us more every day. I fear that if it remains unresolved for much longer, we will cease to exist."

"What curse?" I ask.

He clears his throat, shifting the bundle of scrolls to under his other arm. "Many years ago, during the great battle between the forces of Gaiztoak and us, there was a very powerful Vaelhyrean on our side. She was our queen after Emyr's death. Holding power over the element air, she could only be challenged in strength by Zeldek himself." He pauses. "She was our sister."

"Oh!" I exclaim. "You mean Batuel?"

Of course, she would be his sister too. I didn't think to make the connection until now.

He looks surprised. "Where did you hear that name?"

For a moment, I almost tell him about my deal with Bellator. But no, I shouldn't. Not only would Bellator quite literally kill me if I did, but I would rather that the council not find out about it. Ulmer would disapprove of letting Bellator

near such power and would probably take action to prevent us from leaving.

I clear my throat. "Zeldek mentioned her. I know that because of her death,

the goddess of life – it's Irla, isn't it? Because of her death, Irla cast a curse that

weakened him."

"He has no right to speak of her!" Banner growls. "I suppose you know what

he did to her?"

I nod. "I heard that he killed her and her family."

"Her husband and children, right before her eyes," Banner confirms. He's

angry, bitter; emotions I've not yet seen in him. "Then he cursed her soul so that it

would live on and forever feel the pain of losing everything she loved."

I rest a comforting hand on his dusty, robed arm. "I'm sorry."

"It was barbaric! The work of a monster. Irla was kind simply to take his

power from him."

"But... I don't understand. How does Irla's curse on him have anything to do

with you?"

"Irla didn't only curse Zeldek with the removal of most of his magic. She

cursed us all, leaving us with only enough magic to survive." His eyebrows draw

upward as he observes me. "Don't look so horrified. She had every right to do so.

We Vaelhyreans, together as a people, brought war to the land. We swore to her

when we came that we would maintain the peace we disturbed by our presence, but

we broke that oath. Starting with Caderyn's revolt and continuing for centuries afterward, there was much bloodshed. The misery and pain caused by our feuds tore her apart. Zeldek's massacre of Batuel's household was merely the last straw. Many of the others won't admit it, but we are *all* to blame."

"And the spell remains to this day?"

He nods. "It is probably for the best that it does. Irla was merciful in saying that if the spell on Batuel's arrow is removed, thus revoking Zeldek's curse on Batuel's spirit, our magic would return to us. But I fear that war would follow swiftly."

"It doesn't really seem like the war ever ended," I remark. "Perhaps it would be best just to allow it to play out."

"What do you mean?" he asks.

"Well, what if one of Batuel's children escaped? What if their descendant breaks the spell? A war to get rid of Zeldek wouldn't be all that bad, would it?"

His brow darkens. "The war would spread across Theara, whether you wanted it to or not. No one would be left untouched."

"You wouldn't condone the removal of the curse, then?"

There is a pause, and his eyes slide closed. "I wouldn't say that," he says amid his contemplation. "I've spent a lifetime living a half-life because of that curse. I long to feel alive again. But would it be best for Theara? I don't know. I'm not sure that anyone but our warrior is qualified to make that decision."

I raise an eyebrow. "Your warrior?"

"There is a prophecy," he says. "One which we have all studied over the years since Zeldek's rise to power."

"Go on," I urge.

He turns to look at me with a weary smile. "I won't bore you with the details, but the gist of it is that one day a great warrior will come, fight hand to hand with Zeldek, and destroy him once and for all. Once we have seen that happen, we may have hope of atoning our sins to Irla."

I try not to sound as sceptical as I feel. "When is this warrior going to come?"

He shakes his head. "Like all prophecies, this one is vague."

So that's why they've remained hidden for so long. They're waiting for some phantom warrior to come and save them. Typical.

Banner's voice breaks a lengthy moment of silence. "What price has she set out for you?"

"Hmm?"

"The girl. What price did she set out for rescuing you?"

I avoid his gaze. "Who says there's a price?"

"I know her kind," he says. "They never do something like this unless they're getting something in return."

"She did," I admit. "Set forth a price, that is. But it's between her and me."

His brow darkens. "You're a smart lad, and very brave. In my years keeping watch over you, I know that much. I trust you know what you're getting yourself into. I only worry what her influence might do to you."

"I'll be fine," I reassure him. "I promise, I have everything under control."

"Half-wit!" Bellator's voice suddenly booms from somewhere up the hallway. "Half-wit, get over here now!"

I cringe. "Well, almost everything."

"It's a complicated road you tread upon," he warns with a sad smile. "Please, be careful."

"I will," I promise.

Pulling out his papers again, he observes them with a yawn. "Well, I've got to get to the library with these. I look forward to our next meeting," he says, and walks away.

"Half-wit, I'm waiting!"

I follow the sound of her shouting and soon find her leaning against the doorframe of a nearby corridor. The last time I saw her, she was wearing the grey robes that the elders provided for us. Now, she is dressed once more in her black armour, which she has mended and cleaned. The hole in the shoulder-guard has been patched over, and the newly polished metal glints in the light.

She straightens up as I approach. "What took you so long?" she demands.

I gesture back to where I came. "I was—"

"I wasn't asking for an answer, half-wit," she says irritably. "It's time for us to leave this place and get back on track."

"Are you sure? I spoke to the physician this morning. Your shoulder is still on the mend..."

Bellator glares at me. "I'm stronger than that fool realizes. We leave today. The ezixs will have lost our trail by now. We only have a short window of time to get out of here before they decide to retrace their steps. We've wasted enough time as it is."

I suppose if anyone could bounce back so quickly from such an injury, it would be her. But I also worry she might put her own health aside to fulfill her goals.

"I agree," I say, lightening my tone. "But you might have a hard time convincing Uri and Annalyn."

She smirks. "Actually, they're already packed. Even little Ann is getting tired of this barren place." Looking around with growing vexation, she adds, "Besides, if we stay here any longer, I doubt I'll be able to remain civil to these magical imbeciles for much longer."

"I doubt that too," I agree.

Her irritation grows. "I know you fancy to have saved my life the other day, but that doesn't give you leave to be friendly with me, half-breed! If you hadn't stepped up, I might have died, yes. But I would've taken the whole place down with me!"

"Then I saved everyone else's lives from you." I flash a grin. "You're welcome."

We announce our intentions to leave to the council within the hour. It seems as if they are both reluctant and eager to let me go; reluctant because I'm not going to be under their constant surveillance, and eager because they won't have to be afraid of my 'spontaneous' bursts of magic.

Ulmer appears to be masking boiled rage, and his words are thick with resentment as he bids us farewell. I hope that I'm not right, but I'm certain I have made another powerful enemy.

Once the four of us are together in the same place, we are blindfolded and magically transported back to the clearing they found us in. We find our horses saddled and waiting for us. They have been well fed and groomed until their coats are sleek and glossy, and their packs have been stocked with provisions for our journey.

As Bellator gives orders for us to mount up, Banner pulls me aside. He speaks to me in a low tone, so as not to be overheard by the others.

"I know I've already said this, but please, be careful. Do not trust that girl."

"I don't," I assure him.

He puts his hand on my shoulder. "Whatever she has told you to do—"

"I'm going to do it," I say. "I gave my word."

"A noble gesture, but I worry she'll take advantage of your honesty. She will put her own interests above anything else, above any cost – even if that cost is your life."

I ponder that. He has a point, I will admit. I know she's probably going to take the arrow from me the moment I break the spell, and that she'll use it to exact her revenge against Zeldek. But even if my life is the price for my freedom, I'm willing to risk it.

"I gave my word," I repeat firmly.

With a friendly squeeze to my shoulder, he lets me go. "Whatever the future holds, it was an honour watching over you. If you ever find yourself in a tight place, know that I will always be on call. I am your guardian, after all."

"About that," I glance back at the others to ensure they aren't listening, then lower my voice considerably. "Why do you and the others keep calling me Elroy?"

He shrugs, and says simply, "It's your name."

"Come on, half-wit!" Bellator calls impatiently. "We want to leave *today*."

"Go on," he says with a nod. "You will understand all in time. A word of caution; don't pull on that string just yet. It will only cause you pain."

What could hurt worse than not knowing?

"Zeldek told me that my father abandoned me," I prompt. "But I was never told who he was."

His smile is a poor mask for pity. "Now is not when you learn these things. Allow your mind the ease of ignorance for a little while longer." He nods solemnly, folding his arms in his robes. "Farewell, child."

And then he disappears into a puff of purple mist, leaving me even more confused than before.

Chapter Nineteen

T he Master paced slowly along the rampart atop the circular wall surrounding his fortress. Lava simmered and spat in the pit to his right, rearing up occasionally to spout a fountain of glowing obsidian into the air. But even in this state, it was calm.

His hands were clasped behind his back and his composure was one of dignity, though there was nothing dignified about the present crisis. His plans had been momentarily put on hold. But of course they had been! He would have been a fool not to have expected something like this to happen. This Ealdred had only proved himself to be what Zeldek already knew – formidable and, in time, a dangerous asset.

The two servants, however, were a surprise. He had not thought his staff to be so ungrateful for his hospitality. Perhaps that was a failure on his part. But the fact that Bellator had taken them along was what surprised him most of all. Perhaps she saw something in them that he had overlooked.

Bellator's escape was, regrettably, inevitable. It was natural for one so young as she to have longings for a different life. Such fancies would fade in time. She would be bound to despair and resign herself to her destiny at some point in the future. Then her mind would be clear enough to unlock her full potential.

A horn blast rang out across the vast plain of pits, disturbing the Master's contemplations. The rumble of the gate opening in the distance followed.

The Master smiled to himself.

They had returned, then. The ezixs had not failed him, as the outlaws had. Soon he would be welcoming his guests back from their unprecedented travels.

He'd let the servants off with a minor scourge, he decided. They had most likely been goaded into fantasies of freedom by the two ringleaders. Them, he would have to deal with more harshly. They would find themselves cellmates in the abyss for a couple of years. It may pain him, but they had forced his hand.

The dark forms of the procession of ezixs could be seen making their way toward the long stairway leading up to the portal to the palace. With a wave of his hand, Zeldek vanished from his place on the wall and appeared at the top of the stairs. He began to descend, and both parties reached the bottom at the same time.

The leader of the arriving company stepped forward, his red eye gleaming. He thumped his chest with his fist, the ezix way of showing respect, and then fell to one knee before the Master. His thick black hair was tied in a knot behind his head, and the long, dreaded tails fell down his back in a tousled heap.

"Durgarra! You have returned," Zeldek said in his mother tongue, the only language the majority of these magical creatures could understand. "What news do you bring me from the south?"

Durgarra looked up. "My lord, things did not go as planned."

Zeldek stiffened, but he would feel no anger.

Durgarra's gaze fell and his shoulders slouched. "My master, we have failed you."

"I can see that. What happened?"

"We made it through the thorns only hours after them, and we were making good time. But their tracks vanished without a trace. We searched the area, even miles around it, but found nothing."

"Whereabouts did they disappear?" the Master asked.

"It was near the ruins of Buentoak, my lord."

Zeldek scowled. It was no surprise to him that Ulmer would stick his nose in business not his own. But he had not counted on Bellator going anywhere near that place.

The Master turned away. "Thank you, Durgarra. You have done well."

A weight lifted off of the ezix's shoulders. "Thank you, sire. I only wish I could have done more," Durgarra said, and rising, he ordered his company away.

The Master watched them retreat. The wind whipped his hair about, and his robe flew out around him. He furrowed his brow, searching for any memory that might help him understand what Bellator could be planning. Why had she sought the help of Ulmer? What could she seek that would benefit her so much as to risk such punishment? The questions circled in his head until he could not stand the dull glare of ignorance any longer.

He raised his hand, slowly clenching it into a fist to ease his anger. He must alert his faithful consuls of this new development. With their intelligence, he would have his answer soon enough.

He opened his hand, and dark mist spewed from it until it shrouded him in blackness.

Chapter Twenty

"The River Tireth," Bellator shouts over the roar of the river sweeping through the ravine below us. "It flows from the Handia Mountain and divides the boarders of Zandelba and Valamette."

"Does that mean that we're in Valamette?" Annalyn asks hopefully.

After almost a week of traveling with Bellator, I'm hopeful too. She is certainly a hard taskmaster. Even when Buentoak was far behind us, she wouldn't allow us to so much as whisper for fear of alerting the enemy. Though it was clear the ezixs were long gone, she threatened us with pain if we objected. I didn't argue. Everyone knows that these lands are crawling with outlaws; more specifically, the infamous Crimson Shadow – an outlaw so deadly that no one's ever seen him and lived to tell the tale. Bellator may be a good fighter, but I wonder if even she would risk running into such a character.

"Depending on who you ask," Bellator replies, leading us away from the water's edge. "On the map, it says that we've been in Valamette for about an hour now. But since no one comes here and the nearest population – a few mere towns – is miles away, I still consider this to be wilderness."

"How far is the city of Kenwardton?" Uri asks, looking as if he's drawing up a mental map of the area.

"Kenwardton is a two-day journey from here," Bellator replies. "Why? Is that where we're dropping you?"

"What do you mean, 'dropping' me?" Uri demands, indignant. "Where are *you* headed?"

"Along the Tireth with the half-breed." She turns, walking backward as she speaks, and nods to Annalyn. "What about you?"

"Bynvantalyn," Annalyn says dreamily.

She arches her eyebrows. "That's the little town in the valley near the bridge, right?"

Annalyn nods.

"Oh, good!" Bellator smirks. "It sounds like you'll be home before nightfall."

Bellator turns on her heel to walk forward again, but as she does, Uri grabs her arm and jerks her back to face him.

"You ain't over us no more, but you act like you're still in charge!" he cries, his knuckles turning white as he digs his fingers into her arm.

"That's because I *am* in charge, imbecile!"

"No! No, you ain't! Ain't no one the boss of me but me!" He jabs his thumb into his own chest to assert his point.

Bellator clenches her teeth, and with a deadly calm, she tries to twist her forearm out of his grasp.

"No you ain't!" he shouts in her face, giving her a violent shake, and then he slams her back against a tree. "You're gonna answer my question, and you're gonna do it fast! What's with you trying to get rid of us all the sudden?"

I can see a light growing behind her eyes, and it scares me. It's a look that goes beyond rage, beyond fear. A hunger, or thirst, perhaps. She's going to hurt him, badly.

"Uri, leave her be!" I cry, starting toward them.

Bellator glances at me with a disdainful scowl. Uri gives her another shake, as if to remind her that he is still there, and the look intensifies. In a sudden blur of movement, she has turned the tables. Uri's face is mashed into the tree, his nose bloody, while Bellator twists his arm behind his back, holding her knife to his throat.

"I've put up with you long enough, Uriah!" she growls in his ear.

My heart is in my throat. "B-Bellator, calm down. He didn't mean it..."

"Stay out of this, half-wit!" Her voice has changed to a low, vicious snarl. "I don't make meaningless threats!"

My heart pounds furiously in my ears, but I force my voice to be calm. "We made a deal, remember? You told me that you would help me return them safely to their homes. That's my side of the bargain."

"Oh, I'll send him home," she growls, her blade nicking his neck.

Uri whimpers as blood runs down his collarbone from beneath the shining blade.

"Bellator, please," I plead, my voice strained. "Let him go."

Her eyes are feral, untamed. "Why do you care anyways? He treats you like dirt!"

I swallow. She is right, really. He hasn't said a civil word to me since leaving Buentoak, and has treated me like his personal slave. Two evenings ago, he even tried to make me eat the leftover scraps of meat off of his squirrel bones. Had not Annalyn put a stop to it, I'm sure that I would still have the taste of bone marrow and his rotten breath in my mouth right now.

With that memory fresh in my mind, I have to force my voice to remain gentle as I reply. "That doesn't matter. I told them they would be free, and I mean to make that happen."

Her hand trembles with rage. She's losing what control she has over the devouring beast always present behind her eyes. "And you think that *you* can stop me?"

I lick my lower lip nervously. "No. No, of course not."

Her smirk is just as savage as her voice. "Then stop trying, or I may have to hurt you too!"

I dare to try again. "We made a deal. Doesn't your word mean anything to you?"

"You're right we made a deal," she spits. "A deal to get you and the rest of these idiots out of Gaiztoak. Since my word means *so* much to me, I'll spare him. But let's make another deal, shall we? A deal that will ensure his safety for the rest of the time that we are together."

My voice is so feeble that I am barely able to get out the words. "What do you want?"

Still pressing the knife against Uri's neck with one hand, she releases his wrist and grabs the front of my shirt, pulling me so close that her face is only a few inches from mine. Her breath smells like the mint leaves she has been chewing all morning.

"From now on, you're going to do everything that I say without question and without comment." Her voice is quiet, yet her words are as clear as if she is shouting. "When I speak, you obey! Got it?"

My heart hammers in my chest. "I-I'll try," I stammer.

"You'd better do more than just try," she snaps, and releases the front of my tunic with a shove.

I stumble backward, and she turns to Uri again.

"Next time, I won't hesitate," she says to him, and draws the knife away from his neck.

The monster within has been placated, for now.

Uri backs away, putting his hand to the cut on his throat. Bellator continues into the woods and he glowers after her.

She laughs harshly. "Your compassion makes you weak, half-breed!"

I cringe, but don't let myself think on her words. *She's wrong. Compassion may be a weakness, but it's a weakness the world needs more of.*

"You alright?" I ask Uri.

He shoves me backward so hard that I trip over a root and smash my head into the tree that's behind me.

"Next time, stay out of it!" he bellows, spit spraying everywhere. He kicks leaves at me, adding with menace, "Stupid half-breed!"

He snatches Nimro's bridle and stalks after Bellator.

I stare after him, not sure whether to feel hurt or angry. "He would still be in that hell hole if it wasn't for me," I mutter to myself as I struggle to my feet.

"I know," says Annalyn, and I jump. She'd been so quiet during the entire ordeal that I'd forgotten she was still here. "And I am grateful to you for that," she continues. "It's just that some people can't appreciate help when it hits them between the eyes."

"Sure," I say bitterly, "but even you see me as just a means to get you home."

"No," she protests.

"Really? You see me as an equal to yourself now?"

She hesitates. "You know I have always seen us as equals."

But, judging by her averted gaze, I know that she isn't entirely telling the truth.

"Hurry up!" Bellator calls. "I'd like to deliver Ann home before sundown."

I take Majax's reins from Annalyn, and we start after them. The forest thins as we cover more distance, the sounds of the river growing fainter with each step. A heavy silence hangs over Annalyn's shoulders, and I know she's preparing to say something. It's only a matter of time before she speaks.

"So," she begins, a bit timidly, "you made a deal with her so that she would take us with you?"

I shrug. I don't want to talk about it.

"What was it?" she persists.

"It doesn't matter," I mumble. "But it's worth your freedom to me."

She doesn't say any more, and soon goes up to walk with the others. When the fire in my chest dies down, I feel bad for being so harsh to her.

She wasn't the one that hurt me.

Dusk is falling when we are at last standing on the hill overlooking the little town of Bynvantalyn. The town is nestled in a bowl-shaped valley beside the sparkling waters of a little lake. Hues of orange, purple, and pink darken the clear sky above. The air is fresh and cool, and I breathe it in deeply, allowing it to drive away the unpleasant feelings that have been nagging in my head all afternoon.

"This place ain't that bad," Uri says grudgingly.

Bellator casts him a sideways glare.

"Papa's tavern is right on the edge of the lake," Annalyn says, an excited sparkle in her eyes.

"Let's go then," Bellator says irritably. "Perhaps you could get your papa to give us some ale for our troubles. That is, if he's still around."

But Annalyn's mood is not so easily shattered. She nods, her face glowing. "Of course! He'll be happy to."

Bellator leads us along the ridge until we come to the main road, and we follow it down the steep hill and into town. There are hardly any people on the streets, and those who are duck out of sight as we pass.

"I thought the people here were known for their friendliness," Bellator remarks, emerging from her brooding as her curiosity is sparked.

"They are," Annalyn says, glancing around with a confused frown. "That is, they were before I was taken. Things could have changed."

"It could be because we're all wearing black," I suggest. "They might think that we're some kind of outlaw group."

"No," Bellator says with surprising firmness. "My outlaws never attacked this village. If we ever stooped so low as to pillage, we would go for the bigger, more rewarding towns."

"Yeah, but your outlaws ain't the only ones in Theara," Uri mutters, and it's clear he's still angry with her.

"Yes, they are," she counters sharply. "Those that aren't are made to join us or die. Your father does the same with the pirates too, if you recall."

"Yeah," he acknowledges. "But I didn't think you'd be that smart—"

"The question is," I cut in, hoping to avoid any more quarrelling, "what's got them all so scared?"

Bellator shrugs, glancing around with a frown. "I don't know, and I don't like it either. Be on your guard."

We continue in silence down the main street. A feeling of danger lurks in the air, and a shudder of uneasiness rises in my gut.

"There's papa's tavern," Annalyn whispers, stopping at the entrance to a street that turns toward the lake.

At the end of the street, next to a small dock that stretches out over the lake, stands an old, rustic tavern. As we draw nearer, I see a battered sign hanging over the door. In painted, faded letters it reads, 'P'ter's Tavern and Hostelry for the Weary and Footsore Traveller'.

Uri sniggers. "Looks like an old shack—"

Bellator shuts him up with a sharp elbow to the ribs. But Annalyn doesn't seem to notice. She's walking toward the door with slow, apprehensive footsteps. A few feet from the collapsing porch, she falters.

"What is it?" I ask.

She shakes her head, a tear rolling down her cheek. "It's just... I'm scared. It looks so different! What if they aren't here? What if—"

"It will be alright," I interrupted gently. "They'll be here. We won't leave you until we've found them; I promise."

She nods, wiping away her tears. "Will you come with me, please?"

I nod, but I don't want to. I'm afraid of what we'll find.

"Wait a moment," Bellator calls, approaching us.

We both turn to her, glancing at each other. Annalyn attempts a small smile, and for a moment, I feel a connection. Almost like she might be someone I could call my friend. But the moment is brief, and the walls go up again. She betrayed me once. She might again.

"Listen," Bellator says in a low voice, "I don't care how you feel or who you think you can trust. Don't tell anyone about Zeldek, or Gaiztoak, or anything out of the ordinary that you've seen otherwise. I don't care what you have to tell them, but do *not* mention him. Do you hear me?"

"Why not?" Annalyn asks. "Shouldn't people know what is out there? That all of what they think are myths are actually true?"

"No, they shouldn't! People don't believe anything unless it's right in front of them, and sometimes not even then. You tell them, and things won't go well for you. Do I make myself clear?"

Annalyn lowers her gaze. "Yes."

"I hope so, for your sake." She takes Majax's reins from me and turns back toward Uri, calling over her shoulder as she does, "Oh, and make sure that we get that ale, half-wit."

Annalyn takes another deep breath and starts up the steps to the door. The wood creaks, sagging beneath her feet. I follow with careful footing. When we reach the door, she stops and runs her fingers down a patch of splintered gouges in the wood.

"Looks like someone took an axe to it," I remark, noticing that the latch has also been broken.

Her face whitens, and I realize it wasn't a very good thing to say, all things considered.

Annalyn puts on a brave face and pushes the door open. It creaks on its hinges and bumps into the wall behind it. We pass through the small entranceway leading into the dining room. An old coat hangs from the only remaining peg on the wall, and the wooden doorframe has been hacked apart – another sign of a forced entry.

"No," Annalyn whispers, her voice breaking apart.

She pushes through the pieces of furniture that appear to have been piled in front of the door to create a mean barricade. Reaching the centre of the room, she turns in a circle, her breath coming shorter and faster. Her stunned gaze comes to rest on a spot of floor by her feet, and I move closer to see what she is looking at. But when I do, I put a hand to my mouth.

The floor is stained with blood.

Annalyn's face crumples. "Mama!" she cries at the top of her lungs, running to the counter. "Papa! I'm here! I've come home!"

Silence is the only reply that she receives.

"Please! I've come back!"

"Annalyn," I begin, reaching a hand toward her, "I don't think—"

But before I can finish, the door behind the counter opens a crack. A face peers out at us, muffled breathing coming through the opening. I get Annalyn's attention, gesturing towards it.

She takes a step toward the door. "Mama?"

"Annalyn, be careful," I warn in a whisper. "You don't know who is behind that door."

She heeds my warning and stops. "Hello?" she calls hesitantly. "Is anyone there?"

The door is pushed open, revealing a short, portly fellow with wire spectacles propped on his nose and a head of thinning salty-brown hair. His face is a splotchy mess of white and red, and his body trembles as he stumbles out into the open.

"Annalyn?" he says, gaping. Then he shakes his head, turning to face the counter. "No, it can't be you. You're a phantom sent to haunt me! My girl's gone for good."

"Papa," Annalyn whispers, her lip trembling. "What's happened?"

"I can't take anymore of this, you hear?" he cries. "Leave me be!"

"Papa, it's me!" she cries, dashing around the counter toward him. "It's your Annalyn! I've returned. Please believe me!"

But he won't look at her. "My daughter's gone. She's not coming back."

"She is! Please, look at me! You'll see that it's me." She grasps her father's shoulders, turning him gently to face her. "Look at me."

P'ter cringes, but does as she says. Recognition dawns. "C-can it be?" he whispers, reaching up to touch her face. "It- it is you!"

Annalyn beams, relief spreading over her features.

He wipes a glistening tear from her cheek. "Where have you been all this time? Why did you leave us? You didn't even leave a note!"

Annalyn hesitates, and I know that Bellator's warning is running through her mind. "There was this man," she says at length. "He took me away, far from here. I only just managed to escape."

He opens his trembling arms to receive her. "Oh, my baby girl. You're safe now. You're home."

She throws her arms around him, and he pulls her close. Tears stream down his round, cherry red cheeks. "My little Ann, all grown up."

She nods, tears of joy in her eyes. "I'm not going anywhere again."

Their reunion is sweet, but it leaves me with a feeling of emptiness inside. I doubt that I will ever find my family, and even if I do, I've reason to think it won't be a happy occasion.

Annalyn laughs through her tears. "Where's mama?"

His joy fades at her words, and he looks up into her face, his lower lip trembling. "She's gone."

Her grin disappears in an instant. "Gone? What do you mean?"

"She's- she's dead," he says, suddenly breaking down.

"Dead?" Her voice cracks.

"It was... only yesterday. They came in the night. They attacked us. We... we were unprepared, defenceless! They... they killed her."

"Who did?" Annalyn cries, grabbing his hands. "Who attacked? Who killed mamma?"

He heaves a huge, shuddering sigh. "We don't know. But I think that they were some kind of raiders."

Chapter Twenty-One

"Raiders?" Annalyn gasps, her face turning ashen.

Her father leans against the counter for support. "They came once before... sometime last winter. That time they only stole things... went through the whole town taking whatever they wanted. But this time... this time they were after something else. We don't know what. They broke into the tavern... tore the place apart. Well... you know your mother – how fierce she is – could be. She stood up to them. You should have seen her. She was so... so brave." His voice cracks, becoming a mess of broken sobs. "I... tried... to get her... to stop... to just let them search... but she wouldn't! And they... they... killed her. I could... do nothing... to stop them—" He buries his face in his hands and weeps freely.

Tears roll down Annalyn's lightly freckled cheeks, and she reaches out to comfort her father. "It's alright, papa." Her voice trembles with emotion. "It's... it's not your fault. You did what you could."

My own eyes sting and I step back awkwardly. I want to make this all better, but what can I do? Her mother is dead! There is no comfort or consolation for such a loss.

No, it is best if I leave them alone to grieve.

I turn to leave. I would've passed unnoticed from the room had my foot not caught on a broken table leg as I turned to go. It rolls across the floor, and I cringe.

Her father looks up, noticing me for the first time. His bloodshot eyes sweep over me with growing agitation. "Annalyn, who is this?"

She turns to me, still in shock. "Oh. Papa, this is my friend, Ealdred."

I nod to him, my breath coming short. *She just called me her friend.*

"He's a half-breed!" her father spits.

"Papa!" she chides. "He was the one that rescued me from the man who kidnapped me."

"No!" he cries, made belligerent by grief. "You don't understand. It was one of his *kind* that took your mother from us!"

My mouth drops open in alarm. "I am sorry for your loss, sir," I blurt. "Truly, I am. But you cannot blame me for another person's crimes, half-breed or not!"

"Your kind is all the same!" he growls, putting himself protectively between Annalyn and me. "Animals! The king would do well to banish the lot of you!"

"Sir—"

"Get out of my house," he bellows, "before I make you leave!"

"Papa, stop it!" Annalyn cries, grabbing his arm. "I know you're hurting! I am too. But Ealdred is a good person! You have to give him a chance!"

But P'ter is beyond listening to reason. He picks up a large, jagged piece of wood from the floor and raises it threateningly at me. "Get out, now! And stay away from my daughter!"

Recoiling, I stumble backward, then make a run for the door.

"Ealdred, wait!" Annalyn calls after me. "Don't go, please."

I stop with my hand on the latch and look back. "Annalyn, you don't have to defend me," I say.

"Yes, I do!" she cries. "He shouldn't be treating you like this!"

"Excuse me?" her father cries.

"You know, I don't care how he treats me," I say, struggling over the words. "But Annalyn, your father loves you. Cherish that."

I pull open the door and exit the tavern, letting it slam shut behind me.

"Hey, where's the ale?" Uri demands as I approach.

Without a word, I change directions and walk down the creaky, water damaged planks of the wharf. The shame has gone, but I feel as rotten as the boards beneath my feet. A line of old fishing boats is docked at the end of the wharf, and a bundle of tattered netting lies in a heap with a trident resting against it. I approach the side and stare down into the deep, turbulent water of the lake. It laps against the boards of the wharf and the sound is comforting in a way.

The wood creaks as soft footsteps approach from behind.

"I don't want to talk," I mutter.

"Neither do I," Bellator replies, coming to stand beside me. But she doesn't come as close to the edge as I do. "I just came to see if you're alright."

I shake my head with a bitter chuckle. "Don't act like you care, Bellator. I know you don't. I'm not stupid. I know that all I am to you is something to use until you no longer have need of me."

"To be fair, half-wit—" she begins.

"Don't deny that it's true!" My voice is higher than I mean it to be, and I quickly lower it. "It isn't like you actually care about anyone other than yourself."

She snorts. "I'm not denying anything. But like you said earlier, we made a deal. No matter how we feel about it, we both have to fulfil our ends of the bargain. So, stop feeling sorry for yourself so we can get this over with and never have to look at each other again."

I clench my teeth and shrug. "Whatever."

She takes a deep breath of the misty air. "Now, tell me; was the girl's family there?"

I nod.

"What about the town? Did you find out what is ailing it?"

I nod again. "Raiders."

The word is barely out of my mouth when a shrill horn blast rings through the chilly evening air. Bellator's bow is nocked in her hands before the blast has ended, and I spin around, scanning the ridge that surrounds the town.

"See anything?" she hisses.

I begin to shake my head, but then I do see something. Black shapes appear on the eastern hill, descending toward the town as thick as ants.

"Is that—" I begin.

"The raiders," she finishes with a nod.

"Uh, guys," Uri calls uneasily. "I ain't sure you saw, but we got a problem here."

Bellator snatches the trident from beside the fishing net and starts toward him. "You know how to use a trident, right Uriah?"

He swallows, eyeing the trident as if she might run him through with it. "Yeah..."

"Good." She tosses it to him. "You'll need this where we're going. Half-wit," she turns to me, "tie the horses up to the post. We'll be back for them."

I oblige, tying them to the post at the entrance to the tavern's stables. I don't have to ask where we are going.

But apparently, Uri does. "Where are we going?" he asks, staring down at the trident in his hands with a mix of anger and excitement on his freckled face.

"To find out who these intruders are," Bellator replies, "and what they want with this town."

She turns to me. "Do you have a weapon?"

"Sure, if this counts." I pat the dagger at my side. "Not that I'm going to be doing any fighting."

A smirk turns her lips.

I grow uneasy. "I'm not going to be fighting, right?"

She undoes the strap that keeps her sword belt at her side, and holds it out to me. A quick glance over the weapon tells me that it is designed to look like a larger replica of my dagger. I also notice for the first time that Bellator's bow and quiver are very much like it too. It would seem she made herself a matching set.

I back away. "No, Bellator, wait. I'm not a fighter! I've never hurt anyone in my life, and I don't want to start today."

"Take it, half-wit," she orders.

I shake my head. "Please, I'll do anything else you ask me to. Just... not this."

"Take it, or I'll stick it through your useless gut!"

I swallow hard and take the sword from her outstretched hands. It is heavier than it appears, but the weight lessens slightly once I've strapped the belt around my waist.

"Ha! Coward," Uri sneers.

Maybe I am a coward, but I know what these things can do. I'm not ready for this.

"Be careful with it, because I'll be wanting it back." Bellator pauses, and then adds, "And try not to hurt yourself."

I draw the sword and my gaze travels up the shining blade. I can see my unnaturally blue eyes reflected back at me in the steel's manipulated ripples.

"I'll try," I say.

"That's settled," she replies in her usual officious manner. "Now, let's go kill some raiders, shall we?"

"Right behind you!" Uri cries with new enthusiasm, gripping his trident in both hands.

"Don't let me spoil the fun," I say miserably.

We walk back up the lane and turn onto the main street. Bellator leads the way toward the clamorous hooting of the approaching mob. We reach the town entrance opposite to the one we entered by. The mob bears down on us, growing louder as they near, while flaming arrows explode in the thatched rooftops of the houses along the boarder of the town. In the face of a disaster, it feels nice to have a fighter like Bellator by my side.

In a few moments, the blaze is bright enough for us to finally get a clear glimpse of our attackers. There must be at least thirty men in the group, dressed in uniform dark green clothing, with black masks over their faces and black cloaks wrapped around their shoulders. Their weapons vary, but each man carries himself with a wild confidence that screams death to all in their path.

Unfortunately for them, we are in their way. By 'we', I mean Bellator and Uri. They stand in the centre of the road with a confidence to match that of our attackers. I, on the other hand, feel small and insignificant as our assailants approach, as if I were an insect at the feet of giants.

Bellator aims an arrow in their direction, while Uri points his triple spiked spear with malice more intense than I've seen in him before. I grip my sword in both hands and hold it up, hoping that I don't look too puny.

The foremost attackers stop mid-whoop and stare at us as if they've never encountered resistance like this. Those behind follow suit, their hollering fading to confused muttering. A masked man, most likely their leader, pushes to the front of the group, a double-sided battle-axe slung casually over his shoulder.

He laughs when he sees us – a loud, mocking laugh that ripples through those that follow him. "Well, well, ain't this a pitiful sight, lads!" he jeers. "The men of this town sent their children out to fight us."

Barks of laughter echo reply, but I stiffen. Anger flashes through me, and I raise my sword higher in defiance. I know that voice and I know it well.

Ralcher.

What the hell is he doing here?

Bellator straightens up. "I am no mere child, you insolent swine! I am Bellator, known to you commoners as the Crimson Shadow. I demand to know who you are and what your purpose is with this town!"

There is a ripple of confusion and exclamations of fear throughout the crowd.

"Wait!" I exclaim, a shudder of dread going through me. "*You're* the Crimson Shadow?"

She glances sideways at me. "A title passed down to me from Reevan, but yes, I have been the Crimson Shadow for a time."

"Nonsense!" Ralcher pulls down his mask and swaggers toward her with a wobble in his step, and I realize that he's had a bit too much to drink. "A brilliant move to try to frighten us away, beautiful, but you can't fool me." He turns to his men, spreading his arms. "Right, lads? The Crimson Shadow ain't no girl!"

His men shout their agreement.

"Are you calling me a liar?" Bellator says through her teeth, and I know without looking at her that she is plotting his swift demise.

He turns back to her, almost falling over his own foot. And yet somehow, he is able to keep his movements smooth. "No hard feelings, sweetheart," he says, strutting toward her. "You are a feisty one, I'll admit. I think I'll keep you—"

There is a vibrating twang, and Bellator's arrow pierces his gut. He gasps, blinking stupidly as the pain clears his fogged brain, and then he falls to his knees, clutching at the arrow.

No matter how hard I try, I can't find it in me to feel a single shred of pity for him.

Bellator draws another arrow from the quiver at her side, and sets it on the string. "No one else has to die tonight! Be gone! Never step foot in this town again, and you will live to see another day!"

The crisp air falls silent, and the crackling of flames is the only sound. A low murmuring ensues. One man is pushed forward, and the others look to him for guidance.

"Listen, girlie," he calls, "we ain't afraid of a group of children playing at being heroes."

Bellator clenches her jaw, her eyes flashing. "I am not playing, and I am no hero! I am the Crimson Shadow. You know my reputat—"

She is abruptly cut off as a poorly aimed arrow flies past her and clatters to the cobblestones far behind us.

"Uri, Ealdred," she says to us with a deadly calm, "you may kill as many of these useless curs as you would like. Half-wit, I advise you get in as much sword practice as you can. Have no pity, have no mercy, for none will be shown to you. These men are ruthless, dishonourable, and would destroy this entire town if they could."

"Since when do you care about this town?" Uri asks.

I am wondering the same thing, although I'm not foolish enough to voice it.

"I don't," she replies defensively. "But these idiots have personally insulted me, and I'm going to make them pay for it!" She says the last part loudly enough for the raiders to overhear her.

As a group, they find the courage to laugh at her words.

"Just try!" their new leader jeers as the men brandish their weapons wildly in their drunkenness.

Just as fast and loud as a clap of thunder, the skirmish begins.

Chapter Twenty Two

Bellator unleashes a fury of arrows in rapid succession, each one hitting its mark. Uri charges into the midst of the mob with a wild, unearthly set of whoops and trills. His trident rips through his first opponent's chest, and as he jerks it out he slams the butt into another man's stomach.

This passes in an instant, and I know that it is my turn to enter the battle. But I find myself looking away. I can't do this. Even if I wanted to, if I could stand the sight of torn flesh and gushing blood, I'm small and weak. I always lose in scraps. Even now, these men seem to tower far above me. The only advantage I might have is my quick reflexes.

Is it cowardly to turn away from a fight? I don't want to be a coward. I want to be brave, but how can I be brave if I won't even fight to protect a town of innocent people?

A flaming arrow whips past me, exploding into the side of a nearby house. The dry wood catches fire, darkening to coal as the flames leap up, spreading upward to the thatched roof. A shrill cry comes from within the house.

There's someone trapped inside!

I bound to the door and try to push up the latch. It doesn't budge. Bracing my shoulder against the door, I push with all my might. Still, it doesn't open. The inhabitants probably barricaded it to keep the raiders from entering. I step back, searching for another opening into the house. There's a window to the right of the door, but it's blocked with shutters. I look around for something to open it with.

Suddenly, a battle axe slams into the wood near my head, burying itself in up to the handle. A loud bellow follows, and I spin around to find a huge, burly man charging toward me with a spiked mace in his fist. Fear shoots through me and time slows to a near halt as he raises it above his head and begins to bring it down with a mighty force. I feel icy adrenaline shooting through my veins and in an instant, everything changes. It is as if I have just opened my eyes, and I can see his every weakness mapped across his body.

I throw myself to the side, swinging the sword into his knee to trip him. It cuts through his trousers, leaving a deep scratch in his flesh. With a cry, he stumbles, his mace breaking through the shutters.

More screams come from inside the house.

My attacker turns to me, his face red with anger.

"Come and pick on someone your own size!" I yell.

He observes me for a moment, blinking, then throws back his head and laughs. "Sure thing, little man," he says. "And when I'm done, I'll use your bones as toothpicks!"

I grimace, disgusted. "Why would you say something like that?"

He swings his mace at my head, and I dodge, finding myself suddenly trapped between him and the house. The mace comes at me again, and I put up my sword to block the blow. I do, but the force sends me back into the wall. I hit my head, and fall to the ground. Just as my clarity appeared so too it has gone, and I am left defenceless.

"Do you even know how to use that?" the man jeers.

I try to pick myself up, but he kicks me back down again.

My prickling vision is clear enough to see him loom over me, his mace raised to strike. Then he thinks better of it, and his weapon falls to his side. "You know, I should just leave you here to watch your town burn around you. Hero."

He spits at me and turns away, only to stagger back as an arrow pierces his chest. I roll out of the way as he falls back into the wall, then slumps to the ground, dead. About twenty metres away, Bellator nods to me, then turns and knifes another raider in the gut.

I get to my feet and stagger over to the window. Inside, the flames are already making their way through the walls. A woman and two children are huddled in the centre of the room, coughing and gagging from the smoke. The barricaded door is already in flames.

"Over here!" I cry, beckoning to them.

The mother sees me and starts to her feet, hope filling her eyes. But it fades almost instantly, and she shakes her head. "I'd rather we die in here than let those monsters butcher my children!"

"It's all clear," I assure her. "The fighting is moving away from us."

Hesitantly, she moves toward the window, leading both children by the hand. She looks past me long enough to confirm my words, then hastens over, putting her daughter through the window, then her son. I help them to the ground and then stand guard as she climbs out herself.

"Get to the tavern," I tell her. "You'll be safe there."

She observes the battle for a moment, her face pale but determined, and she takes both children up in her arms.

"Bless you," she says, and hurries away along the building's edge, then off the main street out of sight.

With renewed resolve, I start toward the fray, determined to do the most that I can. But the battle is over by the time I arrive. The dozen or so survivors are running for their lives back into the forest, and the rest lie dead or injured at our feet. I let the tip of my blade fall to the slippery, crimson cobblestones and watch them leave. The overpowering smell of blood fills my nostrils, and I have to fight hard to keep from vomiting.

Uri moves to follow the fleeing survivors, but Bellator puts out a hand to stop him.

"We've accomplished our mission," she pants, pulling her bow over her shoulder. "Let the rest go crying home."

Uri wipes a smear of blood from his forehead with a vicious scowl. "But we don't know who they are yet!" he cries.

"Yes we do," I say. "We know exactly who they are."

They both turn to me, as if to say that *they*, in fact, do not know.

"Those men are from Zandelba," I explain. "That is, their leader was. I would assume that the rest are as well."

"How do you know that?" Bellator demands. She seems displeased that I know something she doesn't.

"That first man you killed was an old master of mine," I reply. "He's an official in the king of Zandelba's army."

She narrows her eyes. "Zandelba, is it?"

Spinning on her heel, she strides over to where the prone body of Ralcher lies face down in the street. Once she has rolled him onto his back, she crouches down beside him and puts a finger to his wrist, feeling for a pulse.

"Is he alive?" I ask tentatively.

She nods, her mouth twisting into a diabolical smile. "He's about to wish he wasn't."

Whipping an arrow from her quiver, she slams it into his arm. Ralcher's eyes fly open with a shout, and his face twists in pain. He gasps for air, stifling another cry, and then bursts into a fit of coughing. Blood dribbles from his lips.

"Remember me?" Bellator says.

"Hey, beautiful," he says through gritted teeth. "I knew you wouldn't forget about me."

She looks him over with disgust. "Another word, and you'll get an arrow in your other arm."

He swallows. "What do you want?"

"You have information that I desire, and you're going to give it to me."

"Promise you'll spare me first!"

She snorts coldly. "You're dying anyways."

A faint smile twitches his crimson lips. "Oh, I'll live. And when I do, I promise, we'll meet again."

Bellator grabs the shaft in his arm and twists it. He howls in agony.

"Alright, alright!" he sputters when he can speak again. "I'll talk! What do you want to know?"

"I have it from a reliable source that you work for King Sedgewick of Zandelba. Is that true?"

"Your source is mistaken."

"Don't lie to me!" Bellator shouts in his face.

"I swear! I know nothing of the court of Zandelba! We're common raiders trying to make a living!"

"He's lying," I say, coming forward.

Ralcher's face betrays his disbelief before he can conceal it. "You!"

"You know this boy?" Bellator demands.

He nods, cringing from the pain it causes him. "That *thing* is my slave."

I feel a sudden urge to hurt him, and hurt him badly. "I am not your slave! Not anymore."

"How dare you speak to me!" he spits. "Worthless half-breed!"

I can't stop myself from flinching at the insult. "I am not worthless," I say through clenched teeth.

His black eyes dart to me with a cruel glint. "You're afraid of me."

I shake my head, but my breath catches in my throat.

"Do your new friends know that you are a sorcerer? That you almost levelled a city in your *terror*?"

Uri gapes at me, backing away. "You got magic?"

"Yes, Uri, he does," Bellator snaps. "Now shut the hell up while I interrogate this piece of filth!"

Ralcher sneers at me. "A half-breed sorcerer fugitive! How free are you really? Come on, tell us!"

"You're wrong," I say.

He laughs. "Coward!"

"Enough!" Bellator bellows, twisting the arrow until he screams. "I want an answer, and I will have one! Do you work for the king of Zandelba?"

"Yes! Alright, yes, I do!"

"Did he send you to raid this town during a time of peace between Valamette and Zandelba?"

He sputters. "What peace? It has never existed!"

"I am aware of the old feud between Valamette and Zandelba! What's your point?"

"My king called me personally for this mission, though I don't know what he means to accomplish by it. I suspect he's looking to see how much your king'll take before declaring war on us and sealing his kingdom's fate."

"He's *not* my king!" Bellator snarls. "If you make it home alive, you can tell your king that if he plans to attack this town again, I will be here to defend it! Now, be gone!"

Ralcher struggles to push himself up with his good arm, but it proves too much for him. He doubles over with a cry, grasping at the arrow in his stomach.

Bellator rolls her eyes, and grabbing his injured arm, she jerks him to his feet. He screams in pain, sways, but remains standing.

"Get out of here before I kill you," she spits.

He jerks his head in a nod, and then glances at me. "You! Here, now!"

A black wave of fear seizes me and all I can do is shake my head.

He grits his teeth, that mad light entering his eyes. "Attend me at once!"

"N-no," I stammer.

Even in such a weak state, he still manages to find the strength to charge toward me.

"Stay back!" My voice comes out in a pitiful squeak. I stagger back, pointing my sword at him, all pretence of courage gone. The prospect of going back to being a slave – *his* slave – brings me more terror than an army of ezixs.

"Get away from him!" Bellator snarls, leaping between us. Her bow creaks as she pulls back her bowstring, a killing blow aimed at Ralcher's heart.

"You would deny me my property?" he demands, incredulous.

"I have been merciful thus far. Do not test my patience."

He quickly thinks better of his protest, and his jaw tightens. "This isn't over," he says, jabbing a finger at me. "I'll be seeing you again."

"Eh, I wouldn't count on that," Uri says, thumping his trident on the pavement.

Ralcher glances from Uri to Bellator and then makes a run for it back up the hill.

I lower the tip of the sword, rather shaken. "Why'd you let him go?"

Bellator raises her eyebrows in mock surprise. "It's unlike you to be screaming for someone's blood, half-wit. Perhaps you've seen enough of the stuff for the day."

My face grows warm with shame. "I'm not screaming for his blood. But you saw him. He's a maniac! It's not like you to let someone like that live without a reason."

"You don't know what I would or wouldn't do," she snaps. "As it happens, I *want* him to deliver my message to the king of Zandelba. There is no other way to ensure Annalyn's safety."

"What?" Uri exclaims. "You mean she ain't safe here?"

"She *wasn't*," Bellator corrects. "Once that knave relays my message, as well as the mission report, King Sedgewick will think twice before attacking this town again. Although," she adds in a lower tone, leaning forward, "I have a feeling that dearest Master Zeldek was the one who initially put them up to this. What way better to punish us for escaping than to hit us each where it hurts most?"

"You think he was behind this?" I ask.

"It has his name written all over it. The brutality, the ignorant pawns, even the use of Zandelba – they're always ready to bully Valamette for their own reasons."

"You don't s'ppose the king of Valamette knows about this, do you?" Uri asks.

"Oh, he definitely knows," she replies spitefully. "But he's a coward and a fool. As long as he stays in power, he doesn't care what happens to the people!" She spits at the ground. "War will come yet, and I say let it! He deserves what's coming."

With those biting words, she turns on her heel and starts back down the street toward the tavern.

"Sheesh! Remind me not to get on her bad side again," Uri says.

I'm pretty sure he's not talking to me, and even if he is, I know he wouldn't listen if I did remind him.

"Hurry up!" she calls over her shoulder.

We start after her, making an effort to avoid stumbling over dead, bleeding bodies as we go. This time, as we pass through the street, the people of the town peer out at us from behind curtains and from the doorways of their houses.

"Ignore them," Bellator advises. "They'll find out what happened after we leave. It'll save us from being detained by their well-meant grovelling."

"Why?" Uri demands. "I'd be glad for some 'preciation for a change."

A sharp glance from Bellator is the only explanation he needs.

We soon stand in front of the tavern once more. Bellator leads the way to the water's edge, and kneels down on the wooden boards. She must have been gathering her arrows as she fought, because her quiver is full of bloody shafts that she takes out to clean in the water.

Uri follows her example and dunks his trident into the lake, swirling it this way and that until the water around it is red.

I look at their clothing, their faces, all splattered with human blood, then down at the clean blade of my own sword. In the reflection, my face has a noticeably green complexion. My stomach churns, and now that my energy is gone, there is nothing to stop my most recent meal from coming back up. I throw myself to the lake's edge and vomit into the water.

Uri barks with laughter. "I told you he'd be sick! Didn't I tell you?"

Bellator glances at me, unsmiling. "You alright there, half-wit?" she asks.

I try to nod, but I'm a bit too disoriented to make any sort of reply.

She slides an arrow into her quiver. "You did good today."

My stomach heaves, but there isn't anything left in it. I straighten up, wiping my face on my sleeve.

"I know it was hard for you," she continues, a bit absentmindedly. "But people like us need to learn to survive in this world. Sometimes that means doing what is necessary to ensure that security."

"Don't we have to also be able to live with ourselves?" I rasp.

She gives me a sharp look. "I suppose you think you can just talk your way out of every situation, then? I can see how well that's worked for you so far!"

"I wasn't saying—"

"Learn what you will from what I am trying to teach you! Just don't blame me when the maniac running at you with a sword doesn't want to negotiate!"

She goes back to cleaning her arrows.

Uri clears his throat. "So, uh... I'm just gonna go over by the horses, in case you need me..."

Bellator ignores him. "Half-wit, clean my sword. And try not to retch on it."

"But I didn't—"

"Clean it!"

I do as she asks, using the edge of my cloak to polish the blade. I sheathe the sword and unbind its belt from around my waist.

"Take it," I say, holding it out to Bellator. "I hope not to have anymore need for it."

She glances from it to me, a malicious glint in her eyes. "Oh, I think you will," she says. "Why don't you hold onto it for a little while longer?"

I grimace, but I wrap the belt obediently around my waist once more.

I proceed to untie the horses from the posts where I left them and lead them from the stables. Darkness has set across the sky, and numerous stars twinkle merrily down at us, oblivious to the suffering so far beneath them. I can feel the weariness of sleep coming over me, but I know that even if I could sleep, I won't be able to keep the visions of today's battle from troubling my dreams.

Bellator approaches, her weapons clean and in order, and takes Nimro's bridle from me.

"Redhead," she says, swinging herself up onto the black stallion, "you'll ride with the half-breed until we drop you off in Kenwardton."

"Actually," Uri replies, jutting out his jaw defiantly, "I changed my mind. I ain't going to Kenwardton no more. I wanna go to Twylaun."

Bellator stiffens, but her voice remains toneless. "Then we'll take you as far as we can, and you can travel the rest of the way on foot."

The door to the tavern swings open, and Annalyn rushes down the steps toward us. In her hands are two large skins of ale.

"Wait!" her voice rings out. "The lady inside told us what you did for our village. Papa sent me to give you these in thanks for that and for bringing me safely home."

"That's more like it," Uri says, snatching up the skin that she offers to him.

She reaches the other up to Bellator, who takes it with a suspicious frown.

"Father said that any time either of you comes to town again," Annalyn continues, "feel free to stop by the tavern, and he'll give you both food and a place to stay for free."

"Tell him we thank him for his kindness," Bellator says.

Annalyn smiles. "I will. Thank you once again for your assistance."

Bellator nods and then takes a swig of the ale.

Annalyn turns to me, her smile fading. "Ealdred," she says, "I would like to thank you, even if my father won't. I'm so sorry about what he said—"

"Don't be," I cut in. "I wasn't your fault."

"I know. But it was wrong how he treated you, and he knows it. He's still in pain over my mother's death, that's all."

"You don't have to make excuses for him. I understand."

But I don't. Since when does causing another person pain get rid of one's own?

She sighs. "Father wouldn't let me bring anything out to you, so you'll have to share with the others. That is, if they will allow you to. I'm sorry—"

"It isn't a problem. Thank you," I say firmly.

She shakes her head, and throws her arms around me. "No. Thank *you*! It was you that got Bellator to take me along, even though I was the reason you were captured in the first place, what with spying on you for Zeldek and all."

"It's alright," I mumble, my face growing warm. "Really, it is."

She pulls away with a shy smile and slides a strand of hair behind her ear. "Well, I'd best let you be off. Goodbye, then."

I nod to her. "Goodbye, Annalyn."

She turns back toward the tavern and walks slowly to the door, a weight to her steps. I watch her go. A heavy feeling of foreboding settles on my shoulders as I venture to wonder if I will ever see her again.

"Well, that was sweet," Bellator scoffs as soon as the tavern door has closed behind Annalyn.

My cheeks flush with embarrassment. "What was?"

"That!" She gestures in the direction that Annalyn retreated.

"I can't have been the only one expectin' them to kiss," Uri sneers.

"Shut up," I snap. "I was just trying to be gentlemanly. Not that you would know anything about that."

"Ain't no such thing as a gentleman, 'cept in books," Uri retorts.

"Not that you'd know anything about that," Bellator mimics, "because you can't read."

I look away, humiliated. "How about we get going now."

There is a slight pause. "But you *can* read, can't you?"

"Yeah," I grunt. "I thought that you knew that already!"

She gives me a nasty smile. "Oh, I must have forgotten."

"What?" Uri exclaims. "*I* can't read!"

"Then maybe you should've learned," I retort, climbing up onto Majax's back.

"Don't you talk to me like that!" he snarls. "Even a pirate knows it's death for a half-breed to know to read!"

I cringe as a painful old memory – one that I have kept locked away for years – breaks free and floods my mind.

His name was Kellagh and he was the only friend that I've ever had, as well as the only other half-breed I've ever met. I was ten at the time and he was thirteen. We were both slaves in the house of a very wealthy merchant who held great influence in the king of Zandelba's court.

Kellagh and I got along really well, and in the few moments of stolen free time that we could get, we would cause all kinds of mischief. Our master threatened us with selling one or both of us on numerous occasions, but we knew he wouldn't. Since half-breeds are so rare, even though we are hated, owning one reflects a high social status. So he would resort to having us beaten, which we both agreed was worth the trouble.

One night, Kellagh took me to our master's library, and informed me that he taught himself to read in one of his previous master's homes, and he was now perfecting that ability by filching some of our master's books and reading them. He said that the books weren't wanted anyways. Then he offered to teach me to read. I was already intrigued by the wonderful stories he'd been telling me, so I agreed. Over the next few weeks, he taught me by candlelight at night.

But one night, one of the maids caught us and dragged us before our master. Kellagh confessed to teaching me, and although I tried to claim my fair share of guilt, he took all the blame for the situation. The next morning, he was beaten to death right before my eyes. Even now, I can vividly remember his screams of anguish, his pleading tears, his face splattered with his own blood.

After they carried his limp body away from the stake, they beat me almost as bad. The next day, I was taken to the market again and sold to an unsuspecting master. Apparently, it is a disgrace to own a half-breed who can read, so I have had to continue to hide my knowledge ever since.

I stare at the leather straps of the reins in my hands, feeling sick again. "I have already paid the price," I say quietly.

"What happened?" Uri taunts. "Did your master beat you? Is that how your face got so ugly?"

"Uri!" Bellator reprimands sharply, and for some reason, the malicious look in her eyes is subdued.

He rolls his eyes in irritation. "What?"

"Not another word or I'll tie a stone to your feet and throw you in the lake!"

Uri shuts up.

Part Two

"The Prince"

Chapter Twenty Three

D ust rose in the evening air as a carriage clattered up the front drive of the castle grounds. Six spoked wheels slowed as it pulled up before the cracked stone stairway, blocking the golden light of the setting sun from reaching the bed of flowers along the castle's foundation. Petunias, violets, and daffodils flourished still even at the close of summer. Age wore at the face of the castle, yet it stood as iron, a testament to the centuries it had served the royal line of Valamette. And it would live on for centuries more.

I am home.

A smile broke out over the face of the new arrival as the carriage came to a full halt. He didn't wait for the footman to dismount and open the door, but threw it open himself, stepping out onto the cobbled floor of the courtyard. He inhaled the sweet country air, filling his lungs to the brim, and savoured it.

"Are you well, sire?" the footman called from where he sat atop the carriage, holding the reins.

"Quite well, thank you," the prince replied. "Long trip home?"

"Ah, nothing to worry about, your highness. The missus is expecting me not long after dark." The footman glanced about, a bit of a crease in his brow. "Not much of a welcome party."

"Oh, I'm not expected," the prince replied with a grin. "Just leave my things on the steps. I'll send someone out for them."

"Very good, sire."

The prince started toward the garden, taking the well known path around to a side door of the castle. Even when he was a child, he never used the front door. It seemed too pretentious. Besides, he'd rather slip in unnoticed and surprise everyone.

As he neared the garden, he heard the unfamiliar sound of music and laughter swelling from an open window. He frowned. No one ever came here.

Continuing toward an opening in the hedge, he scanned the windows for an explanation. A flicker of movement here, a flash of colour there. It seemed as if someone was throwing a dance.

That is peculiar. In all my time growing up here, no one has ever thrown—

Buried in his contemplation, he didn't see the girl sitting just around the bend on the other side of the hedge until he tripped over her. The girl gasped, and the volume she was reading was knocked out of her hands. The prince barely caught himself from falling face first in the grass.

"My apologies," he exclaimed, bending over to pick up the book. Dusting it off, he held it out to her.

The girl clambered to her feet, taking it from him. "No need to apologize," she said quickly. "I should've known better than to sit by the walkway."

"But I should have stayed on the path."

She smiled, her lovely green eyes sparkling. There was an odd deepness to them, like a portal to a vast store of knowledge. The prince felt suddenly nervous and struck with a strange feeling of delight all at once. She was the first one to look away.

"I apologize, but it seems we haven't met," she said lightly, pulling a strand of blonde hair behind her ear. "May I ask who you are?"

The prince straightened out his overcoat with an air of dignity. "Hamish, at your service," he said with a bow. "Very pleased to make your acquaintance."

Alarm registered on the girl's face, and her cheeks blushed a dark pink. "H-Hamish," she stammered. "As in the prince? They told me you were studying in Lavylli."

"I am a quick study," he said, clasping his hands behind his back. "There was nothing more I could learn at this time, so I returned home for the duration of the summer."

A loud peal of laughter came from within the castle, and Hamish cast an uneasy glance in its direction. "It seems this place has been put to good use while I was away."

"Uh, yes, it seems so," she said, following his gaze. "Of course, I'm only here because my father said time in Valamette would be good for me, so your father agreed to take me along. I—"

Hamish's brows furrowed. "The... the king is here?"

She slid a braid of grass between two pages of her book and closed it. "He's come here for the past three summers. Didn't you know?"

He shook his head. "He never comes here."

"Well," she cleared her throat, the rouge of her face only deepening, "you see, I only agreed to come because I thought it would be nice to finally meet *you*."

"Me? Why would you want to meet me?"

She opened her mouth to respond, but just then, the door to the garden opened, and a crowd of nobles poured onto the lawn, ruddy from their dancing. They paired off, pink faced ladies leaning on their gentlemen's arms, the noise of their chatter disturbing the spell of nature's silence. The prince was quickly able to pick out the man he knew described his father; tall, handsome, golden. Hamish had not been able to picture him in his mind for some time now. A dainty woman as beautiful as a goddess leaned on the king's arm, feeding him a piece of cake and cooing loudly.

The prince frowned.

"Ugh," the girl scowled from beside him. "*Algitha*. What am I saying? Of course, you already know her."

"No," the prince said slowly. "Should I?"

The girl looked confused. "She's your stepmother. She and your father were married last year. Didn't you attend the wedding?"

Hamish scratched behind his ear. "Ah, no. I have been in Lavylli for three years."

"But King Fendryl attended."

Prince Hamish felt shame creeping in as his ears flushed, and his shoulders slouched in defeat. "I suppose I was not invited," he admitted. "Father does not like it when I attend public occasions. He would rather I studied."

The girl understood more than he was saying. "When was the last time you spoke to him?" she asked.

"I... I do not remember," he stammered. "He... never comes to visit..."

A sudden determination grew in her eyes. "Well, we should fix that, don't you think?" She put a hand on his arm. "Come. I'll introduce you."

Hamish planted his feet, shaking his head. "He is busy now. He will not want to see me."

"Then shame on him," she said. "But you should at least try."

The prince sighed, giving in with a nod. He straightened up, squaring his shoulders, and the two of them walked toward the stairway. The king didn't notice them approach, and when he finally did see them, he looked from one to the other, his golden brows furrowed in confusion. Hamish could tell by the red of his nose that he'd had far too much to drink already. Yet even in this state, the smile left his face.

The girl gave Hamish's arm a reassuring squeeze.

"Hello, father," the prince said.

The king looked him up and down, setting down his glass of wine on the banister. "What are you doing here?" he demanded. "I thought you were supposed to be in Lavylli for another month."

"They let me return early, father. They said there was nothing left to teach me."

The king snorted. "You should've stayed the month. There's always more knowledge to be had. A king would think of that."

Hamish bowed his head. "I suppose so."

"Oh, Leo honey, you said you'd show me the little fishies," the woman on the king's arm simpered.

"Yes, of course." He started to leave, but hesitated, then patted Algitha's hand. "You go on, love. I'll be there in a moment."

With a giggle, Algitha floated down the steps, waving a slender hand as she went.

The king glanced from Hamish to the girl. "I see you two have met, then."

"Well, in a manner of speaking." Hamish glanced to the girl, who looked back with those lovely, piercing green eyes. "I apologize. I did not catch your name."

The embarrassed red returned to her cheeks. "It's Marianna," she said.

Hamish pulled away, shocked. "Marianna *Jerousse*?"

The king threw back his head and laughed. "Come now, boy. She's only your fiancée. And pretty as a doll, if you ask me."

Marianna smiled apologetically. "It's nice to finally meet you, Hamish."

"Likewise," Hamish replied, a bit too formally. He took another step back. "Well then. I think I will retire. I have had a long journey."

"Nonsense!" the king said. "Join the party. Have a dance or two with your lovely bride-to-be."

Marianna reddened still more, hugging her book close to her chest.

"I- I will pass," Hamish said, equally as embarrassed. "I really need the rest."

"Ha!" the king scoffed. "Didn't know I had a recluse for a son. I guess that's what happens when you let your boy be raised by a woman."

Anger flared up in Hamish's eyes, and he opened his mouth to speak.

"You have something to say to me, boy?" the king said, cuffing his hand to the side of Hamish's face.

Hamish cringed again. "No, sir."

"Then join the party."

With that, the king turned and strode down the steps after his queen.

"Are... are you alright?" Marianna asked.

Hamish let his shoulders relax. "Yes. I am fine."

He turned and started toward the garden doors into the castle.

"Where are you going?" she called after him.

He turned back, flashing a grin. "To be a recluse and talk to the woman who raised me that way. But I am glad that she did. Without her, I would be just like him."

It didn't take long for him to find her. She was descending the stairway when he walked through the doors, her composure powerful, yet cold, like an empress from over the sea. When she saw him, she stopped, her hand resting on the banister.

"Hamish," she said, surprised, yet unusually reserved. Hamish was usually the one person who could make her smile. "You've returned."

"Yes," he replied. "I have."

"How are you?"

"I am well," he said. "Better before I arrived, but well."

She eyed him as if he were a stranger. "And Lavylli? Did it... did it change you?"

"Change me?" he echoed. "Not as far as I know. I mean, I have gotten into the habit of walking like I have a board tied to my back, but that is not too much of a change."

The woman smiled softly, whatever fears she entertained set at ease. "Always with the humour," she said fondly. "Look how you've grown. You're almost a man."

He smiled. "I feel like a child."

"Good. Don't ever let that be taken from you."

A sly grin spread over his features. "You know, I have not changed enough to dislike a welcome home hug from my Nenda."

The woman opened her arms. "Come here, my beautiful boy."

He climbed the stairs, skipping two at a time, and she pulled him into a hug, laughing softly.

The prince smiled. He was home, right where he belonged.

Chapter Twenty-Four

O ur next objective is to ditch Uri.

At least, that is what Bellator seems to be doing. We travelled all night and halfway into this afternoon without any rest. Throughout that time, she started making snide remarks and comments such as, "Hey redhead, when did you say you were leaving again?" and "Ah, that looks like the perfect turn off for you, Uriah."

At last, Uri is fed up with it.

"Listen!" he shouts. "I said I was goin' to Twylaun, so I ain't turnin' off anywhere! Like it or not, I'm comin' with you for a while yet!"

Bellator reins her horse abruptly and turns to him. "I don't think you understand what I am saying," she growls. "It's time for you to leave! Go to Kenwardton, or Twylaun, or off the face of the earth if you want to! I don't care. Just as long as I never have to look at your smug face again!"

"What 'bout this?" Uri demands, tugging my hair. "Is it leavin' too?"

"That doesn't concern you! Get down off that horse and be on your way!"

He groans. "I can't even keep the horse?"

"Down!"

He remains where he is. "Bellator, I don't got nowhere to go!"

She fakes a surprised look. "Oh! I thought you were going to Twylaun. Don't you remember?"

"Bella, please—"

Her eyes are ablaze. "*Do not call me that!*"

"You won't shoot me," he says, more out of hope than actual certainty.

"Oh really?" she snarls. "And what makes you so sure?"

Uri jerks my knife out of my belt and grabs me around the chest, putting the blade to my throat. The cold edge bites into my skin, and I go very still.

"Uri, what are you doing?" There's a slight panic to her voice as reaches for her quiver.

"Don't!" He tightens his grip on the knife. "Put it back. You know I'll kill *it* if I got to!"

There is a long pause, in which Bellator remains completely motionless.

"What do you want?" she demands.

"I wanna know what you two are up to!" he says. "I know you leavin' Gaiztoak weren't just to help us. It ain't like you care 'bout no one but you!"

"We are on a strictly secret mission. Not only do I not trust you with further knowledge, but I cannot risk telling you out in the open like this."

"You can't trust me?" he echoes. "We just fought side by side only yesterday! You trusted me then!"

She huffs. "Uri, your curiosity is going to get you – and more importantly, *me* – into a lot of trouble. I don't have time for your foolishness!"

"And I s'ppose you need this one for your mission?" he growls, spitting on my face. "Don't you deny it. It ain't like you to keep him and us alive just 'cause he asked you to!"

Her eyes flash. "You don't know anything about me, Uriah!"

"I told you not to call me that!" he bellows. "It ain't my name!"

"Please," I manage to squeak, "just listen to her. It's for your own good."

"I don't take no orders from you," he snaps, drawing the point of the knife to beneath my chin.

Bellator lurches in her saddle. "Uri, enough! Let him go!"

"Ain't I just as good as him?" he cries. "You don't need him! I can help you with whatever it is."

"No, you can't!" she snaps. "Let him go now, or I swear that I will kill you!"

"Or," he says through his teeth, "I can cut his throat and make your life hell instead."

"You kill him, and you die instantly," she threatens. "I doubt the odds are much in your favour."

He seems to think this over. "And if I let 'im go, you'll kill me anyways!"

"Aren't you wishing you'd listened when I told you to go in the first place," she says with a smirk.

"No!" I croak from under the pressure of the blade. "Please, Bellator. Let him go. No one has to die."

The feral glint returns to her eyes. "What if I want someone to die?"

"But we made a deal!"

"We did. We also made a deal that you would do everything I say without question, and so far, you haven't kept up your end of the bargain!"

"I can't! It's not that simple—"

"You've been a slave for your entire life. If anything's simple for you, it's this."

I take a breath, the weight of Uri's crushing grip pressing on my chest. "If I swear to it, will you let him go?"

She considers this. "You have my word."

I sigh. "Then until this quest is over, I swear I'll do whatever you say without question."

"Splendid." She jerks her head to Uri, lowering her bow. "You'd better get out of here, Uriah, and fast, or I *will* kill you!"

Uri doesn't dare test his luck. Tossing my knife to one side, he shoves me from the saddle. I fall to the dusty road, jarring my arm underneath me. Uri turns Majax and I scuttle clear of the hooves, rolling to the grass along the roadside. Kicking his heels into Majax's sides, they bolt off down the road at a full gallop.

Bellator stares after him, her eyes narrowing. A smirk curls her upper lip, and I'm almost certain she's going to whip out her bow and shoot him down as he flees. But she doesn't. Instead, a wind I cannot feel gathers around her. The hair that has escaped from her braid goes from a flutter of movement to wildly flying about her head. Her cloak whips this way and that, and the hair on Nimro's neck is caught up with it.

As I watch, the whites of Bellator's eyes disintegrate into black holes, and the ocean blue rings of her pupils swirl white.

"*Vanesco!*" she cries, jerking her palm out toward his retreating form.

Uri vanishes from the saddle.

A cry of alarm fills my throat, and I struggle to my knees. Confused, a now riderless Majax slows to nibble on a bush. I turn to Bellator, only find the wind has vanished and her eyes returned to normal.

"What did you do?" I cry.

"Oh, don't fret," she says with a sly grin, dismounting from her horse. "He's not dead. He'll just wish he was when he awakens in a few minutes. I transported him back to his father's ship, so he should be quite at home."

"But doesn't he hate his father?"

"Would you rather I'd killed him? I can bring him back, if you'd prefer..."

I shake my head, picking myself up off the ground. "You... you never mentioned you had magic."

And honestly, it never occurred to me that she might possess the extraordinary gift as well. Now that I think about it, it makes perfect sense. No wonder she felt she could teach me how to control my magic. It is because she knows from the experience of controlling her own.

She shrugs. "I didn't feel you needed to know before now."

I look at Majax, then back to her. "You can teleport people. Why didn't you use it to help us escape Gaiztoak?"

"If only it were that simple, half-wit," she says. "There is a barrier of magic surrounding Gaiztoak that cannot be passed through using extraordinary means by anyone who doesn't have his say so. It would've been futile trying. Besides that," she adds, "I haven't yet figured out how to teleport myself, so what good would it have done any of us? None of you would've made it without me to protect you, and you know it."

"True," I say with a slight smile. "So, was all of your magic learned, then?"

"What?"

"What I mean to say is, you're not a half-race like me?"

She gives me a sharp look. "I never said that I wasn't."

"You are, then?"

"I never said that either," she snaps. "Really, half-wit, learn to mind your own business."

"Sorry," I mumble. "It's just, you seem to know everything about me and my past. I don't see why you won't tell me this one thing about yours."

"I do *not* know everything about you."

"Really? You knew about Batuel being my ancestor. You knew my father abandoned me. How do I know you don't know his identity too and just aren't telling me because it doesn't suit you at the moment?"

She throws up her hands. "I don't know who your father is, and frankly, I really don't care. The only things I know about you are what Zeldek told me. I've already shared everything relevant with you."

"Relevant?" I echo. "Is there more you haven't told me?"

She winds Nimro's reins around her hand. "Really, we don't have time for childish arguments. We have an artifact to locate before the day is out."

I shove my hands into my pockets. "Do you know where it is?"

"Oh yes. That was the easy part."

Reaching under her shoulder-guard, she pulls out a bloodstained parchment and opens it up. I recognize the drawing of the arrow on it.

"It says here, *'Deep in vaults of hidden gold, caverns steep and halls of old.'* The castle of Arnon, Lady Batuel's home, was ruined by Zeldek in his pursuit of her weapon. It was said that she stored a great fortune in the hidden vaults beneath her castle. I would bet anything that's where the arrow is. The only difficulty is that no one has been able to locate the ruins in centuries. Which means—"

"That there's some kind of protective spell over it," I finish.

She grins. "Exactly. See this next part here: *'Hidden from the fires and coal rests the arrow and my soul'.* Zeldek's element, if you haven't already noticed, is fire. So that line practically means 'hidden where Zeldek can't get to it'. Now,

where would you suppose someone whose element is fire wouldn't go?"

I think about it for a moment. "Near water," I decide.

"You're catching on quickly, for once," she jeers, but it isn't a cruel jeer this

time. It's almost... playful? "Some legends say that the castle of Arnon was located

by a great water source, and that the underground vaults were constantly flooded to

keep him away."

"And you think it's the Tireth River." That much is obvious. "Why?"

"That is just a simple matter of knowing about Batuel in general," she

explains. "See, she and her four siblings, Zeldek included, were each given a country

to be the guardian over and protect from all harm. Incidentally, Valamette was the

country placed in Batuel's care. And since the Tireth is the only large flowing

source of water in Valamette—"

"You're certain that it is the one," I conclude.

"Exactly." She pauses. "And that's where you come in. I understand you don't

know what you're doing, but even so, I'm fairly certain that the descendant of

Batuel would have an easier time uncovering the ruins than most. Don't you think?"

I shrug. "I'll see what I can do."

"You'd better!" Her smirk grows unpleasant again.

"What's the thing it says about the stars?"

She glances down at the paper, rereading the line. "*Three bright stars of

purest form do await the coming storm.'* I don't really think that we have to worry about that line at the moment. It seems to be referring to something that we will find guarding the arrow once we get inside." She tucks the paper away again. "We should get off the road."

She puts her fingers to her lips and whistles. Majax pricks up his ears, and bounds toward us. She grabs his bridle, and leads him over to me.

"Here," she says, and I take the reins from her. "Follow me."

I stroke Majax's mane, wrapping the leather straps around my hand a few times. Then I lead him after Bellator into the underbrush. We push through it until we are out of sight of the road. Bellator pauses, listening. There is a faint sound of running water nearby. We follow it until we come out into a small clearing with a brook running through a mossy patch of ground.

"We'll leave the horses here," she says, leading Nimro to the creek's side. "They'll have everything they need here for at least a few days."

She pulls off Nimro's bridle, and then follows suit with his saddle. I do the same with Majax and soon both sets are in a heap beneath the shade of a tree.

Bellator fishes through the saddlebags, producing the rest of the ale and remainder of the food. She splits it between us, and tells me to eat up.

"Don't know when we'll have our next meal," she adds with her usual mysterious look.

After we have eaten, she uses magic to weave a large fence out of living tree branches and bushes around the horses to keep them from wandering off too far.

The horses don't notice, instead busying themselves with nibbling at the moss near the water's edge.

"How are you doing that?" I ask, gaping in wonder.

She glances back with a bit of smile. "Spells," she said. "Anyone can do them if they have the skill. But for now, it is best to keep using your magic just to sharpen your reflexes. The rest will come with time and practice."

We start out soon afterward. As we make our way through the maze of trees, Bellator seems to grow more and more impatient. She's getting close. I know she can feel it.

The sky darkens through the leafy rooftop that canopies us as the sun creeps toward the horizon. Crickets chirp, beginning their evening serenade. It's been a long time since I've had the time to just listen to them. Not since I was five, when I was still young enough to have a small amount of free time at the end of each day. I would sit by myself on the rooftops and listen to the night sounds as I watched the stars come out.

Life was so much simpler then. I hope that once the arrow is found and I am truly free, it will be like that again.

Chapter Twenty-Five

"Bellator," I call. Her pace is taxing, and I struggle to keep up.

She steps over a fallen tree, ducking under an overhead branch. "What is it?"

I take advantage of her slowing pace to catch up with her. "When I met you before in Sustinere, you were living on the streets. How did you end up in Gaiztoak with Zeldek? You mentioned you were captured..."

She casts a sharp glance over her shoulder. "I told you I didn't want to talk about me," she snaps.

"You said you didn't want to talk about the source of your magic," I point out.

The muscles in her jaw tense. "I'm a good fighter, half-wit. I've never met an opponent in hand-to-hand combat that I couldn't beat. That thing that drives me... well, I've had it since I was a child. Zeldek found it useful. Unique. Not to mention his interest in my strong magical abilities. I led him to believe that he could control me." She hesitates, her pace only quickening. "He marked me when I was only a baby. He thought I might be of use to him, but didn't want the responsibility of raising me. I was thrown out on the streets until the time was right, and then I was taken to Gaiztoak."

"One of his followers took you to him. You mentioned that before."

There is a dreadful silence, and I feel a heavy tension growing around her.

When she finally brings herself to reply, her voice is riddled with bitterness. "I was betrayed by the only person I have ever considered a friend. That's all anyone need know."

That explains why she has trust issues.

"I'm sorry," I say.

The moment the words exit my mouth, she whirls on her heel, her face blazing with anger. "Why do have to be so *nice* all the time?" she demands. "Why can't you just leave me alone?"

I open my mouth to speak, but she isn't finished yet.

"Get it through your thick skull! We're not friends. I barely even tolerate you. I don't want your sympathy, or your questions, or your kindness!"

"What do you want, then? For me to be silent and obey your every word?"

"What I want," she says, giving me a shove, "is for you to hate me! After everything I've done, I know you hate me, deep down. Why do you hide it? Show me!"

She shoves me again, harder this time. "What are you waiting for? Hate me!"

I shake my head, stumbling back. "I don't hate you, Bellator."

"I know," she spits. "You pity me. If there's one thing I can't stand, it's pity! Hatred, mistrust, betrayal: I understand them! But useless, unconditional kindness? It's brainless!"

"That doesn't make sense! Most people want to be loved, not hated."

She grabs my face with both hands, digging her fingernails into my temples, and bares her teeth. "Don't get too close, half-wit," she hisses.

Terrified, I try to pull away, but her grip only tightens. "Wh-what's that supposed to mean?" I breathe.

"It means that—"

She falls silent mid-sentence, and straightens up, listening. There is a long pause, and then she releases me with a shove. I stumble back, grabbing onto a branch to stop my fall. By the time I've regained my balance, she is creeping away.

What is it now?

I start after her, my steps soft on the grassy forest floor. I feel like a predator as I walk through the tall, slender, yellow grass. I listen, but cannot hear what has made Bellator prowl; I can only hear the breeze as it whispers through the leaves on the trees. She's like a fox, darting from cover to cover, not once hesitating. Her footsteps are silent and swift, and she holds her bow notched in her hands as she pursues her invisible prey.

At last, she stops and flattens against the trunk of a large tree, motioning for me to do the same.

"What is it?" I pant as I reach the tree.

She puts a finger to her lips. I muffle my breathing in my sleeve and listen. That's when I hear it. Soft voices, coupled with the snapping of twigs and the quiet rustle of fabric.

Bellator peers out from behind the tree. I crouch down behind a bush next to it, peeking through the gaps between the leaves.

Two figures stroll into sight, engaged in what seems to be a cool, reserved conversation. It is a boy and a girl in their mid-teens, yet with the stiff, graceful bearings of someone twice their age. In the dimming light, it's hard to make out much of their features, but I know at once that they more than common peasants. Their attire is much too rich for that.

As they draw closer, I can make out the words of their conversation.

"—if you knew my father, you'd understand," the girl is saying, twisting a lock of blonde hair between her fingers. "He's too set in his ways, if you ask me. He thinks that putting on a good face is more important than actually living."

The boy holds a leaf up toward the sky, examining it intently. "That sounds dull." His voice has the rough touch of manhood to it, and he speaks with a naturally rigid accent that strikes me as familiar. "For myself, it is hardly possible to put on a good face." He chuckles. "Besides that, I was raised away from the bustle of city life, in a strictly sheltered environment. I suppose I have always just lived."

"You did, of course, have a circle of playmates?"

"I suppose for a time, some of the lords sent their sons to take lessons alongside me," he says blandly, and I realize his accent is so familiar because it has the stiff inflection that characterizes the Lavyllian tongue. "But we were never close. In fact, I found it hard to get along with them at all, mainly because of their overly competitive and sometimes downright hostile attitudes toward me."

The girl looks down at her gloved hands. "I'm sorry."

They are very near to our hiding place now; so near that the girl's skirt brushes against the bush I hide behind.

"Do not be," the boy responds. "I assure you, it is not a loss on my account. They were all the arrogant sort. Besides, I had Jambeau. You have met him, correct? He has been a good friend to me since he was station here. Before I went to study in Lavylli, that is."

Bellator starts from beside me, flattening back against the tree. She takes a deep, silent breath, a bitter scowl curling her lips.

I fall back behind the tree as well. "What are you planning to do?" I whisper.

She sets her jaw. "What's necessary."

Drawing back the string of her bow, she prepares to step around the tree.

I put out a hand to stop her, but halt myself from touching her arm. "Bellator, don't."

A light flares behind her eyes. "Did you just give me an order, half-wit?"

I alter my voice to something more supplicating. "Please, let them be."

"You swore to obey me," she warns. "Don't allow your fickle compassion to get in the way of that, or you'll regret it. Now, follow my lead."

Pushing off from the tree, she leaps up the trunk and summersaults out in front of them. Amid the cries of surprise, I hang back, drawing out my sword. It feels heavy in my hand.

Yet I sense that it will be the nobles, not myself, who will suffer if I dare to disobey. With a reluctant sigh, I step around the bush, coming out at the other side, blocking their escape.

"Hands where I can see them!" Bellator is saying.

"Hamish!" the girl cries, grabbing hold of the boy's arm.

The boy, Hamish, draws his sword, stepping between us and the girl. "Get back!" he orders. "We do not want any trouble."

"Put the weapon down, boy," Bellator scoffs. "Before you hurt yourself."

Hamish raises his sword in a simple act of rebellion. "Believe me, I won't be the one getting hurt."

Bellator snorts with laughter. "Your courage is commendable, yet lacks intelligence. Don't you know who I am?"

He raises his chin. "I don't need to know. I'm not afraid of you!"

"A brilliant façade, your highness. As the crowned prince of this country, you really should've been smarter than to wander so far from home. And with your betrothed, no less."

Fear enters the prince's eyes, and he withdraws a step.

"Oh yes," she says, covering the distance he retreated. "I know who you are, *half-breed.*"

"What?" I ask, not quite sure how the conversation had changed to me.

Bellator rolls her eyes. "Not you, idiot!"

And that's when I see it.

The prince. He has the pallid skin, his eyes are a pale lilac, and his hair, although slicked beneath the circlet on his head, is distinctly ebony.

The prince of Valamette is a half-breed.

Chapter Twenty-Six

"How is that possible?"

The words come before I can stop them. To most, I might sound nosey, even rude. But to my kind, it is a logical question. Half-breeds don't become great. It just doesn't happen.

The prince's gaze falls on me, and a look of sympathy passes through his eyes. "I have heard of others like me that are held captive," he says. "Only, I've never met one until now."

I try my best to look independent. "Oh, I'm not a slave anymore."

"Actually, you are," Bellator says, turning her head slightly as if to acknowledge an especially irritating insect. "Your will belongs to me. What do you think that makes you?"

"My will is my own," I object. "I'm just—"

"You serve me, half-wit! From now until we gain our prize, you're my slave. From there, we'll negotiate the terms for your freedom."

I am distracted from making an immediate reply as I notice the prince leaning over to whisper in the girl's ear.

"It's not your call to sacrifice yourself to protect me," the girl hisses in response to whatever he said to her.

Bellator spins to face them again, her bow rediscovering its original target.

"Marianna, I said to keep your voice down," the prince says through his teeth, facing us again with a defiant scowl.

"Drop your sword!" Bellator orders.

He brandishes his sword, ending with a flourish that leaves it pointing at her. "Never!" he says with a slight toss of his head.

Bellator bursts into a peal of mocking laughter. "Do you honestly think you have the advantage here, little prince? My arrow will strike you before you can even *think* of blocking it. And then who will be left to protect your beloved from me?"

"No one needs to protect me," Marianna says. "Hamish, we can talk this through without anyone getting hurt."

The prince hesitates.

"You should listen to her, boy," Bellator says.

His jaw clenches, his eyes blazing with indignant anger. But even as he does, his decision is made.

He throws his sword at her feet.

"Wise choice, half-breed," Bellator sneers. "Get down on your knees!"

"Bellator," I intervene, "do you need to humiliate him?"

"Down on your knees!" she shouts, ignoring me.

"Must you be so cruel?" Marianna cries, going to stand by the prince's side. "We are willing to listen to what you have to say."

"Get back, girl!" Bellator barks. "Or you will be the cause of your prince's death!"

Marianna recoils at once, throwing up her hands in submission. The prince glares at Bellator and slowly, with as much rebellion as he can safely muster, he gets down on his knees.

Bellator lowers her bow, removing the arrow from the string. She slides it back into her quiver and pulls her bow over her shoulder.

"*Ligar!*" she cries, her eyes changing briefly into black and white swirling holes.

In an instant, the grass at Marianna's feet rises around her and braids itself together, forming a rope. Bellator flourishes her hand. The makeshift rope binds itself around Marianna's hands and winds around her body. She opens her mouth to scream and the rope snakes into it like a gag. Bellator closes her hand into a fist. The ropes tighten.

"You're a witch!" Prince Hamish exclaims.

Bellator laughs harshly. "No, my prince. You have it all wrong! I'm just a poor girl well versed in the art of magic."

"Whatever you are, I demand that you untie Lady Marianna at once!"

"I don't take orders from a spoiled palace brat!"

"And I don't take orders from a bloody outlaw!" Snatching up his sword, he turns to cut Marianna free.

In an instant, Bellator's arrow is on the string again.

"Don't!" I shout as she releases it.

The arrow whizzes through the prince's hair, nicking his ear before it slams into the tree right behind Marianna.

He freezes, putting his fingers to his ear.

Bellator throws out her hand toward him, reaching as if she is grabbing for something, and then jerks it back. He flies forward and hits the ground on his face at her feet.

"Isn't it better," she says, shoving her bow into my hands, "to do as you're told?"

Prince Hamish tries to push himself up, but she places her foot in the centre of his back and shoves him down again. His hands snap together and a pair of leather handcuffs appears on his wrists.

"Did you really think you could free her?" she says, jerking him to his knees by the collar of his doublet. "I could've shot you both dead in a second!"

"Why did you not, then?" Hamish demands.

"I need answers."

The prince narrowed his eyes.

"And if I don't get them, I'll make you watch as I cut your lady apart piece by piece!"

"No, you won't!" I snap.

Hamish fights his bonds. "You touch her, and I'll kill you!"

"That's adorable," Bellator retorts. "Unfortunately, I don't have time to listen while you say your vows. While you were walking, you mentioned a name. Jambeau. Is he with you, or did your worthless father leave his useless hide in Twylaun?"

The prince scowled. "He is here in Gerithold."

"I hear they made that imbecile captain of the guard. How fitting."

Understanding dawns on his face. "This is personal. Isn't it?"

"Very much," she says, passion saturating her words.

The prince waits, examining her face with new interest. "You're the Crimson Shadow."

"Ha!" she cries with contempt. "Does he really call me that?"

"No. But he's told me enough about you to recognize you anywhere. And my father... I heard him mention you once. It seems you've met as well?"

"Yes." Her voice has an amused, yet hateful edge. "We have a too history, your father and I. Let's just say, it will end with fire and blood!"

The prince pales. "So— so you plan to kill me to exact your revenge on my father?"

Bellator scoffs. "He'll suffer for his own crimes. No, I'm actually in the middle of an urgent quest and have come to you for assistance."

The prince looks like he's going to decline, but thinks better of it. He heaves a sigh. "What do you want from me?"

"I'll cut straight to the chase. Do you know where the ruins of the ancient castle of Arnon are located?"

Hamish stares at her. "Arnon is a myth."

Bellator flips her knife in her hand. "You're not a very good liar."

Putting the blade to his neck, she slits the laces of his tunic and jerks apart the folds of his shirt to reveal a long, jagged scar that starts at his collarbone and makes its way down his chest.

"What about this, then?"

He gulps. "How do you know about my scar? And why would it have anything to do with Arnon?"

"Why do you think, son of Leonel?" She spits out the king's name with added venom. "I was the monster that gave it to you!"

"You?" he stammers. "But I thought—"

"That there was a savage beast guarding the scary castle?" she scoffs. "Don't be daft! My old master doesn't appreciate little boys wandering around in places they shouldn't be. Naturally, he sent me to scare the little boy away, and hurting you was the only way to keep you away for good."

"Then you should know where it is already! Why do you need my help?"

"My master never trusted me with all the information. He teleported me there, and when the task was done he used the same method to bring me back. I'm honestly going off of guesswork that the castle is even in this forest."

Hamish shudders in spite of himself. "I pray that nothing so dark lurks anywhere else in this land." His voice descends into unconscious despair as he delves into his memory. "The emptiness. The cold. All this time, it has clung to me like a leech, remaining to haunt my dreams. Once it has touched you, it... it does not let go."

His eyelids close, his features twisting in an expression of deep pain Marianna's face melts and she looks like she wants to reach out and comfort him.

"I know of the darkness of which you speak, young prince." Bellator's voice has gone unusually soft, hoarse almost, and her eyes are haunted with the same pain that riddled the prince's voice. "My goal is to end this spot of darkness. I *long* to. But you need to tell me where the ruins are."

I can't tell whether she's truly genuine.

"Ha!" the prince scoffs. "I feel the evil you claim to fight shrouding you and every action you take!"

"I use whatever means I must," Bellator responds, the chill returning to her tone. "Tell me where the ruins are located, now!"

Hamish shakes his head. "You don't understand! Even if I showed you where the castle is, you wouldn't be able to find it."

"Explain!"

"After I recovered from my injuries, I tried to relocate the castle to show it to Jambeau. But it was nowhere to be found. The space where it had been was empty."

"All I need is the location of the castle. I have all I need to proceed beyond that point right here." She glances sideways at me.

"You honour me," I say acidly.

"Shut up!"

The prince turns his lilac eyes up to Bellator. "I have read the myths surrounding the castle," he says. "I would not trust someone like you with such power."

"Better me than the Lord of Gaiztoak, who will use us to get to the arrow if we're not careful. Besides," she jerks her head toward me, "the arrow belongs to him, not me."

He glances at me, unconvinced.

"Listen," I say, stepping forward, "I swear, if you lead us to where you last saw the castle, we'll let you go. On my word of honour, whether Bellator wants to or not."

Bellator narrows her eyes at me.

Hamish glances from me to her. "You will free both of us? Let us return home unharmed?"

Bellator gives a nonchalant shrug. "If we find the ruins, yes. If not, I'll finally have the leverage that I've always wanted against your father. And if you even think of betraying me, your lovely lady will be the first to go."

"I do not intend to trick you. I have that much honour." His gaze wanders back to me. "But if something happens to me in the process, you have to promise that you will return Marianna home safely."

Although he acts as if he is addressing Bellator, I know that he is asking me, half-breed to half-breed. I give him a hardly discernible nod.

Bellator raises an eyebrow in mock sympathy. "No harm will come to her so long as you both cooperate." She bends down and picks up his sword, sliding it into the sheath on his belt. "Now, lead the way, lord prince."

Chapter Twenty-Seven

"I'll bring up the rear with the damsel in distress," Bellator says as she snatches her bow out of my hands and arms herself with it once more. "The half-prince will lead the way in front with you. Understood?"

I nod.

"Make sure to guard him well. If he escapes..." Her voice trails off, leaving me to imagine all of the horrible things she might do to me if he does. Then she turns back to the others.

I put my hand on her bracer to stop her, and instantly regret it. She grabs my wrist, her eyes fiery.

"Give me one good reason why I shouldn't break your arm," she growls.

"I'm sorry, I'm sorry!" I blurt. "It's— I was just— I was wondering about— about your magic!"

It is an obvious lie, but I'm afraid she really would snap my arm if I followed through with my plan to confront her about the way she's been treating our prisoners.

She raises an eyebrow. "What about it?"

I talk fast. "Just... how it works. You're incredible with it, and I just wanted to know when I'll... I'll be able to do similar things with mine."

Suspicion rises and she glances at the prisoners to make sure they're staying put. Satisfied, she releases my wrist.

"It's complicated," she says gruffly. "As an elemental, you will learn that there are many elements, most of which are only able to be used by their specific Vaelhyrean keepers. Most magic wielders simply tap into the basic earth elements using spells. I can do this, as well as use the small shreds of elements I inherited."

I hesitate. "What element do you think I'll be able to use?"

"My assumption is that, because of the power my old master claims that you possess, you will have the ability to use one of the five key elements; fire, lightning, water, earth, and air." She eyes me carefully. "I haven't seen enough of your magic to have an idea. Who knows? You might've inherited an element all your own."

"Which means...?"

"It means the element your Vaelhyrean parent used will be passed to you through blood." She glances at the royals again. "But enough with the questions. We have a castle to find before nightfall."

We rejoin the captives.

The prince looks at us through the clump of ebony hair sticking in his eyes. "The castle should be located approximately two miles east from here, at the edge of the Tireth River."

Bellator squints in the direction that he gestured. "Anything to avoid?"

He shakes his head. "No. Gerithold is south from here."

"You'd better hope that's true." Turning to me, she jabs her thumb in the prince's direction.

I nod, shoulders sinking, and gesture for him to take the lead. "Take us to it," I order.

Hamish turns east, and plunges into the foliage, but not before casting me a disappointed glance. As if he expected more from me. As if I should expect more from myself.

I follow close behind him, while Bellator keeps Marianna in the back with her, showing enough kindness to remove the gag from her mouth.

I don't like this. Any of it. I mean, kidnapping? I never signed up for that! Did I?

I know I swore to end the spell on the arrow, no matter what. I can't break my word.

But how far is Bellator going to go? How far will she force me to go? Then again, how far am I willing to go? If it were just my life on the line... but it's my freedom! I'm so close to getting the one thing I've ever dared to dream of.

Is that why I'm going along with this? Do I place my own freedom above the lives of others?

It disturbs me that I cannot answer.

As we go on, I find myself walking beside the prince. He certainly holds himself admirably. Though his hands are tied, his step is sure. His back is straight, his head held high as he struggles to retain as much of his pride as he can. Somehow, he maintains his confidence amid his fear.

"Why?" Hamish asks abruptly. "How could you willingly submit yourself to be her slave?"

"I'm not her slave," I say, but my words sound hollow.

"So you mentioned. And yet you do as she says like she is your master."

I glance over my shoulder. "She and I have an understanding. I work only for my freedom."

"Yet for a cause you do not believe in?"

I stiffen. "What makes you think I don't believe in it?"

"Your heart is not in what you do."

I recoil at the thought that I could be so easily read.

"Is there not a better way to achieve your goal than this?" he presses.

"If there was, I would be doing it. I owe her a debt, and this is the only way to pay it back."

He seems to understand. "I am sorry."

I sigh heavily. "No, I'm the one that's sorry. I should never have gone along with capturing you."

"Do not take this the wrong way, but I am unsure there was much you could have done to stop it."

"No, I guess not." I wait. "I'm Ealdred, by the way."

"Hamish. If it were other circumstances, I am sure I would be delighted to meet you."

"Likewise." I glance over my shoulder to make sure Bellator is out of earshot. "I don't mean to pry, but how is that that you're a prince and also a half-breed? I didn't know it was possible."

He frowns, lines of sadness forming in his brow. "I am surprised you have not heard of me before. My father is considered extremely unfortunate, having a half-breed for an heir."

"Why you?" I ask. "I've never heard of a half-breed ruling before."

"Most kingdoms shy away from intermarrying with Lavylli, but it has been done before. One of my ancestors married a princess of Lavylli, and their son became the next king. The difference was that he had the golden hair. I do not."

"Golden hair?" I echo.

"Yes," he confirms. "Legend says it is a sign from the divine that the eldest son is worthy to rule Valamette. Every ruler of Valamette has had it. Even the half-breed king." He sighs bitterly. "I will be the first king of my line in our history without it."

"Oh." I hesitate, not wanting to pry. "Why don't you have it?"

He shrugs. "I am not the eldest. I had a brother: a twin, who was stillborn. The hair was supposed to pass to me upon his death, but it never did. I wish that it did not matter, but I know it does. One day, I will be king. I just need to prove myself to the people so they will want me."

"I do not think it will be that hard," I reassure him. "You're kind and brave, and that means more than all of the charm in the world."

He smiles faintly. "Thank you. That means a—"

"Enough with the chatter already," Bellator interrupts. "We want to get there before next month!"

The prince stiffens.

"Would it help if I told you she's usually not this mean?" I say in an undertone.

The sky is a canvas of colours as the sun sits on the horizon. Thunder lingers in the distance, growing louder and louder as we near another bend of the Tireth River, filling the air around us and blocking out all other sounds. The trees thin, disappearing altogether as we come out into a wide clearing.

Hamish stops next to the last tree and glances around. "Yes. This is it."

The clearing is barren and rocky, stretching out before being cut off by the gorge through which the river sweeps. There is no sign of life, or previous life, and there are certainly no ruins of a castle.

"There's nothing here," I mutter.

"I told you," Hamish replies, turning to Bellator. "It is no longer here."

"Yes it is," she says, stepping past us. "We just have to wait for it."

Only a sliver of the sun peeks from the horizon now, leaving a yellow line to light up the world. In a moment, that too is gone, and the cool darkness of night sets in. With the loss of the sun's light, the moon appears in the sky, white and full. Under the light of the moon, the landscape before us slowly changes. The sound of the river is abruptly cut off, almost as if it has stopped flowing. Any wisp of grass growing on the rocky hillside disappears, and the dark skeleton of a castle materializes in the moonlight. Massive cut stones are scattered around it, and heaps of what used to be a wall skirts the only thing that remains standing: an iron gateway. The metal grate has long since been smashed through in the centre, but the edges stretch out their claws to bar the way.

Hamish takes a step back. "There it is."

"The ruined castle of Arnon," Bellator announces.

"It's beautiful," Lady Marianna says, breathless.

"Of course," I say to myself. "The spell makes it so that it can only be seen during the night."

"Indeed," Bellator beams. "This quest has been planned exceptionally well, if I do say so myself. The light of the full moon opens the portal into the realm where the spell has trapped these ruins – a realm between the land of the dead and that of the living. Today is the first of four days that we have entry to this place. If we'd missed this window, we would've had to wait another month."

"Which we can't really afford to do," I conclude.

"Exactly. Now come. We don't have any time to lose."

"Wait!" Hamish says, stepping forward. "You said that if I brought you here, you would let us go."

"And I mean to," she replies. "But I never said *when* I would do so. I'm not going to risk having your father's soldiers trap us inside. You're coming in with us."

Turning, she steps toward the castle. As she does, a chilling screech rips through the air from within. She freezes, reaching for an arrow. The screeching begins again, but is cut off by a loud hiss that echoes into the night.

"What was that?" Lady Marianna whispers.

No one answers and no one dares move.

"Bellator," I gulp. "This place is a death trap. I was the only one that committed to go in there with you. Let the others go."

She tears her gaze away from the ruins and shakes her head. "Don't cross me on this, Ealdred. I've gone too far to risk this mission being ruined. This is our chance and I'm going to take it. If they die, so be it. But we're *all* going in there."

Chapter Twenty-Eight

T he gateway of the castle was not left unguarded. Although the two creatures that stand guardian over either side of the crumbling archway are made of stone, their appearance alone is enough to repel visitors from joining their ghostly company. Half-gargoyle, half-serpent, their grotesque heads rear back as if to strike, while their feathered tails coil in heaps around the base of the broken archway.

"A deterrent to keep out the faint of heart." Bellator glances back at Hamish, her eyebrows raised. "Which you, apparently, are not."

Hamish stares into the darkness beyond the gate, looking ill.

Bellator follows his gaze. "Now's not the time to faint," she says. "Come, we'll take the first steps together."

Reluctant, yet obedient, the prince walks with her through the gate. I find myself left with Marianna. Her jaw sets with determination, and before I say anything, she charges in after them. I can only follow.

It seems as if we step from one world to another as we pass under the arch of the gateway. A world with very little darkness is traded for one that is made of it. The air is stale and eerie, and the heavy stench of death lingers in every breath we take.

Bellator pulls out the firestone in her gloved hand and lets it dangle from its chain. She mutters something, and it ignites, casting its light to our surroundings. Shadows press around us in a ring. The area of ground illuminated is littered with rubble from the walls and fallen towers, cracked pillars of different heights both toppled and left standing, and something even more terrible.

"Bellator, are those—" I falter.

"Skeletons," she confirms.

The ground is scattered with decrepit human skeletons that would be unrecognizable if not for the suits of rusted armour that holds their forms. Weapons pierce the bodies, some stuck fast in pieces of armour, some lying beside their victims, and very few remaining in the hands of their masters. Spider-webs have been woven over the bodies, serving as nature's shroud for the dead.

"This is no place for the living," Hamish says, his voice echoing in the darkness beyond what we can see. "Terrible things have happened here."

"Indeed," Bellator says. "Here took place the ancient battle of Arnon."

"What happened?" Lady Marianna whispers.

Bellator hesitates. "People died."

The prince clears his throat. "Legend speaks of this place as belonging to the first settler to come to our land, perhaps the very same person the mythical phoenix was modeled after—"

"Legend is wrong," Bellator cuts in, abruptly ending the prince's account.

Her bitter mood returning, Bellator hurries through the courtyard, either leaping over the remains of dead bodies or kicking them aside as she passes. Her gaze flits to and fro as she searches the rubble for something only she knows. The air is filled with tension as we follow her, each of us anticipating our own swiftly approaching demise.

We reach the large, circular foundation of what used to be a tower. Most of the wall has joined the rubble around the base, but a good ten feet from the ground has been spared. Strangely, it doesn't appear to be damaged.

Bellator steps up to the door that bars the entrance to the tower. "This is it."

"What is it?" I ask, following.

She turns to me, an eager light in her eyes. "This is what we've been looking for." Stepping aside, she gestures to the door. "Open it."

I look at the old, seemingly wooden door. Scorch marks cover it, especially surrounding the handle, yet it remains as sturdy as ever. "Are you sure?"

"Well, I doubt that anyone else could open it, or it would probably be open by now."

I step forward and reach out my hand toward the door. I pause, my fingers only a few inches away from it. Then I grasp the cold metal of the handle and try to pull it open.

"It's locked," I mutter.

No sooner are the words out of my mouth than a sharp hiss cuts through the air. I jump back, whirling to face Bellator. She locks her gaze with mine, a look very much resembling fear passing through her eyes.

"What was that?" I whisper.

She opens her mouth with a slight tremor. "It's... it's calling you!"

My eyes widen, and I allow myself to panic. "*What* is?"

"I- I don't know..." her voice trails off, but then comes back with fierceness. "Draw your weapons!"

I draw my knife with my left hand and my sword with my other. Bellator spins around and cuts Hamish free of his bonds.

"You're freeing me?" Hamish asks.

"Yes! Now draw your sword if you want to use that freedom!" she says, nocking her bow with an arrow.

The prince quickly gets over his shock and draws his own sword. His eyes are wide with fear, but he stands with us to help fight the beast.

The creature hisses again. Pain shoots from my left hand, searing up my arm. I cry out, dropping my knife, and look down at my palm. The brand on my hand glows red and heat scorches like it had when I was first burnt.

"Ealdred, look out!" Bellator shouts.

I look up. A massive black creature springs up in front of me, as high as a tower, rearing its fearsome head back and hissing ferociously. Two shining yellow eyes the size of shields glare down at me with a wicked grin. A long, forked tongue darts in and out between two razor sharp fangs as it opens its jaws, preparing to strike.

"By the goddess!" Hamish exclaims. "What is that thing?"

"S-snake!" I cry, snatching up my sword in my right hand.

The vibrating twang of a bow sings through the air, and Bellator's arrow strikes the beast's skin. But instead of sinking in, the arrow splinters on its iron scales.

With another hiss, the serpent sweeps its long tail at my sword, catching the blade and ripping it from my hand.

I jump back and search frantically for where my dagger had fallen. I see it and leap for it. As my hand closes around the hilt, the snake's tail coils around my legs and pulls me into the air.

The world spins, and I let out a strangled cry as I find myself hanging upside down far above ground. I try to reach up and cut myself loose, but my arm isn't long enough. My dagger cuts fruitlessly through thin air. Again, the snake hisses, and deliberately slams me into the side of a pillar. Light flashes. Everything goes dark as pain resonates through me, and all I can do is search for a way through it. When I come back to full consciousness, I am once again dangling in the air.

"Hey!" Bellator shouts, and the beast swings around to assess her. "You want a fight? Here I am!"

The serpent goes to swipe her away with its tail, carrying me along with it. Bellator summersaults out of the way, shouldering her bow. Down on her hands and knees, she looks up at the serpent, a smile turning her lips.

"Finally," she says. "A real challenge."

With a leap, she lunges for the beast, swinging onto it with the agility of a wildcat. She climbs up its body, reaching the top of its head with ease. The beast thrashes about, trying to throw her off, but she clings to its scalp with remarkable balance.

The snake grinds its head into a mound of rubble, lowering me almost to the ground. I reach out for something to grab onto, but am hoisted up again almost at once. Feeling satisfied that it has removed the pest, it swings me closer to its open jaws, preparing to swallow me whole.

I take my knife in both hands and hurl it at the creature with all my might. The knife pierces the oversized viper between its two fangs and sinks in up to the hilt. The beast rears backward, shaking its head, trying to escape the pain. While it does, Bellator rises up from a torn scale over its brow, and brings the firestone into the creature's eye.

A shriek emerges from the serpent and it gives a sudden, violent thrash. Bellator loses her balance and tumbles into the creature's open mouth. She catches herself on my knife, stopping her fall. For a moment, it holds, and she tries to swing herself back up. But then the knife slips, beginning to cut through the thin anchor of viper flesh.

The snake rears back, its mouth open wide, preparing to strike at me. Bellator dangles upright inside the creature's mouth, directly above its bottom fangs. I look at her over the empty space, and for the first time since we met, I see terror in her eyes.

"Ealdred," she breathes.

"Hold on!" I cry, reaching for her.

"No! The poison—"

The creature's tongue flits through its teeth and her hand slips a little.

"Find the arrow!" she shouts, her voice unusually high. "Whatever it takes, find it!"

Then the knife gives way. In that same moment, the snake throws me into the air and dives forward to swallow me whole. For a brief instant, we are both falling in the same direction. Her mouth is parted in a silent scream as she sails toward the black hole that is the creature's throat. Then the snake snaps its jaws shut between us and I slam into its nose. Its tongue shoots out and I tumble over its head, rolling down its body until I collide with the ground.

The snake rises above me, hissing furiously. Then it jerks back, and whipping around, slithers into the darkness.

"Bellator!" I cry as soon as I have breath.

Silence is the only reply that I receive.

Blinding pain shoots through my ribs as I push myself up, and stumble to my feet. I grunt, pressing my hand to my side.

"Bellator!" I shout again, hoping that somehow, someway, she was able to escape.

"Where is she?" Hamish groans from the darkness nearby.

I blink back tears that I can't explain. "She saved me." It is a strange, yet simple fact. A truth that I would never have expected of Bellator. "She saved me!"

"Did it—" He grunts, and I can tell that he is in pain. "Is she— dead?"

I turn in the direction of his voice and the tears escape. The truth isn't registering in my mind, even though I know the answer.

All I can do is nod.

Chapter Twenty-Nine

Moonlight pierces the darkness around us, lighting the courtyard with a cool, clear glow. I look around, hoping to catch some glimpse of the snake, of Bellator. But all that I see before me is rubble and the ancient dead strewn as far as can be seen.

Hamish is on his knees nearby, his left hand pressed to his right leg, which is dark with blood. Lady Marianna lies sprawled on the ground a few metres behind him, not moving.

"Is she alright?" I ask, staggering toward them.

The prince glances back, then cries out in alarm. "Marianna!"

I rush past him and kneel down beside her, cutting her free of her ropes with a rusty knife I find on the ground nearby. Blood runs down her face from a gash in her forehead. Taking her hand, I press it between my own. It is limp, but still warm.

"Is she alright?" the prince asks, trying to get to his feet. "Please, tell me that she is alive!"

I press my finger to her wrist and feel a slow, languid heartbeat. "She's alive, but barely. You have to get her to a physician right away."

"I cannot," he stammers hopelessly. "I cannot walk. She will die before I can get her back."

My heart is conflicted. Bellator's dying wish was for me to get that arrow, and frankly, now I owe it to her more than ever. But, I also can't let the future queen of Valamette die.

"Please," Hamish begs, "help me!"

My gaze catches on the glinting blade of my sword. If only I had been strong enough to keep it in my hand! I am struck by the thought that no matter how much Bellator professed that she hated me and only needed me to get the arrow, in the end, she died saving me.

It is time to follow her example. She turned aside to save a life. Now I will do the same.

I pick up my sword and sheathe it in its scabbard. Then I turn to the prince. "Let's get out of this forsaken place."

Relief washes over his face and he struggles to his feet, leaning on a rusty spear that he pulled out of a nearby skeleton.

"Thank you," he says.

I stoop down and lift the lady up in my arms. She is much heavier than I expected her to be – almost too much for me to carry – and with her whole body limp, I am careful to support her neck. Hamish reaches out his hand and gently presses the back of it to her cheek.

"It is funny," he says as if to himself. "We have been engaged our whole lives, but I only just met her yesterday. She is actually rather charming."

"Ready?" I ask.

He nods quickly and draws his hand away, abashed.

We start back toward the gate, which looms out of the darkness like a beacon of hope in a world of despair. But as we draw nearer, two red glowing eyes appear directly in our way. A shadow fills up the gateway.

I stop short and turn to Hamish. "You have to take her," I hiss.

His terrified gaze breaks off of the obstacle ahead of us. "But I cannot—"

"You have to try!" I return forcefully. "I'll keep it off as long as I can."

"I'm not going to leave you to fight it alone!"

"You must! If you don't, the Lady Marianna will die. You have to save her. I will try my best to save you."

"But it will kill you!"

I attempt a smile. "Have a little faith, will you?"

He isn't amused. "I will not let you sacrifice yourself. Not for me."

"I will try my best to save you," I say again. "Perhaps by doing so, I will forgive myself for allowing you to be brought into danger in the first place. Please, at least give me that."

He takes a breath, his lips white as he presses them together.

I look down at the unconscious face of the lady. Her complexion has grown frightfully pale. "I would have you save her if you can."

He gives a wavering nod. "You have my thanks."

I place her gently in his outstretched arms and support him as he braces his leg against the weight. He takes a step, grappling under the strain on his leg. He sways, but regains his balance swiftly.

I turn back to the gate, drawing out my sword with my right hand. Truth be told, it is not as strong as my left, but I cannot risk losing my weapon again.

The creature rears back its head and howls a long, chilling howl that brittles my bones, and stalks into the moonlight. Although its shape resembles a wolf, it is the size of a bear. Claws like curved daggers extend from its giant paws, its teeth spearheads bared in a vicious snarl.

Fear as strong as an ocean tide channels through me, but I fuse myself to the spot. I close my eyes and coax the cold energy into my veins so that I may have the courage to face this thing.

The beast lets out a low growl, its gaze piercing me, and I find myself captivated by it. Something inside of me connects with the soul of the wolf, and my heart swells with pity.

"It's beautiful," I find myself muttering aloud. "How can I harm something so beautiful?"

Footsteps shuffle nearby, and somewhere in my consciousness I understand that Hamish has taken the opportunity to slip past the creature.

The beast crouches low to the ground, readying to pounce.

"I won't," I say, bewildered. Then, to the wolf, "I won't fight you, creature – it's wolf, isn't it? Wolf, I will not fight you!"

I lower myself slowly, and set my sword on the ground beside me.

"This is stupid," I say, both to the wolf and to myself. "Probably the stupidest thing I've ever done. Put down my sword when death is staring me in the face." I laugh, shaking my head. "If Bellator could see me now... she'd kill me herself."

The wolf creeps toward me, and I straighten up, putting out my hand to stop it. It recoils defensively, snapping its jaws and foaming at the mouth.

"Maybe they're right," I say, the words coming faster and more distractedly. "Maybe I *am* a coward. But does that matter? I won't fight you, but why? Why not? There's something more." I stop, the realization hitting me. "What if... what if it's not only that I *won't* fight – it's that I *can't*. There is something holding me back. Something that..."

Hot breath hits my face and my voice trails off. I look up. The wolf stands before me, its face distorted in a fearsome snarl.

Trembling, I turn my head to the side, bracing myself. "D-do it! If you can, do it. Take me, and let them go. That's the way it works, isn't it? A life must be sacrificed as payment for the safe passage of the rest?"

Its muscles tense and I squeeze my eyes shut.

"I'm ready!" I say.

The wolf snarls and lunges. Its jaws snap, but the blow never comes. Instead, a cold breeze washes over me. I open one eye and then blink, turning in a circle. The wolf is nowhere to be found. Instead, a white mist surrounds me, lingering in the windless air.

I realize that I'm not breathing and let out my breath in a rush.

It wasn't real! It was a cruel phantom of the mist, like before. If only we'd been so lucky with the serpent...

Retrieving my sword, I slide it into my sheath and pass under the archway. Hamish is stumbling over the rocky ground toward the forest, still bearing Marianna gallantly in his arms. I press my hand to my side, breathing hard, and hurry out through the gate, leaving Arnon behind.

As soon as I have passed between the gargoyles, the cool evening breeze hits my face and fresh, clean air fills my lungs. I drink it in, then take off at a sprint after Hamish. It doesn't take me long to catch up with him.

He turns to me with a surprised, yet pleased, smile. "You live!"

"How is she?" I wheeze, slowing to walk beside him.

His smile dims. "She is not moving. I am not even sure that she is breathing."

"You have a physician at your palace, right?" I don't wait for a reply. "Can he help with something like this?"

He nods. "Lesley is the best healer in the land."

I force air into my pressured lungs. "Tell me the location of the palace. I'll run ahead and get him."

"It is a few miles southwest from here. Please hurry!"

"Alright. Take her into the forest far enough to be out of sight of the castle, and then don't move. I'll be back as soon as I can."

With a wave, I take off into the woods. The river is to the east of me. As long as I know its direction, I should be able to locate the palace without a problem. I bound through the rugged foliage, pushing through branches that whip my face and leaping over the occasional fallen tree. The pain in my side grows so intense that I can hardly breathe, but even then, I slow only to make sure that I am going in the right direction.

At last, I enter a clearing. The ground is blanketed with grass, which I notice is nicely trimmed. At the opposite end of the lawn from where I stand is a stone stairway leading into a massive granite building with windows of coloured glass. The entrance to the building is barred by two wooden double doors. The doors are surrounded by three decorative mouldings that repeat the original pillared architecture of the doorframe. Guarding the door are two soldiers bearing the crest of Valamette – a golden phoenix on a blue backdrop.

I take a step toward them, but a tall man wearing a similar uniform steps in my way, cutting me off. I slam into him before I can stop myself and tumble back into the grass.

The sound of grinding metal rings in the air, and he puts his sword to my throat.

"It is not that simple to acquire an audience with the king, filthy half-breed," the man sneers.

"Please," I gasp, "I've come for the physician, Lesley—"

"I'm sorry to disappoint," he replies. "He only practices for the royal family."

"But the pr—"

"Enough!" he snaps, jabbing at me with his sword. "Be gone before I have you flogged for your insolence!"

"Alright. Alright!" I bat his blade away with the back of my hand and struggle to my feet. I turn as if to leave, but then whirl back around, drawing my own sword.

"How dare you?" the guard exclaims.

I cross my sword with his. "You have to listen to m—"

"Enough!" a voice shouts from the top of the stairs.

The guard spins around and solutes the newcomer. "Captain."

A young man, also dressed in a blue and gold uniform, descends the stairs. His shoulder-length brown hair is tied back at the nape of his neck, revealing a long burn scar starting halfway up his scalp and crossing down one half of his long, boyish face to the thin growth of whiskers on his chin. As he draws closer, I notice that his right hand is missing. In its stead is a large, silver hook.

"Officer, what is the meaning of this?" His tone is soft, but he has a confident, solemn bearing that gives him an aura of authority.

The officer points at me. "This half-breed dog was trying to break into the palace to see the royal physician, sir."

"We do not discriminate here," the captain warns. "And did you bother to ask this *boy* his reason for needing the physician's assistance?"

"Sir—"

The captain puts up a hand. "You are dismissed. Continue your patrol."

With a click of his heel, the guard is gone.

The captain turns to me and opens his mouth to speak, but stops. His brows pull together in a frown. "Who are you?"

"I don't have time to explain," I blurt, "but the Lady Marianna has been badly injured and Prince Hamish sent me to get the physician to help her."

He looks toward the woods, alarmed. "I thought they returned hours ago!" Spinning around, he bolts for the castle, calling over his shoulder, "Stay there!"

He bounds up the steps and disappears into the castle. I sheath my sword and wait. In a few minutes he returns, a lit torch in his hand. A surprisingly spry elderly man follows, carrying a satchel under his arm.

"Where are they?" the captain asks.

"At the edge of the woods, near the Tireth, northeast from here. That's where I told them to stay, at any rate."

The physician looks at me, his bushy grey brows furrowed. "And who's this scrawny little fellow?" he croaks good-naturedly.

"Never mind about him." The captain nods to me. "Bring us to them."

We find the royals in the woods just out of sight of the castle, as I directed. Hamish sits with his back to a tree, hugging his knees to his chest. Lady Marianna lies on the ground in front of him, her head lolled to the side and her mouth parted in sleep. Hamish has taken off his overcoat and spread it over her in a feeble attempt to shield her from the cool night air. He looks up when he hears us approaching, picking anxiously at the threads of his boots.

Lesley bends to his knees beside her and opens his satchel. "This does not look good," he clucks.

"What happened?" the captain asks Hamish.

"We were attacked," he mumbles, staring at the ground in front of him. "By a wolf. Lady Marianna tripped. I think she hit her head."

The captain raises an eyebrow in a way that very much reminds me of Bellator. "A wolf?"

Hamish looks at Lesley. "She'll be alright, won't she?"

"If she dies, her death will be on you."

This voice is entirely new, and all three turn to acknowledge the newcomer's presence. A middle-aged man attired in clothing far richer than that of the prince steps into the small clearing from behind us. The firelight of the torch catches on the sparkling chain around his neck, but even more so on the locks of golden hair that curl around his scalp. Arms crossed, he glares sternly at the prince, his eyes made terrifying in the glow of the torch.

The captain quickly falls to one knee, gesturing for me to do the same.

Hamish's face goes suddenly white, and he bows his head. "Father? You... you came looking for me?"

"Irresponsible!" The king's voice rings out through the trees. "If I'd known your head was so empty, I wouldn't have bothered paying for your special education. No son of mine should be so careless as to risk our treaty with Lord Jerousse by letting his daughter come to harm!"

Hamish ducks his head. "I am sorry, father. I tried to protect her—"

"Not hard enough, it seems, or you'd be the one at death's doors! Your brother wouldn't have been such a coward!"

The prince cringes, looking away.

The king's disapproving gaze turns to me and I feel a sudden need to disappear. "And who is this urchin?" he demands.

"A friend, your majesty," the captain replies with a bow, and I'm surprised – yet grateful – that he's standing up for me.

"Silence, Jambeau!" the king snaps, glaring at the captain. "My son has a mouth, if he has backbone enough to use it."

Jambeau. Isn't that the name of the fellow Bellator was so spiteful about?

The captain bows again, his fist to his chest. "I apologize, my liege."

"My king," the physician interrupts, "I have done my best to stabilize the lady's condition. We must get her back to the palace immediately."

"Your assistance is required, captain," the king says.

Jambeau salutes, then lifts up the unconscious Marianna, bearing her away after Lesley and back toward Gerithold.

Once they have gone, the king turns back to us. Hamish stands up, his back still pressed to the tree. His injured knee trembles, and he puts a hand down to brace it. He keeps his gaze low, his shoulders tense as if awaiting a dreaded explosion of tempers.

But the king doesn't even glance at him. Instead, he turns back to me. "Who are you, half-breed?"

The cold tone in which he utters the words sends a shock of anger through me. Does he really despise us so much, even though he has one for a son?

Out of the corner of my eye, I notice Hamish shrink even more.

"M-my name is Ealdred, sire," I stammer.

"He saved us, fa—" Hamish begins.

"Speak up, boy! I can't hear you when you mumble."

Hamish clears his throat. "Ealdred saved us," he says, louder this time. "He fought the wolf and then ran to fetch Lesley."

The king's gaze hardens. "And how, Ealdred, did you just *happen* to discover them in the middle of my forest?"

I scratch my ear. "I was lost."

"Do not be angry, father," Hamish tries again. "If he was not there, Marianna would be dead right now."

"Hold your tongue, boy!" the king snaps, turning to loom over him. "You're a disgrace! If you were anything like me, you wouldn't need to be saved by some wandering urchin! Does the courage of Gryphem run in your veins, or were you cursed with the pansy blood of Lavylli? Man up! Do not speak again until you have something to give other than excuses!"

The words hurt him, I know, but Hamish does well to hide it.

The king turns back to me, his voice less severe. "Tell me about yourself, Ealdred."

My mind sharpens with suspicion. "What do you want to know?"

He waves his hand carelessly. "Whatever story you're willing to tell me."

"Well, uh... I'm an escaped slave from Zandelba. I was in these woods to keep off the roads." I bow my head. "I didn't know that the forest belonged to you, sir, and if I offended you, I'm truly sorry."

The king rubs his chin, flattening the loose hairs of his beard. "Well, Ealdred of Zandelba, I appreciate you saving Lady Marianna's life, but we do not harbour runaways. I bid you be gone from my country and never return, or I'll drag you back to your masters after having you flogged!"

"Father!" Hamish exclaims, his boldness returning.

The king turns on him. "I told you—"

"I will not be silent!" the prince exclaims, clenching his fists. "He saved Marianna's life, and this is how you intend to repay him? This country values justice above all else. Justice is not only for the condemned, but for those who deserve a reward!"

"I see." The king eyes him carefully. "Your king's justice is not to your satisfaction. Well then, tell me; what would *you* have me do?"

Hamish doesn't let his father's ridicule discourage him. "We can start by offering him a warm place to sleep for the night. From there, I would assume he could stay with us until he is ready to be on his way. It's the least we can do."

I open my mouth, shocked speechless. *He wants me to stay with them?*

"Out of the question!" the king cries.

"Why not? It would be nice to have someone around who understands me."

"So that's what this is about! The lonely prince wants a playmate?"

"No! Well... perhaps." Hamish looks down at his bleeding leg, his shoulders slouching. "You have no idea what it has been like to grow up as this," he gestures to indicate his entire body. "Everyone has such high expectations of me, yet there is no way I can reach them. Ealdred? He's a half-breed, like me. He will not mock me. Already, I know I can trust him with my life. People like that are hard to find."

The king growls.

"All I am asking is that you let him stay, at least until he finds somewhere else to go."

I look from one to the other, my breath held. Part of me wants the king to decline. Bellator has been right so far; he really is a nasty character. But for Hamish's sake, I hope that he agrees. There's something about the prince that feels safe, that reminds me of myself.

The king glances from Hamish to me, his internal struggle visible on his face. Then he sighs in defeat. "Fine. He can stay for a couple of days, as long as he behaves himself."

Hamish draws his hands together and bows. "Thank you, father. You will not regret this decision."

With a wave of his hand, the king turns his back to him. "Go and see to it that Lesley fixes your leg. I'll make sure Ealdred gets there safely. But first, I wish to speak with him in private."

The smile beginning to form on the prince's face fades and we exchange a worried glance. But he turns obediently and hurries away, leaving me alone with the king.

Chapter Thirty

While the sounds of Hamish's footsteps fade, the king remains patient, still, his crystal gaze fixed on my face. It is hard to discern anything from his strikingly good-looking features besides the strong sense of dislike that increases as he ponders me.

A cricket chirps nearby. The breeze rustles through the trees. The moon has risen full in the sky and is now directly overhead.

The king puts a hand on my shoulder, and I jump.

"Walk with me," he says, and we turn toward the castle at a slower pace.

I wait, unease stirring in my stomach.

He breaks the silence with a low, dry chuckle. "Ealdred," he says, contempt saturating his tone. "Such a brave lad you are in the eyes of my son."

"Believe me, sire, I didn't intend for any of this to happen."

"Oh really? You just 'happened' across my foolish son while he was in danger, rescued him, and now you're being welcomed into my palace with open arms. And you tell me you didn't plan any of it?"

"I did not."

"I know a liar when I see one," he says with the same irritating chuckle. "Do you think the eyes of the king of Valamette are so easily blinded? I know as well as you do that my son was lying about how Lady Marianna was injured."

My heart stumbles over a beat. "I don't understand—"

His fingers dig into my shoulder. "Think carefully before you lie to me again."

I give in. "You know what happened, then?"

"You are unusually smart for a slave of your race, aren't you?" His words are mocking. "Oh yes, I saw you and my son leaving that damned place when I was searching for him. I wonder what business a boy like you could possibly have in the cursed castle of Arnon?"

I think quickly, speaking the words as they come to me. "It wasn't by choice, sir. My master brought us all to the castle by force. He was after some of the treasure he claimed was inside. But he was killed, and we were able to escape."

"Upon which time you bravely stepped in to save the day." He snorts. "Predictable."

My temper flashes and I shove his hand off of my shoulder. "Stop playing games with me! What is it you really want?"

His smile has a sharp edge to it. "I want to know what you know."

"About what?"

He stops and looks me hard in the face. "I think that you know exactly what I'm talking about."

"No," I say slowly, unable to imagine what he could possibly be speaking of. *The arrow, perhaps?* "I don't."

He strokes his beard. "It doesn't matter, as long as Hamish doesn't find out. Because if he does, I will make your life very miserable."

Too late. Hamish knows about the arrow.

"Whatever you wish, your highness," I say with a mock bow. "Though it may be difficult to carry out your order, seeing as how I have no idea what I'm supposed to keep from him."

The king scowls at me. "It won't matter anyways, as you don't intend to stay for long."

It isn't hard to catch his meaning.

"Are you even trying to be subtle about your dislike for me, or do you actually want to make it this clear?"

"You do have an attitude about you," he says, gripping my shoulder again with threatening malice. "Beware that you do not use it to your own disadvantage."

A twig snaps in the darkness nearby. I halt, straining my ears.

"Hurry up, boy," the king orders, walking on ahead. "Or you might find the palace doors closed to you when you finally arrive."

"Wait!" I say, but he either doesn't hear or chooses to ignore me.

The burn on my hand begins to ache, and when I look down at it, it is again outlined in a red glow. My spirit sinks.

Not again...

I draw my sword and turn in a circle, searching for the immediate danger.

The king spins around. "So you're an assassin, are you?" he says, brandishing his own sword.

"No," I say, stepping back. "Danger!"

He suddenly goes very still, his eyes widening. Raising a trembling finger, he points at something behind me.

I freeze, tightening my grip on the hilt of my sword. Breath bated, I whirl around, slashing wildly through the air with my sword. The tip grinds against the iron breastplate of an ezix that materializes out of nowhere, towering above me. Its mouth twists into a horrid grin, and it swings its spiked sword at me. I don't have time to get out of the way, so my branded hand leaps up to block the blow. The sharp iron hits my palm. But instead of cutting into it, the blade stops as if my hand were protected by an iron gauntlet.

"What is this foul creature you have brought into my land?" the king demands.

"Ezixs," I gasp, tearing my bewildered gaze from my hand. "Run!"

But as I turn, I see the others. We are surrounded by a ring of about a dozen of them. Their hideous faces jeer at us from behind heavy iron helmets.

"Never mind," I say, backing toward the king. "We'll go back to back!"

There is no reply.

I glance over my shoulder, only to find that he's backing away from me. He sheaths his sword and throws up his hands.

"Sorry, lad," he says with a sudden grin, "but this is your fight."

Fear twists my gut. "What?"

The king walks toward the ezixs. "Put in a good word for me to the Master when you return to Gaiztoak, won't you?" he calls over his shoulder.

The ezixs part for him, and then snap together once he has passed through their ranks.

Of course! The king didn't detain me so that he could talk nonsense to me. He detained me so that the ezixs could trap me.

My veins are cold with energy that is waiting to explode, but I try to quiet it.

"Congratulations, Zeldek!" I say calmly, turning in a circle. "You really fooled me. I thought for a moment that you couldn't reach me here. I guess I was wrong."

An unusually short ezix steps forward, holding up a hand as if in greeting. Its appearance differs to that of the others, not only in stature, but also in complexion. Its skin is a sickly brown colour instead of slimy grey, and its hair is a light chestnut instead of black.

"Hello," it says in a broken form of the basic language of Theara. Its voice is rough, but feminine. "I am Tzaile, the translator. Are you the one we seek?"

"I- think so?"

I didn't know there was any such thing as a friendly ezix.

"We have come from the Master. He wishes that you return with us. If you refuse, we may take you by force."

I blink. "He *wishes?*"

"Will you come?" Tzaile asks.

I step away, only to back into another ezix. It brings its fist down on my arm, wrenching the sword from my hand.

Tzaile looks impatient. "Will you resist?"

I try to answer, but the surging in my veins has rapidly grown into an ache that is filling me up to overflowing. Still, I keep it back. If I let it out, I may hurt them.

"We will take you then," Tzaile says, and gestures for them to seize me.

The pressure intensifies and grows unbearable, and when I look, my veins are raised, glowing with blue light.

"No!" I gasp, confused and terrified. "Get away. Leave, quickly! I'm— *ah!*"

My palms are trying to open, the dragon brand a swirl of red and blue light. Shaking, my knees weaken, and I fall to them.

"Run!" I shout, my voice amplified in my own ears.

The freezing surge of energy overpowers me. My hands open and power unlike anything I have ever felt pours from me. Blue light, pale and pure, explodes around me with powerful force, throwing back the ezixs and engulfing everything until even I am blinded by it. Grunts and shrieks fill the air and I feel as if my breath is being sucked out and forced into me at the same time.

I look to the sky and a spiral of light shoots to the stars. Panicked, I open my mouth to call for help, struggling to make my frozen limbs move. My voice does not come.

Then, all at once, it's over. My limbs free themselves, the light fades, and I fall forward into a clump of grass.

Grunts rise in a chorus, and a shout goes up to the boughs of the trees. Branches snap as heavy footsteps retreat, echoing to silence.

It takes me a few moments, but I am finally able to pull myself to my feet. My knees begin to buckle, but I grab onto a nearby branch to regain my balance.

Only one semi-coherent thought comes to mind, rooted from deep within: I need to get to the palace. Whether the king wants me there or not, I have a strong feeling that I need to be there, whether it is to confront him or to support Hamish. In such a state of mind as I am in now, it is hard to reason with myself.

Once I retrieve my sword, I continue my journey to the castle. I reach it in a manner of minutes, and stagger across the lawn toward the portal to the palace.

Jambeau and the king stand at the top of the stairs, conversing in hushed tones, staring at the sky above the trees from which I just came. I stop at the base of the steps, sticking the point of my sword in the ground, and rest my hands on the hilt so that I look steady.

"I trust you arrived safely, my king," I say, not able to help but smirk up at him.

The king jumps at the sound of my voice and he turns to face me. Prudence takes hold, and he straightens up before his shock displays itself.

"I did."

"Very good, sir. Shall I retire for the night?"

He stiffens, but smiles through his teeth. "You look faint. Perhaps a little medicine would do you some good."

"Thank you," I begin to ascend the stairs, "but I think I'll manage without any 'medicine'."

The king flicks his hand and Jambeau retires indoors.

I stop in front of the king and sheathe my sword. "Next time you decide to attack me, be man enough to do it yourself!"

He seizes my arm, his eyes alight with rage. Yet beyond his anger, he seems afraid. "I had no choice."

I try to jerk my arm from his grasp, but he holds on tight. "I know. You have to obey your master Zeldek's every wish, don't you?"

He clenches his jaw. "It was not wise to come here, boy."

"Ah, but no one ever said that I was wise."

There is a lethal glint in his eye as he releases me. "Have a nice rest, Ealdred. Beware that it isn't your last!"

Chapter Thirty-one

I t was long after midnight when the cloaked figure passed through the dark forest. His steps were brisk, and he didn't take the necessary precautions to ensure that he was alone. His mind was too filled with confusion, too clouded with fear.

He reached his destination: a cracked stone basin brimming with water in the middle of a small glade in the thickest part of the woods. The sound of running water from the Tireth River accented the still night air as the figure stopped before the basin. He peered into the dark water for a moment, and then uttered the only magical word that he knew how to use.

"Ertain."

The water in the basin began to swirl, and sparks of red, yellow, and orange filled it. The figure took a step back in anticipation. Flames exploded from the surface of the water, swelling outward, but quickly settling down to one flickering tongue.

The figure covered the distance between himself and the basin once more, and peered into the flame, waiting.

"Leonel!" the Master's voice boomed from the fire, and the figure cringed in spite of himself. "What is the meaning of this? Why have you disturbed me?"

Leonel cleared his throat, bowing his head. "Sire, I would not have done so if it were not completely necessary."

"Yes?" The Master's voice was impatient.

Leonel glanced around and then spoke hurriedly in a whisper, "This evening, a boy entered the courtyard of my palace seeking the help of my physician. My captain allowed him to leave with him, but accompanied them into the woods. Now, as you are aware, my son arrived from Lavylli only yesterday—"

"Leonel," the Master interrupted impatiently. "If you have disturbed me for some petty family matter..."

"No, sire! Not at all!" Leonel's voice was urgent, and the Master paused to listen. "I don't know the details of what happened, but this boy—"

"Get to the point!"

"His name is Ealdred, sire."

There was a long moment of silence, and Leonel took the opportunity to speak once more.

"He is a half-breed, from Zandelba, and I noticed that he wore a sword that bears the crest of the Crimson Shadow."

"Bellator?" Zeldek's voice did not sound surprised. "Is she not with him?"

"No, sire. I believe that she is, in fact, dead."

"Dead?" Zeldek echoed. "That's not possible!"

"That's what I have gathered. I saw the four of them — my son, the Lady Marianna, the Crimson Shadow, and this Ealdred – enter the ruined castle of Arnon, and some time later, only three of them emerged. That girl was not with them."

"Arnon?" the Master repeated, incredulous. "So she thought that she could take the arrow for herself, did she?"

"It doesn't matter, sire. She is gone, and the arrow is as it was, waiting for you."

"No! You don't understand. Without her, I will never regain my full strength! She is key to my plan!"

"Sire—"

"Silence! I want proof of her death! Get me proof!"

"I will. I shall not fail you."

"See to it that you don't."

Leonel hesitated. "In the meantime, what of the boy?"

The Master pondered this. "Watch him closely. I want a full report of his activities. Then, when the time comes, I will want him back."

"Why not take him now, sire? It would be safer for all of us."

"I have a feeling that his being there is not a coincidence. I want to see what his plan is, if there is one, and I want to know it as soon as you discover it."

Leonel bowed. "Yes, sire. I must return before I am missed. Are there any last orders?"

"Do not fail me."

"You know that I won't, sire."

The flames in the water were put out. Leonel tucked his cloak around himself once more and began to retrace his steps through the woods.

He did not see the figure flattened against a nearby tree, nor did he realize that it had heard every word of the conversation.

Chapter Thirty-Two

I *am still alive!*

Light streams in through the window to my room, casting its rays on the wooden floorboards. A warm breeze blows through the lattice, brushing aside the white sheer curtains and filling the room with the sweet scent of summer air. I relax, putting my head back on my pillow, and sigh. My ribs still ache from last night's encounter with the snake, but at least they don't feel like they are broken anymore.

I am lying on the floor beneath the bed in one of the guest rooms in the palace. The king had specifically allotted me this room to stay in, causing me to assume the worst – that being a knife through the heart while I slept. Despite being exhausted, I was only able to fall asleep after I moved a pillow and a few blankets down under the bed. I slept with my sword ready on the floor beside me.

The door to my room creaks open, and footsteps halt at the door. After a moment, they enter the room. My hand finds the hilt of my sword in an instant, and

I pull it quietly out of its sheath. Finely polished boots approach my bed, and I hold my breath.

"Where did he go?" mutters the familiar voice of Prince Hamish.

I let my breath out in relief and roll out from under the bed on the opposite side that he's on.

"I'm right here," I say, standing up.

He blinks, glancing down at the floor, and then back at me. "Why—"

"You wanted to speak with me?" I interrupt, sheathing my sword.

He glances at my weapon, raising his eyebrows. "I came to wake you. It is almost noon. Father wants you to join us for dinner."

"Is it noon?" I ask, uninterested.

Oh yes, the thought of spending a meal with the man who threatened to kill me last night is very agreeable. Especially the poison that will certainly accompany the sweet cakes.

The prince nods. "You did earn the extra sleep, what with everything that you went through yesterday."

I am very glad to hear someone say it.

"That is kind of you to say," I reply more humbly. "But it does make me feel sluggish."

"I am sure you will feel even more so after a few days here with us," he says with a grin. "But I should leave you to get cleaned up. I had the servants put some of my old clothing in your wardrobe. It should be around your size."

I hesitate. "I don't want to sound disrespectful, but wouldn't it be better if I wore something more... well, suited to my status? It wouldn't feel right to go about as royalty when I'm not."

"Nonsense! You have earned it, Ealdred. You saved me and – more importantly – Lady Marianna. My family owes you a great debt."

I bow my head. "Thank you. How is she, by the way? Lady Marianna. Is she well?"

"Actually, she's in perfect health." He beams. "She does not remember a thing from yesterday, though. It is for the best, I suppose. Father really would hate me if he knew that I had allowed myself to be captured, and by a girl no less." He seems to notice the tense look on my face because he adds quickly, "Not that I see anything wrong with it. She was an excellent fighter. Better than I could ever be. And she turned out to be noble in the end, despite everything she put us through."

"Yeah," I mutter.

It all still feels too unreal. I keep expecting to hear her voice at any moment, shouting at me to get downstairs and probably shooting a few uncomplimentary names my way while she's at it.

"Well," Hamish says after a moment, "I had best leave you to it."

He turns toward the door.

"Hamish," I call after him.

He turns back. "Yes?"

"You were going to ask why I sleep under my bed," I begin, and we both chuckle. "It's because I'm afraid."

He looks surprised. "Of what?"

I realize too late that I don't actually want to tell him. But I force myself to continue. "I've never lived in a place where there wasn't constant danger around me, and people who wanted to hurt me. I have a hard time trusting anyone; actually, to rephrase that, I never trust anyone. Even the people that I find out too late that I should have trusted." I pause. "Even here, I feel unsafe. Your father... well, he doesn't seem to like me, does he?"

Hamish puts a reassuring hand on my shoulder. "You will be safe here. My father can be... rough at times – sometimes even hostile – but I firmly believe that inside, he is good at heart. He will not harm you."

I wish that I could believe that, but the king's actions last night proved otherwise. I decide to drop the subject for the present. I see no reason his trust in his father should be destroyed on my account.

"And just so that you know," he adds, "you can trust me. We are friends now, right? I won't let anything happen to you."

It isn't that I don't believe him, but I know that if his father was to take any action against me, Hamish would have no say in the matter.

"Thanks," I say.

He smiles. "Now, get yourself cleaned up."

Then he turns and leaves the room, closing the door behind him.

Once he is gone, I peel off my dirty tunic, and assess my aching ribs. My whole right side is badly bruised, and there is a clotted cut across it. My ribs show just as much as ever and my skin sticks to their shape like glue.

I sit down on the edge of the bed, sinking into the soft mattress. Something clinks against my skin, and I look down to find my amulet resting on my chest. I've gotten used to its weight over the past few weeks, so much as to not notice it anymore. I pick it up in my grimy fingers to examine it. After all of the trials I've been through, it remains unharmed. I am glad. It is precious to me. It and my family seem to be one and the same in my mind. By wearing it, I keep the only link that I have to them close to my heart.

Letting it fall again, I cross to the basin of water on my nightstand, rinsing the dirt from my hands and face, and splashing water on my bruised side. As I turn, I catch sight of the ugly S-shaped scar that was singed into my shoulder many years before. The mark is raised and streaked with the long scars that also cut across my back, induced by the steel barbs at the ends of my masters' whips. I feel sick to the stomach and turn away. Taking the towel, I begin to pat myself dry, glancing into a pane of glass that hangs on the wall before me.

A boy looks back at me. The same scrawny boy with the wide, unnaturally blue eyes, sunken cheeks, deathly pale skin, and a shock of tousled black hair that always reflects back at me. His face is touched with sadness and hardened by fear. He really isn't anything to look at, and would probably be considered ugly by most.

But I feel comfort when I see him. I reach out and press my hand to the glass, putting my forehead to his.

"We'll make it," I whisper to myself. "I promise."

A knock sounds on the door and I start, dropping the towel on the stand beside the basin.

"Who is it?" I call, preparing to draw my sword.

"It's Lesley, lad. The palace physician," croaks the voice of the old man. "We met last night."

I run to the wardrobe and pull on the first tunic that I see. "Come in!" I call.

The door creaks open as he pokes his head into the room. "I was told that you had some injuries that needed attention, and that I was to come and tend to them when you awakened."

I straighten up. "Thank you, sir, but I'm alright. I've dealt with them myself."

"Are you sure? You don't look like the physician sort."

I attempt a smile. "Yes, I'm sure. I've handled far worse before."

"Hmm." He eyes me for a moment, stroking his chin. Then his face lights up. "Can you read, young man?"

I hesitate. "Why do you ask?"

"Well," he croaks with a strange sort of chuckle, "when I'm not attending to my duties as a physician, I also care for the royal library. If you would like, you can come by at any time and read for a while."

It sounds nice, but I am still suspicious. *Did the king put him up to it? If so, what could he possibly be trying to accomplish by it?*

"Thank you," I say out of politeness, making a mental note to stay as far away from the library as possible.

He nods, looking pleased. "Alright then. You'd better hurry up. Your dinner is about to be served."

Lesley exits the room, closing the door behind him. I listen until I can no longer hear his footsteps, and then turn back to the basin. I quickly wash my hair, dry it with the towel, and then change into one of Hamish's old outfits. He was right; they do fit me pretty well. I find some perfume on my nightstand, and put it on as well. Finally, I strap my sword to my side and pull on a pair of black gloves.

Taking a deep breath, I put up all of my guards again, and open the door to my room. I half expect there to be an ambush waiting outside the door, ready to kill me as soon as I exit. But instead, all that I find is a little dark-skinned boy standing against the wall across from the doorway.

"Hello, lad," I say. "Do you know where dinner is taking place?"

The boy nods and beckons for me to follow him. I double-check that all is clear before stepping out into the hall. He leads me down the passageway until the stone walls end, and a polished wooden banister takes their place. A flight of curved stairs laid with purple carpet flow down into the floor below us.

"What's your name?" I ask as he approaches the first step.

He looks back as if to acknowledge that I spoke, but still doesn't answer.

"Hey," I coax, "you don't have to be afraid of me. I'm not going to hurt you."

"He cannot speak," says a bold, feminine voice from behind me.

I turn, my hand immediately going to the hilt of my sword.

At the entrance to another hall directly across from the stairway stands a middle-aged woman whose features, though weary, display the fading beauty of her youth. Her skin is light, marred with wrinkles of age and turmoil, her clothing worn and all different shades of blue, and her blond hair falls over her shoulders in straggles. But the remarkable thing about her is her eyes. A swirl of grey and white, they remind me of the foam of the ocean on a windy day.

Her slender hand rests against the wall, while her other is tucked around her waist. She looks at me with a grim expression.

"A bit on edge, aren't you, stranger?"

"Uh, no." I swallow, quickly relaxing my grip on my sword.

She coughs, pulling her shawl closer around her shoulders. Then she nods to the boy. "We call him Kenet. He came here two years ago, when he was only five years old." She looks at me, her eyes narrowed scrupulously. "He cannot speak because his tongue has been cut out."

I gasp, unable to comprehend for a moment the horror of her words. "What? Why?"

She runs her hand down the wall. "He attempted to steal the king's sword. For that, Leonel had his tongue cut out, and made him his slave for life."

I am repulsed. "That's— that's horrible!" I sputter. "It's just a sword! I'm sure that he could easily get another one."

The woman raises an eyebrow. "I'm afraid he could not. This sword is no ordinary weapon. It is said to have been made by the people of Vaelhyre at the beginning of time, and contains magic that only the king can wield. But King Leonel is not worthy of it."

"I would agree with that," I mutter.

"Keep that attitude and you won't be here for long," she warns. "Anyone who gets in that man's way is destroyed very quickly."

My stomach twists, but I shake it off. "I don't plan to stay long."

She shrugs. "Enjoy your dinner with the brute. It may very well be your last." With that parting remark, she wanders back up the hall whence she came.

I turn back to Kenet. He is still standing on the first step, staring at me with wide, sad brown eyes. I attempt a comforting smile.

"Lead the way, little one," I say softly, resisting the newly fuelled anger that is rising in my chest.

He turns and continues down the stairs, holding onto the railing as if it is the only support that he has in this world.

The room we descend into is large. The floor is carpeted by a burgundy and purple floral velvet rug, which is set over polished wooden boards. The stone walls are hidden by bright and colourful tapestries that depict the most beautiful scenes of kings and queens in the olden days. Across from the stairway is an open door that leads out into a luscious garden. The light which it lets in sparkles off of the crystal

chandelier that hangs from the ceiling.

I try to imagine what it would be like to have grown up in such a place; to be

happy, with everything that I could ever want. To never have been a slave. It is

blissful beyond anything that I can comprehend.

When Kenet reaches the last step, he stops, still clutching the railing, and

points toward the door. I step onto the carpet, which seems too fine to be something

made to walk on, and look out through the door.

Out in the centre of the garden is a round stone table set under the shade of a

large apple tree. Five tall-backed wooden chairs have been set up around it, in

which the royals now sit, enjoying their dinner.

I turn back to the little boy.

"Thank you, Kenet."

He just stares at me, his eyes empty, his face blank. I know that look. It

reflects the way I feel when I am trying to block out pain, but am still hurting

anyways.

I don't know what else to say. I can't tell him that everything is going to be

alright, because I know that it isn't. I can't tell him that I share life experience

because I still have my tongue. And I can't imagine what it would be like to have

my voice silenced forever.

Kenet turns and starts back up the stairs. My opportunity is gone, but I

doubt that it would have done any good anyways.

I turn toward the door, stumbling over the doorstop as I step out onto the stone path. The warm breeze brushes across my face and rustles through my hair. Patches of clouds float across the glorious azure sky as the sun gladly lends its rays to all beneath it. I pass through rows of blue anemones, red carnations, yellow chrysanthemums, and purple limoniums. They blend nicely together, giving the garden a bright and cheery feel. At the table, the royals all burst into laughter over something that was said, and my step falters.

I don't belong here. Even if the king *had* welcomed me without hesitation, I still would not feel right about stepping in like this. Trouble seems to follow me wherever I go, and I don't want to bring it to this family.

I probably would have turned and snuck away if the king had not seen me at that moment. He stands up with a charming smile. "Hello, young man. You are welcome to come and eat with us."

His masquerade makes me feel even sicker than before. But I can fake this just as well as he can. I put on a shy smile and approach the table.

Lady Marianna turns and smiles at me, her eyes bright and very much alive. The only remaining indication of last night is a small gash bordering her hairline. Hamish glances up from his food and gestures for me to sit in the empty chair beside him before digging in again.

I glance at the king, who assents with a nod. I quickly make my way to the empty seat and perch gingerly on the edge of it.

The table before me is laden with the most scrumptious foods and drinks, none of which I recognize. They are like nothing that I have ever made for any of my previous masters, and certainly nothing like anything that I have ever eaten. There are pastries of all sorts, jellies of all colours, and creams that pile flat breads and the tops of brown sweet drinks.

"What is *this*?" demands a sour voice with dulcet tones as sweet as sugar.

I look up from the food. Across from me, sitting right beside the king, is a woman more beautiful than any of the flowers that surround us. Her skin is flawless, her hazel eyes sparkle, and her blonde hair is perfectly put together. She wears a lot of makeup, giving her the appearance of a woman in her late twenties, though something tells me she is older than that. In spite of her beauty, I feel a strong aversion toward her. The reflection of pomp is pooled in her eyes, and she carries herself like every other pampered mistress that I have served in my lifetime.

The king caresses her arm. "Don't fret, my love," he replies in a honeysweet tone. But his face does not reflect the sweetness of his words. "This is the lad that saved the children in the forest last night. He deserves our respect and appreciation."

What a hypocrite!

The queen pouts. "It's lower than a peasant! Couldn't you express appreciation without having it sit at the same table as me?"

The king looks like he wholeheartedly agrees with her, yet opens his mouth to object. But Marianna speaks first.

"Algitha," she scolds, "*he* is a friend. Do not treat him with such disdain!

Don't you see that you have upset him by your words?"

I open my mouth in alarm, and shove a random pastry into it before I do

anything stupid like cry. I grimace as the taste of liver fills my mouth, but I force it

down anyways.

"Ugh!" the queen sniffs. "It eats like a pig!"

"Algitha," the king warns.

I feel like getting up and just running far away from this place. Somewhere

where I won't have to meet any people. Somewhere where I won't have to hear

their hurtful words any longer. But I know that I can't leave just yet. I have an

unfinished mission that I need to accomplish first.

Chapter Thirty-Three

"Ealdred, hold up a moment!" Marianna's voice rings through the evening air behind me as I walk briskly down the lane away from the castle of Gerithold.

Her footsteps beat against the dirt road as she hurries to catch up to me, jerking her bothersome skirts clear of her feet. Behind us, the faint sound of shouting seeps through the closed windows of the stone palace. I shove my hands further into my pockets. The wind is uncharacteristically cold, and somehow finds its way through the many layers of clothing demanded by high society.

I slow my pace, but I keep my eyes trained on the ground. My shoulders sag from the guilt that bears down on my chest.

"Please, I don't want to talk," I say through gritted teeth.

"Listen," she says breathlessly as she falls in stride beside me, "you can't blame yourself for what just happened. The king often blows up over such nonsense."

Anger boils in my veins. "Does he not realize that Hamish is more than just a pawn in his game of power? He's his son, yet he treats him like barely an acquaintance! It isn't right!"

"No, it isn't," she replies with a sad frown. "But in prestigious families, it's quite common for the parent not to pay much attention to their child."

"Yes, but to practically ignore that they exist for fifteen years?" I cry. "It's outrageous! Shouldn't one's family be the highest priority? Doesn't he realize how lucky he is to even *have* a family?"

She rests a hand gently on my shoulder, but I pull away.

"Ealdred, listen," she begins. "I can see why this is angering you, but—"

"Why?" I interrupt, my indignation only increasing. "Why is the king so cruel to him? It's not Hamish's fault he was born the way he was. He is kind, brave, and has a good heart. He's twice the man his father could ever dream of being, and I believe he'll be twice the king too!"

Marianna purses her lips thoughtfully, blonde ringlets falling from the carefully pinned net of braids on her head. "I agree," she begins slowly. "But saying so will not help Hamish's case. He is a half-breed and not very many people can see past that. Unfortunately, that includes his own father, who I've gathered resents him because his hair never changed to golden after his twin brother died."

"That shouldn't make a difference!"

She sighs. "It does to him."

I shake my head. "When I was a child, I would spend long nights staring at the stars through the bars of the cages that I was kept in, imagining what it would be like to be royalty. I always thought that they were the happiest people in the world. They have everything! And yet now that I've gotten a chance to observe them, I see that they live in misery."

"You are right. By rights, we should be happy. And yet power brings enemies; enemies masquerading as friends. A person cannot have peace if they are in constant fear of those around them. Fear drives people to do terrible things."

"Sage words."

She gives a small smile. "My father says that I have a keen intuition that allows me to sense a person's character just by looking at them."

"Really? What do you sense about me?"

She hesitates. "You're hard to figure out, actually. But from what I've seen, you and Hamish aren't all that different from each other. I will not liken his suffering to yours, but he too has been alone his whole life, without any true friends to stand by his side. As I read in you, he too is desperate to prove himself in hopes that one day someone will come to love him for who he is inside."

A question pops in my head, and I ask it without thinking. "What about you? Do you love him?"

She stops walking and I stop too, turning to face her. Her cheeks have gone strangely pink and her mouth is turned down in a confused frown.

"I'm sorry," I blurt. "It's not my business."

"Oh, it's alright." She pauses, inhaling deeply. When she speaks again, her answer comes rather abruptly. "Well, we are engaged, aren't we? It really doesn't matter how we feel about it. Don't take me wrong. I think he's a very good young man, and I could not hope for more in a husband. The fact that he is a half-breed never once bothered me. But—" she hesitates. "But if I wasn't engaged to him, I would never have considered marrying him at all."

"Sounds... complicated."

She nods, heaving a sigh. "It *is* complicated. I was engaged to him at birth, but in the fourteen years of my life, I did not meet him until his return from Lavylli. He is certainly admirable, and I will be happy, whatever happens. But," she pauses, looking dreamily into the sky, "I crave independence. Adventure! If I had a choice of what to do with my own life, I'd follow the rivers, chase the wind to the corners of Theara, climb the mountains to their highest peaks, and touch the sky itself!"

"Of course," she adds gloomily, "most girls of my status are desperate to marry a prince, half-breed or not. For the wealth and the honour it would bring their families, you know. Society expects us to be content to settle down and get married and spend our lives looking after husbands and households and children. I don't see myself being content with that. I need adventure, even though I now know that I don't know what to do with myself when it *is* given to me."

I smile faintly, the thought of Bellator coming to mind. She knew exactly what to do with herself when an adventure presented itself. I am certain that she would create her own adventures the moment she found life too boring.

"What are you smiling at?" Marianna asks, bringing me back to the present.

"Oh," I say casually, keeping in mind that she has forgotten Bellator and the escapades that came with her. "Just a girl I used to know. She was a lot like you. Only, tougher." That's an understatement. "A lot tougher."

An odd grin plays at the corner of her lips. "You mean the Crimson Shadow?"

I stare at her. "You remember?"

She laughs. "Of course I do. I only said that I didn't because I wasn't sure what story you and Hamish had been spreading. I didn't want to get either of you into any more trouble than you were already in."

"Does Hamish know that you remember?"

"Not yet. I wanted to leave him thinking that I didn't remember his reckless attempts to protect me for a while longer before I have to thank him for it."

I can't help but smile at this.

"I've just been dying to know what happened after I was knocked out," she adds with sudden eagerness. "The outlaw was holding onto the snake's head, and then a shower of rocks hit me, and that's all that I remember. What happened to her? She was still there when I was knocked out and now she isn't. Did she manage to get what she came for?"

I recount to her everything that she missed, up to when Hamish asked his father for me to stay with them in Gerithold for a while. I omit the part were Leonel tried to capture me, as well as the events closely surrounding it. When I am finished, she scowls at the ground.

"I wish that one of you had thought to untie me so I could've fought too. Then I wouldn't have been uselessly standing there, just asking to get hurt."

I shrug, folding my arms on my chest to shield from the chilly breeze. Then I realize that the breeze isn't really all that cold, and that the icy feeling inside of me is what I am trying to shield myself from. "I'm not sure that any of us were thinking straight."

"I'm sorry," she says quickly. "I see that it's a painful subject for you."

"What? No..."

"I know that look. It's like the one that my father gets when he is talking about my mother. She... left us. A few years ago. He still misses her deeply."

"Yeah, but that's different," I say, startled. "Bellator was nothing like that to me. We actually hated each other."

"That's not what I meant," she replies softly. "And I don't think that you hated each other, either. I know it sounds crazy to say this, considering how horrible she was to us, but I really did admire her now that it's over. She was strong, driven, and fought for what she wanted. How many people do you see that are like that? Who have that much power at their command?" She gazes thoughtfully into the sky again. "Bellator was the picture of everything that I have always dreamed of being, but know that I can never become. Without the cruelty, that is. But even when she was cruel, it was all an act. She never did us any harm. And though she did tie us up and force us into that horrible place, I don't think she expected anything to happen to us. She was just ensuring that his majesty's men didn't trap her inside." She looks back at me. "What I am getting at is this: you two

may have argued a lot, and she may have treated you like a slave, but she had to

have grown on you somehow, and you on her. She died for you, after all. And I can

see that you are sad, and that you have an empty place inside now that she's gone."

Her words are so simple, and yet they perfectly describe the unexplainable

feeling that rises in my throat every time that I think about Bellator. Could it be

that somehow, I had actually started to care about her?

"It sounds like they're done shouting now," Marianna says, and I notice that

the air has grown quiet. "We should probably get back before it grows dark. Will

you return with me, or are you planning to leave for good?"

I pause, thinking it over. The only thing in my mind when I stormed out was

that I had to leave before I said something to King Leonel that I would later regret.

I feel an unusually fierce desire to protect Hamish, but I also know that my

prolonged stay may only serve to hurt him.

It's only for a little while longer. Where else can I go?

"I will return, for now," I reply heavily.

We turn and start back toward the courtyard outside of the palace. As we

approach, I hear low voices coming from behind the wall. I gesture for Marianna to

quiet her walking. Together, we creep closer to listen. But as we near the wall, we

both begin to regret coming to eavesdrop.

The tones belong to none other than Hamish. His voice is shaky, and I realize

with a start that he is crying.

"—no matter what I do or say, he always finds something to shout at me about," he is saying. "Since I arrived, he has not said a civil word to me. Nothing that I do pleases him."

"I know," a woman's voice replies wearily. "He's a very selfish man. But he has chosen it for himself."

I recognize this voice too, surprisingly. It is the same guarded, unfeeling voice of the woman I met in the hall with Kenet.

"Why?" Hamish sputters. "Why does he hate me so much? I need to understand. How can I prove myself to him?"

She sighs. "Don't bother with him. He's engulfed by his own pride and there is nothing that anyone can do to change him. All that you can do is focus on being the good man that you want to be."

"But it is hard! I've been away for three years! Three years, Nerienda, and he acted like I had been gone a minute! He barely said two words to me, and since then he has treated me like a failure. A disgrace! As if I live only to disappoint him!"

"He has no right to be disappointed in you. Believe me, Hamish, you'll be a much better king than he could ever be."

"Do not say that," Hamish says uncomfortably.

"But it's true. You are kind, something he hasn't been in a very long time. Yet still you listen to his criticism."

I can hear a weak smile in his voice as he replies, "Well, he is my father. I do not really have a choice in the matter, do I?"

"Then there's no use crying about it, is there? Dry your eyes and I'll see if I can get you one of those cream puffs that you like so much from the scullery."

"I am not a child anymore," Hamish says, but he sounds more cheerful now.

"Nonsense. You'll always be my little prince, even if you live to be a hundred and fifty."

That coaxes a quiet chuckle out of him, and their footsteps start toward the palace.

I glance at Marianna, whose mood has been dampened. Sympathy is etched into her face.

"Who is this Nerienda?" I whisper once I'm certain they have gone.

"She's his nurse," Marianna explains. "That is, she *was* his nurse, when he was much younger. They've formed a bond, though. You see, the day Hamish lost his brother, he also lost his mother. She passed away while giving birth to them. Nerienda had recently lost her own child, so she was brought in to nurse him. Eventually, she became a mother figure to him. But the king would rather Hamish not be so attached to a servant, so I have gathered, and Hamish thinks it may be one of the reasons he was sent to study in Lavylli for the past three years. He believes his father was trying to break their bond, trying to force Hamish to 'grow up'." She heaves an indignant sigh. "The thing is, he is already more grown up than any fifteen year old has a right to be."

"I've noticed," I say, forgetting that I myself am fifteen.

There is a long veil of silence as Marianna delves deep into her thoughts again.

"Oh dear," she says suddenly, turning her gaze to the dusky sky. "It's getting dark quickly. We should return."

We hurry toward the gateway and find Jambeau in the process of closing the front gate.

"You're both late," he says with a frown. "My lady, the queen has been looking for you for quite some time now."

"We're deeply sorry," Marianna says with a polite curtsey, but there's a look of annoyance behind her smile.

"Well, get inside then, the both of you," he says, and the gates creak as he swings them shut.

I take note of her quiet irritation. "Do you dislike Jambeau?" I ask as we walk toward the main doorway.

She shrugs. "I don't *dislike* him. There is just something about him that I don't particularly *like*. It's probably just me. He is, after all, the closest thing to a friend that Hamish has."

"Hmm," I say. "Bellator also had misgivings about him. But he seems alright to me so far."

"He is. He's very kind." She hesitates. "It's probably his missing hand that throws me off. No one really knows where he lost it... But speaking of Bellator, that reminds me; are you planning on going back to Arnon to finish recovering the arrow?"

"Yes."

"Oh, good!" And with a delighted bounce to her step, she skips the rest of the way inside.

I don't have the heart to tell her that this time, I intend to go alone.

Chapter Thirty-Four

"You want to go back?" Hamish exclaims incredulously.

"Shh!" I hiss, glancing across the lawn from beneath the shade of the apple tree under which we are crouched.

Nerienda is barefoot in the grass, bent over a patch of carnations growing along one side of the garden door. We haven't spoken since our encounter on the stairway, but after hearing her comfort Hamish following his fight with his father, my respect for her has deepened.

Hamish lowers his tone. "But why leave so soon? Do you not like it here?"

"Oh, of course I do," I reply quietly. "I have been treated better here in the past three days than I have been in my whole life. But you don't understand. I have to finish what I started. And tonight is my last chance to get into the castle for a month."

His eyes are alert with interest. "Why is it so important to you? You can trust me, you know."

I glance over the lawn again to make sure that no one is listening. Then I lower my voice even more. "Have you heard of Zeldek?"

He frowns. "The mythical master of fire and darkness, right? The traitor."

"Yes, that's him. Well, he actually exists. He lives in a fortress in the far north."

Hamish barely bats an eyelid. "The stories never did tell how he died."

I pull off my glove and show him the mark on my palm. "He kidnapped me, and gave me this. Bellator helped me escape. We were after the Arrow of Arnon, which is supposed to contain enough power to keep Zeldek from destroying the world. I made a promise to her that I would recover it, and I will do anything in my power to keep that promise."

He stares at my burn, horrified. "Once you have the arrow, how do you plan to stop him? Will you fight him?"

"Well," I gulp. I'd never really thought of what I would do after breaking the spell on the arrow. "Honestly, I don't know. I'd never be strong enough to fight Zeldek alone. Besides, I'm not really the fighting type. I suppose I'll find someone else who can wield the arrow if it comes to it. But first, I have to break the spell."

"What about me?" he says. "I can come with you, if you will have me."

"I'm not putting you in danger like that again."

"You would not be putting me in danger," he says with a smile. "I would be putting myself in danger."

I shake my head. "It's too risky."

He's not persuaded. "You might have escaped the wolf, but that snake is still lurking around there. If the Crimson Shadow could not defeat it, neither can you. You will need help."

He has a point.

"But if you come it'll eat both of us," I point out.

"Look, we do not have to go alone. I shall talk Jambeau into coming with us. He would commit murder for me if I told him to."

"Oh? So that's how it is, is it?"

The disembodied voice comes from the tree above us, and we both look up Jambeau is sitting on a thick bough, mostly concealed from view by a thick array of emerald leaves and ruby apples. He gives us an impish grin, and pulls an apple from a branch above him, taking a slurping bite.

"Yes, you would," Hamish shoots back good-naturedly. "Pass down two of those red ones, would you?"

Jambeau shakes his head disapprovingly, but plucks two more apples from the tree and tosses them down to us. I catch mine, but Hamish's bounces off of his forehead and rolls onto the ground. He bends down to retrieve it.

Jambeau scrambles off of the branch, using his hook as an anchor, and scurries down the trunk of the tree. At the bottom, he turns to us, his humour fading.

"Hamish," he says slowly, "I only heard bits and pieces of your conversation, but I don't like what you are planning. Whatever reason you have, I don't think it wise for either of you to go back there. The two of you and the Lady Marianna almost died last time. And from what I've heard, Ealdred, your master did die."

He seems oblivious as to whom my 'master' was and I realize that Hamish must not have told him the full truth.

"Besides," he continues, "what would your father say about you repeatedly endangering yourself like this?"

"Fine," Hamish says, dusting off his apple. "I will not go if you insist. You just have to go along with Ealdred and keep him from getting himself killed."

Jambeau doesn't look convinced. "Hamish, that place isn't safe. I'm not going to turn a blind eye to anyone who wants to go back there; not even at the behest of the crowned prince."

Hamish frowns, his mouth full of apple now. "Some friend you are."

"I *am* your friend," Jambeau continues calmly, "and for that reason, I don't want to see you hurt again. What's more, I am a knight of the realm and the captain of the guard in Gerithold. I mustn't abuse my authority. You know that I can't risk losing my position. I've worked too hard and given up too much."

There is a sense of loss in his tone that is reflected deeply in his eyes.

Hamish grows more sympathetic. "I know," he says, "but there is a lot at stake here. All you need to do is get him in there without anyone finding out. I am sure that he knows what to do from there."

I try to look as if I do, but I don't. In fact, now I don't even have the prophecy to go by. Besides that, there is a growing unease in the back of my mind regarding

Jambeau. True, he defended me against Leonel that first night when I met them, but Bellator had been enraged at the mere mention of his name. She had been right about Leonel. Could it be that she is also right about Jambeau?

Jambeau frowns. "I'll think about it. For now, why don't the two of you stop consorting and go and do something less suspicious. Perhaps show Ealdred the armoury or something."

Hamish brightens up, throwing away his apple core. "Good idea!"

I smile in gratitude, and hurry after him as he runs toward the palace. As I approach the door, I slow down. Norienda is still bent over her flowers, running her hands through the dirt around their roots. She glances up as I pass by and I stop. I look down at my apple, which I'd been turning over in my hands while Jambeau and Hamish were arguing, and hold it out to her.

"What's this?" she asks, a mixture of annoyance and confusion on her face.

"For you," I stammer. "I- well, I just thought you might want it."

She pulls her hands out of the dirt and wipes her hair out of her face, leaving a streak of dirt across her forehead. There is a slight tremor to her hand as she takes the fruit from me.

"Thank you," she mumbles, setting the apple on the ground beside her. Then she buries her hands in the rich earth once more.

Feeling a bit stupid, I turn and enter the palace. Hamish leads me down a flight of winding stairs into the vaults under the palace. He pushes open a door that is streaked with dust and cobwebs and lifts an already lit torch from the wall.

I take a few steps into the room and then turn in a circle, my breath leaving my lungs in amazement. The walls are lined with swords, spears, axes, maces, bows, quivers of arrows – any and every kind of weapon that you could imagine. Suits of armour glisten along the walls as the fire dances from the torch in Hamish's hand.

But he doesn't seem to notice any of it. Instead, he walks toward a stone table set in the centre of the room. I follow him, marvelling at the different shields and crests. There is something about it all that both thrills and horrifies me at the same time.

On the table, set on a white and gold embroidered cloth, is a sword. It is indeed stunning. The blade shines as if it were made of the purest silver. Two poised, golden dragons with eyes of pearl make up the cross guard, and a blue sapphire sits between them. White velvet is bound around the grip, held in place by bands of gold studded with tiny sapphires, and the pommel is a small sapphire with waves of golden fire encasing it.

"This is Stormcrest," Hamish announces with pride, "the sword of the kings of Valamette."

I whistle. So this is the sword that Kenet tried to steal. I understand now why he wanted it.

"It is said to have been enchanted by the Vaelhyreans long ago and holds power that only the king of Valamette himself can wield."

"Is that true?" I ask.

He shrugs. "Father says that when he is holding it, the blade glows a faint blue and feels as light as a feather in his hands. If anyone else tries to wield it, it will grow so heavy that they will be unable to bear its weight. As for the power that the myths claim it holds, nothing of the sort has been documented for centuries."

"Does it glow for you yet?"

He shakes his head. "My father says that I am unworthy of it. I must make myself into a king before I will be able to wield it." His tone is light, but there is doubt in eyes as he gazes wistfully at the sword.

"Don't worry," I assure him. "It will glow for you soon."

He shrugs, clasping his hands behind his back, and changes the subject. "He will agree, you know. Jambeau, I mean. He is just cautious. After all that he has sacrificed, I would be too."

I want to ask what he means, but I don't want to pry. Instead, I ask, "Why didn't you tell him about Bellator?"

Hamish turns away from the sword. "Because, it would have hurt him terribly to know that she's dead."

"*Hurt* him? I thought they were enemies."

He shakes his head. "Oh no. From what I have gathered, they actually used to be friends. But he refuses to talk about it, even with me."

I recall her mentioning that she had once had a friend, and that he had betrayed her. I wonder if that friend had been Jambeau.

The air resonates with deep, thoughtful silence for a time. Then Hamish starts toward the door.

"Come on," he says. "Perhaps we will have time for a ride before dinner."

We retrieved Majax and Nimro from the woods the day after I came, and now they are enjoying the luxuries of the palace stables. Nimro seems to have taken a liking to Hamish already, and I've decided to leave him with the prince when I go.

I follow Hamish out of the armoury and we turn back toward the stairway leading up to the main level. Out of nowhere, a great weight falls on my chest and I vault forward. My amulet falls from my tunic, suddenly gaining a mind of its own, and jerks me in the opposite direction. I cry out, groping for a place in the wall to hold onto and stop myself, but it overpowers any strength that I possess. I am forced to follow its lead.

"Ealdred!" Hamish calls after me. "Where on earth are you going?"

Shock renders me speechless as my amulet drags me away.

I hear his footsteps charge after me, but the amulet is forcing me to run faster than I normally would ever have been able to. I reach out and grasp the pendant in my hand, pulling on it with all of my might, trying to halt it. It doesn't work. Thinking quickly, I grab the chain on which it hangs from the back of my neck and try to jerk it off. But the chain is twisted up to my throat and won't fit over my head.

A flight of stairs drops in the darkness beneath my feet, and I would have tumbled down them had not the amulet been holding me up. At the bottom of the stairs, my feet splash through a puddle on the floor. The air has grown musty, and the walls that I grab onto are slimy with mould.

"Ealdred!" Hamish calls from somewhere behind me.

I know it's no use even trying to answer. I am already further underground than I am sure is allowed for someone of my status.

At last, the medallion seems to reach its destination. It lurches to a stop before a set of double doors. They swing open before me, and the amulet throws me forward. I stumble into a large room and the pendant drops to my chest with a thud. I blink, looking around.

A massive cavern opens up before me, lit by a stream of light coming from an opening in the ceiling somewhere far above. Stone monuments that look disturbingly like coffins are set in even rows all throughout the room and the air is scented by some kind of putrid spice. I shudder as I realize the purpose of the hall.

It is a tomb.

I want to turn and leave at once, but something holds me back. A voice as quiet as the wind whispers through the air, echoing in the corners of the hall, and the hair on my neck stands on end. The words are muddled together, but from what I can tell, it's some kind of chant.

I step cautiously toward the nearest row of coffins, which is only half finished. They are newer and are less covered in dust and cobwebs than the other rows. At the end of the line is a large, elegant coffin that is different from the rest. It is clearly styled with the intricacy that characterizes Lavyllian craftsmanship. A bouquet of faded flowers has been set on top of it and most of the spider webs have been cleared away. I lean closer to see the name carved into the top of the stone covering. It reads:

QUEEN ARROSA SOLANGE-GRYPHEM

BEAUTIFUL ROSE, ANGEL OF THE EARTH

BELOVED WIFE AND MOTHER

Sadness claws through my present state of fear. This must be the resting place of Hamish's mother. I reach out and wipe a bit of gathering dust from the plaque with her name on it. A spider the size of my hand scuttles out from the flowers, and I jerk away with a shudder.

The whispering swells, as if reproving me, and I can make out a word here and there.

"Electus... Gryphem..." it hisses. "Electus... Lerroa..."

I take a step back from the dead queen's coffin and notice something beside it that I hadn't seen before. A little coffin is set beside Queen Arrosa's, made for a child. It is a plain, simple stone box with no designs. It is untidy and streaked with cobwebs, as if no one has bothered to tend to it for a long time.

I feel compelled to step toward it, so I do. As I approach, the voice grows still louder until it is a howling in my ears, as if coming from the coffin itself. I see a name roughly carved into the stone and I reach out a shaky hand to wipe away the dust. I feel my heart rising to my throat. When I see the name, I drop to my knees and stare at it, my whole body going numb.

"Ealdred!" Hamish cries, bursting into the room. "What has gotten into you? This is a tomb!"

"Whose grave is this?" I ask, not able to look at him.

I hear his footsteps approaching cautiously behind me. "That is the grave of my older twin brother." He pauses. "Why? What is wrong?"

Everything seems to click at once and I simultaneously understand and don't understand more than I could ever imagine. I finally allow myself to look up at him, trying to keep the alarm from showing on my face.

"Oh, nothing," I say casually. "My- er, my amulet brought me here. I really can't explain how." I force myself to stand up. "I am feeling very ill. I think that I should rest for the duration of the afternoon."

He nods, glancing warily at the hall around us. "Yes, I think you should. Let us get out of here, shall we?"

I follow him toward the door, trying to find my way through the maze of questions in my mind that's making it difficult to breathe.

As we pass through the doorway, the eerie voice follows me. This time the words ring clearly in my head, repeating over and over the name on the grave of Hamish's stillborn brother who had withheld from him his birthright of golden hair.

"ELROY ELECTUS LERROA GRYPHEM!"

Chapter Thirty-Five

I enter the damp cool of the palace and hurry toward my chamber, my mind spinning. Hamish parted ways with me after seeing me safely to the main level and I cut through the garden instead of going around through the halls. Nerienda was no longer there, but the apple I'd given her lay abandoned in the dirt.

I climb the stairs wearily and continue down the hall toward my room. The faint sound of shouting comes to me from up the hall, only growing louder as I draw nearer to my chambers. When I reach the door to my apartment, I find it closed. The shouting is coming from behind it.

I put my ear next to the crack in the door and listen. There are two voices railing at each other from inside, one of which I instantly recognize as King Leonel's. Uncontrollable anger washes through me and I want to know what he is doing in my room.

"He's a runaway half-breed slave," the king is saying. "That's the end of it!"

"Is it?" The second voice belongs to Nerienda. "No, I know you too well. You're hiding something, and you will tell me what it is!"

"I don't have to tell you anything!" the king bellows. "Another word and I will silence you, this time for good!"

Nerienda laughs coldly. "You think that you can silence me, son of Leonard? You have repaid me ill after a lifetime in your service, and I am sick of it! I should never have—"

"Silence, woman!"

"You dare—"

There is a loud crash followed by a scream.

I throw open the door, letting it slam into the wall. "Stop it!" I shout at the top of my lungs, releasing all of my anger with it.

The mirror on the wall shatters, and both the king and Nerienda stare at me, astonished. My room has been ransacked. The wardrobe is wide open, and my things are scattered all over the floor. The blankets have been pulled off of my bed, and my sword is lying unsheathed on the bare mattress. The drawers of the nightstand are pulled open, and the basin, evidently hurled by the king, lies in pieces at Nerienda's still bare feet.

The king takes a frantic step toward me, his eyes wide. "How much of that did you hear?" he demands.

"It doesn't matter!" I spit. "I don't care what your status is, your highness, but you have no right to treat her like that!"

He grabs my shoulders and gives me a violent shake. "How much did you hear?" he shouts in my face.

I look him in the eye and revulsion is all I can feel. "Only the last few words."

His jaw relaxes. "Very good. And no one will hear of this, will they, Ealdred?"

I shake my head, my blood boiling.

"Excellent." He throws me toward the broken pottery. "I think there's a mess for you to clean, slave."

I stumble to the floor at Nerienda's feet and the king strides out of the room. Gingerly, I pick myself up from the sharp pieces, relieved to find that I wasn't cut by any of them. I dust off my sleeves and turn to Nerienda.

"Are you alright?" I ask.

Teeth clenched, she pulls the hem of her skirt aside. Blood streams from her foot where a thick shard protrudes from the top of it.

"I'll be fine," she growls.

I offer her my arm. "Here, lean on me. I'll take you to Lesley."

She nods distractedly, taking my hand. Her skin is cold and clammy to the touch. Despite her steady composure, she is trembling uncontrollably. I help her pick her way through the shards, supporting her as we walk toward the door.

"You're going to have to tell me where to go," I say.

"Turn right," she directs, and we turn up the hall away from the stairway.

It is slow going, but I allow her to take her time. She leaves a trail of bloody footprints on the floor behind us. At the end of the hall is a closed door, and beside it, a narrow stairway that ascends upward. Nerienda motions to the door and I help

her to it. She lets go of me, lifts the latch, and pushes the door open.

Inside, Lesley looks up from a bottle of yellow liquid he is examining.

"My dear girl!" he exclaims when he sees her. "What has happened?"

She falls into his embrace, tears falling down her cheeks. "Oh, father," she

sobs.

"Did he hurt you again?" he asks, stroking her hair.

"Has he ever stopped?"

Guessing that I'm not wanted here anymore, I back out of the room, closing

the door softly behind me. I turn down the hall, only to stop abruptly.

"It's time for you to leave," the king snarls, looming over me. His eyes are

alight with the same wild fury that seems to have taken hold of his golden hair,

which flies about his head in an unkempt fashion so contrary to his usual majestic

array.

"Why?"

"You interfere in things that are none of your business, strutting about as if

you own the place! I've had enough of it! If you don't leave at once, I will make you

leave!"

"Why do you hate me so much?" I demand, anger welling up inside of me

again. "I never did anything to you!"

"Enough!" He is so close now that his hot breath hits my face. "You will

leave, or I will have your head!"

"Go ahead and try!" I hiss right back. "Just remember, Zeldek wants me alive."

He looks down at me for a moment and then steps away. "We'll see," he says, and turning on his heel, he strides away.

Once he has disappeared around the corner, I lean back against the wall beside Lesley's door.

Don't worry. I'll be leaving tonight anyways.

The door opens and Nerienda exits the room. Her foot is bandaged now and she glances at me as she passes by. But she quickly turns away.

A moment later, Lesley comes into the hall.

He stops when he sees me and tilts his head to the side. "What is it, lad?"

I glance up at him. "Nothing."

"You want to talk about your nothing?"

I shrug.

"Well, I'm about to go to the library for the afternoon. Would you like to join me?"

I shrug again.

"Come on then."

He turns and starts up the steps. After a moment's hesitation, I start after him. The stairs wind in a narrow spiral upward as we ascend into a tower.

Lesley glances back at me and chuckles. "You like reading, do you?"

My friend Kellagh comes to mind, and I shudder. "It's not something I do often."

"Ah yes, the half-breed thing. Well, you're lucky to have come here. This is the only place in all of Theara that is accepting of your kind. Mostly because our future king is one."

"I have heard that many of you aren't so keen on that," I mutter, recalling the king's animosity toward his own son.

"It'll be a change, that's for sure," he muses. "But Hamish is a good and wise young man, whatever his flaws may be. He will serve the kingdom well." Under his breath, he adds, "Anything is better than the way his father is running the place."

He pauses at a door at the top of the stairs, and I hear the lock grind open. The door swings on its hinges and we enter.

The library is nothing like the one where Kellagh taught me to read. Though that one was much grander, this one is quaint and homey, and every space is stuffed with books. I am greeted by the scent of wood and old parchment. Iron candelabrums dripping with used wax stand all around the room, and dust layers everything.

Lesley closes the door behind us and lights a few candles. Then he sits down at a desk in the centre of the room and leans back in his chair.

"Hamish used to come here and entertain me often when he was younger," he says with a weary smile. "The last couple of years have been lonely with him gone, and since his return, he hasn't had time to come up here. The Lady Marianna has been kind enough to visit me in the short time that she has been staying with us. Even with such a wealth of books, an old man can get tired with no one to share them with."

"Ah," I say, trying to look interested. But my thoughts are elsewhere.

He seems to guess this. "Something is troubling you, isn't it?"

I nod.

"Can an old man help you sort things out? Or is it something you need to figure out for yourself?"

I look up at him. "Did you ever see Hamish's older twin brother?"

His eyebrows arch, and he watches me carefully. "Why do you ask?"

I swallow. This isn't going to be easy. "I- need to know."

"I was the one who pronounced him dead."

"But—" My throat is dry, and it is hard to get the words out. "But he *was* dead, wasn't he?"

"Very much so." He sounds almost offended. "What on earth are you getting at?"

"I think—" My voice breaks off, and I try again. "I think that—" I put my face in my hands.

Lesley leaps suddenly from his chair. "Where did you get that?"

I look up at him, startled. He points at my chest. My amulet has fallen out of my shirt again.

"I've always had it," I say, sliding it back under my tunic.

But Lesley looks as if he has seen a ghost.

"Lesley," I swallow. "Lesley, am I who I think I am?"

Before he can answer, the door swings open, crashing into the bookshelf behind it. Jambeau enters the room with two armed guards behind him. I spring to my feet, clenching my fists.

"You're going to have to come with us, Ealdred," Jambeau says uneasily.

"Why?" The word barely exits my throat.

"The king has ordered your arrest. You have been accused of being a sorcerer and conspiring against him and his family."

My mouth goes dry. "I didn't. You know I haven't."

He shakes his head sadly. "I don't like this either, but I have to take you in for questioning. Just pray to the Vaelhyreans of old that he will find no fault in you."

"He will," I say, not moving.

Jambeau looks worried. "You're not a sorcerer, are you?"

I pause, and then nod. "I was born with the ability to use magic."

His face grows even more downcast. "Then I'm afraid that there is nothing that can be done to save you."

He gestures for the guards to take me. They seize my arms, clapping an iron cuff around each wrist. Jambeau leads the way out of the tower as the guards push me toward the door.

"Ealdred!" Lesley calls.

I look over my shoulder.

He sighs wearily. "I fear you may be correct."

Chapter Thirty-Six

King Leonel is already present when I am dragged into the room in which I will inevitably be interrogated. Given the number of staircases we descended to get here, I know that I am once more deep within the vaults beneath the palace. The room is twice as long as it is wide and is outfitted with the devices required for certain forms of interrogation. Shackles and large metal yokes stained with what I pray is rust dangle from the ceiling and walls. But from the dark splatters on the uneven stone floor below, I know that an interrogation or two must have gone rather badly.

The king's deep blue eyes are indifferent as they pass over me, and a catlike smile curls his lips. The frigid hollow that has carved itself in my chest since I was arrested grows still more at the sight of him. It is hard to resist the urge to spit on his feet when I am thrown to my knees before him.

I glare up at him, a defiant tilt to my chin. A challenge plays in his eyes as he stares back.

"Chain him to the wall," he orders, not breaking his gaze for a moment.

"But sire," Jambeau says, "he's just a boy! I believe that he will cooperate—"

"Do it!"

The guards pick me up again by the arms and drag me to the back of the room, where two shackles hang from the wall. I look to Jambeau for help as they force my already cuffed wrists against the rough surface of the wall, but he looks away. We both know that he can't help me even if he wanted to.

Shackles are clapped onto my wrists, and the metal is cold against my skin. My shoulders are pressed against the wall by the weight of the chains, and when the guards release me, I have to keep myself from falling forward, twisting my arms back still more.

The guards leave the room upon command, and the door clangs shut behind them. Jambeau melts against the wall as the king comes to stand in front of me.

"Ealdred, you injure me," he says, shaking his head with a feigned look of bewilderment. "You have betrayed my trust. Even worse, you have betrayed the trust that my son put in you. At his request, I allowed you, a runaway slave, to invade my family home, though it was against my better judgement. And what have you done to repay such kindness? You've turned around and stabbed us in the back!"

"What are you talking about?" I grunt. "I have done nothing!"

"Keep your lies to yourself, half-breed! I am not blind. The night you arrived, a blast of light was seen spiralling into the sky nearby. Moments later, the surrounding landscape was enveloped in blue mist that sunk into the ground. I do not know what kind of curse you have cast on us, but your insistence on lagging behind that evening has forced me to conclude that *you* are the sorcerer behind it. Even worse, I have proof that today you, in a fit of anger, blew out a mirror that I was standing by. Will you deny this action?"

"I see that your mind is already made up," I say bitterly. "There is no poin—"

"Do you deny it?"

"You know that I can't!"

He nods, satisfied. "It has also come to my attention that you consorted with an outlawed person known as the Crimson Shadow."

"The Crimson Shadow?" Jambeau echoes, his eyes widening.

"Indeed," the king says. "This was found in his room."

He draws Bellator's sword and throws it down at my feet. The air rings with the sound.

Jambeau stares at it. "Where did you get that?"

I glare at the sword.

"Answer him," the king warns, raising his hand to smite me.

"It was a gift, to keep until I got a sword of my own," I say gruffly. "And I wasn't trying to hide it! I had it at my side for all to see when you invited me to stay with you."

"It was dark and the Lady Marianna was injured!" the king replies. "None of us were looking at the design of your sword!"

"When did you have dealings with the likes of her?" Jambeau asks, his tone not quite matching the hostility of his words.

"We travelled together for a time." I hesitate, the memory of her death still too fresh in my mind. "Up until she died."

Jambeau inhales sharply. "She's dead?"

I nod. "She died saving my life."

All pretence of hostility is gone. He takes a deep, shuddering breath and presses his hand over his gaping mouth. His eyes well with tears and his gaze darts around, looking for a safe resting place.

"This is no time for past sentiment, captain," the king snaps.

"She's dead," Jambeau says, his voice raw with emotion. "She's—"

"Why should you care? I thought you lost all feelings for her when you abandoned her for this position years ago!"

Jambeau flinches. "She wasn't supposed to die," he whispers. "She was supposed to come back. I was going to—"

"She never would have come back and you know it!" the king interrupts. "She allowed her heart to be darkened by her bloodlust and it destroyed everything good that had ever been inside of her. You should be glad that you left her when you did."

"Who are you to talk about evil?" I explode, my sorrow channelling into rage. "You who have already sold your soul to Zeldek and will stop at nothing to do his every bidding!"

Both the king and Jambeau stare at me.

"Silence, boy!" the king snaps, blanching. "You don't know what you're saying!"

But I won't be silent. I want him to know exactly how I feel about him. "I'd be willing to bet my life that I'll be on my way back to Gaiztoak in the morning."

King Leonel's face reddens and he balls his fists. "Leave us," he hisses to Jambeau, his voice trembling with fury.

Jambeau is too overwhelmed to care and quickly does as he is told. As soon as the door is closed behind him, the king turns on me and slams my shoulders into the wall

"You are smarter than you look, half-breed!" he growls. "Yes, Zeldek wants you back! He wants your allegiance, and in the end, he will have it. Tomorrow morning, I will send you back to him under the pretence of having you sent to the mines of Lavylli. Then you'll be out of my life forever!"

I stare back at him, hoping that he can see his own rage reflected in my eyes. "I don't know what I did to you to make you hate me so much!" I pause, and then force out the word, "Father."

He glares down at me, his eyes glazed with deep hatred. "Do not call me that. I have no son but Hamish!"

I nod, pushing back the bitterness that sours my mind and the pain that fills my heart. "Yes, Hamish. My brother."

His glare turns to a cruel sneer. "How did you figure it out?"

"I saw my grave."

Confusion flickers across his face. "But how did you know of your true name?"

"Zeldek told me. He also told me that my father abandoned me as a baby. I worked everything out from there." I take a deep breath. "That's why nothing is working out for Hamish, isn't it? Why his hair isn't golden? Why the sword won't glow for him?"

"You were supposed to die! All of that was supposed to transfer from you to him!"

"What happened, then? If I was meant for the throne, I would have the golden hair!"

"You did, once," he says, and his gaze drifts off as he stares into a past only he can see. "I see that you are confused. I'd be surprised if you weren't. Perhaps it would be best for both of us if I sated your curiosity."

I don't object.

"Its funny how life finds a way to foreshadow things yet to come," he begins with a bitter laugh. "The day you were born was bitingly cold. Winter had come a few weeks early that year, and so had you. You were so tiny, so sickly. You could barely move or make a sound other than a pitiful squeak. Your mother was hopeful, of course, but I knew that you wouldn't last the night. She told me that you were to be named Elroy, for you were 'the chosen king'!" He snorts, and revulsion sharpens his words like whetstone does a blade. "But my Master had other plans. He was convinced that you would survive, and that you would be a danger. He told me what to do, and I did as he commanded. While no one was looking, I gave you a potion that had been given to me by my master. The potion stopped your heart long enough for that oaf Lesley to pronounce you dead, and even your mother was convinced. She fell ill in her grief, and by the time Hamish came along, she'd lost her will to live."

His gaze passes over me, landing on the amulet, which glints out from behind the folds of my tunic. He takes the pendant in his fingers, a look of deep pain creeping behind his eyes.

"After she died," he continues with more of a struggle, "she commissioned me to bury this amulet with you. My Master ordered that I let you keep it, as it may one day prove useful to him. I do not know why."

He lets it fall to my chest again and turns away, clasping his hands behind his back.

Though my anger is great, I cannot help but pity him. Somewhere deep inside, there is good in him that struggles to get out.

When he speaks again, the spite has returned to his voice. "According to my Master's wishes, you were taken to a sorceress called Siena, who cursed you with the appearance of a normal half-breed, ridding you of your golden hair. You were put in the charge of one of my closest friends to look after until you had grown a little. When you were old enough, the lord sold you as a slave into Zandelba, where I assumed you would be worked to death. And yet here you are."

"I don't understand," I stammer. "You got rid of me just because Zeldek told you to?"

He spins to face me, his eyes wild with the passion that saturates his words. "My loyalty is to Zeldek and Zeldek alone!"

"What about love? Decency? Did none of that stop you? I was an innocent baby! I was your son!"

"You were never my son! Never! My blood may flow through your veins, but I will never bear the disgrace of calling filth like you my son!"

"Filth like me?" I echo, confusion binding me more than the shackles that hold me to the wall. "I need to understand. Hamish and I are twins! And yet you chose him? I need to know why!"

An odd smirk turns his lips. "You have every right to be jealous—"

"Answer me!" I shout, my voice going hoarse. "I don't understand! What is the difference between us?"

He glowers at me with that same hatred, but doesn't reply.

"Please," I cry desperately, trying to make sense of it all. "Tell me!"

"You are weak!" he shouts. "Hamish is strong! I glimpsed into the future. I saw what you might become! My master was right. The only thing that you will ever be good for is slavery! Because of my sacrifice, you will never rise above that. Because of me, you will never become the king that Hamish will!"

My gaze falls to the ground, weighed down by intense shame. What future horror could Zeldek have shown him that would turn cold even the love of a father? I realize that my face is wet with tears.

"You could have done it, you know," he adds quietly. "You could have redeemed yourself in my eyes if it wasn't for your stubborn pride!"

He pauses, as if waiting for an answer, but I don't give one.

"Did you hear me? I could have called you my son again! If only you had joined Zeldek when he asked you to! If only you had accepted his offer and given him your allegiance. That's all that it would have taken. But now we are stuck on opposite sides of a war!" His voice becomes more and more strained. "I have to disown you once again because of what you are and what you have chosen! I have to call you a disgrace to the line of Gryphem!"

I look up at him. For the briefest of moments, there is a glimmer of remorse behind the mask of rage. Then it is gone.

"I cannot wait to see my master destroy you!"

The words pulse through my body in a current of despair. In all of my recollection, nothing has hurt this much. "He will never destroy me," I choke.

"Yes he will! And I'll be there beside him, watching him shape you into what you should have been. Only then might I have reason to be proud of you. Because right now..." he shakes his head. "Right now you make me wish that you had died as an infant."

He turns on his heel and exits the room, throwing the door closed with a thunderous slam. The noise resounds through the hall outside and the flames in the torches flicker. The echoing of his footsteps fade away and I let myself slump forward in my chains. I barely notice the sting of the metal cuffs as they dig into my wrists, or the ache of my arms as they are pried back.

And for the first time since it all began, I allow myself to cry.

Chapter Thirty-seven

I t is a while before the door swings open again, and Jambeau re-enters. Even through the swelling of my own eyes, I can see that he too has been crying. His eyes are red but he tries to hide it by squinting through the torchlight as he searches for the right key to unlock my chains.

"You alright?" he asks, noticing the tears that streak my face. His voice sounds strained, like an eggshell preparing to crack.

I nod slowly.

"He didn't hurt you, did he?"

Physically, not much. Emotionally...

I shake my head.

The key rattles as he unlocks my shackles. One by one, they fall from my wrists.

"Come," he says, thrusting the keys back into his belt.

He turns and his foot bumps Bellator's sword. It clatters, skidding across the floor. He freezes, then takes a few hesitant steps toward it. Bending down, he picks it up as if it were a delicate rose petal.

"It's beautiful," he breathes, examining the hilt. "They say she was evil, but it's not true. There must have been beauty in her heart to have created something like this."

I make no reply. I don't need to add the memories of Bellator's death to my torment.

Jambeau shakes his head, struggling to regain his composure. "Best get you to your cell," he mutters, taking my arm.

He guides me down a corridor and into a hall with heavy doors and barred windows. He brings me to the very last door. Opening it, he pushes me inside. The cell is small. A built-in bench barely big enough for me to lie down on takes up the width of one wall, and a grungy bucket in the opposite corner serves as a latrine.

The door screeches on its hinges as Jambeau begins to close it, but stops halfway. There is a moment of silence. I refuse to turn back to face him, to meet his gaze. I don't want to see the pain he is feeling.

"Did she suffer?" His voice is very near the breaking point.

I look over my shoulder, but focus on the wall beside the door.

"I don't think so."

He takes a shuddering breath. "I'm sorry, Ealdred. Truly, I am."

I turn to stare at the wall before me again.

There is a pause, and then the door snaps shut, cutting off all light. The key grates in the lock. His heavy footsteps fade slowly. I wait until I can no longer hear them and then throw myself angrily at the door, kicking it as hard as I can. I only hurt myself, but I don't care. I scream out all of the anger that is inside of me. Tears follow swiftly, and I break down into uncontrollable sobs. I collapse against the door, letting myself cry. My family was the one hope that I always clung to. The one hope that there might be someone out there who loved me. But now even that small hope has been taken from me and crushed before my eyes.

"What's wrong?" says a soft, wispy voice in the darkness.

A shudder runs through me. I know that voice all too well.

"Look at the pain you have brought upon yourself by your own stubbornness. All that you had to do was give me your allegiance! That was it."

"Leave me alone, Zeldek!" I scream.

"Oh, but you are alone! Is there one person in all of Theara that cares about you now? You, who are so odious that not even your own father can bring himself to feel anything for you!"

Tears choke me.

"I'm giving you one last chance. Give me your allegiance, and I will welcome you when you return to Gaiztoak. I will treat you kindly and give you a high position in my house. Perhaps then your father will welcome you with open arms. If not... well, I will enjoy hearing you scream!"

"Leave me be!" I shout, pressing my fists over my ears. "Just leave me be!"

"You are a fool!" he growls, his voice growing fainter. "Embrace the consequences of your words, half-race! This is the last drop of kindness you will ever receive from me."

"Don't flatter yourself! You have never been kind to me!"

But he doesn't reply. I kick the ground in fury, the anguish inside of me almost too much to bear.

I can't go back there! I can't!

As the hours pass, I begin to greet the familiar faces of my old enemy hunger and his twin sister, thirst. But I know that it will be a while until I'll be able to eat again. Just as I am drifting off into a troubled sleep, I hear light footsteps running down the hall outside. Moments later, a key fumbles in the lock.

I crawl away from the door and put my back to the stone bench. The fumbling continues. I grit my teeth and wait. The lock finally clicks open. The door swings on its hinges. I squint through the bright torchlight that streams in from the outside hall. As my eyes adjust, I recognize Nerienda standing in the doorway, sliding two hairpins back into her braids.

"Get up boy, quickly!" she whispers, beckoning to me. "It is almost midnight. The king has retired to his chambers for the evening. You must leave immediately!"

"You're- you're here to help me?" I stammer.

She nods. "Be swift!"

I scramble to my feet and exit the cell. She eases the door closed again. Then she turns to me, crossing her arms over her chest. Her critical gaze passes over me and compassion softens the worn lines on her face.

"Hamish tells me that you are innocent of the crimes charged against you," she says. "Is that true?"

I lower my gaze. "I'm a sorcerer."

A kind smile fills her eyes. "There is no crime in that."

"You think so?"

"You have a gentle heart, Ealdred. I believe that you will use your power to help instead of injure."

"Why? You barely know me."

"Hamish believes in you, and that is reason enough for me." Her expression regains its usual frost. "I ask only that you don't let him down."

Without waiting for an answer, she turns back up the passage and leads the way to the guards' quarters. The prison guard lies sprawled out over a cot, snoring loudly. A mug dangles from his hand, the last dregs leaking onto the stone floor.

"Poor fool had too much to drink," Nerienda remarks, shaking her head. "Leonel will have him flogged for this."

I feel sad for him. My escape will serve only to increase the severity of his punishment. Yet my hunger for freedom combined with my fear of Zeldek outweighs my compassion.

We return to the main level. Although the hall is empty, Nerienda keeps close to the walls, peering around every corner before she turns it. I begin to recognize my surroundings as we draw closer to the castle's scullery.

Kenet suddenly bursts around the corner, looking frantic. He sees Nerienda, and his hands fly as he communicates urgently with her.

"Algitha?" Nerienda exclaims. "What is *she* doing down here?"

He makes some form of response, his fingers forming sentences that only Nerienda understands.

She sets her jaw. "Alright. Leave her to me. Take the boy out the gardener's way, and make sure he isn't seen."

Kenet nods.

She looks fondly at him. "I'm counting on you, little man."

A grin lights his face and he puts his thumbs up.

She gives me a curt nod, and then sweeps around the corner out of sight. Kenet gestures for me to follow him. He leads me in the opposite wing of the hall she left through, and a few minutes later we emerge into the cool night air of the garden.

Kenet stops in the doorway. Tugging on my sleeve, he points toward a thick grove of trees.

"Thanks, little sir," I say.

He smiles shyly and skips away.

I hurry across the lawn in the direction he pointed.

"There you are!" a voice calls as I approach.

"Hamish?"

He ushers me further into the thicket. "I was worried that Nerienda might not make it past the guard."

"Oh, there was no need..." My voice trails off as Jambeau emerges from the shadows behind him. "Wait! Why are you both helping me? The king — he's made me a criminal."

Hamish puts a hand on my shoulder. "And he is wrong to do so. You may be a sorcerer, my friend, but you haven't hurt anyone. You don't deserve to be treated in this manner."

Friend. The word warms me inside like a ray of sunlight. Yet a deep sadness is cast over my heart. I don't deserve such loyalty and I'm afraid that I can never repay it. *He has risked so much for me. Will I be able to do the same for him?*

"Besides," he continues, "Jambeau told me the charges that my father made against you. You may have lost control for a moment, but Jambeau says that's natural for someone who doesn't have full control of their magic yet."

"How would you know that?" I ask Jambeau.

He shrugs. "You aren't the first sorcerer I've met. Your powers have developed much later than hers did, but I can see the same beginning stages in you."

I don't need to ask whom he is referring to.

"Speaking of which, you'll be wanting this back."

He holds out Bellator's sword to me. As I take it from him, his hand lingers on the hilt for just a moment before releasing it.

I strap it to my side. "Thanks."

"Shh! Someone is coming!" Hamish says, and we all crouch low to the ground.

"Relax. It is only me," calls the voice of Lady Marianna.

Hamish breathes a sigh of relief and beckons for her to approach. "You have brought our provisions, my lady?"

She appears through the rising mist, her netted hair draped with a hood of forest green. Marianna told Hamish about her deceit regarding Arnon the same evening that she told me. At first, he was annoyed that she hadn't told him sooner. But his irritation didn't last for very long.

"And some water too," she confirms. "It isn't much, but it is enough for a day, at least, in case you get trapped in there."

Hamish takes the three satchels from her and tosses one to each of us. "Thank you, my lady," he says, slinging his own over his shoulder.

"Please, call me Marianna," she says with a bashful smile, sliding a stray ringlet of hair behind her ear. "It's less formal."

"If you wish it."

"We're set to go now, my prince," Jambeau says.

Hamish acknowledges this with a nod and turns back to Marianna. "We will continue on from here. You must go back and cover for us."

Marianna hesitates. "I know it won't be safe, but I still want to come with you."

"You mustn't. If anything happens to me, Valamette will need an heir to rule them. I wouldn't want the throne in anyone's hands but yours... Marianna." He smiles. "Besides, father will kill me if he catches us."

She rolls her eyes. "Don't be so dramatic. Nothing's going to happen to you."

"That might be the case," he replies softly. "But I will not have you harmed again."

She sighs. "Alright. But I will not see you hurt either. After all, we are betrothed."

It seems to be a wry joke between the two of them, and they both grin. Then she turns to me and smiles. "You stay safe too, Ealdred. Watch over Hamish, will you?"

I return her smile. "Certainly."

Hamish pretends to scowl at me, but a smile twitches the corner of his lips.

Lady Marianna turns to say a formal goodbye to Jambeau, however, he is staring off into the woods in the other direction. So she turns and disappears back around the bush.

"Come on," Hamish says. "We have little time to lose."

Chapter Thirty-Eight

We stand between the two gargoyles at the entrance to Arnon Castle, looking once more at the ancient battlefield before us. The air has the same dark feeling of death that it had the last time we called.

"Not much has changed," Hamish remarks in a whisper. "I hope that means that no more creatures have been lurking about since we were here."

"Let's keep our voices down anyways," Jambeau advises uneasily.

Hamish nudges my elbow and points past me. "Perhaps we should try that door again. Bellator seemed to think it was the way in."

As soon as Bellator's name is out of his mouth, he looks as if he regrets saying it. Both of us glance back at Jambeau, who merely blinks, examining a pile of corpses.

"Yes," I mutter. "But let me go first."

We start toward the foundation of the tower, our footsteps echoing through the courtyard despite efforts to muffle them.

"How did she die?" Jambeau asks suddenly.

Hamish and I exchange looks.

"It was a heroic death," Hamish says.

"Was it painless?"

Hamish glances at me. He doesn't want to say that it wasn't.

"There was a beast," I explain hesitantly. "A serpent, larger than anything I have ever seen. She fought bravely with remarkable skill... but it got her in the end."

He grimaces and runs a trembling hand over his whiskers

"There was nothing that you could have done," Hamish says gently.

"Yes, there was!" Jambeau cries, and I wince as his voice echoes off of the skeletal walls. "I could have gone with her when she asked me to! I could have given this up instead of leaving her all alone like I did! Then she'd still be alive."

Hamish frowns. "You don't know that."

"Yes, I do," he says, and thankfully, his voice is quieter now.

"Come now," the prince whispers, "if you keep this up, we'll all soon be joining her." He tries to sound jocular, but his words ring a little too true.

Jambeau falls sombre and silent. We are almost at the door now, and from where I stand, I can see that the handle is smashed and the door is ajar. The snake must have broken it when it was flailing about trying to get Bellator off of its back.

"Halt!" The word pierces the air like a thunderbolt from behind us.

The three of us spin around in unison. King Leonel stands in the gateway, his sword drawn in his hand. The blade of the sword glows faintly blue, and I realize that he must be holding Stormcrest. Behind him, little red dots glow out of the darkness, and I can make out the huge shapes that accompany them.

"What are those?" Hamish breathes.

I swallow, trying to keep my voice calm. "Ezixs. Don't have time to explain. On my signal, get to the door as quickly as you can. Do you hear me?"

Both Hamish and Jambeau nod.

Leonel steps toward us, the click of his boots echoing throughout the courtyard. "Hamish!" he calls. "Hamish, listen to me. Come here at once, my son."

I can't help but feel that the 'my son' was a gibe at me, because in all my time in the palace, he has never once called Hamish 'my son' to his face.

Hamish falters, but doesn't respond.

"Now, son!" Leonel orders.

My heart stings as if a dart were sent through it. "You should go, Hamish," I say, struggling to get the words out. "This isn't your fight."

"Yes, it is," Hamish replies. "You are my friend, and I'm not leaving you to face my father alone!"

"We insist," Jambeau says, taking my side. "Ealdred and I are in enough trouble now as it is, and neither of us would see you harmed. Not at your own father's hand."

But he remains stubborn. "It's my fault that you're in this mess. If I hadn't been too blind to see my father for the tyrant that he is, I would have known that Ealdred wasn't safe here, and I wouldn't have pressed for him to stay. I endangered him, and so I must help him out of danger."

"I'm not asking you to do that," I respond.

"But how am I supposed to prove myself if I am never given the chance?" he cries, and I can hear desperation in his tone. "I need to prove myself! I need to show them that I'm worthy!"

"Hamish!" his father – that is, *our* father – calls, agitated now. "I am warning you, come now!"

"That's your final decision then?" I say in an undertone.

He nods.

"Fine. We run now!"

Turning, I take off toward the door as fast as I can, and hope that they are right behind me. I reach the door and push on it with all my might. It is large and much heavier than it looks. Hamish and Jambeau almost plough into me as they force themselves through the small opening. It begins to close as I try to pull myself in after them.

"Stop!" Leonel cries, raising his sword in the air.

Lightning flashes from the clear night sky and strikes his sword. Power glows from it as streaks of electricity rush up and down the blade. With a cry of rage, the king thrusts the tip into the stone ground. The stones erupt, exploding from the ground and creating an avalanche that rushes toward us.

I pull myself inside just in time, and the door slams shut behind me with a thud, cutting out all light. Seconds after it is closed, the door rumbles with the sound of stones slamming against it. The earth shakes. I stumble back, tripping over something, and find myself on the ground.

As the rumbling dies, I push myself to my knees.

"Is everyone alright?" I whisper.

"Yes," Jambeau grunts. "Your highness?"

"I'm alright," Hamish's voice comes from right behind me. "Did you see what my father did?"

"I did. So much for his stance against sorcery," Jambeau replies grimly.

There is a pause.

"We're trapped down here, aren't we?" I say at last.

"Yes," Hamish replies. "We need to find a way out."

"Stay where you are for the moment," Jambeau whispers. "I'm almost certain that I saw some sort of a drop as I ran in."

"We will need a torch," Hamish adds.

"I'll see if I can find some wood." I hear shuffling in the direction that Jambeau's voice came from.

A sudden thought occurs to me and I pull the glove off of my right hand. Clenching it in a fist, I close my eyes, and concentrate on that icy chill that is always present somewhere inside of me. I open my hand, slowly but deliberately.

My fingertips tingle with cold, and I open up my eyes. A small blue light flickers in

the palm of my hand. The light swells until it forms a glowing ball that illuminates

the room around us.

It might have been larger in its former glory, but now, after the walls have all

caved in, the room is the size of a large broom closet. There is a stone stairway

leading down into a dark pit near where Jambeau is groping about on the floor.

Hamish squints up at me, his mouth open in amazement.

Jambeau stands up. "Convenient," he says with a nod of approval.

"So much for torches," Hamish says with grin. "Now, let us find a way out of

here."

"I think," I say, "that our only option at this point would be to take the stairs,

and quickly. I don't doubt that those ezixs will tear this place apart in no time and

I'd rather be long gone before then."

Hamish and Jambeau glance at each other.

"What exactly is an 'ezixs'?" Jambeau asks for both of them.

I start down the stairs, and they follow me. "An ezix is a horrible creature

that lives in the far north, in Gaiztoak. Because they live there, I'm almost certain

they have to do Zeldek's bidding."

"You're *almost* certain?" Jambeau asks.

I shrug. "That's really all that I know. This is the third time I've encountered them, and I haven't had time to stop and ask their life stories on either of the other occasions."

The staircase continues to go deeper and deeper underground, sometimes twisting, sometimes winding, but always going down. It seems like hours before we finally come out into open space. After that, the staircase continues on without railings, stretching over bottomless ravines until finally ending at the entrance to a large cavern of dusty pillars. The floor glints with heaps upon heaps of bronze trinkets, which mostly consists of coins, but there are also plates, eating utensils, goblets, candlesticks, weapons, and countless varieties of other valuable objects.

"Oh!" Hamish breathes. "If Valamette had access to this, the kingdom would never, ever want for anything! Zandelba would be furious!"

"They would start a war over it, that's for sure," Jambeau mutters.

A cold breeze hits my face, and I hear that same unsettling, whispering voice that I heard in the tombs. "Don't touch anything," it hisses, repeating its order four or five times before fading away again.

I put up my hand. "Did you hear that?"

"Hear what?" Jambeau asks.

"The voice," Hamish replies, his eyes wide. "It said not to touch anything."

"Then let's not," Jambeau says, looking around cautiously. "Who knows what we may unleash if we do?"

Hamish and I nod in agreement, but his eyes are still wide in amazement, and he looks around, taking in as much of it as possible. I watch him, and a smile twitches my lips. My own little brother. He looks so innocent, so childish, no matter what worries seem to weigh him down. Then a thought comes to me. *If he and I are brothers, that would mean I'm not the only descendant of Lady Batuel here. He is too. He could also break the curse on the arrow. Is that why he could also hear the voice?*

If that's the case, I wonder why Bellator never mentioned it, why Zeldek only wanted me. Why my father only cast me away.

"Look," Jambeau calls as we near the bottom of the stairs. "There's a door across the hall."

He points across the mountains of copper coins, and I spot a set of decaying wooden double doors. There is no path through the vast wealth to it. We stop on the bottom step of the stairs, which is littered with coins.

"We'll have to walk over them," I say. "I don't think that anyone will mind, so long as we don't take any."

They both nod, but I can see that they are uneasy. Gingerly, I set a foot down on the heap of treasure. The coins slip and clink under my feet, but the ground remains sturdy, and nothing jumps out to swallow me up.

"It's fine," I call over my shoulder.

They start after me, and we all silently agree to hurry over the treasure. It is slow going, but we finally make our way to the other side. As we near the door, the coins begin to clear away, leaving just enough room for us to slip through. But when we have passed through them, we stop short. There, piled in front of us, is a sea of silver coins.

"By the goddess!" Hamish gasps, awestruck.

It takes us much longer to pick our way across this pile, but there seems to already be a path indented into it and we follow it to another set of double doors. When these are opened, even I have to be amazed. Before us is another room, only this one is full of gold and sparkling jewels.

"This is enough to make gold worthless!" Jambeau exclaims.

"And we have had this beneath our feet for how long?" Hamish gasps in amazement. "Father would kill for this!"

I know what he is probably thinking. He could return with word of this and be called a hero. Once his country was wealthier than even Lavylli, the people would finally love him, and would practically beg for him to rule over them once his father was gone. He would rightfully be among the greatest kings ever to rule Valamette.

As for me, all I would need is a handful of this, and I could live in freedom for the rest of my life! I would be lying to say that I'm not tempted.

"Come on," I barely manage to say, and we start across the glittering pile.

We are all eager to see what we will find in the next room, and we practically run the whole way through the golden hall. But when the next set of doors is opened, my heart drops in disappointment. The adjoining hall is narrow and empty, and seems to stretch for miles beyond the light cast by the blue flame in my hand. Water trickles down the walls and gathers in pools on the floor. Moss and other such fungi sprout across the cracked stones, and my nostrils are filled with the pungent smell of earth.

As soon as we have passed through the doors, they slam behind us, forcing us to move forward. Within minutes, my feet are wet, and I begin to feel very miserable. We travel like this for at least an hour before there is even a slight change in the walls. After maybe two hours, the smooth, cut stones evolve into rough stone that glitters like the sand on the seashore. Coincidentally, the air also smells strangely like the ocean.

The passageway ends abruptly, and a large, rusted metal door bars our path. Although it looks to be made to keep things out, the door is unlocked and it opens very easily. We enter the small, dank, grimy room, and the door slams shut behind us. There is a grating sound, like a key in a lock, followed by a click. I turn back to the door, but as I do, the blue magic of my light is extinguished.

I hold my breath and concentrate on the light again. It flickers up for a second and then goes out. But as it does, I catch a glimpse of a dark figure crouched on its hands and knees between us and the door, ready to pounce.

Chapter Thirty-Nine

My hand flies to the hilt of my sword, but the creature assails me before I can pull it out. I am thrown back against the wall, and the ragged breathing of the creature wheezes over me, its foul breath hitting my face. An acrid, acidic scent oozes from the creature, like it's been bathing in a tub of rotten lemons for a decade. Its hands grope for my throat and I grab its boney wrists, shoving it back with all of my might. It weighs much less than I expect, and I hear it slide across the floor to the other side of the room.

"Ealdred!" Hamish cries, and I can hear the zing of metal as he draws his sword. "Are you alright?"

Before I can answer, the creature is upon me again, pinning my chest to the wall with its sharp elbow and pressing a grimy hand over my mouth. I try to kick it back again, but this time it is prepared, and it dodges out of the way of my feet. Then it pushes on me with crushing force, digging its claws into my face.

"Hold still," its raspy voice hisses in my ear.

I stop fighting.

"Now," it continues, "I will uncover your mouth in a moment, and you will tell me who else is here with you. Understood?"

I attempt to nod.

"Good," it says, and uncovers my mouth.

But instead of betraying the names of my friends, I blurt, "What are you?"

It growls in annoyance. "Just answer my question, half-wit, before I lose my overly long-held patience!"

Half-wit. There is only one person in all of Theara that calls me that!

"Bellator?" I exclaim, joy flooding my chest.

She huffs, releasing me. "You *are* stupid!"

The room erupts with white light as she holds up the firestone in her cloak. Once my eyes adjust to the light, I see that it is indeed her. She is standing in front of me, and she looks terrible. Her hair hangs about her face in matted, grimy straggles, and her complexion is as pale as death. Her eyes are bloodshot, her clothing torn, and her armour is tarnished with a green and slimy substance. Her face is so gaunt that her cheekbones stick out; she looks more vicious than ever as she scowls down at me.

"But how—" I stammer. "I— I saw it eat you!"

She snorts. "Did you really think that I could be bested by a snake?"

"I saw it eat you!" I repeat.

"Which was the biggest mistake that it ever made," she says with a crooked grin.

"Um, Ealdred," Hamish says hesitantly, and I remember that he and Jambeau are here as well. "Isn't that the girl that died?"

Bellator turns to him, her sarcasm at the ready. "Well, if it isn't our little prince. Truly, I am impressed. And who's the..."

Her voice trails off as her gaze lands on Jambeau, who stares back at her, ashen faced. Mouth parted, his eyes widen with fear. His lips move as he attempts to say something, but no sound comes out. Her name, maybe? But no, it looked like something else.

"You!" she snarls, starting toward him.

She shoves Hamish out of her way, and I instinctively press my back into the wall.

"You!" she shouts again as she slams Jambeau back against the wall. "You son of—"

"Briella," he says, his voice hoarse.

"Do not call me that!" she roars. "You have no right! No right to that name at all!"

There are tears in his eyes. "I'm sorry," he whispers. "I'm so sorry."

"You're *sorry*?" she shouts. "You left me! You left me all alone! I was helpless without you, and you left me!"

"I know," he says miserably. "You were right. I was a fool."

"A fool?" Her voice is shrill. "You were cruel! I was nine years old! *Nine!* I couldn't survive by myself, and you left me!"

"I tried to find you," he says weakly. "Really, I did! But you were gone."

"I was gone because of you! He took me to Zeldek the next day, and it's your fault!" She sucks in her breath, and then snarls, "I hate you!"

He looks hurt, but says nothing as he lowers his gaze to the floor.

"You were my only friend," she goes on, her voice wild and full of more emotion than I thought her capable of feeling. "My *only* friend! How could you? How could you do it?"

"I thought—" His voice cracks, and he tries again. "I thought that after I made a name for myself, you could come and live with me too. I just couldn't stand to live on the streets anymore. You know how much I hated it. So... so I took the first opportunity."

"We were supposed to do it together! We were supposed—" She takes a gulp of air before her voice returns with full vehemence. "You're despicable!"

With a vicious shove, she releases him, then swipes her hand through the air. An invisible force jerks him to the side, slamming him into the corner. His head bashes into the wall and he falls to the floor in a heap.

Crying out in alarm, Hamish rushes to his side. "What have you done?"

"Only what he deserves."

Bellator turns on her heel, charging toward me. I shrink back, wishing I could sink into the wall. She grabs my arm, and jerks me toward the door opposite the one we entered by.

"Wait—"

"We're going, half-wit!"

Throwing open the door, she shoves me through into a narrow hallway. The door slams shut behind us. She utters a phrase of indecipherable magic, waving her hand over its wooden surface. A thin veil of black mist curls over it.

"What are you doing?" I cry.

"Locking them in that room until the spell is broken. I won't have them getting underfoot."

She turns and shoves me down the winding hall, and into another large cavern. This one, unlike any of the others beneath the castle, is empty except for the large, dusty pillars that hold up the ceiling. Directly across the room from us, however, are two golden doors. Light shines down from somewhere above us, casting a single ray down on the floor before the doors. As we near it, I can make out what the light is illuminating.

An emblem stretches across the floor, reflected in the smooth surface of the doors. Three raised stone serpents knot in a circle around two crossed arrows. The heads of the serpents are raised from the floor, mouths gaping. In each mouth is the impression of a different symbol. One is a dragon with a teardrop stone clasped in its claws, one is a pear-shaped gem with vines entwined around it, and the last

one—

I look up at Bellator, alarmed. "What is this?"

"Three bright stars of purest form," Bellator quotes, her anger seemingly

forgotten. "They are the key."

"The key?"

"You know, I really did miss your stupid questions, half-wit," she says acidly.

"Yes, the key. You see, at the beginning of time, before the Vaelhyreans decided to

start killing each other, there were many wondrous things in their possession that

they brought from over the sea. One such object was called the Firestone. Now, at

around the same time that Lady Batuel was given the arrow that we now seek,

King Emyr decided to make use of the captured Firestone. He bottled up the power

of it into three precious stones, and gave one to each of the three great ladies living

at the time. The first was given to the Lady of Sylvaria, Batuel's little sister; the

second was given to Zeldek's wife, the future Lady of Gaiztoak; and the third was

given to Batuel. When Batuel created this hiding place, she asked the two other

bearers of the Firestone to lend her their stones so that she could guard her weapon

against Caderyn, who, if you were paying attention before, you'll remember was a

powerful and evil lord. All three of them agreed, and handed over their stones to

make this key. To unlock this door, we must have all three stones. The Light of

Sylvaria..."

She pulls the firestone from around her neck, and places it in the symbol of the pear-shaped jewel with vines twining around it. They are a perfect match.

"...the Breath of the Dragon..."

She pulls the dragon necklace from around her neck, and places it in its slot. It too is a perfect match.

"...and the Eye of the Storm."

She holds her hand out to me.

I reach to the medallion around my neck. "How did you know that I had this?" I ask, bewildered.

"I saw it when I was beating you up in the arena," she replies. "Now take it off. Zeldek knows what we are after now, so we don't have much time before he comes for us."

Reluctantly, I pull it off and drop it into her hand. She sets it down in the last slot. Like the others before it, it is a perfect match.

"Step back!" she orders, and pushes me away from the symbol.

At first, nothing happens. Then light begins to pour from around the outline of the snakes, and the entire symbol on the floor starts to revolve. Slowly, jerkily, the doors open.

"There's something you need to know before we go in there," she says. "Do you remember that story I told you about how Zeldek discovered you?"

"Yes. What of it?"

"Well," she hesitates. "I wasn't completely honest with you when I was telling it."

I cast a wary glance in her direction. "What do you mean?"

"Well, my story was true, with one exception. You see, Zeldek did search for Batuel's descendants, and he did kill all of them but one. But, it wasn't a little boy. It was a little girl." She hesitates again. "It was me."

I gape at her. "You?"

She nods, looking away.

"But," I am at a loss for words. "Isn't that why Zeldek wanted me?"

"Oh, no," she says. "That's why Zeldek wanted me. He wants you for a different reason entirely."

I feel helplessly confused. "If you knew that, why did you risk so much to break me out and take me with you? If you just wanted my medallion, I'm sure you could've stolen it off of me or killed me for it."

She purses her lips. "I can't tell you yet. But once we enter that room, I am going to need you to do exactly what I say as soon as I say it. Can you do that?"

I hesitate, and then nod. "But why didn't you tell me in the first place?" I ask.

She fiddles with her grime-coated dagger. "The truth is, I didn't think that you would have agreed to come with me if I'd told you that the arrow would have been mine."

To be honest, I'm not sure what I would have done. I've always had the feeling that it would end up belonging to her anyways. For me, the quest was more about my freedom than finding the arrow.

"Come on," she says, and starts around one side of the symbol.

I walk around the other, and we meet in the doorway. She straightens up, pushing her dishevelled hair out of her face, and we start into the room together. As soon as we have passed through, the doors close behind us.

The room we find ourselves in is like nothing else that I passed through in all the rest of Arnon. The walls, pillars, and floor are made of white speckled marble that is as smooth as glass. It is spotlessly clean, as if the floors have been scrubbed a hundred times over, and the only furnishing is a marble altar in the centre of the room. There are steps leading up to the altar, and a light shines on the surface of it. Something glimmers beneath the light.

Bellator steps toward it, her eyes alight with a strange, hungry curiosity. The heels of her boots click on the tiles, and the sound echoes throughout the hall. I follow cautiously, hoping that Bellator hasn't brought me along because breaking the curse requires a sacrifice or anything like that. That would be just my luck.

As we approach the altar, I can see what is on it. On the bare surface of the marble lies an arrow. That is, two halves of an arrow. The golden shaft and iron arrowhead shine as if newly polished, and the white feathers at the end of the shaft are smooth and unmarred. Below the arrow, carved into the stone surface of the altar, is the same prophecy that's on the parchment that Bellator showed me.

Bellator stops a few metres from the altar, and falls to one knee. "My lady," she says reverently, "I have brought the boy and received the final piece of the key."

There is a whispering like the wind through leaves, and then the same voice that spoke to me in the tomb says, "You have done well, my daughter."

Suddenly, a shimmering figure appears on the steps of the altar. A pale, transparent woman in a glittering white dress stands before us. Her face is delicate and beautiful, but it is marked by pain and sorrow. Blonde hair flows about her face in perfect wisps and her hands are clasped at her waist. Transparent chains stemming from the altar hang from her wrists and clink against the floor.

"Is that—"

"Lady Batuel," Bellator confirms, bowing her head again to the woman.

"Are— are you a ghost?" I ask Lady Batuel.

She casts her weary gaze on me. Her pupils are almost completely white. "I am the spirit of Lady Batuel, left as an imprint on Theara. My soul has been cursed to eternal torment until the spell that I placed on this arrow is broken. And yet I will gladly wait many more years if it will prevent this weapon from falling into the hands of my brother, Zeldek."

"It won't," Bellator says confidently.

Batuel eyes her. "The curse can only be lifted by one who is worthy. Are you sure that you are that person?"

Bellator holds her head high. *"'She of dark and she of light, for her own soul she shall fight',"* she quotes, and then takes another step toward Batuel. "I am of light, as your heir, but also of dark, having been trained in black magic by Zeldek. I have fought hard to keep him from stealing my will, and have come out with full control. What more can I do to prove myself?"

Batuel purses her lips. "You may have won control of your will, but have you won the battle for your soul?"

Bellator looks unsure. "I never gave Zeldek my complete loyalty."

Batuel sighs. "I hope for your sake that what you say is true. You are my last descendant, my child. If the arrow rejects you, then nothing can save the world from its impending downfall."

"I will use the arrow to fight Zeldek," Bellator assures her.

Batuel clears the way for her, gesturing up the stairs.

Bellator hesitates, glancing at me. "My lady, there is one request that I ask of you."

"I will grant it if it is within my power," the spirit replies.

"May the boy come with me? It would be nice to have his support, even if I fail."

Batuel gives me a searching look. "It is a strange thing that you have asked. The only other to have tried relied only on his strength alone to break it, and he did not succeed." She frowns thoughtfully. "I see no harm in it. He may go up with you."

Bellator starts toward the stairs, gesturing for me to follow. I keep a safe distance, hanging back at the foot of the steps. She ascends and her lips move as she quietly repeats the words of the prophecy.

Batuel's gaze remains fixed on me, curiously. "Why you, I wonder? You are still a child."

"What do you mean?" I ask.

She adjusts the chain on her wrist. "Your destiny is a great one in the eyes of many."

That only makes me feel more uneasy. Is that the same destiny to which my father referenced? If so, I want no part in it.

I grow uncomfortable under Batuel's gaze and move around the stairs to stand beside Bellator. Bellator turns to look at me, and I am surprised to find a hint of nervousness in her eyes. I nod to her. Taking a breath, she tightens her jaw, and reaches out her hand toward the arrow.

"Give me your hand," she says under her breath.

"What?"

"I said, give me your hand!"

I reach up and grasp her left hand with my right. Her palm is sweaty, and she stiffens at my touch. Her index finger presses into my wrist.

Cold shoots through me, freezing my veins. The cold fills me up and then drains into my right arm. On the altar, the golden shaft of the arrow glows blue.

"*Befugnisse umschlingen,*" Bellator whispers.

"What are you doing?" Batuel cries out, alarmed.

"*Befugnisse umschlingen!*" Bellator says, louder this time.

The cold begins to leave my body through my hand and into hers. Yet at the same time, I can feel a burning sensation filling my veins, and surging through me, giving me strength like nothing I have ever felt.

"*Befugnisse!*" she shouts at the top of her lungs. "*Umschlingen!*"

And I realize what she is doing. She is joining our powers together, both our strengths and our weaknesses, and putting it all toward mending the arrow. It is brilliant, really, but terrifying if it doesn't work. The arrow considers us to be the same person right now, and if she fails to break the curse, the fate that would have been hers alone will become mine too.

A wave of light shoots out from the arrow, blinding me as it ripples to every corner of room. My knees wobble. I'm growing weaker and weaker by the second, like water drained from a bucket, and it feels like the bucket is almost empty.

I try to say her name, to tell her to stop, but my words come out unintelligible and garbled.

"Bellator, enough!" Batuel cries from somewhere nearby. "You'll kill him as well as yourself!"

But her hand is frozen on my wrist, and I doubt that she could let go if she tried.

"Please!" Bellator's voice is a weak echo in the centre of the light. "Please mend."

The moment the echo has died, the light fades. Bellator releases my hand, buckling forward into the altar. Everything is dark and splotchy. I grope for something to steady myself, but feel the cold floor against my back and realize I've already fallen. The next thing I know, Batuel is bent over me, her cool, breezy hand beside my cheek.

"Are you alright?" she asks, concerned.

I blink, and my vision clears a fraction. "I- I think so."

A sinister chuckle rumbles through the floor. "Let's hope that he is. It would be a shame to lose him before the battle has even begun."

Alarmed, I jerk upright as Zeldek sweeps into the room, his red robe billowing about him. The golden doors slam shut behind him with a bang.

With a shriek, Batuel throws herself against the altar, her eyes widening in terror at the sight of her brother.

"Well done, Bellator," Zeldek says, approaching the steps. "You have exceeded all of my expectations and then some. Bringing me both the arrow and the boy in one stroke? Your loyalty will be greatly rewarded."

Bellator remains motionless, inattentive, not seeming to notice the intruder.

"Is that true, Bellator?" I demand. "Have you been working for him this entire time?"

"Of course she has been," Zeldek scoffs. "You're too naïve and trusting, half-race! Bellator is and will always be my most loyal pawn."

Batuel shakes her head, staring at the weakened warrior with numb shock. "You lied to me," she whispers, the hurt of the betrayal saturating every word. Then her voice erupts like a thousand gales blowing. "You lied to me! You told me it wasn't for him!"

"Trust is a funny thing," Zeldek says, his voice strangely bitter. "When you give it, it may turn around and destroy you."

Batuel looks up at him, her empty eyes flashing. A wind I cannot feel begins to blow around her and for just a moment, I can see the resemblance between her and Bellator. "You are wrong!" she hisses. "I cast the spell! The arrow will remain broken if she is unworthy!"

"But my Bellator was never one for following the rules," Zeldek sneers. "She found a way around your idealistic 'pure-of-heart' guideline. By channelling the power of the most innocent soul through herself, she has manipulated your spell into thinking she was pure of heart. It will have mended."

"No!" Batuel roars, and I know that if she wasn't a ghost, this entire place would be falling on us by now. "You cannot fool the spell! It knows! It always knows!"

Zeldek gestures toward the altar. "Let us see if that is true."

Batuel turns to Bellator. "Did it mend?"

There is a long moment of silence as all three of us wait with bated breath. Then Bellator straightens up, lifting the slender shaft from its resting place.

"Yes," she breathes. "It has."

Chapter Forty

S he turns to us, the arrow of Arnon lying across her outstretched hands. The broken pieces have been welded back together and the golden shaft is lit with the iridescent glow of the remainder of our combined magic. But there is a bitter taste in my mouth as I behold it now.

A greedy look enters Zeldek's eyes and he takes a swift step toward Bellator. "At last!" His voice trembles with emotion. "All of your efforts have come to nothing, my sister. Your arrow is finally mine!"

He reaches out his hand toward it. Batuel winces and looks away, unable to bear the sight of her long-protected weapon going into the hands of her murderer.

Bellator snatches it out of his reach. "*Please.* If you think I'm going to just hand it over to you, you're a bigger fool than I realized!"

I let out my breath in a rush, and Batuel utters an exclamation of joy.

Zeldek's mouth drops open. "How dare you? You foolish girl! You cannot control the amount of power that weapon contains!"

"Oh? Do you want to help me test that theory?" she says, drawing her faithful bow from her shoulder.

"It is not your destiny to kill me," Zeldek warns. "You know that just as well as I do."

"I don't intend to kill you," she says through her teeth, setting the glimmering arrow on her string. "But if you test me any further, my finger might just slip!"

Zeldek wisely takes a step back.

Bellator pulls back the bowstring to her ear. "Return home now while you still can and wait for the full extent of your power to be restored to you! Then come seeking vengeance."

Rage burns on his face. "You stupid girl! You cannot overpower me!"

"I *couldn't* overpower you," she corrects. "But you said yourself that this weapon contains great power."

"It does," he snarls, drawing his sword. "And I will not lose it again!"

He raises his weapon above his head and swings it in a full circle. Fire blazes from it, casting a ring of flames around us. Bellator keeps a centre of calm as he attempts to entrap us, her bowstring held back, waiting to strike the killing blow. Sword in one hand, Zeldek holds out his other, palm up. A tongue of flames flares, forming itself into a rolling ball. He hurls it at her, and she flips backward onto the altar to evade it. The flames hit the base of the stairs, cracking the cold stone.

"You amuse me," he taunts. "You know that you cannot win. Why do you continue to fight?"

Uncertainty flickers over Bellator's face, but she quickly shakes it away. "You do not control me anymore! With this arrow, no one will ever enslave me again!"

"You seal your own fate!"

He thrusts his sword at her and fire shoots from it. Without thinking, without deliberation, I whip out my sword, and leap between them. Power that I thought was drained while breaking the spell shoots through my hands and into the sword. The tinted metal shines with blue light that flashes like lightning and the flames extinguish.

My strength fails me and I fall to my knees.

Zeldek steps toward me, anger and humour playing in his eyes. "Your power weakens you, boy! If you had let me teach you how to control it, you might actually be worth my time!"

He swipes his hand to the side. It is as if someone has hit me with an invisible wall. I am thrown into the air, hurtled over the ring of flames, and then crumble to the floor on the other side, skidding until I hit the wall. The whole left side of my body is paralyzed with pain and my head aches blindingly.

Through the tears that blur my eyes, I can make out Zeldek advancing toward Bellator. She stands her ground, setting the arrow on the string once more.

But instead of attacking again, he begins to skirt the altar, keeping his sword pointed at her.

"You won't shoot me," he announces.

"I wouldn't be so sure," she growls, keeping the arrow trained on him.

"How could you? You are weak. Too weak to be able to handle the power that arrow possesses."

She shakes her head. "I know what you're trying to do."

"Oh?" he asks with a tone of surprise.

"It won't work. Not this time."

He smiles as if appeasing a child. "You know that it would be safer in my hands. You know that I am the best person to have it. Why do you continue to resist the truth?"

Her uncertainty grows and her hand begins to relax the string.

Zeldek's voice is low and rhythmic, as if he were performing some ancient chant. "Give the arrow to me and come home. I will forgive your insolence. Things will go back to how they were and all will be... *forgotten.*"

I feel a disturbance in the air as he enunciates the last word and I know that something is wrong. Bellator's face has lost its defiance. Her eyes are blank and empty as she lowers her bow. The arrow dangles carelessly from her hand.

"That's it," he says. "Hand it over. Now."

Bellator stares down at the arrow without seeing it and holds it out to him.

"No!" Batuel cries, throwing herself between them. Her hands grasp for the shaft of the arrow, desperate to pull it out of her brother's reach forever. But they only slide through it.

"Silence, witch!" Zeldek snaps. "Your time is long over!"

"Perhaps," she says bitterly, "you should have thought of that before you cursed my spirit to walk the earth for eternity!"

With a flick of his hand, Zeldek throws the ghost aside. She cries out as her chains are tightened and she disappears in a shimmering veil. Then he returns his attention to Bellator.

"That's it," he coaxes. "Give it to me."

"Bellator!" I cry, pulling myself to my feet. My head spins, and I have to grab onto the wall to keep from falling over. "Don't do it!"

She turns distractedly and I see hopelessness in her eyes. "It's no use fighting," she says. "He's too strong."

"Not for you—"

"You don't get it! I'm not like you. I can't fight him like you can."

"That's not true!"

"I'm not strong enough."

I stare at her in disbelief. "Bellator, you're the strongest person I know!"

"I don't think you understand," Zeldek says, closing his long fingers around the golden shaft. He pulls it from her hand and holds it up to the light. "Bellator is strong in many ways that are beneficial to me. It's when she starts thinking for herself that there's a problem. So I've ensured that she can't fight back, even if she desperately wants to."

"What have you done to her?" I demand.

"The Aemurel can be used for many things, half-race. It creeps into the mind, twisting thoughts and ensnaring the will to its own command. I've been able to use this to my own advantage. Bellator is completely and irrevocably under my control. She will come to accept this in time. As will you."

"You will never control me!"

"As always, I admire your courage." He smiles, coming around the altar. "But you are wrong. You think you can match my power, but you've seen nothing yet!"

The arrow is an illuminated golden line as he raises it in the air. Thin streaks of light form in a ring around the tip, expanding and ricocheting off the walls with a rumbling buzz.

"Bow!" he says, pointing the arrow at me.

A spear of light hurtles out and strikes me full in the chest. Pain vibrates through me, sharp and refined like a thousand honed knives. It throws me back against the wall with a force that knocks every ounce of air from my lungs. The pain circles through me and exits from my throat as a tortured scream.

"You will know more pain than anyone who has gone before you and any that will come after!" he cries, the flashing of the light casting eerie shadows over his face.

"No!" a voice, deep and savage, echoes through the room.

Zeldek begins to turn, but in a blur of movement, a fist hits him in the jaw, and he flies back. The arrow slips from his hand, clattering to the floor near his attacker's feet. Bellator stands over him, her eyes alive with hatred.

"You will not control me and you will not hurt him!"

Zeldek puts his hand to his jaw, staring at her in surprise. "How—"

"You will never control me again," she growls. "Leave now, and I will allow you to live."

"You'll *allow* me to live?" he scoffs, rage reddening his face. "The boy will beg for mercy over your mangled body!"

"Come on then! I dare you!" she retorts, an unearthly rumble to her voice.

He is on his feet in a second, but she's faster. The arrow of Arnon is on her bow, and she lets it fly. It finds its mark in his chest.

He staggers back, stumbling over the train of his robe.

"What have you done?" he cries.

She lowers her bow, straightening up with grace. Her jaw is set, yet a smirk curls her lips.

Zeldek reaches up a trembling hand and grasps the golden shaft. Blood seeps through the crack in his armour, staining the pale skin of his hand. He draws in his breath with a hiss that seems to echo through the timelessness of the room, and lifts his hand up in front of his face. He stares, horror-stricken at the sparkling blood that runs down his arm. A sudden and violent shudder goes through him and his legs buckle. He falls forward, catching himself on his hands and knees. The ring of flames that surrounds the altar sputters and dies.

Bellator leaps toward him, seizing the shaft of the arrow in her hand. Her eyes sink into swirling pools of loathing and she pulls him forward so that his face is inches from hers.

"This is for Fyra!" she says through her teeth, and rips the arrow out of his chest.

He shrieks in agony, stumbling backward. "You will regret this! I will have my vengeance!"

Black smoke billows from his hand, cloaking him from view. When it evaporates, he is gone.

Bellator straightens up, panting, and runs a dirty hand through her hair. I can tell that she's exhausted, but she hides it beneath a sturdy composure. I can't help but admire her for it.

And me? Well, I'm sprawled back against the wall, knees trembling, keeping as still as I can for fear of falling over.

"Well done, my child," Batuel praises, materializing beside the altar once again. "You have avenged our family's honour and earned the right to bear the weapon of your ancestors. Use it with pride!"

Bellator acknowledges this with a nod. "And you? Will you be freed from this curse?"

Batuel looks down at the shackles on her wrists, and her elation fades. "I know not. His curse would only be broken if the arrow was his."

Bellator quirks an eyebrow. "It *was* his, for however short a time."

The ghost smiles sadly. "I'm not sure that the laws of magic work that way."

"Who cares? Any law can be broken."

"My dear child, you are clever and brave, but you must not grow conceited in this small victory. Zeldek will be back with more power than ever before."

Bellator raises her chin. "And I will be ready for him."

"I hope you're right." Batuel bows her head. "I admit, I still have misgivings about you. To bear the weapon of an archer, you must be level headed and slow to violence, both of which you are not. The manner in which you broke the spell undermined the tests the spell would have given you, and thus you did not prove yourself worthy."

"You think I'm not worthy of it?" Bellator challenges.

"When the arrow was mine, I was young, but I thought myself wise. I was blinded by own arrogance and sense of serenity. As a result, I thought that my violence was justified and I ended up hurting someone very close to me." She sighs deeply. "That is why I locked it away; I could no longer trust myself. Beware the corruption of power, my daughter. Beware that you use it only for good."

Bellator shrugs, unmoved. "I don't have anyone close to me, so what do I have to lose?"

The ghost shakes her head. "I see a great darkness in you, and deep pain. You are guarded and cruel to make yourself feel stronger. This will be your downfall if you aren't careful."

"Tell me how I may set your mind at ease."

"Gaining the arrow comes with a great responsibility; one which you must be true to. If you do this thing, you will earn the right to the power the weapon carries."

Taking a breath, Bellator prepares herself. "What is this responsibility?"

"Valamette is now under your jurisdiction, as it was once under mine. You must watch over it as a guardian, to serve the people, and – should trouble arise – to be willing to give your life to protect it. Are you up to the task?"

"I am," she says at once.

"Hmm," Batuel frowns. "Know that you will be held to this oath for the remainder of your life. I warn you, do take it lightly and do not break it. Valamette may need you before the end."

"Right..."

"I have a warning for both of you," the ghost continues, casting a foreboding glance to me. "Dark things are coming. The war for Theara is just beginning, and the war against the Aemurel is long overdue. It has been foretold and it will come to pass. Woe to all caught up in its destruction."

A chill creeps down my spine at her words.

Her gaze pierces me. "So great a burden has been cast upon you, child. How heavy still it will become."

"What do you mean?" I ask, my hand going up to clutch my aching chest.

She reaches her hand toward me. "Would that another had been found to carry this burden, to ease the pain fate has chosen for you."

"That's quite enough of that," Bellator says sharply, stepping between us. "Batuel of Arnon, I free you from your bonds. You may go in peace to the land of the dead."

Batuel's hand falls to her side. "I'm afraid that's not quite—"

"*Aske izan!*" The arrow is a blur in Bellator's hand as she swishes it through the air, ending with a flourish that leaves the tarnished arrowhead pointing at Batuel. A star of white light gathers around the tip.

Weariness passes over Batuel's face, and she shakes her head. "I applaud your attempts, child, but you do not understand. My bonds were forged through Zeldek's magic and so Zeldek's magic must set me free."

A sly smile forms on Bellator's lips. "I know."

Sparkling blood drips from her hand, making a splattered blot on the marble floor. Black mist rises from the blood, twisting around the speck of white light at the arrow's tip. Dark and light entwine, the twisting elements moving out from the arrow and suspending in midair. They form a small sphere and spin through the air, lodging themselves in the lock of the shackles. A loud snap resounds off the walls. The chains fall from Batuel's wrists and clatter to the floor before vanishing entirely.

Batuel stares down at her wrists, her mouth agape, and then turns her gaze to Bellator with renewed admiration. "How did you—"

"I told you," Bellator cuts in. "Zeldek trained me in the use of dark magic. I know a trick or two."

Batuel's eyes shine with tears and she spreads her arms out like a bird. "May the blessings of our house be upon you, Bellator, daughter of Arnon! Let your name be remembered to all future generations!"

"Sure," Bellator says with an uncomfortable smile.

Batuel turns her godlike gaze to me. "As for you, you have much to learn in so short a time. Go to my brothers in the north and train under them. They shall prepare you for what lies ahead."

"If you mean Ulmer and Banner, I'm not sure that's the best idea. We don't really get along."

"Do not see enemies where there are none! It is in my brothers' destiny to keep you safe."

I nod, but I still doubt that Ulmer's protection would help me any more than Zeldek's wrath would.

She turns to Bellator. "Your castle has been restored to its former glory. My work in this world is finished. I go now to take my place of rest with my family in the land of the dead. Farewell, and be strong."

She dives into the air, spiralling into the ceiling. There is a flash of light that reverberates over the white marble dome of the ceiling, passing down the walls and into the floor. By the time it disappears, she is gone.

Bellator lets out her breath in a rush, and wanders over to sit on the steps of the altar. She looks conflicted, and I realize that she probably never expected that her golden trinket would come with so great a responsibility.

My own mind is overwhelmed with both fear and confusion, and my body is riddled with pain. While Bellator seemed to be shielding me from the brunt of Batuel's words, I can feel the weight of the truth that Bellator is trying to conceal from me.

I clear my throat, cringing at being the one to have to break the silence once again. "That was impressive."

"Hmm?" she mumbles, distracted.

"You fought Zeldek by yourself and won!"

She sighs, putting her face in her hands. "Batuel's right. This fight is far from over. I have injured him, yes, but it will take much more than that to kill him. Now that I've angered him, he'll be back with triple the strength. I must be ready."

"You will be."

She glances at me, a look of wonder etching itself into her dirty face. "Ealdred, I lied to you, took advantage of your ignorance, and used your power to further my own ends. How are you not angry with me?"

I shrug. "I don't know. I guess I just suspected it of you all along. But that doesn't mean that I wouldn't mind an explanation of why you did it."

She laughs quietly. "I suppose I do owe you that. You see, I discovered that I was Batuel's heir not long after Zeldek took me in, and it took me less time to figure out that I didn't want a weapon like that in his hands. Since then, I have been seeking a feasible way to ensure that when Zeldek forced me to break the spell, not only would I succeed, but I would also have enough strength left inside of me to keep it from him. It was obvious to me that, considering all of the crimes that I have committed, my heart wasn't even close to pure, and I needed a way to trick the spell into thinking that it was. When I heard you refuse Zeldek's enticing offer, I knew that if anyone had a spotless heart, it would be you. It was very convenient for me when I discovered that only Zeldek seemed to know who your family was, and I thought that if you thought you were Batuel's descendant, you would be more willing to come along. I decided to test you, discover your strengths and your weaknesses, until I was satisfied that I could indeed use your magic to help break the spell."

"And you also knew that you could sap up all of my magic to keep yourself strong enough to fight him."

"That too," she admits. "But I desperately needed the arrow. It was the only chance I had of freeing myself from Zeldek's control. In the months leading up to your arrival, I could feel that Zeldek was trying to strengthen me for the moment that I would mend the arrow, and this was only confirmed when I discovered that he had been studying the prophecy.

"It was when I found the prophecy in his study that I knew my time was running out. He was planning something big, something that went beyond breaking the spell on the arrow. Something that involved both of us, and I did not want to wait around to see what it was. It was the day we fled Gaiztoak that I realized he had also gathered the three keys together in one place, although it is possible that it was unknowingly. However, I will not count it as a coincidence that both Annalyn and Uri also carried a piece of the key when they were kidnapped and brought to Gaiztoak."

"Uri?" I echo disbelievingly. "*He* had a piece of the key?"

"The Breath of the Dragon," she confirms. "He said his mother gave it to him to remember her by, but Zeldek had me confiscate it from him nonetheless. At the time, I just assumed that Zeldek didn't want him to have anything personal that would make him want to leave."

"But why would he keep them there if he only wanted their necklaces?" I muse. "Do you suppose that Uri and Annalyn could have some kind of special power that we don't know about?"

She snorts at this. "Even if they do, Annalyn is too soft to hurt anyone with it and Uri's too stupid to even discover that he had it. Believe me when I say that we are in no danger from them." Rubbing the bridge of her nose, she grows more serious. "However, it is a possibility, and I do think that Zeldek kept them enslaved so he could find out if they did have special abilities. He's always looking for powerful people to subjugate and use to his own advantage."

We fall silent. A thought comes to me, and I find myself smiling.

"What?" she demands.

"Oh, nothing," I reply with a grin. "I'm just flattered that you thought that I was pure of heart."

She looks at me, squinting slightly. "There is something about you, Ealdred. Something that I can't, as of yet, understand—"

It would have been nice to hear what she was going to say next, but unfortunately, she is unable to finish. The golden doors burst open and King Leonel strides into the room, flanked by a dozen ezixs.

Chapter Forty-One

"Halt!" the king cries in his irritating, self-important way. "Hand over that arrow at once, or I will have these beasts tear you to shreds!"

Bellator arches an eyebrow and turns to him, bowing mockingly. "Oh yes, yes, anything you say, your divine majesty," she says, her voice dripping with spite.

The king scowls at her. "Oh, *you*. I knew that I shouldn't have believed the rumours of your death."

She straightens up with a harsh laugh. "I'm sorry to disappoint, my liege. But, as you should already know, it takes a lot more than serpents to kill me!"

He rolls his eyes. "If I had known that a girl so young could keep such a grudge, I would have killed you then and gotten it over with!"

"Because locking a nine-year-old girl in a pit of poisonous snakes for days without food or water just wasn't cruel enough for you, was it?"

"You survived it, didn't you? And you are stronger because of it," he says, as if the accusations are nothing to feel guilty about.

"Stronger? You made me into a beast that needed to be caged!" she spits, her voice passionate with hatred.

Leonel laughs. "'Zandelba' may be afraid of you, witch, but I can see past your façade! You're still that feeble little brat huddled in the corner, petrified of the dark."

"I *am* the dark!" she snarls.

"Such an imagination," he says with vague annoyance. "Give the arrow to me, or I'll put you back into that pit. And this time it will be for the rest of your worthless life!"

"You apparently haven't heard," she sneers, "but your precious master was just here, and I sent him home with a wound that won't quickly mend. If he couldn't take it from me, do you really think that a petty mortal like you can?"

A look of doubt passes through the king's eyes, but then he raises his sword so that she can see it. "You may have your arrow," he says, "but I have this!"

"Ah yes," she scoffs. "A magical sword that you can hardly use. I'm terrified now."

His face turns red and he points at her. "Kill her!"

The ezixs rush toward us.

I begin to hoist up my sword, preparing to fight, but Bellator is quicker than I am. She takes the arrow in her hand, and points it at them, shouting, *"Hiltzeko!"*

A streak of white light flashes like forked lighting from the end of the arrow and disintegrates the entire line of ezixs into ashes that scatter in all directions.

The king throws up his sword, deflecting the lightning with the blade. He looks around, fear flashing through his eyes as he finds that he is alone.

"Well," he says, forcing a chuckle, "I see that your magic has greatly improved. But what about your skill with the sword? Have you even practiced that, or will you forever resort to hiding behind your bow?"

Bellator takes his bate. She throws down her bow and quiver of arrows.

"We fight hand to hand." She turns to me. "Take the arrow, half-wit, and give me my sword."

"Half wit?" the king snorts, finally acknowledging my presence. "It does suit you, doesn't it?"

My face grows warm even as I pretend to ignore him, and I draw the sword, handing it to Bellator. She thrusts the arrow into my hands and faces the king once more, pushing her bangs out of her eyes.

"We fight to the death," she says. "Winner gets the arrow. I'll throw in the half-breed too, since I've heard you've condemned him for sorcery or something of the like."

The king nods his agreement to the terms.

I am really starting to resent the way that she continues to endanger me like this.

"Hypocritical, if you go into detail," she adds acidly, "since your bloodline has been mingled with the magical blood of the Vaelhyreans for centuries."

"It is for the king alone to have the power of the gods," he replies arrogantly, and they face off, crossing their swords between them.

That is the sign for the fight to begin, and begin it does. First the king slashes at her and then she slashes at the king. That's how these things always start, it seems. I observe both of their bearings as the battle continues with ferocity on both sides. Bellator is agile, but the king is stronger and obviously a very skilled fighter. Adding to that, the magic of his sword sends blue sparks at her face every time their swords clash.

As the murderous dance wears on, it grows clear that King Leonel has the upper hand. Bellator is getting slower, and he frequently gains ground, while she loses it. Her strength is still drained from breaking the spell, and the fact that she was eaten by a snake only a few days ago certainly can't be helping. At last, the outcome is inevitable. Leonel rips her sword out of her hand, and points Stormcrest at her chest.

"Ha!" he taunts breathlessly. "You have lost, as I knew you would. My master will be pleased that I have avenged him."

He runs the tip of his sword up her neck, forcing her to look up at him. She flinches, breathing heavily. There is a flicker fear in her eyes, but there is something different about it this time. Nothing like the fear I'd seen when she was falling down the snake's throat. It's almost... artificial.

"Please, don't kill me!" she whimpers mockingly, and then her voice grows callous. "Is that what you want to hear? Just as it was before, with me at your mercy!"

And that's when I see what she is doing. Before I can say or do anything, she jerks out a knife that is strapped to her leg, rolls out from under his sword, and thrusts her knife into his stomach. He doubles over, his sword falling from his hand. There is an alarmingly savage glint in her eyes as she shoves him onto his back, still holding onto the knife.

"Oh, vengeance is sweet!" she says through her teeth. "I always imagined that it would end this way. With fire and blood. Isn't that what you said to me once?"

He gasps, trying to pull out the knife, but she presses it in more.

"Now, now, don't touch it," she chides. "I need time for the venom to take its hold in you."

"V-venom?" he stammers, his face turning ashen.

"Aye, the venom. Compliments of Ealdred."

I have been standing paralyzed until this point, but when she says this, I break out of my stupor.

"What?"

She pulls the knife from him and throws it at my feet, blood splattering the floor around it. I bend down and pick it up. She's right. It is mine. It is the knife that she'd given to me. The one that I threw into the giant viper's mouth. She must have retrieved it when she escaped and laced it with poison from the creature's fangs.

I swallow. "Bellator, that's Hamish's father."

"Yes, it certainly is." She rises to her feet, looking down at him. "And Hamish will make a much better king than he ever has been!"

I feel panic rising in my throat. "You are supposed to be protecting Valamette!"

"You're right, I am!" she spits, snatching the arrow from my hands. "The king is dead! Long live prosperity!"

I shake my head and push past her, falling to my knees at the king's side. He turns his gaze to me, his sapphire eyes clouding.

"Sir?" I say, touching his arm.

He shrinks away, and even now disgust crosses his face. "Get away from me!" he chokes. "You caused this!"

"Please," I say, "let me help you!"

"No. I want my son! I want Hamish!"

"He's— not here..." My voice falters, and I back away, feeling suddenly very lost.

A loud bang jolts me from my confusion, and I turn in the direction of the sound. Any sorrow that I am beginning to feel fades into horror as Hamish himself rushes into the room.

"There you are!" he says, looking relieved. "I tried to follow right away, but the door..."

His voice trails off as the scene before him registers on his countenance. A cry of alarm escapes his throat when he sees his father's gasping form, and he rushes to his side. He kneels down beside the king and puts his hand to his father's cheek.

"Father?" he whispers.

"H-Hamish," the king gasps, his breath coming short. "M-my son. My brave, precious son."

"I am here, father," Hamish says reassuringly, tears spilling down his cheeks.

"I said not to trust him," the king wheezes. "Didn't I tell you not to?"

"What— what are you talking about?" Hamish asks, his voice trembling. "I do not understand what you are saying."

"The half-breed!" The king's gaze darts to me. "He did this to me—"

He breaks into a fit of coughing, and Hamish helplessly pats his shoulder, assuring him that everything will be well.

I feel myself going cold all over. He's blaming me. He's blaming me for this. And to make things worse, he's trying to turn Hamish against me before he goes.

"Avenge me," the king rasps. "Promise me."

Hamish shakes his head, taking a shuddering breath. "Father, you're not—"

"Swear to it!"

"Father—"

"Do it!"

Hamish closes his eyes. "I swear."

The king is labouring to breathe now, and it seems to be taking great effort for him to speak. "Do not fail me this time..."

His breath leaves him and he goes very still.

Frozen in place, Hamish stares unblinking at the body of his father. The very air is hushed, and even Bellator remains unmoving, giving the prince a moment to grieve. Hamish sits back on his knees, trembling all over. He swallows and presses his hand over his mouth, and I know that he is trying to be brave. But his composure dissolves and he slides down to his hands and knees, collapsing into heartbreaking sobs.

Sorrow washes over me, more for him than for his – for *our* – father. How could I have let this happen? I should have stopped Bellator before she killed him. I should have done something! But if she hadn't killed him, Leonel would have killed her.

Hamish straightens up and turns to us. His face is streaked with tears.

"You!" he shouts, pointing at Bellator. "You killed him!"

"What if I did?" she retorts, reaching for her quiver, which is once again strapped to her side.

He draws his sword. "I made a promise to my father that I would avenge him, and I will die before I break that oath!"

No! If he attacks her, Bellator will surely kill him too!

"Are you deaf?" I shout indignantly, turning my expression as cold and unfeeling as the walls around me.

Hamish and Bellator turn to me, surprise apparent on both of their faces.

"What?" Hamish demands.

I hold up the dagger, which is still dripping with my father's blood, and try my best to imitate Bellator's chilling sneer. "Did you not hear what your father said? *I* killed him! I killed King Leonel!"

Hamish gapes, horror stricken. "You?"

I look down my nose at him as I take a step in his direction. It hurts, but I force the words out. "Perhaps you're merely daft!"

His lower lip quivers. "But- but why?"

"Do you really think that I would forgive him for the way he treated me? Never! He deserved what he received!" My words come out with such passion that I am convinced their truth is rooted in me. I doubt that I could ever have forgiven him. That I ever will.

"But we trusted you! *I* trusted you!"

I look directly into his glistening eyes and sneer. "You should be careful who you trust, little prince. Your father was right about me, though you were too gullible to see it! I am more dangerous than you can possibly understand."

He charges toward me with a scream of rage, brandishing his sword wildly. I don't know what I would have done had not Bellator cried, "*Vanesco!*" at that moment. Hamish vanishes into thin air, along with – I notice moments later – the body of King Leonel.

I turn to Bellator, completely dropping my harsh composure. "Where did you send him?" I ask, my voice breaking in my throat.

For once, she doesn't have a quick retort ready on her tongue. She stares at me, her brows furrowed in confusion and her mouth parted in shock. Then she shakes her head, dropping her gaze to the floor.

"Where did you send him?" I cry desperately.

She looks back at me. "I sent them back to Gerithold..." Her voice trails off.

I heave a sigh of relief.

"Why?" she asks abruptly. "Why did you do that? I would have been happy to take the credit for that, and I would be tempted to feel threatened by you stealing my thunder had it not been *you* that did it! You're such an idiot. You finally had a chance at being happy. The king was gone and you had the trust of the crowned prince! Hamish would have let you stay with him for as long as you wanted!"

I grow angry. "I did it to protect him from you!"

"I wouldn't have killed him!"

"Wouldn't you have?"

She hesitates.

"It was the only way to ensure that both of you remained safe."

She snorts. "He wouldn't have been able to scratch me."

"That's not what I meant! Batuel charged you with protecting Valamette. It is your duty!"

"You don't have to tell me, half-wit. I know what is required of me!"

"No, you have to listen to me!" I cry. "You have to stop caring only about yourself. It is *your* country now, Bellator, whether you like it or not. *You* are the protector of the people of Valamette and you must fulfil that duty, because there is no one else that will! And how do you expect them to accept you if they find out that you killed their king?"

"I get it, alright?" she snaps. Then she smirks. "Thanks to your play-acting, they'll be on the lookout for you instead. Even *I* thought you had lost your mind, you played it so well."

I don't take it as a compliment.

It is better this way, I tell myself. Hamish was born to rule. He may be hurt now, but it's nothing compared to the pain that I may cause him if I stay and my true identity is revealed. I will not take away his chance to prove himself to the people. And even if Bellator doesn't see it yet, Valamette needs her. Hamish will need her. My one hope is that my faith in both of them is not misplaced.

"And another thing," I add.

She rolls her eyes. "What now?"

"You must promise me that you will bring no harm to Hamish, and that you will give him your full support and undivided loyalty for as long as he is king."

She shrugs. "Sure. My grudge was against his father alone."

"Please! You *must* protect him, whether it goes against your own interests or not!"

She stares at me for a moment, weighing her options. "I will."

"Swear it on the thing you hold most dear!"

Our gazes meet, and she sighs. "I swear on my mother's grave, I will protect him with my life."

I feel reassured, because for once, I know she is telling the truth.

Chapter Forty Two

"Half-wit," Bellator's voice comes softly from behind me. The evening sky is dark and starry, and moonlight shines down into the garden. I slide off of the bench that I am sitting on and turn to Bellator. She is outfitted in a long black jerkin, a simple white shirt with armguards over it, and trousers. The firestone, which is not illuminated at the moment, hangs around her neck. We retrieved the three stones on our way out of the underground cavern, and she returned my amulet back to me with only feeble resistance. No doubt the third necklace is locked away in the same place that she's hidden the arrow of Arnon.

The walk back to the castle was long and tedious. My spirits were low the entire time. Bellator seemed to guess it because after she transported Jambeau's unconscious body back to Gerithold, she tried small talk in an attempt to cheer me up. The problem was, she isn't all that great at cheering people up, and she gave up pretty quickly.

When we returned to the surface early this morning, the castle had indeed been restored to its previous splendour. Batuel certainly outdid herself. The walls, ramparts, and gates rise protectively around a courtyard, a huge keep, and the palace. Even the clearing outside of Arnon has been replenished, and is now green with flourishing grass. Inside the palace is well furnished and decorated like some haunted castle, which thrilled Bellator. We spent the entire day exploring it and the grounds outside.

As evening drew closer, Bellator allotted me a room in the guest quarters that was equipped with a bathhouse. We both cleaned up and then met in the dining room for a silent dinner, after which she retired to her rooms for a rest. I went out to the garden to clear my thoughts, which is where I am now.

"Hello," I reply glumly.

"I think," she says, glancing around, "that I'm going to rename this place."

"Really?" I ask, trying not to sound too depressed. "What do you have in mind?"

"Well," she says, twisting a ringlet of hair around her finger. "I was thinking something that would keep the name similar, and yet also add my own personal twist to it. What do you think of Quincarnon?"

"It does have a nice ring to it. What does it mean?"

"Renewed Arnon," she replies with an odd smile.

"That works."

I sit back down on the bench and resume staring into a pool of water a few feet away from us. The moonlight shines on the water, and I can hear the lulling sound of the Tireth River rushing through the ravine on the other side of the garden wall.

"So," I say, shaking the heaviness from my voice, "how did you escape the snake?"

"Well," she says, and I can hear the pride in her voice, "however brave jumping down a snake's throat sounds, it isn't a party once you're inside. I had the knife ready, and I managed to stop my fall somewhere in its throat. But once its jaws were shut, there wasn't enough air for the both of us, so I used the magic radiating off of the firestone to energize myself while I hacked away at anything I could find. It took time, but I finally managed to kill the beast. Then I crawled back up through its throat and out of its mouth."

I shudder at the thought.

"But when I came out," she continues, pacing now. "I found myself in a dank cave system – the beast's home, no doubt. When I finally managed to make my way back to the courtyard, you were gone and the entrance was still locked. I wandered through the forest, searching for you, and came across the king communicating with Zeldek. Through them, I learned that you were staying as an honoured guest in the castle, and that Zeldek now knew what we were doing in Arnon. Once the king was gone, I contacted the Master and told him I was alive, and that our escape was all an act to get the arrow for him. My plan was to draw him in so I could end him, and he believed me. All that was left to do was wait for you to come, so I returned to Arnon. I managed to break open the door of the tower, and found the halls of treasure. I followed the passageway from there. When I reached the chamber that you met me in, I had to wait for days."

"Yeah, sorry about that."

"That's when I met Batuel," she continues. "I spoke with her through the door, and told her about my problem. She assured me that she would see to it that you would come with final part of the key, and so I continued to wait. It kills me to admit this, but I could do nothing without you there."

I try to smile, but the realization that Batuel *had* been the whispering voice and that she forced the knowledge of my past on me solely to get me back to Arnon weighs me down still more. "Well, it was nice to be needed for once."

She watches me for a moment and an uncharacteristic look of understanding passes over her face.

"I expect I'll be leaving tomorrow," I say after a moment of awkward silence.

"Are you sure you want to leave so soon?" she asks. "Because you're welcome to stay here until you have fully rested."

Her sudden spurt of generosity is unnerving and I decline easily. "Hamish will be looking for me," I say. "He'll want me arrested."

"Maybe you should tell him the truth," she says, giving me a reproachful glare.

"No!" I snap. "He must never know! You must promise me that you will never tell him."

She raises an eyebrow. "Alright then, if you're certain it is for the best. But I don't understand why you so freely throw away any opportunity for a better life."

"You may someday. But, just like you have your secrets, I also have mine." I pause, sighing deeply. "Besides, I doubt I will ever enter Valamette again once I am gone."

A frown crosses her face. "You're a good person, Ealdred."

I look back at her and see sincerity in her eyes. "So are you."

With a chuckle, she sits down on the grass at the foot of the bench, sticking her thumbs in the tops of her tall boots. "No, I'm not."

"Yes you are," I insist. "I don't think that you're as heartless as you want people to think. Why else would you save Bynvantalyn from those outlaws? There really was nothing in it for you."

She shrugs. "I like killing things."

"And yet you let some of them live," I remind her.

She gives a frustrated growl, her shreds of sympathy evaporating. "You know, there was a reason I came out here, and if you would shut up long enough, I might be able to get to it!"

"Hmm?"

"You see, while we were down there, and you asked me what Zeldek wanted with you—"

"Let me guess," I interrupt. "You lied to me."

She nods, glancing up at me with a hint of a smile. "Technically, I never said anything for certain. I just didn't want to burden you before you helped me with the curse."

"Well, try me," I say, sinking back into my dismal mood. "I doubt that anything could dishearten me any more today."

"See, there is this prophecy. I discovered it when I was looking through Zeldek's notes a couple of years ago. It speaks of a half-race warrior who is destined to destroy Zeldek one day and rid Theara of the Aemurel."

I look up, startled. "Banner mentioned that same prophecy to me while we were in Buentoak. But he said that he didn't know who it was speaking of."

She clicks her tongue. "Apparently you have more than one person lying to you. It seems as if they are all afraid that *you* are the one that the prophecy speaks of, and I think that's why they have been watching you so closely. I know that's why Zeldek was trying to gain your allegiance. He might even try to strike you off the list if you get too dangerous."

I groan. "I was hoping that I could be done with Zeldek after this. Maybe have a bit of peace in my exile."

She shakes her head. "If you have his mark, he will never leave you alone. Just remember this, half-wit; no one can escape their destiny, no matter how hard they may try."

"I'll remember."

"There is another thing. I think I might have figured out what your element is."

"What?"

"Well," she says, "I have only seen flashes of your magic here and there when it comes out in its colour form of blue light. But you did make something happen once without that. You know – when you exploded the ground of your master's house. Zeldek told me about it." She rubs her chin thoughtfully. "Of the five key elements, the ones involved were earth, which is Banner's element; air, which was Batuel's element; lightning, which is that idiot Ulmer's element; and water, which was Sylvia's element. But she died during the second great war, and the element hasn't been able to be used since. However, it could be possible that you somehow have been able to gain the use of this element."

"You think that my element is water?"

She shrugs. "It is as likely as any other theory I've come up with. It would help if you knew anything about your parents."

I look away. "Yes..."

But even knowing what I know about them, I still can't figure it out. I don't know much about Queen Arrosa, but from what I gathered, she was an ordinary princess of Lavylli. And while Bellator mentioned that Leonel's line had some magical blood in it, that wouldn't make me *half* Vaelhyrean. It doesn't make any sense.

And to add to that, why is everyone so interested in just me? Hamish is my twin brother, which would make him a half-race too and every bit as powerful as I am. He did hear Batuel's voice in the halls of treasure, after all...

"Well?" Bellator's voice is impatient.

"Well what?"

"I said, 'The only way to know for sure is to try it out'. Weren't you listening?"

"Oh... no. Yes. Good idea."

I turn to the still waters of the pond, and reach my hand out over the lily pads that adorn the surface. I concentrate on the cold sensation and direct it toward the water, picturing what I want it to do. I wait a second, ten seconds. The cold is pounding through my veins before the surface of the pool even begins to ripple, but it isn't me that's doing it. Rain has begun to sprinkle from the clouds gathered overhead. Thunder rumbles in the distance. A sphere of blue light surrounds my hand and I know that if I don't let up now, it might explode again like it did that time in the forest.

I release my concentration and turn back to Bellator.

"Nothing," I say wearily.

Her lips are pursed into a hard frown. "Interesting. It almost seems..." her voice trails off, and she sinks into her thoughts again.

"Almost seems...?" I ask.

"As if you don't have an element. But that isn't possible. You need to have either an element or the use of spells to even be able to use magic." She shakes her head, rubbing her chin thoughtfully. "There must be an element I'm overlooking."

"Oh." I pause, thinking this over. "Well, what about you? What's your element?"

"Wouldn't you like to know?" she says shortly, and it doesn't take a wizard to know that the subject is closed for further discussion.

There is a moment of silence as we listen to the music of the crickets in the air and the rain in the leaves.

"What are you going to do now that you have all of this?" I ask at last.

"Oh, me?" She smirks to herself. "I am going to join the Counsel of the Lords of Valamette as soon as Hamish is king, and force them into making decisions that will benefit the country instead of their own pocketbooks. I will then proceed to generously give the new king my full support and funding. With my help, Hamish will make the kingdom prosper, and no one will dare say that he is unworthy of his title."

I smile. "He'll appreciate that."

She raises an eyebrow. "Why are you so concerned about him, anyways?"

"He's my friend," I reply without hesitation. "I want to see him succeed."

"Then you and I have a common goal once again," she says with a smile, and I can't help but smile back. "Well," she adds, "I'd better get some rest."

"Goodnight, then, Bellator."

She rises to her feet and brushes herself off. Then she starts slowly toward the palace. She halts, and turns back to me. "Oh, and Ealdred," she says.

"Yes?"

She pauses, opening her mouth to speak, but closes it again. Then she smiles a little. "…goodnight. Friend."

Chapter Forty Three

A commotion in the courtyard below my window wakes me the next morning. Yawning, I roll over, and would have gone right back to sleep if I hadn't recognized Hamish's voice. I bolt upright, throw aside my blankets, and rush across the cold stone floor to the window.

In the courtyard below, Bellator is standing in the centre of the stairs leading to the great door to the palace. The courtyard is full of guards in blue and gold phoenix uniforms. Hamish stands at the foot of the stairs, speaking to her in harsh tones. Something about him has changed since I last saw him, as if he has aged five years in just one day.

Jambeau is standing behind him, apparently finding the stables very interesting, because that's where his gaze is fixed. His face is badly bruised and he wears a bandage around his head.

"Where is he?" Hamish demands. "I know that he was here with you!"

"I have no idea, sire." Bellator's tone is agreeable, but I can tell that she is getting frustrated. "I told you; after I got you out of there, he ran off without another word to me. Thankfully, he was too frightened to remember the arrow. It is safely in my possession still."

The prince doesn't look convinced. "I would trust you with the arrow just as much as I would trust him with it," he replies coldly. "Now, if you will step aside, we are going to need to search the entirety of your estate until I am satisfied that he is indeed not here. And that includes your vaults."

Even from where I stand, I can see her grow tense. But her voice is still as pleasant as before as she replies, "By all means, go right ahead. But if I find that even one coin is missing, you and your men will answer to me."

I dodge out of sight of the window, and fly toward my wardrobe. I hurriedly change into a drab outfit and travelling cloak, and strap my dagger to my side. Bellator hasn't yet returned the sword to me since her fight with Leonel, and I doubt that she will.

Within moments, I hear footsteps rushing about on the level below me, and they soon migrate upstairs. I rush to the window again. The courtyard outside is empty besides the trio of soldiers left to guard the entrance to the palace. They should be easy to slip past.

I begin to push open the lattice, but then have to duck out of sight again as a dozen more guards come into view from the direction of the stables. I back toward the door, but stop when I hear Hamish's voice ring clearly from downstairs. My heart hammers in my chest.

I'm trapped.

The door to my room creaks open, and I let out my breath in relief when I see that it is only Bellator.

She closes it softly behind her and turns to me.

"Oh, good! You're up. I was hoping that I didn't have to send you away still dressed in your nightclothes."

"They're here for me," I whisper, shaken. "There's no way out."

"There's always a way out." She looks over her shoulder. "However, seeing as you are now wanted in all of Valamette as a murderer, it won't be so easy getting back in if you ever feel so inclined."

When she looks back, her smile is gone, and there is regret in her eyes. "You were right in what you said last night. You will never be able to come back here again. Ever. Even if your sentence is revoked, even if they find out the truth, I doubt that we will ever meet again." She hesitates. "No, I'll rephrase that; we can't ever meet again."

I furrow my brow. "Why not?"

She glances over her shoulder again. Footsteps have started in the hall outside my door. "When you're around, you make me want to be a better person. You make me feel compelled — no, that's not it. You make me *want* to do good. And," she takes a deep breath, "I can't afford to do that. Not with war between the

Vaelhyreans coming. Not with conflict between Zandelba and Valamette impending. I have to do what needs to be done without you here being my conscience. I need to live my life without... well, without you."

I understand her perfectly, and even though I had been the one to pronounce my banishment first, hearing these words from her hurts. "So now that you're done using me for your own ends, you're just going to throw me away?"

She nods, but she doesn't wear her usual smirk. "Well, yes."

I shake my head and look away.

"This one service I owe you," she says, and her voice is unusually gentle. "But it will be the last. The end of it all. The close of our journey together."

Tears are forming in my eyes, and I try to block them. I should have known that she hadn't meant it when she called me her friend. I just wanted so much to mean something to her.

Bellator takes my left hand, and presses a leather satchel into the gloved palm.

"Here. Some copper from the vaults. It should last you a while."

I shove it into my belt, not wanting to look her in the eye. But I do, and she holds my gaze. Her voice comes so softly that I can barely hear the word.

"Vanesco."

Her hand comes up, her palm out to me. A tear escapes my eye and races down my cheek as everything around me begins to fade away. The carved stone walls shift into a wide, open clearing, and the floor beneath me slopes at my feet, becoming a steep, rocky ravine. The last thing to disappear is her face, and her voice echoes as she says, "Goodbye."

I jerk to the present, and look around. Water rushes through the deep ravine before my feet, and I can see a castle sparkling in the sunlight, perched on the opposite shore from where I stand. The castle of Quincarnon. There is a deep thicket behind me made of huge, red trees, and I know exactly where she sent me: across the gorge to Zandelban soil.

I feel like I should be panicking, but instead, there is a strange calm inside. Also, loneliness. I am very much alone. But how is that different from usual? Only this time, a wave of happiness mingles with my tears. I may be alone, but I am free to choose my path for the first time in my life.

As I take my first step into a brave new future, the path ahead grows clearer. There is much danger ahead of me. I can sense it in the air itself. I know that no matter how long it takes, I will have to face Hamish once more. My only hope is that when I do, he will somehow find it in his heart to forgive me.

But even more pressing is the knowledge that I will have to face Zeldek again. And when that day comes, I have to be ready for him. Even though I know little of the destiny set before me, I can feel it in my heart. I have to do the best that I can to destroy the evil that he creates. Not because I am powerful, or strong, or even brave, but because I have been chosen by the Vaelhyreans.

I am Elroy.

Chapter Forty-Four

The Master was in a rage. His eyes glowed like hot embers, and his cries of agony could be heard even from the forest beyond the mountain ridge. Smashed pottery, broken glass, burning papers, and charred books scattered the floor of the throne room. A dark liquid splattered in a trail across the red carpet from the doorway to the throne. Upon the throne the Master was slouched, gasping for air, a hand pressed over the wound that still bled on his breast. His armour glinted with blood as black as ebony, and his white hair mingled with it on his breastplate.

This was the state in which Warrick found his lord as he entered the throne room in response to his summons. He still wore his travelling cloak about him, and his gait, although weary, was as stately as ever. He approached the stairway, and bowed stiffly from the waist.

"My lord, what has happened?" he inquired, his terse voice edged with concern. "Why such urgent summons?"

"I have been betrayed!" the Master roared, and even though his anger was great, Warrick noticed the weakness in his voice.

"By whom, my lord?" he asked, truly surprised.

"Bellator! I thought that I knew her mind, that I owned her very soul! But she is clever, more so than I could ever have predicted! How could one so small, so weak, trick one such as I?"

Warrick chose his words carefully. "If you don't recall, I did warn you of her deviousness, sire. Considering her lineage—"

"Silence! I will not have that brought into this! She has become a powerful adversary, and she will pay dearly for what she has done to me!"

"You mean that she is still out there, my lord? Unchecked and unchallenged?"

Zeldek took a loud, shuddering breath. "Against my will. But I am too weak at present to do anything about it. I only barely escaped her treachery with my life! And worse, she has attained the Arrow of Arnon! She has become a force to be reckoned with."

Warrick glanced down at the splatters on the carpet, and understanding dawned on his face. "Then she resides in Valamette, in her ancestor's castle? I am beginning to understand why you have summoned me here."

"I want you to find her weaknesses! She must have some."

Warrick grew uneasy. "My lord, I assumed that her only weakness was that dragon."

"It was," Zeldek admitted. "And I had it shot down right before her eyes when she escaped with three of my prisoners. I thought that doing so would break her, but I was wrong. I only succeeded in removing the only leverage that I had against her." He gasped, and continued with more of an effort. "You must find any kink in her armour that can be found, and if there are none, create some! Do you understand me?"

Warrick nodded. "I do."

"Good! And I don't want you to stop with just her! I want to see her country burn! The cities, the villages, down to every rock and every tree, will be razed to the ground. The people will be slaughtered and every river poisoned for the rest of eternity so that never again will anyone say that they found refuge in Valamette!"

He stared at his master. Warrick did not wish to risk Zeldek's disfavour, but he wanted to point out the distinct lack of benefit this plan would offer his own ambitions. However, he wisely set his own cares aside for another time. "I will do what I can to assist you in subduing them."

When Zeldek did not respond, Warrick continued. "I too bring grave news, sire."

"What news?" Zeldek demanded.

Warrick hesitated for effect. "Leonel is dead, my lord. His younger son will be taking his place on the throne in two weeks time."

"Leonel is dead?" Zeldek repeated, curiosity filling his voice in place of any sort of concern. "How did *that* come to pass?"

"His body was found in the courtyard of his residence in Gerithold, my lord. They say he was murdered in cold blood by a young half-breed boy called Ealdred. You and I both know who that is."

Zeldek slammed his fist into the armrest of his throne, a crazed look entering his eyes. "No! That isn't true! If he is the one of whom the prophecy speaks, he will not have done something so evil!"

"And yet Prince Hamish swears to it, sire, and has sworn revenge against him."

"Where is he, then? Is he dead? Is he behind bars? Have you brought him here before me to appease my anger?"

Warrick bowed his head. "No, sire. He managed to escape, and somehow disappeared without a trace."

"NO!" Zeldek roared, and the two burners flew in both directions, the coals in them scattering all over the floor. "I want him found, and I want him back here the moment that you find him! He will learn to rue the day that he ever chose to defy me!"

Warrick bowed hurriedly. "I will begin the search at once, my lord. Will that be all?"

Zeldek growled. "One more thing; call forth Siena and bid her to come to me at once! I will need her magical arts if I am to make any sort of recovery. And send for the Alliance of Shadows to make haste. We must begin our preparations for war!"

Acknowledgements

I would like to thank my mother Lindsay for raising me to believe in myself, to work for what I want, and to never give up; and my father Cory for encouraging me every step of the way. I would like to thank my sisters Tabitha and Zailynne for those long hours sitting up late at night talking out the characters and scenes with me, and Tabitha for always being there to give me advice on character development, plot, world-building, and whatever other random snag my story was caught on. I would like to thank my little sisters Tirzah and Gabrielle for being my guinea pigs, on which I tested the impact of the story. I would like to thank all of my reviewers and everyone who critiqued my book who helped to make it what it is today, as well as my team of editors, Julie Sutherland and Kate Sabler, for their work getting this book ship-shape and ready for sale. A special thanks to my friend, Michayla Kerley, for all of the unexpected character development.

About The Author

Azaria M.J. Durant is a passionate writer of fantasy with plans to branch out into sci-fi and dystopian. She enjoys writing stories with lots of adventure, unexpected twists, and fleshed out characters that challenge gender roles and expectations.

Azaria lives in Atlantic Canada with her family, cats, and dogs, and her big dreams to travel the world. In the moments when she isn't writing, she is sketching concept art for her stories, participating in community theatre, or curled up with a good book and a box of mint chocolates.

Connect with Azaria!

Facebook: https://www.facebook.com/azariamjdurant/

Instagram: https://www.instagram.com/hermajestymj/

Twitter: https://twitter.com/HerMajestyMJ

Blog: https://ofswordsandquills.wordpress.com/